DATE DUE	

10/07

Day by Day

**Center Point
Large Print**

**This Large Print Book carries the
Seal of Approval of N.A.V.H.**

Day by Day

Delia Parr

CENTER POINT PUBLISHING
THORNDIKE, MAINE

This Center Point Large Print edition
is published in the year 2007 by arrangement with
Harlequin Books, S.A.

The text of this Large Print edition is unabridged. In other
aspects, this book may vary from the original edition.
Printed in the United States of America.
Set in 16-point Times New Roman type.

ISBN-10: 1-60285-051-8
ISBN-13: 978-1-60285-051-4

Library of Congress Cataloging-in-Publication Data

Parr, Delia.
    Day by day / Delia Parr.--Center Point large print ed.
        p. cm.
    ISBN-13: 978-1-60285-051-4 (lib. bdg. : alk. paper)
    1. Grandparents as parents--Fiction. 2. Grandmothers--Fiction. 3. Female friendship--Fiction.
4. Large type books. I. Title.

PS3566.A7527D39 2007
813'.54--dc22

2007017636

Dedicated to
Peg O'Hara,
My Summer Friend
in Ocean Gate

Acknowledgments

During the writing of *Day by Day,* I relied heavily on friends and family for inspiration and information. They deserve all the credit, but I'll take responsibility for any mistakes I may have made sharing their wisdom within the pages of this book.

Laurie Cohen, who owns the delightful Sweet Tooth Candies store in Collingswood, N.J., graciously explained the candy business to me. Laurie is an amazing woman of faith who truly does see operating her store as a ministry. I thank her for spending the afternoon with me, for showing me around Sweet Tooth Candies and for the bag of chocolates I ate on the way home!

My coworker and friend Monica Segrest is my colleague as well as a hairstylist who has made a very real difference in the lives of her clients and her community. I am very grateful for the time she spent giving me information about hairdressing as a career and a ministry.

Arlene B. Rubin, Esquire, is an outstanding school administrator, colleague and friend who provided answers about the legal system that kept me writing on the beach and saved me countless hours in a law library. Marty Barrett, security coordinator for our local school district, helped me learn the process of enrolling a grandchild in school.

In addition to my incredibly dedicated agent, Linda

Kruger, I have a very talented family, who helped me a great deal. My daughter-in-law, Ileana, is a gifted family counselor who shared her professional understanding of children and family dynamics during the writing of this book. My sister, Carol Beth, as always, was my first line editor and shared her summer home with me again so I could write at the beach, and my sister friend, Jeanne, never let me doubt I would finish the book by deadline. Pat and Joanne are always there if I need a word of encouragement, too.

And finally, my children: Matt, Brett and Liz. You are the real sunshine in my life.

Thank you, all. You are all such wonderful blessings!

Day by Day

Prologue

Hot, humid days and sultry nights each summer slowed the pace of everyday life in Welleswood, a small suburban town in Southern New Jersey. Despite the renaissance that had breathed new life into this once-dying town, many families fled the suffocating heat and escaped to nearby mountain retreats or beach resorts for a few weeks at a time. Others remained to take advantage of townwide recreational and cultural events organized by an old-fashioned network of women who worked together to make Welleswood a good place to live, even in the throes of summer.

Within the predictable cycle of summer this year, however, the early days of July would bring heartache and tragedy, as well as new challenges to grow in faith and love, to three very different women in Welleswood.

"Daddy can't come."

At the sound of her granddaughter's voice, Barbara Montgomery looked up from the travel brochures that littered the dining room table. Her husband of thirty-four years, John, was standing in the doorway holding their twin granddaughters, one in his arms, and the other at his side. "Jessie! Melanie! What a surprise!"

Barbara pushed back from the table, rose to her feet and quickly set aside all thoughts of the sailing adventure she and John were planning two years from now

11

when they launched into retirement as members of a crew on a two-year sailing trip around the world.

"Daddy can't come," Melanie repeated. Her little six-year-old face was strangely solemn, and she held tight to her Pappy's shoulder.

Jessie tugged free from his hand. The eldest by all of three minutes and the more dominant by leaps and bounds, she folded her hands on her chest and stomped her foot. "Daddy had to go away, and Pappy says we can't go with him, but I want my daddy. Why can't me and Melanie go? You'll take us, won't you, Grammy? You know the way to heaven, don't you?"

"Heaven?" Confused, Barbara looked up and studied her husband's features. She froze the moment she saw his tearstained cheeks and the grief that shadowed his gaze. The world stopped for a moment. Time stood still. Her heart pounded against a wall of denial that refused to be cracked. Their son Steve was in heaven? Steve was gone? No, that couldn't be true. Impossible. Not Steve. He was only thirty years old. He was a health fanatic. He had these two precious little girls to raise—little girls whose mother had deserted Steve and abandoned her babies shortly after their birth.

No. Steve could not be in heaven. Barbara had just talked to him this morning. She locked her gaze with her husband's, praying he would put her worst fears to rest. "John?"

Fresh tears coursed down his cheeks. "Our Steve's gone. He's been . . . murdered," he croaked. "Our boy has gone Home, and the girls . . . the girls need us, Barb, now more than ever."

Pain seared the very essence of her spirit. The look of absolute grief in her husband's gaze melted the wall of denial protecting her heart, and she rushed to embrace him. With one arm around Melanie, she pulled Jessie against her, too, as her soul clung to her faith in God—faith that would somehow have to sustain them all.

Late Saturday afternoon, Judy Roberts quickly scanned the empty beauty salon and searched for signs of any cleanup task she might have missed. Satisfied that all was ready for Tuesday morning when her shop would reopen, she flipped the light switch and watched each of the green neon letters in Pretty Ladies sputter and flicker into darkness.

She let out a sigh and arched her back while every muscle in her legs and feet protested against each of the fifty-seven years she had spent on this earth, especially the decades she had spent as a hairdresser turning other women into pretty ladies. "Time for this pretty tired lady to drag herself home," she mumbled. She opened the door, turned, and locked the door behind her, stepping from the relative comfort of the air-conditioned shop into a never-ending wall of hot, humid air.

Fortunately, home was only a few blocks away. She worked her way down Welles Avenue and eased through the influx of Saturday-night diners who crowded the brick sidewalk en route to a host of new eateries that were part of the trendy "new" Welleswood. There were some families out tonight, but mostly couples and mostly strangers to her, she noticed, and quietly turned off the avenue toward the row house she called home.

Row house. She chuckled to herself. Newcomers called the vintage row houses built during the Great Depression town houses now, but more than the name had changed. Prices of these homes had nearly quadrupled in the years since she and her husband, Frank, had purchased theirs some thirty-five years ago. With Frank gone four years now, God rest his soul, she was barely able to afford the taxes, but she did own the house, free and clear. Any plans she had for spending her golden years comfortably, unfortunately, had died with him, along with the hope she might one day be reconciled with their only daughter, Candy, or see her grandson, Brian. She stopped at the corner to let the traffic pass and patted her thigh. "Looks like I'll have to struggle through, best as I can on my own. Don't need much for myself. Good thing, too," she mumbled before crossing the street.

Dog tired, she got a boost of energy as she started down the block where she lived and thought about taking a shower. A long, refreshing shower. Then a quick bite to eat and off to bed where she could fall asleep watching television, but only after she had set the alarm so she would not oversleep and miss Sunday services. Walking against the glare of the late-afternoon sun, she could just make out her row house on the corner at the end of the block, and it appeared that one of the neighborhood children was using the railing on her front porch like a balance beam.

Again.

Another boost of energy hastened her steps, and her purse swayed faster as she hurried toward home. She loved the neighborhood children. She did not mind if they played on her front lawn or climbed the backyard fence to retrieve a lost ball. She even let them skateboard in the driveway along the side of her house, since she could not afford the insurance for a car and the driveway served no real purpose for her.

Her front porch railing, however, was definitely off-limits. Visions of one of the children falling off the railing now and getting hurt sent her scurrying as fast as her tired legs could carry her. From behind, the boy only appeared to be five or six years old. Didn't anyone keep track of their little ones any more?

"You there! Get down! You'll really get hurt if you fall," she cried as she passed the front of the house next door.

If the boy heard her, he ignored her and continued his daredevil antics by leaping from the front railing to the side one. He landed hard, bobbed a bit, then pitched headlong off the railing toward the driveway below.

Shock halted her steps and her heart skipped a beat, but instead of a scream of terror or the horrible sound of his little body striking the asphalt driveway, she heard a man's harsh voice. "Do it again, and this time, try harder so you don't fall!"

Her eyes widened. Her pulse quickened, and she charged past her front lawn, ready to give a good tongue-lashing to the idiot of a man who was letting the boy use her front porch like an old-fashioned playground. She rounded the corner of the yard and faced the man who was lifting the boy back up to the railing, but the diatribe she had planned died before she could utter a single word.

The man was indeed an idiot.

He was also her son-in-law.

Was the boy with him her grandson, Brian? She had not seen the boy for four years, and he had only been a few months old when Duke and Candy had first moved to California with him. Her heart leaped with hope. Was Candy here, too? Was she inside, ready to reconcile, or at least explain why she had gone back to California after that terrible scene at Frank's funeral?

"Duke?" was all Judy could manage to say.

At the sound of his name, he turned his head, gave her a relieved smile, and pulled the boy down to stand on the ground beside him. At six foot four inches and weighing close to three-hundred pounds, Duke was a massive man. His arms bulged with muscles covered with tattoos that stretched to his knuckles, and he sported half a dozen earrings in his left ear. In the distance, at the far end of the driveway, he had parked his Harley.

He nodded at her. "Me and Brian been waitin' awhile. Just drove cross-country, and I'm plain tuckered out."

She swallowed hard and tried not to imagine her son-in-law driving her grandson cross-country on a motorcycle. She approached her grandson and crouched down to gaze at him face-to-face. A layer of dirt and grime covered his features and the dark curls on his head were matted, but the blue eyes twinkling back at her were the same color as Frank's. "Do you know who I am?" she asked.

"You're Grandmom," he answered, squaring his little shoulders. "Dad told me."

Duke nudged the boy with his knee. "Go on. Give her a kiss hello, boy. Time's a-wastin'."

Brian flinched, but obeyed his father and planted a kiss on her chin. "Hi, Grandmom."

Judy closed her eyes for a moment and melted with joy. She kissed him back. "Hi, yourself. Is your mommy here, too?"

"Candy's not here. She's back in the hospital. Again." Duke spat the words without giving Brian a chance to respond.

Concerned, Judy stood up, but before she could ask for a full explanation, Duke shoved an envelope into her hand. "What's this?"

"Papers. Legal papers. You'll be needin' 'em if you're gonna raise him. I can't tell you exactly where Candy is stayin', 'cause I don't know, so don't bother tryin' to grill me."

She turned the envelope over and over in her hand. "I don't understand. If Candy is back in rehab, then why—"

"I'm leavin' Brian with you. I don't know whether or not she'll ever show up for the boy, but until she does, you need the papers to put him in school and stuff."

She edged closer to Brian and put her arm around his narrow shoulders. "Why?"

Duke snorted. "Kid's six now. He started school last year, and Candy—"

"No. I meant why are you leaving Brian with me? Why aren't you going to wait for Candy to come home and raise him? You're her husband and his father."

He shrugged. "Havin' a kid was Candy's idea, not mine. Doesn't look like she'll be able to take care of him anytime soon. Besides, I got plans now, and he's not part of 'em."

When Brian tried to squirm free from Judy's grip, Duke nailed the boy to the spot with a glare that sent shivers down her spine. "You behave, boy. Don't make me come back if I hear you've been bad."

Brian froze and his features paled.

Judy held him tight. She did not know whether to throttle her idiot son-in-law senseless for being such a brute or for abandoning his own flesh and blood. She was even tempted to thank him for bringing her grandson home to her, instead of leaving him to get lost in the maze of foster care. Without giving her a chance to do anything, however, Duke simply got on his motorcycle and drove off.

He never looked back.

He never even said goodbye to his son.

Ginger King and her husband, Tyler, emerged from their house with their cooler packed and ready to leave for some tailgating with their friends from church before today's doubleheader baseball game between the Philadelphia Phillies and the Chicago Cubs. To her surprise, they ran straight into their daughter Lily, and her eight-year-old son, Vincent.

At thirty, Lily was their youngest child. A single mom, she and Vincent lived in Chicago where she taught elementary school. She had never spoken of Vincent's father or even revealed his identity, and she had not been home for a visit for nearly two years. Their oldest son, Mark, was in Nashville recording demo tapes and waiting for his big break into country music, while their middle child, Denise, enjoyed life as a flight attendant, headquartered in San Francisco. All were still single, but it was Lily who Ginger worried about the most.

Ginger squealed with delight, hugged her grandson with one arm and her youngest child with the other. "What a surprise! I can't believe you two! What are you doing here?" Without giving either one the chance to answer, she tussled Vincent's hair. "Look how tall you've gotten. Don't tell me you've become a Cub fan and Mom flew you here from

Chicago for the doubleheader today. We were just headed over to the stadium," she gushed. She knew they would have to ditch those plans now, but her excitement at seeing Lily and Vincent quickly erased her disappointment.

Vincent blushed. "You know I don't like baseball, Grams."

Ginger winced. As endearing as the term *Grams* might be—it was better than *Grandmom*—yet she was still tempted to look around, as if Vincent were talking with someone else. At fifty-five, she felt and acted twenty-five. She was too young to be a grandmother, by any name. When she looked at the way Vincent wrinkled his nose at the mention of baseball, any hope that he had developed an interest in sports also died quickly, a major disappointment to both Ginger and Tyler, whose social lives revolved around professional sports, especially baseball and football.

"If I remember correctly, you like hot dogs, though," Tyler prompted. He nodded back toward the house. "How about we go out back and fire up the grill?"

Vincent beamed. "I love hot dogs, Gramps."

Tyler gave Lily a kiss. "Welcome home, sweetie."

"Thanks, Daddy, but don't go just yet. There's someone I want you both to meet." She turned and looked toward the curb where Ginger noticed, for the first time, a young man standing next to a Hummer convertible. When Lily smiled and waved for him to join them, the man quickly approached and placed his arm possessively around her. Beaming, Lily took a deep breath. "This is Paul Taft. Paul is my husband. We were married last week."

Ginger's heart skipped a beat. "Married? You're married?" When Lily held out her left hand and the sun flashed on a set of rings beset with diamonds, Ginger's reaction shifted from surprise to denial and stayed there. "I can't believe it! You're married? Really married? Without a word to us first?"

"Yes, Mom, married."

"Oh," was all Ginger could manage. Thankful that Lily would no longer be alone and Vincent would finally have a father, albeit a stepfather, Ginger hugged her daughter tight. She also embraced the fact that her daughter's secretive wedding was only the latest in a long line of disappointments in their relationship.

Tyler set down the cooler to shake hands with their new son-in-law, but his expression was sober and reflected his own disappointment. "You could have told us when you got engaged."

"I could have helped you with plans for the wedding," Ginger added. "At the very least, we could have flown out for the ceremony. Mark and Denise would have wanted to be there, too," she admonished, only too aware of how easily Lily had always been able to set aside her parents, as well as her brother and sister, in favor of her friends. "Besides, you know how much your father and I love to travel," she teased.

Lily glanced at her parents and edged closer to Paul. Her cheeks were flushed pink, which added a little color to her plain, girl-next-door looks. "Especially since I got married in a sports town like Chicago," she retorted. She slipped her hand into Paul's. "Under the circumstances, we just wanted a private ceremony," she murmured. "We thought we'd stop here first for a day or so to tell you both, then we need to go to Boston to tell Paul's family."

"We can call Mark and Denise while you're here," Ginger suggested, "but you can stay as long as you like." Eager to speak to Lily alone, she looped her arm through her daughter's. "Tyler, why don't you take Paul and Vincent out back to start the grill? Lily and I will get the plates and things from the kitchen," she suggested.

Tyler nodded and picked up the cooler. "This way, guys. We're probably all better off if we give these two women time for some girl talk in the kitchen."

While he led them around the side of the house, Ginger took Lily inside to the kitchen. Instead of focusing on her own disappointment, however, she needed to appease her concern that Lily had married someone neither Ginger nor Tyler had ever met. "Tell me all," she insisted. "Where did you meet Paul? How come you didn't call and tell us about him? What does he do for a living? Will you still work?"

Lily laughed and held up her hands. "One question at a time, Mom, but for starters, we met on a blind date last year. I didn't tell you about him because I never tell you about my social life or the men that I date. Paul's an attorney who spends all of his time representing some of his family's interests. And finally, no, Taft women do not work."

With her eyes dancing, she shrugged. "I'm not really sure what the Taft women do with all their time, but Paul assures me that his mother will take me under her wing once we settle in Boston."

Ginger nearly dropped the stack of napkins she was loading into the holder. "The Taft women? You don't mean . . . you couldn't possibly mean *that* Taft family."

"Yes, Mother, I do mean *that* Taft family."

"As in Edmund Taft, the head of the family that owns Taft Publishing and . . . and a major TV network, not to mention all the cable . . . *that* Taft family?"

"Edmund Taft is Paul's uncle." She toyed with her rings and let out a sigh. "There's only one slight problem," she whispered. She looked directly at Ginger with a troubled gaze. "They're a very proper kind of family, Mom. They're not going to take it very well when they find out that Paul and I have gotten married without all the hoopla that usually surrounds one of their weddings." She looked around the room, as if making sure no one would overhear her, and lowered her voice to a whisper. "They're especially not going to like welcoming a daughter-in-law with baggage."

Ginger's eyes widened and she shoved the napkin holder aside. "I hope you're not referring to Vincent."

Lily's eyes flashed defiantly. "I'm a single parent whose child was born out of wedlock. I'm not exactly the kind of woman who marries a Taft."

"Paul chose you to be his wife, and he married you, I hope, because he loves you. That should be reason enough to welcome you into the family, with Vincent an added blessing," Ginger insisted, quickly losing the fight against the disappointment and anger attempting to rise and cloud her thoughts. "If Paul can't stand up to his family to defend the woman he loves and an innocent child, then maybe you shouldn't have married him in the first place."

"He will, Mom. I know he will." Lily squared her shoulders. "Please don't ruin this for us. I haven't met his family yet, but Paul is certain that once they get to know me, they'll love me and then we can tell them about Vincent and—"

"What do you mean, 'once they get to know' you? How are you going to explain who Vincent is when you get to Boston?"

"Well, that's one of the reasons I'm glad we have a chance to talk privately. Paul thinks it would be better if Vincent stayed here with you and Dad. Just for the summer. By the time school starts in September, we'll be able to bring Vincent to Boston. In the meantime, Paul's parents can get to know me, and we can find a place of our own. It's only for a little while, Mom. Please. Won't you let Vincent stay with you and Daddy for the summer?"

Disappointment in her daughter and her new husband ran deep in Ginger's heart, along with the reality that all of the plans Ginger and Tyler had made for this summer would have to be changed. But neither disappointment ran deep enough to slice through the love she had for her grandson, or the regret that she and Tyler had never been to Chicago to visit Lily and spend time with their only grandchild. "I'll talk it over with your father," she murmured, "but I suppose we could manage, as long as it's only for the summer."

Chapter One

For the first time in over twenty years, Judy Roberts once again welcomed the start of another school year with open arms and a huge sigh of relief. After a long, frustrating summer juggling her job, getting to know her grandson and almost depleting her meager savings to keep him in day care while she was at work, he was now in school in first grade.

Less than a week later when she hurried to work, she was not sure if her life had gotten more or less complicated now that Brian was in school. She had to get out of bed an hour earlier than usual to get him up, dressed and fed, and walk him to school before she could go to work.

"My life's just complicated. Sometimes more, sometimes less," she muttered as she unlocked the front door to the beauty salon and slipped inside. She let up the shade on the door and hit a series of wall switches. As the neon sign, Pretty Ladies, flickered to life, bright lights illuminated both sides of the salon. Behind the reception desk, on either side of the room, two stations sat opposite one another, with a row of six hair dryers and seats stretched across the rear wall. Behind that wall, there was a customer lounge and a ladies' room. Throughout the salon, a fresh coat of dove-gray paint-covered walls cracked with age that matched the well-worn tile floor. Mauve accents, including baskets of dried flowers hanging in between the stations, offered a soothing atmosphere that helped ease her flustered state.

Her mind raced through a list of things she needed to do as manager, to get the salon ready for business. She stood behind the main reception desk that anchored the converted storefront on Welles Avenue, the main street that the town locals simply called "the avenue," and opened the appointment book. No computers here. Pretty Ladies was just an old-fashioned beauty salon that had survived through the lean years, during the sixties and seventies, when one business after another had closed along the avenue only to reopen a short while later in nearby malls. In addition to the standard appointment book, the desk held an old, battered recipe box that held index cards for individual customers, recording the specifics of their hair dye colors, preferred brands of permanents, and personal preferences.

Unlike the new and very trendy unisex hair and nail salon just a few blocks away that drew newcomers to town, Pretty Ladies catered mainly to the elderly residents who lived in the senior citizens' complex, Welles Towers, or longtime, loyal customers who preferred to remain with the owner, Ann Porter, or Judy, the only other hairdresser at the shop.

She quickly counted the appointments for the day and smiled. Ann was only working in the morning today, with her first appointment at ten o'clock, but Judy had eight appointments, starting with one of her favorite clients here at nine o'clock and ending with an afternoon at the Towers. Not a great day in terms of what she might earn, but decent, although she was still worried she might have to get a second job now that she had another mouth to feed.

Still smiling, she answered the phone when it rang, even though the salon did not open for another half an hour. After making an appointment for one of Ann's customers for tomorrow, she stored her handbag at her hair station and went directly to the customer lounge in the rear of the salon. Within ten minutes, she set up the coffeemaker and a kettle of water for tea, put a fresh tablecloth on the snack table, and set out the packets of sugar, both natural and artificial, powdered creamer, napkins and paper plates.

At eight forty-five, she answered the usual knock at the front door and signed for a box of goodies from McAllister's Bakery that held the standard order of three dozen assorted baked goods. By design, these were far too many doughnuts or Danish or sticky buns for the customers to consume, but she would take whatever was left to the Towers for the seniors, a daily ritual that almost always ended her day on an upbeat note.

Before she had a chance to carry the box back to the lounge area, Ann arrived a full hour ahead of time. At sixty-two, she was only five years older than Judy, but she was no longer the vibrant, tireless woman who had spent the past thirty years working side by side with Judy as both employer and friend. Beyond the common bond of their vocation, they had shared the challenges of raising a child and the sorrows of widowhood. While Judy had maintained her health, Ann had packed a good extra forty pounds on her once-slender frame and had battled recurring bouts of gout over the past year that had zapped her energy, although her sense of humor was still intact.

"You're early," Judy remarked, holding tight to the box.

"Alice Conners called me at home last night. She's not feeling up to coming in for her ten o'clock, so I promised I'd stop by her house instead. I just need to get my bag." She paused, stared at the box in Judy's hands and pointed to the back of the shop. "Take that into the lounge. Quick. Before I gain another three pounds just thinking about what's inside or my big toe turns bright red and starts throbbing again."

Judy chuckled. "Just thinking about treats from McAllister's isn't the problem. It's eating two or three a day that gets you into trouble, in more ways than one. Baked goods are off-limits. Doctor's orders, remember?" she insisted before she turned and started toward the lounge.

Ann followed her for a few steps, but turned to get

to her station. "No baked goods. No coffee. No tea. No chocolate. And that's just a tip of the forbidden list. Boy, isn't living with gout swell?" She sighed. "Still, it has been a couple of months since I've had any problems, and I've been dreaming about Spinners for weeks. All that sweet, buttery dough laced with cinnamon and topped with a mound of chocolate icing." She sighed loudly again. "Set aside a chocolate-iced one for me, will you? Just one couldn't hurt."

Ann was off her diet more than she was on it, and Judy was loath to encourage her to do something that would adversely affect her health. When she got to the lounge, she set the box down, lifted out the tray, set it on the table and grinned. "Sorry. No Spinners today," she replied, relieved at the day's offerings.

"Any cheese Danish?"

"No. Just miniature sticky buns that you don't really like. There's still some fresh fruit in the refrigerator," she suggested, hoping to convince Ann to follow her diet and try to prevent another debilitating episode that would either keep her off her feet for a few weeks or trigger another eating binge that would add even more pounds.

Judy stored the box away and opened the refrigerator. "I have a yellow Delicious apple, a pear and a navel orange. And there's a quart of cider you can warm up if you want something hot to drink."

"One orange. Three sticky buns. And don't argue. I'm still the boss around here, and just in case I need to remind you, it's dangerous to argue with a post-menopausal woman."

"That's funny. I distinctly remember my boss telling me just last week that I should ignore her when she asked for something she shouldn't eat," she teased, even as she arranged a plate with the orange and three sticky buns and put it back into the refrigerator.

"That must have been your other boss. The one with willpower."

Judy laughed, went back into the shop and grabbed her smock that she put on while she made her way to the reception desk where Ann stood waiting with her bag of tools and supplies. When Judy nearly tripped, she stopped to hike up her slacks.

"New slacks?" Ann asked.

"I got them off the clearance rack. I meant to hem them, but as usual these days, time has a way of running out before all my chores are done." She took a deep breath and smiled. "Things should calm down a bit now that Brian's in school."

"I'm sure they will. Just be careful, will you? I don't want you to trip and fall and hurt yourself."

"I'll be fine."

Ann nodded. "I should be back in plenty of time for my ten o'clock," she said before she headed toward the door.

"I'll be here. I've got plenty to do. It's supply day, remember? In between appointments, I'll be inventorying the stock."

Ann looked back over shoulder and lifted one brow. "What about my goodies?"

"One orange. Three sticky buns. I have them on a plate in the refrigerator, although it's against my better judgment."

Grinning, Ann waved goodbye. Before the door closed behind her, Judy was already reviewing her appointments for today. The first one, for Madge Stevens, a longtime client, brought a lift to her heart that the second appointment with Mrs. Hart quickly erased, and she prayed for an extra dose of patience to get through it.

When Madge arrived a few minutes later, promptly at nine o'clock, Judy greeted her with a smile and a bear hug. "I've missed you."

Madge returned the hug, stepped back and grimaced. "I've missed you, too, but I'm afraid my hair has missed you even more. I was going to borrow that special conditioner you gave me for Andrea when she was getting chemo, but she'd used it all up and neither one of us could remember the name of it."

"No problem. Andrea's still doing well?"

Madge smiled. "It's been two years now, and she's still cancer-free, thankfully."

Judy inspected Madge's blond, shoulder-length hair and grinned. "Sun and salt air might be your nightmare, but they're a hairdresser's best friend. Don't worry. I've got some of the conditioner. I'll use it today and send you home with some, but we'll have to snip off those split ends first."

Madge shrugged. "Getting my hair cut is a small price to pay for being able to rent a place for a month at the shore with my sisters. Jenny and the girls were able to stay for the whole time, and Andrea even managed to get down for a few days each week. What a great month!"

An only child, Judy shook her head and wished she had had a sister or two like Madge. Judy had not had a single day off the entire summer, either. Not since Brian had arrived. "Go on back. I'll give you a good wash, then we'll see about taking care of those split ends."

Within moments, she had Madge freshly shampooed and settled into the chair at her station, and she had a tube of conditioner on the counter for Madge to take home. Judy rearranged the plastic drape to protect Madge's lavender outfit and started to comb her hair free of snags. "We'll have you looking perky again in no time," she assured her.

Madge chuckled. "Now that Sarah is in school, maybe I'll have a little more time to get perky and help Russell at the store, too."

"Business is still good?" Judy asked and wondered how or why anyone would buy the gourmet food or expensive trinkets for cats, all available at Russell's store.

"At the Purrple Palace? It's going perfectly," Madge teased. "I'm so pleased for Russell. He's worked hard to make the store a success."

"And Sarah. Is she is still attending the preschool program?"

"She turned five in the spring, so she's in full-day kindergarten. Remember when my boys and your Candy started school? They had half-day kindergarten sessions back then. That's all changed now, I suppose to accommodate so many working mothers."

Judy's hands stilled as memories of her daughter surfaced. When Candy started school, Judy was young and hopeful, with her husband, Frank, at her side. Now he was gone, and Candy was somewhere in California battling her addiction again.

Madge pointed to the photograph Judy had taped to her mirror. "Is that your grandson?"

Judy looked into the mirror and locked her gaze with Madge's. Although they were very close in age, the two women looked very different. Madge wore her years well. She had a deft hand with her makeup and both the time and the money to make sure her hair was colored well and styled fashionably. Like the proverbial shoemaker's son who had no shoes, Judy had little time for her own hair. She wore it short and shaggy now, and her gray roots reminded her she was long overdue for a color touchup. Struck by the difference between them, as well as Madge's question, she took a deep breath and turned her attention back to Madge's hair. "Yes. He's in first grade. You've been away, so I guess you haven't heard. Brian's staying with me . . . for a while longer."

Madge frowned. "I thought I'd heard he was only going to be with you for the summer and that he'd be going back to school in California."

Judy took another deep breath. "Candy's not well," she whispered, relying once again on the euphemism she had used for so many years now, although Madge knew all too well that Candy had been battling drug addiction for most of her life. Madge had been there through Candy's rebellious high school years, her unfortunate marriage, and the scene at Frank's funeral four years ago that had changed the rift between mother and daughter from temporary to permanent, at least as far as Candy was concerned. Judy glanced up and looked into the mirror again, half expecting to see her broken heart staring back at her, along with Madge's sympathy.

"I'm so sorry," Madge murmured.

Judy blinked back tears. "Me, too. For the past few years, I thought not knowing how she was doing was bad, but not knowing where she is now is even worse. Brian's only six, but he asks questions about his mother and his father that I can't answer."

Madge nodded. "Sarah's had questions, too. She was three when we adopted her, but she still asks me to find her mommy for her. Death isn't a concept she understands yet, I'm afraid."

Judy swallowed hard and started trimming off the split ends. "I think I could handle explaining Candy's death to Brian a lot easier than trying to explain why his mommy doesn't come for him when she's still alive. I've told him how sick she is. Unfortunately, he knows that, too, but he's so young. He doesn't understand drug addiction any more than I do, and I'm afraid he's seen a lot of things he shouldn't have."

"At our age, raising a child isn't easy," Madge murmured. "What about Brian's father? Isn't he able to take care of him?"

Judy snipped another section of hair and let her hand drop. "Duke?" She snorted. "Would you believe he drove that child cross-country on a motorcycle? Then he waited with him on my front porch until I got home from work, handed me an envelope with some legal papers making me Brian's guardian and cycled off into the sunset all by his lonesome."

"He didn't!"

Judy cocked her head and studied Madge's hair. Satisfied with the trim, she worked some conditioner through the sun-damaged strands of hair. "He sure enough did. I'm trying really hard, but raising Brian is a whole lot harder than raising Candy." She sighed. "Or maybe I'm just a little bit older than I was back then, and now I don't have Frank to help me. But at least school's in session now, and I don't have to pay a sitter while I'm working. They have an after-school program, too, so I can pick him up at six o'clock. That helps."

Madge did not respond for several minutes. When Judy picked up her blow-dryer, Madge gripped the end of the dryer and held on to it. "We adopted Sarah, so our situations are different. I know that. But I have a friend who is going through the same thing as you are, raising her grandchildren. She's in her fifties, too, like we are. I'm sure you know Barbara Montgomery, don't you?"

"Not very well. Her granddaughters are in Brian's class, though. She's Ann's customer. Owns Grandmother's Kitchen on Antiques Row at the other end of town. It's so sad about what happened to her son, but she hasn't been in to the salon to have Ann do her hair since the funeral, and I haven't seen her at school much, either."

"It's a tragedy. A true tragedy, especially for the twins." She sighed. "Poor babies. First their mother runs off and disappears. Then they lose their daddy in a senseless crime," she murmured as she shook her head. "I'm really worried about Barbara, too. Between losing Steve, raising the girls, running her shop, dealing with the stress of the continuing police investigation and praying they find the monster responsible for Steve's death, she's having a rough time all around," Madge whispered.

Judy toyed with the cord on the dryer. "To be honest, I've been so busy with Brian and work all summer, I haven't had much time to myself," she murmured.

Madge smiled and let go of the dryer. "Maybe you and Barbara should get together. You have a lot in common, with both of you raising grandchildren. It might help."

"You might be right," Judy said absently while she turned the idea over in her mind.

"You know, Barbara's been a friend of mine for years. She may be too proud to admit it, but she could probably use a friend in the same situation right about now, too."

Barbara Montgomery, along with her husband, were definitely "old" Welleswood, like Judy, but they had been among the town elite for years, while Judy's background was decidedly working class. Would the problems they were each encountering raising their grandchildren be enough to create a bond of friendship? Eager to find out, Judy shrugged. "I guess it couldn't hurt."

"It'd be good for you. For both of you. Why don't I stop by her shop this afternoon before I pick up Sarah from school? I'll talk to her and tell her to stop in to see you on her way home from work. I think she finishes up at four."

"That's all right. I'll . . . I'll make sure I walk over one day later this week. Today's not really a good day for me. I've got to check the supplies and place an order. And somehow I wanted to find time to color my hair, so I may not even have time for lunch and still be at the Towers for the afternoon," Judy insisted and switched on the blow-dryer to prevent Madge from arguing. Whether or not Judy would be able to find a friend in Barbara remained to be seen. Finding support or getting advice from someone else in a similar situation, however, was something she knew she really needed.

Madge could understand the challenges Judy faced—to a point. But she had not walked a single day down the path that led to having a grown child abdicate her responsibilities as a parent or raising a grandchild or making the emotional and financial adjustments that had become a necessary part of Judy's life. Judy did not know Barbara Montgomery very well at all, except to know they lived and worked in very different social circumstances. She suspected she might have more in common with another single working woman trying to make ends meet than she would with Barbara, who was married to a very successful CPA and owned her own business to boot.

Judy finished styling Madge's hair and met her gaze in the mirror. "Better?"

Madge smiled. "Much better. Thank you. I'll need another appointment for early October for a coloring, though. By then, you and Barbara might be friends," she suggested.

"Maybe," Judy replied, but she was not nearly as certain about the prospect as Madge seemed to be. She removed the plastic cape, hiked up her slacks again and swept up while Madge left to use the ladies' room.

When Madge returned, she pressed a bill into Judy's hand and took a bite out of one of the miniature sticky buns that had been in the lounge. "You take care of yourself, and don't forget to go over to see Barbara," she murmured and left before Judy could respond.

She rang up the charge on the cash register and slipped the change, her tip, into her pocket. She was not surprised that Madge had tried to be so supportive, as well as generous. She was surprised, however, when Madge returned half an hour later. "I stopped to see Barbara. When I was talking to you earlier, I forgot that she closes the shop at three o'clock now that she picks up the girls after school. She said she'd have some time around one if you wanted to stop in to see her then. I know you said it was a really busy day for you, but sometimes you just have to leave one thing go because something else is more important."

"Like coloring my hair? Thanks a bunch." Judy chuckled to herself and shook her head. "Do you ever leave anything undone?"

"Of course not," Madge teased.

The phone rang and interrupted their banter. As soon as she answered the phone and heard Mrs. Hart's voice, her heart sank. When the elderly woman canceled her appointment and scheduled another one with Ann later in the week, Judy tried to remain polite. She was more relieved than disappointed not to have to deal with this particular customer today, in spite of the fact that she needed everyone she could get these days.

As soon as she hung up, she looked at Madge and shrugged her shoulders. "Mrs. Hart canceled her appointment for today, so unless someone walks in, I think you're my only customer this morning."

Madge smiled sympathetically, then brightened. "Which means you can get started checking the supplies."

"True. And color my hair."

"And have time for lunch?"

"Also true," Judy admitted.

"Good. I'll pick you up at twelve. We'll celebrate the start of the school year by having a quick lunch at The Diner, and then we'll go to see Barbara together. I've been meaning to stop at the shop next door to order something for Andrea anyway. She and Bill are celebrating their second anniversary in a few weeks."

Lunch at The Diner, the quaint little restaurant that was one of the few businesses like Pretty Ladies that had thrived during the years when Welleswood was just another dying, suburban town, sounded wonderful. Judy's purse, unfortunately, held barely enough to last for the week as it was, even counting Madge's tip.

"My treat," Madge insisted, as if reading Judy's mind. "I owe you lunch, remember?"

Judy frowned. "You owe me lunch? Since when?"

"Since September, 1986. We both went to lunch at The Diner to celebrate when Candy started her last year of high school. Remember? I'd forgotten my wallet, so you paid the bill. When I tried to repay you, you told me I could pay for both of us the next time we got together on the first day of school, which we never did because that was Candy's last 'first day' of school."

Judy laughed. "You're making that up. Your memory might be good, but it's not that good."

Madge narrowed her gaze. "As I recall, you were a redhead back then. On that particular day, you were wondering whether or not to go blond or try frosting your hair."

"So you remember our conversation, too?"

"Tell me you don't remember what happened to your hair that very afternoon?"

Judy opened her mouth to respond, but a memory flew out of the past. A painful memory that flashed a horrid mental image of the disaster later that afternoon that had left her with bright orange hair less than half an inch long over her entire head on the very day that Candy started her senior year. "Oh, *that* day?"

"Exactly that day," Madge insisted. She smiled and patted Judy on the shoulder. "I'll pick you up at twelve," she insisted. "In the meantime, stick to the inventory and if you do have time to color your hair, stick to dark brown. It's more becoming, and it's safer," she teased before she left.

Chuckling, Judy hiked up her slacks again. When she saw the tube of conditioner on the counter, her smile widened. She could give Madge the conditioner at lunch, free of charge, one friend to another. The phone rang again. "Pretty Ladies, this is Judy," she said as she grabbed her pen to either make an appointment or change one.

"Judy Roberts?"

"Yes."

"Judy, this is Marsha, the school nurse at Park Elementary. It's Brian. I'm afraid you need to come to the school immediately. He's—"

Judy dropped the phone, grabbed her purse and ran out the door, barely remembering to lock it behind her before charging down the avenue toward the school.

41

Chapter Two

The nurse's office at Park Elementary School smelled of alcohol and disinfectant and sported freshly painted medicine cabinets with shiny locks. There was a child in one of the four yellow plastic chairs that served as a waiting area for students sent or brought to the school nurse, who was sitting behind a metal gray desk.

Judy shoved her visitor's pass into her pocket and rushed straight to Brian. Ignoring the nurse, she crouched down in front of her grandson and ran the edge of her finger along one of his tearstained cheeks. "Feeling sick?" she asked, too concerned to waste time worrying about how she was going to salvage the rest of her workday.

He shrugged and kept his gaze downcast.

She heard the nurse approaching as she felt his forehead with the back of her hand. "I don't think you have a fever."

"His temperature is quite normal," the nurse quipped.

Judy stood and turned slightly to face the other woman, who had stretched out her hand. "I'm Marsha Chambers, the school nurse. We spoke on the phone."

Judy shook the younger woman's hand and wondered how this woman-child could possibly be old enough to be a nurse. She did not look a day over seventeen, but then, everyone Judy dealt with these days seemed impossibly young. "I came as quickly as I could. I had to walk. I don't have a car," she explained, wishing Hannah Miller, who had been the school nurse here at Park Elementary for as long as Judy could remember, had not retired last year. Or was it the year before?

"I understand. You're Brian's grandmother?"

"Yes. I'm raising Brian. Temporarily. What's wrong? He doesn't appear to have a fever."

The nurse glanced at Brian and hardened her gaze. "No. Physically, he's fine."

"Then why on earth didn't you tell me that when you called?" Judy argued.

The nurse arched her back, and flipped her long, blond hair over her shoulder. "I would have told you, if you hadn't hung up on me," she countered, with just a slight tone of impatience. "Actually, Miriam called me from the front office to let me know you'd arrived. I've arranged for Brian to spend a few moments with one of the secretaries so we can talk. Privately," she added with a nod toward Brian.

Judy swallowed hard and tried to stem the flow of miserable memories that threatened to sweep over her, despite the relief she felt that Brian was not seriously ill. When Candy had been in high school, Judy had been called to the school too many times to count, let alone remember, but that had been high school, not elementary school. When the secretary arrived, Brian left without an argument or a glance at either his grandmother or the nurse, and Judy sat down in the chair positioned at the side of the nurse's desk.

After the nurse took her own seat, she looked at Judy with a gaze softened by pity. "I know it can't be easy to be raising a young child at your age."

Pity? Judy's backbone stiffened. "I was busy raising his mother before you were even born," she snapped. "How many children are you raising?"

The nurse huffed, and her cheeks reddened. "I'm not married so I don't have any children of my own, but I had four years experience at Grace Academy before coming here last year. If you'd rather speak to the principal—"

"No," Judy murmured before their encounter became any more adversarial. "I'm sorry. Your call scared me half to death. I should have given you an opportunity to explain what was wrong. Brian seemed perfectly fine this morning when I walked him to school, so if he had taken sick this quickly, I was afraid it might be something serious."

The nurse nervously twisted her hands, which were resting on top of a manila folder on her desk. "I'm sorry, too. I probably should have been a little more direct when I called you. I certainly didn't mean to alarm you. It's just that . . . well, I've never encountered anything like this before. Our guidance counselor is also assigned to another elementary school, and she was already involved in another incident and couldn't come, so Mrs. Worth, the principal, asked me to speak with you."

Judy swallowed hard again. Mrs. Worth. Another

person at Park Elementary who was new to Judy, but at least she had met Brian's first grade teacher at the Open House in August. "What exactly is the problem?"

The nurse opened the manila folder, picked up a crayon drawing, and slid it across the desk so Judy could see it. "Yesterday afternoon, the children were asked to draw pictures of their parents. This is Brian's picture, which his teacher only looked at last night at home. Given the climate in today's society, I'm sure you'll be able to see why Brian's teacher had to bring this to our attention today. Before anyone contacted the Division of Youth and Family Services, the principal thought it best we speak with you."

Judy's pulse raced. Before she even took a peek at the picture he had drawn, she thought she had a good idea of what she might see, but she was not prepared at all. Despite some very juvenile stick figures and awkwardly drawn objects, the image of what his life had been like before coming to Welleswood to live with his grandmother was devastatingly graphic and pathetic.

Trembling, she examined the picture closely. The largest stick figure had been drawn in heavy black crayon. An assortment of oddly shaped spots on one ear looked far more benign than the dark rainbow of colors streaking down each arm. Judy could not have drawn a more accurate picture of Duke, with his tattoos and earrings, if she tried.

She was shaken, but not overly concerned because

she knew the picture was, unfortunately, very accurate in detail. She studied the small stick figure sitting at the man's feet playing with what appeared to be a collection of weapons of some sort. She could not tell if they were supposed to be knives or guns, but there was no doubt the little figure had one aimed upward, pointing directly at the larger stick figure.

Her heart lurched against her chest, however, when she gazed at yet another stick figure lying in a prone position on the floor behind the tiny figure. Yellow crayon scribbled across the head obviously represented blond hair, just like Candy's had been the last time Judy had seen her. But it was the assortment of crudely drawn bottles, multicolored dots looking very much like pills, and pointed objects that looked like syringes that left Judy clutching her chest as she tried to endure looking at the painful scene which had poured out of Brian's memories onto this paper.

Blinking back tears, she pointed a shaky finger at each of the stick figures and identified them. "This is Duke, Brian's father. The prone figure is his mother, my daughter, Candy." Her voice cracked. "This little one would be Brian."

Without responding, the school nurse left for a moment and returned with a glass of water for Judy. She took a sip, almost too distraught to swallow the water without choking.

The picture Brian had drawn depicting the life Candy had led in California with her husband and child was far worse than Judy could have imagined.

Heartfelt disappointment in her daughter, coupled with concern for Brian, quickly merged into anger. "How could you? How could you?" she whispered, as if Candy might be able to justify allowing her child to be raised in such a dangerous and godless environment. She did not expect Candy to answer. Judy knew that it was not Candy at all, it was the drugs, those hideous drugs, that had robbed Candy of all sense of decency and put Brian in danger.

Any and all resentment Judy had harbored these past few months about being thrust into the role of mother instead of grandmother evaporated at that very moment, and all the inconveniences in her life now that Brian was with her seemed inconsequential, if not petty. Brian was safe now. He was here, with her, where he belonged and needed to be.

She took several sips of water before quietly explaining the meaning behind the picture, as she understood it, as well as the circumstances behind her temporary custody of her grandson. To her relief, the nurse remained sympathetic and nonjudgmental, patting Judy's arm. "I'm so sorry. Brian's very fortunate to be with you."

Judy sniffled and reached into her purse for a tissue. "What do we do now? About the picture?"

The nurse put the picture back into the manila folder while Judy put her glasses back on. "Even though Brian is no longer in that environment, with your permission, we'd like Brian to see the school district's psychologist, of course, but the counselor wanted me to arrange for a time she could speak with you about arranging for private counseling for your grandson." She took a card from the folder and passed it to Judy. "Her name is Janet Booth. If you call her tomorrow morning after nine, she'll set up a time convenient for both of you to meet."

Judy sighed with relief. Finally a name she knew. "Mrs. Booth was Candy's sixth grade teacher. I didn't realize she'd become a counselor. Of course, I'll call her tomorrow morning." She paused to moisten her lips. "What about the Division of Youth and Family Services?" she whispered, frightened that Brian might be taken from her and placed into foster care.

The nurse shook her head. "I'll speak to the principal, but I don't believe that will be necessary now. Not under the circumstances."

Judy looked toward the door and back again. "What about Brian? Should I take him home? I had to close the salon to come here, but—"

"You can speak with him if you like. I know he's still a bit confused about why his picture wasn't hanging up with all the other children's. I'm afraid he got a bit forceful with one of the other students, which is why his teacher, Miss Addison, sent him here. Just to cool down a bit."

Judy shook her head and tried to reconcile the nurse's description of Brian with what she had observed. Over the course of the summer, she and Brian had actually gotten to know one another for the first time. Now that he had filled out, his stocky frame was in perpetual motion, and he had the greatest dimple in each of his pudgy cheeks. At first, he had been wary of her, even untrusting. He seemed more comfortable with her and with his new surroundings now, although she noticed he did not gravitate toward men, especially large men. "He's normally very agreeable. He can get withdrawn once in a while," she admitted, "but he's never highly agitated or pushy, even with the children in the neighborhood."

"All the more reason for you to speak with the counselor. I'm sure she'll have some ideas for you that could help. In the meantime, you can take Brian home if you want, although maybe it would be better if he rejoined his class. The teacher has already taken down all the other pictures," she added.

"I'll ask Brian, but he'll probably want to stay," Judy suggested. While the nurse called the front office to have Brian returned to the nurse's office, Judy worried the strap on her purse. How she might be able to afford counseling for Brian when she scarcely made enough for the two of them now was a problem she would need to lift straight to the top of her prayer list, but she was certain about one thing. Brian would get all the help he needed, even if that meant taking a second or third job to pay for it.

By skipping lunch with Madge, after a brief, but evasive explanation and a promise to meet her at Barbara's shop, Judy was back on schedule by one o'clock. She had a good forty-five minutes before she was due at Mrs. Schimpf's apartment in the Towers to give her a haircut, and she turned down the cobblestone walkway onto Antiques Row toward Grandmother's Kitchen with more than a slight hesitation to her steps.

It seemed like only yesterday when the lumberyard had been on this plot of land. Frank had come here to order the wood to build the fence that still protected the backyard of their home and the swing set he had made for Candy as a surprise for her fifth birthday. Judy made her way past the shops, scarcely four years old now, but designed to complement the vintage storefronts along the avenue.

Grandmother's Kitchen was halfway down the row, and the foot traffic, even on a day as hot as this one, was light. Judy was so preoccupied with happier memories she nearly walked past the shop. Once inside, she paused for a moment to cool down in the air-conditioning and looked around. The shop was smaller than it appeared from the outside, perhaps no larger than fifteen by twenty feet, and the shine on the wooden floor was almost dazzling. Floor-to-ceiling shelves boasted dozens and dozens of rare china canister sets that were breathtaking, both in beauty and price. Protective velvet chains, like the ones used in movie theaters and museums, kept patrons at a safe distance. No problem there for Judy. If she saved her wages for a month of Sundays, she would never be able to afford a single item in this shop, and she held tight to the box from McAllister's and her purse for fear of knocking something over.

Several small antique glass-and-oak display cabinets placed about the center of the room protected more canister sets for potential buyers to inspect at close range. Candles on top of the cabinets added the scent of summer roses to the air. There were no customers currently in the shop but Judy could hear voices coming from a back room, presumably Barbara's office.

Uncertain how to proceed and anxious about the time, she was grateful for a sign that directed her to buzz for assistance. Within moments, Barbara emerged from the back room, and Judy saw for herself how deeply the woman had been affected by her son's tragic murder.

Although still stylish, dressed in a pale pink linen suit and heels, Barbara had obviously been too grief-stricken by her son's murder or too busy trying to raise her twin granddaughters to pay much attention to her hair, badly in need of a good trim and a touch-up. Sorrow had etched new lines across her forehead and down her cheeks, but it was the haunting look in her gaze as she drew close that nearly moved Judy to tears.

Poor Barbara. To lose a child so suddenly and so violently must be a heavy cross to bear. At least Judy could still pray for Candy's recovery, but Barbara had no hope of ever seeing her beloved son again. Maybe she and Barbara could become friends, helping one another deal with their private pain as they each struggled to revert from their roles as grandmothers to become mothers again, despite the obvious differences in their backgrounds and circumstances. Perhaps grief, for a son lost forever and for a daughter lost to drugs, would be the bond that was strong enough to help them both.

When Judy stepped forward, eager to make a new friend, she tripped on the hem of her slacks. With her purse in one hand and the box of bakery goods in the other, she bumped into one of the glass display cases. Fortunately, the case was heavy enough to hold fast and keep her from falling, but her nudge had toppled the contents.

With her heart pounding over the sound of the china rattling in the display case, she closed her eyes, grateful to have kept her balance. Thoroughly embarrassed by her awkward entrance, she prayed nothing more than her pride had been cracked or broken.

Chapter Three

Barbara took one step out of her office and froze. Helpless to prevent the inevitable, she watched near disaster unfold in motion slow enough that it appeared to defy time.

Cringing, she instinctively squeezed her eyes shut. When all was quiet, she opened them and saw that Judy was still on her feet, though her face was flushed as she drew in deep gulps of air.

"Merciful heavens, are you all right?" Barbara managed as she rushed forward.

"I'm okay," Judy insisted, looked over her shoulder at the display case and sighed. "Thankfully, I think your china is okay, too. I can't believe I was so clumsy. I knew I should have hemmed these pants. I'm so, so sorry for bumping into the display case. I can't even begin to imagine how long it would take me to repay you if I've broken anything."

"Nonsense," Barbara countered. "I have insurance to cover everything. I'm just glad you're all right."

Madge rushed up to join them. "Barbara? Judy? Are you two all right? I thought I heard—"

"I'm fine. Just totally and completely mortified. I tripped and bumped into the display case," Judy responded. Holding tight to her purse and the box of baked goods, she turned and scanned the display case again. Smiling, she shook her head. "It doesn't look like anything is broken. Maybe my day is taking a turn for the better after all. I was afraid this was going to be the grand finale to a day that went from bad to awful by noon!"

"Mine, too," Barbara admitted. "I'm afraid having a bad day is become the norm. I've been more than a little preoccupied lately. Between reopening the shop, caring for the girls, and my Steve . . ." Her throat tightened. She choked back the grief still so heavy on her heart and wondered if she could ever function normally again or spend the rest of her days trying to exist with a broken heart.

Madge put an arm around Barbara and Judy. "You both have enough on your plates to warrant a lot of bad days. That's why I wanted to get the two of you together . . . so you could help each other."

Judy sighed and shook her head. "Some help I brought with me today. I can't believe I was so clumsy." She turned and looked down at the display case again. "I'd rather have broken something on myself. Bones heal. But antiques can't be replaced. I don't think any of the china is broken . . . but what if it's cracked?"

"Barbara said that would be covered by insurance," Madge insisted. "Now listen. This may not have been the best introduction, but working together to make sure there's been no damage at all might be just the ticket."

"The display case is pretty solid and the velvet lining should have cushioned the pieces that tipped over," Barbara suggested.

Madge left them for a moment to turn the sign on the window from Open to Closed. "The last thing we need right now is a customer," she explained.

"That's true," Barbara murmured. After walking around the display case, her initial hopes about the lack of damage were substantially reinforced, although she needed to carefully inspect each piece for hairline cracks that would ultimately affect their value.

The flush on Judy's cheeks, however, remained. "Are any of the pieces cracked?" she asked.

Barbara caught her breath for a moment. Telling Judy the display case housed one of the most expensive or the most fragile set in her collection, which primarily contained imports from Germany and Czechoslovakia, would only add to the woman's obvious distress. These white china canisters, decorated with multicolored wild flowers, dated back to the early 1800s. The largest canisters for flour, sugar, barley, rice, coffee and tea were intact, as were the smaller ones for spices ranging from cinnamon to mustard, and a pair of tall matching cruets for vinegar and oil, although most of the pieces had tipped over. "There's no visible damage," Barbara murmured.

Three months ago, she would have been frantic even to think the set might have been damaged, but losing Steve had taught her many lessons, not the least of which was the importance of life over mere possessions. The smile she offered to the other two women now was genuine. "If there's any damage at all, it would be very minor. I still have to carefully check each of the pieces for cracks or chips, but I have to put the canister sets under the light on the work counter in back to know for sure."

Judy's smile was tenuous. "Minor?"

Madge grinned. "That's what Barbara said. Minor."

The distant sound of a tinny melody signaling a call on a cell phone immediately deepened Madge's grin. "That's my cell phone. I just love hearing 'The Purple People-Eater' instead of a standard telephone ring," she explained. "I've been expecting an important call. I'll be right back."

While Madge walked to the back office in rhythm to the catchy tune, Judy checked her watch. When she looked back at Barbara, her gaze was filled with disappointment. "Unfortunately, I've only got about half an hour before the first of my afternoon appointments at the Towers, so I won't be able to stay while you check the pieces for any damage. Why don't you open the display case? At least I have enough time to help you take the pieces back to your office. I'd call to cancel the appointments if they were in the shop. My customers there wouldn't mind a last-minute cancellation half as much, but the seniors . . . well, that's not your problem, it's mine. Anyway, as soon as I finish up at the Towers, which should be by five o'clock, at the latest, I'll pick Brian up from the after-school program. There's no way I can bring that child here, though. I'll see if I can find a sitter. Maybe one of my neighbors would mind him, under the circumstances, and I can come back tonight. That's assuming you can come back—"

"Judy! You're rambling. Stop!" Barbara almost chuckled out loud when the woman snapped her mouth shut and blushed again. "Take a deep breath."

She did.

"Now another."

She did.

Barbara sighed. "Life is a whole lot more complicated for me now, too, especially when John has evening appointments, which he does most nights these days. But don't worry about staying while I check the pieces for damage. Once we get them to the back room, it won't take me long to check them over, and in the meantime, you can go ahead and keep your appointments at the Towers," she insisted and absently smoothed the hair on the back of her head. For the first time in months, she felt self-conscious about neglecting her hair, but blamed her vanity attack on the fact the Judy was a professional hairdresser who certainly must have noticed how wretched her hair had become.

Judy smiled, however, for the first time since she had entered the shop. "I can't thank you enough for being so understanding, but I can do your hair for you. After hours. During hours. At the salon, or your house, or mine. It's the least I can do. I know you're Ann's customer, but I don't think she'd object."

Barbara swallowed hard and focused on retrieving pieces of the wildflower canister set. "I've been too preoccupied and too . . ." She tried to choose her words carefully. Judy was merely an acquaintance, not a friend, and Barbara was not prone to talking about such private issues, anyway.

"Too overwhelmed?" Judy prompted.

Barbara nodded. "Good choice. I was trying to think of a word that wouldn't make me sound like I was whining."

Judy set down her purse and the box of baked goods before carefully lifting a cruet from the display case.

"Overwhelmed is just one of the words that came to mind. I could have said exhausted or overtired or stressed out or pressed for time or too proud to ask for help—"

"Who needs help?" Madge asked as she blew back into the front of the shop.

"Oh, not me," said the hairdresser.

"Not me," said the shopkeeper.

Madge gave each of them a hard stare. " ' "Then I'll do it myself," said the little red hen,' " she said, reminded of the old nursery tale of the little red hen who had to do all the work of making bread by herself because no one would help her until the bread was baked and ready to be eaten. In this situation, however, Barbara and Judy were not offering to help. They just needed someone to help them, and Madge was determined to be that someone. "Look, I've known you both for years, and I've been raising Sarah for two years now, at a time in my life when I thought I'd be enjoying my grandchildren, not another child. So I think I know a little bit about how much your lives have changed in the past few months and how much your lives will change even more in the coming years."

She held up her hand when Barbara tried to respond. "I know my circumstances are also very different. I chose to adopt Sarah. You two are far more noble. You've both accepted responsibility for your grand-children without question and without hesitation, all the while dealing with heartache I can only imagine.

So . . . here's the plan. You two get all the pieces of the canister set to the back room and finish up whatever work you have for the afternoon, but don't worry about dinner tonight. I just talked to Russell about it. Bring the children and meet us at Mario's at six. We'll have a pizza party, then Russell and I will take all the children to the puppet show at Welles Park while you two enjoy a little free time."

Barbara hesitated. Going out for a pizza party tonight was about the last thing she wanted to do. She was not really ready to resume a life quite that normal yet, even for the girls. And free time meant time to think, time for the deep ache in her heart to begin to throb, time to begin to pray, then stop, too full of pain to even remember the words to prayers she had recited since childhood.

"I haven't had much in the way of time for myself," Judy admitted.

"Good!" Madge clapped her hands once, sealing the deal without waiting for Barbara to agree, and headed for the front door. She closed it behind her, then opened it again to pop her head back inside. "Listen, you two. When you're comparing notes and talking about being mothers again instead of grandmothers, there's something you both have to remember, something this younger generation just doesn't seem to understand."

Barbara raised a brow, almost too afraid to ask Madge what she meant. Almost. "Pray tell, what would that be?"

Madge looked around, as if making sure no one would overhear. "Don't even try to be a superhero. They aren't real. In fact, they never existed in the first place," she murmured, and promptly closed the door.

"Amen to that," Barbara whispered. "Amen."

Chapter Four

Just before two o'clock, Barbara let Judy out the front of the shop, turned and leaned back against the door. She took a deep breath and carried the last few canisters to the back room which doubled as both her office and workshop, an odd blend of modern life and yesteryear. Along the right side of the room was a custom-built unit, housing the usual array of modern office equipment: a telephone, fax machine, computer, printer, scanner, coffeemaker, even a small television, DVD and CD player. On the left, a wall-to-wall work counter, set waist high since she preferred to work standing up, held shipping and packing supplies, a case of disposable, white cotton gloves, a hanging shop light and a variety of cleaning solutions and tools, along with the two damaged canister sets.

She set the canisters down, crossed the room and poured a cup of coffee. Carrying the coffee with her, she returned to the worktable, with the familiar sense of walking from present to past, from today back to yesterday. From sorrow back to joy?

She was quite pleased with the way she had handled today's accident at the shop, but she was usually stoic throughout emergencies of any kind. When the dust cleared, that's when she would allow herself to collapse. That's how she had handled news of Steve's tragic murder, the funeral, the media attention and the process of taking in her two granddaughters to raise, even reopening the shop. Two months later, when life had seemingly returned to some sense of normalcy, few people had any idea that she was coming apart or that her grief was still so raw that it swept over her in waves as spontaneous and uncontrollable as they were unpredictable.

When her arms and legs began to tingle, she sensed another episode about to unfold. She set her coffee mug down on the counter. Just in time. In the next heartbeat, a tsunami of grief crashed through the protective wall she had built around her heart. Deep choking sobs filled the room, and she wrapped her arms around her waist. Tears fell. So many tears. How many tears could be left in the deep well of hurt she carried within her? How long would it be before grief would relent and let her live in peace instead of sneaking inside her heart and slicing open old wounds?

"Steve."

She whispered her son's name and groaned. He was her baby. Her dream child. A loving, gifted man. A doting father. A Christian who lived and loved his faith, even when abandoned by the woman he had loved and married.

"Steve."

He did not deserve to have his life snuffed out by a bullet small enough to fit in the palm of a child's hand. He had been an innocent victim, shot while performing the mundane task of getting cash from an ATM, in broad daylight, in the middle of center city Philadelphia. No attempt at robbery had been made. Amazingly, no witnesses had stepped forward.

Steve was simply here one moment and gone the next. His children did not deserve to be orphans before they were even old enough to fully understand that once Daddy got to heaven, he could not come back. Would not want to come back. She choked back tears. She did not deserve to lose him, either. She should not have lost him. In the normal cycle of life, a mother died before her son.

"Steve."

Her legs weakened. She grabbed onto the counter for support as she fell to her knees. Head bowed, she felt grief fuel the nugget of anger buried deep within her soul. "Why?" she cried. "Why Steve? Why my son? Why?"

She drew in deep gulps of air and felt her tears flood her cheeks. She tossed back her head and stared up toward the heavens. "He was a good, good man. He was my *son*. You had no right to take him. No right!" she cried.

She listened to the echo of her words. She was so shocked by the harsh tone of anger in her voice that she caught her breath. Ashamed, yet too heartsick to pray for forgiveness, she concentrated on trying to breathe normally again and waited as her heart finally stopped racing. She held very still, hoping the grief would ebb and the anger would subside. Waiting. Listening to the sound of each breath she drew. Feeling each heavy beat of her heart.

And in the stillness, a gentleness surrounded her. She opened her heart to the Source of all love and forgiveness, yearning for the gift of acceptance and the peace only He could bring to her through His Son.

She bowed her head and gripped the counter even harder. "But the cross is so heavy, Lord," she whispered and let her troubles spill from her heart. "I can't pray. I can't eat or sleep. Thanks to the media, I can't get the image of my son's wrapped body lying on the ground out of my mind. John's buried himself in his work, and my shop . . ."

Her litany of troubles continued to pour forth until she was hoarse and her mouth was dry. Exhausted, she let go of the counter, leaned back on her haunches and closed her eyes. "I'm just a mess. My whole life is a mess. My marriage, my house, my shop—"

She hiccuped and wiped her lips. "And if I really want to win the whining award, I should mention my hair, too." She shook herself and got back to her feet. She reached for her coffee mug, but the echo of Reverend Fisher's words when she met with him last week for counseling stilled her hand. "Prayer can be just having a conversation with God. Talk to Him. He'll listen."

She repeated her pastor's words aloud and wondered if today she might have taken the first step toward prayer. "There are no accidents in life. Only opportunities to open our hearts and accept His will as our own," she whispered, relying once again on the wisdom the pastor had shared with her.

Barbara was waiting outside the elementary school at dismissal time with other parents and caregivers. The school crossing guard, Emmett Byrd, had his large stop sign in his hand, ready to freeze traffic on Park Avenue for his little birds who were almost ready to fly the nest again. Now seventy-six, he had been the crossing guard at Park Elementary since his retirement from the military some thirty-odd years ago, and his devotion to the children entrusted to his care was still as strong and unwavering as he was.

She scanned the crowd. Mostly women. Mostly younger women. Of course. She shook away memories of waiting for Rick and Steve all those many years ago. Rick had always been the first child from his class to rush out the door at the end of the day. Steven had been the last, dragging home a schoolbag filled with schoolbooks and books from the school library.

When the dismissal bell rang, she cupped her hand at her brow and watched the children break rank and fly out the door and down across the lawn. They slowed a bit, once they passed the principal, and again when they either reached the crossing guard or whomever had come to take them home.

The little ones in kindergarten were first to be sent

home by their teacher, but there were only a handful. With so many mothers working full-time today, she assumed the rest had stayed for the after-school program. She could have kept her shop open until five, as always, and signed Jessie and Melanie up for the program, too. Unlike many other women, however, she had the economic freedom, especially with John still working, to make the choice to shorten her shop hours and care for the girls after school rather than have them stay with strangers.

When the first-grade teacher emerged, Jessie was first in line behind Miss Addison, holding hands with her sister. Barbara watched the girls and caught her breath as they waited for the teacher's permission to leave. Jessie and Melanie were fraternal twins, as different in looks as they were in temperament. Jessie was built tall and lean, like her father, with long, poker-straight brown hair she wore in a single braid that coiled halfway to her waist. With a healthy dollop of freckles that spilled across her cheeks and sparkling brown eyes, she was the classic image of the all-American little girl. She was forceful, dominant and easily frustrated.

Melanie was the younger of the two by a few minutes. Shorter and a bit plump, with curly brown hair and pale blue eyes, she reminded Barbara of the children's mother, Angie, who had not made any attempt to contact Steve since the day she walked out three years ago. Even Steve's murder, widely covered by the media, had not inspired the woman to return or contact any of her relatives, for that matter. But unlike Angie, Melanie was so sweet, an absolute darling who wanted nothing more than to please everyone around her.

The bond between the girls was unlike anything Barbara had ever witnessed with her sons, Steven and Rick, who had been born several years apart. She had a number of books on twins which well-meaning friends had given to her. All she needed was the time to read them.

Maybe tonight?

"Grammy, look!" Jessie charged forward, dragging Melanie with one hand and holding up a bag with the other. Her backpack flopped around on her back as she ran, and she was so excited she nearly ran into Barbara while Melanie struggled to keep up. "Look inside! Look!"

"Careful, Jessie," Barbara cautioned. "Give Grammy a kiss. You, too, Melanie. We'll take a look inside your bags when we get home."

They shared kisses while Jessie hopped from one foot to the other. "No, now, Grammy!" she insisted, then let go of Melanie's hand and opened her bag. "See?"

Barbara, deciding to choose another battle to win, stooped down and peeked into the bag. Inside, she saw two large hunks of fabric, each a different shade of green, lying next to what appeared to be a page of instructions. "Oh, my. What's all this?" she asked, even as visions of some sort of costumes that needed to be made flashed before her mind's eye.

"I'm gonna be a frog! So's Melanie. Show her, Mel."

Melanie looked shyly at Barbara for permission first, then opened her bag. "See mine, Grammy? I'm gonna be a frog, too." She wrinkled her nose. "I wanted to be the princess, but I didn't get picked. Susan's gonna be the princess."

Jessie tilted up her chin. "Frogs are better."

"Frogs are my very favorite," Barbara insisted. She took a quick look at the paper inside Melanie's bag and skimmed the teacher's note, but she did not bother to read the directions for making the frog costume. "So, you're going to be in a play during the Book Fair next month. That's wonderful!"

Jessie grinned. "We gotta. Miss Addison said so. But we gotta practice a lot. Like this." She handed her bag to Barbara, squatted down, pinched her features together, and started hopping around. "Ribbit. Ribbit. Ribbit." She stood back up and grinned. "See? I know how to be a frog already, but Mel's gotta practice more." She took Melanie's hand. "Want me to show you how again?"

Laughing, Barbara stood up, rather ungracefully, since her leg muscles had cramped. "You'll both be great little frogs, but we'd better practice at home. After homework." She took one of each of the girls' hands and started them all toward the car. "Then we're going out for a pizza party before the puppet show."

"Pizza! Pizza! Yeah!" Jessie skipped her way along-side Barbara, shouting for joy.

Melanie just smiled. "I like pizza the best."

"Not as best as me," Jessie challenged.

Barbara laughed again. "What about frogs? Do you think they like pizza?"

Melanie shrugged, but Jessie squinted her eyes for a moment. "Frogs don't eat pizza. They eat bugs. Ugh!" she said and stuck out her tongue.

They bantered back and forth until they reached the car. As Barbara buckled each of the girls into their car seats in the rear seat, she heard someone call her name and looked up. When she saw Fred Langley, the police chief, approaching, her heart began to race. Why was it that every time she could actually keep grief at bay, even for just a few moments, reality had a way of bringing it back?

She stiffened her backbone, planted as much of a smile on her face as she could manage as she waved the chief over, and turned back to the girls. "Grammy needs to talk to someone. I'll stay right here next to the car. While I do, why don't you two practice sounding like a frog for a few minutes?" she suggested and closed the door halfway.

With the sound of ribbits behind her, she was satisfied that the girls would not overhear anything. When the police chief finally arrived, her fear that her son's murderer had been caught was almost as great as hearing news he was still at large and no progress had been made in bringing him to justice. As if justice could bring Steve back. "Fred?"

"Sorry to bother you like this, Mrs. Montgomery. I

haven't been able to reach your husband, but I thought I might be able to track you down here."

She swallowed hard and nodded.

He took a deep breath. "I got a call from Detective Sanger, the Philadelphia officer handling Steve's case. She said they've got a possible break in the case. News about possible suspects leaked out, so it's probably gonna hit the news at five, maybe even earlier. She's not gonna be able to get away for a while, and she just wanted me to warn you and your husband so you both weren't caught off guard."

Barbara closed her eyes for a moment until she could find her voice. "Have they found Steve's killers?"

"They're not sure, but Sanger said they had a gun. It's the right caliber, but they're waiting on ballistics, and there's a lot of investigation that still needs to be done before any arrests can be made or charges filed."

She struggled against images her mind had created to bring to life the monsters who had senselessly killed her son. A cold shiver raced up and down her spine. "Can you tell me anything about them? The suspects?"

His gaze softened. "I really don't know much about them, other than one is seventeen and the other is fifteen. Sanger said she'd call you as soon as she has something further to report."

"They're just teenagers," she whispered. "What kind of parents raised their sons to become murderers before they were old enough to graduate from high school or to vote? What kind of mother—"

"They're girls, Mrs. Montgomery, and they're sisters. That's why the media has really grabbed hold of the story."

Girls. Barbara nodded, too numb to even imagine two teenage girls as murderers.

"You'll tell your husband?"

She nodded again.

"Is there anything more I can do for you?"

"No. Thank you." She looked inside the car, wanting to shield the girls from the media. "I—I need to take the twins home," she whispered, turned and closed the car door. Given the notoriety of the case, there was no way she could take the girls out for the pizza party tonight for fear of having reporters approach them. She did not have the heart to disappoint the girls, but right now, she had to call John on the private cell phone he carried for her emergency calls and tell him to come home.

Barbara heard John's sports car pull into the driveway and looked out of the third-floor window to make sure. He was home. She popped the *Finding Nemo* DVD into the player, adjusted the volume, and leaned down to give each of the twins a kiss. "I'll be right back."

Jessie pouted and tried to pull out of reach. "I don't wanna watch Nemo again. I wanna go to the pizza party and the puppet show."

Barbara kissed the tip of her nose anyway and wished she had remembered a lesson she had learned the hard way with her own children: Never mention an outing until you're ready to leave. "I'm sorry, baby. Not tonight. There's ice cream in the freezer, though." She tweaked Jessie's nose and planted a kiss on Melanie's cheek. "If you two eat all of your supper, maybe we can make ice-cream sundaes for dessert."

Ever the one to please, Melanie smiled. "I like sundaes. Can we smash up some cookies to put on our ice cream like Pappy did last time?"

Jessie crossed her arms over her chest. "I don't like cookies on my ice cream. I like caramel sauce, but I like pizza—"

"We have cookies and caramel sauce, but we'll have to have our pizza another night," Barbara insisted. "Now watch Nemo while I go downstairs and see what I can make for supper." She left without giving Jessie a chance to continue to be difficult and met John on the second-floor landing. Her hold on her emotions was so tenuous, she avoided his gaze. "The girls are upstairs watching a movie," she managed.

He took her hand and led her back down the stairs. When they got into the parlor, he let go of her hand and she stepped into his embrace. With her arms wrapped around him, she could feel the tension in his body. She burrowed closer and laid her head on his heart before she let her tears fall.

He pressed his cheek to the top of her head, and they rocked back and forth. No words of comfort were spoken or necessary. Only the heavy silence of sorrow and loss reigned. And the mutual fear that now that the journey toward justice for Steve had begun, each step—the trial, the verdict, the sentencing—would only deepen their grief and accentuate their sense of loss and devastation.

No trial, no verdict, no sentence could bring the sound of Steve's laughter or the glimpse of his smile back into their lives. He would not be there to watch his girls grow into young women, and he would not be there on the their wedding days to walk them down the aisle.

John stilled, took a deep breath and handed her a handkerchief to dry her eyes. Sadness shadowed his gaze, and he cleared his throat. "I called Detective Sanger on my way here," he said quietly. "She couldn't add much to what Fred told you, except a little more background on the girls."

She twisted the handkerchief in her hands. "I can only imagine the kind of background that would give two teenage girls access to a loaded gun and prompt them to use that gun to solve a problem or end an argument. It's reckless and outrageous and it's beyond my ability to comprehend, let alone forgive," she snapped. "But I can tell you what they'll probably discover."

She counted out her assumptions on the fingers of her right hand. "One, a broken home. Two, maybe even a series of foster homes. Three, drugs. Alcohol for sure, probably worse. Four, poor academic and discipline records at school. Five, they haven't been to church for years, if ever. And their defense attorney will use their deprived, miserable backgrounds to defend and make excuses for them so the jury will feel sorry for them. No one will care about Steve and the price he paid for someone else's sins."

Alarmed by the depth and scope of her anger, she stopped, closed her eyes for a moment and forced herself to take a few long, slow breaths to slow her racing heartbeat. When she did, the echo of her words sounded against the very foundation of her faith—a faith built on the belief that the Son of God had sacrificed His own innocent life to atone for the sins of others.

"They're still investigating," John murmured and stroked the side of her arm. "Let's take this one step at a time, one day at a time."

She met his gaze and saw the turmoil in her soul reflected in the depths of his eyes before he dropped his gaze. "I'm really glad you came home," she whispered.

He looked toward the staircase. "I'd better head upstairs. I need to make a few calls and tie up some loose ends."

"Okay. I had made some plans for us to go out for pizza with some of the girls' friends before the puppet show, but I told the girls we'd make it another night."

"That's probably a good idea."

"I just have to make a call or two to cancel."

"Use your cell phone."

She cocked her head.

He shrugged. "I unplugged the phones on the first floor. I'll do that upstairs, too. I'm just surprised none of the reporters have tried to call yet," he explained.

Memories of the media barrage in July that began with Steve's death and continued for days past his funeral were still vivid enough to make her shudder. While he went upstairs, she got her cell phone from her purse and called Madge first and quickly explained why she had to cancel tonight's outing.

"If you can't come to the pizza party, then the pizza party will come to you," Madge insisted. "Good friends, junk food and a few little chatterboxes are just what you need to take your mind off what you learned this afternoon. I'll take care of everything, and I'll call Judy to tell her about the change in plans, too. Just set the table and change into something comfortable, like jeans and a T-shirt," she offered and hung up before Barbara had a chance to decline.

Chapter Five

As the party was winding down, Barbara sat back in her chair and sighed with satisfaction.

Indeed, Madge had been right.

A lot of chatter, a little chaos and a good dose of friendship had been just the prescription to help rescue a troublesome and challenging day and a sure way to ease the ache of *what might have been*. She glanced down the length of the dining room table. Instead of the maps and brochures John had been collecting, now safely stored away in the attic, along with dreams of sailing away into retirement and a life of leisure, empty pizza boxes and antipasto tins littered the middle of the table.

Behind paper plates and beverage cups, all five adults and four children crammed together around the table. Russell and John sat at opposite ends. Madge and Judy anchored one side with Barbara between them, across from the four children on the side closest to the wall, a line of chatterboxes, their little faces smeared with tomato sauce and more than one milk mustache.

Ever the organizer, Madge checked her watch and clapped to get the children's attention. "Who wants to go to the puppet show now?"

"Me!"

"Me!"

"Me!"

A chorus of little voices rose louder and louder until Madge quieted them with another clap of her hands. "Then we need clean faces and hands."

Barbara got to her feet. "And a potty stop. Sit still. I'll get some cloths." While she went to the kitchen to retrieve the box of premoistened, disposable cloths that had become a new staple in her life, John and Russell blocked the two possible escape routes. The children apparently were far more interested in getting ready for the puppet show than they were in avoiding a cleanup because when Barbara returned, they were all in their seats and offered little protest when she started an assembly line.

After washing one pair of hands and a face, Barbara passed the child to Madge who provided escort to the powder room behind the kitchen. John took the next child upstairs to the main bathroom. Then, while John and Madge kept their little charges occupied in the living room, as much to protect the antiques as to keep the children from going back to the table for one more bite of pizza, Judy and Russell took the remaining two children for a potty break.

Barbara tossed the last dirtied cloth into one of the pizza boxes, got a large trash bag from the kitchen and cleared the mess from the table, including the plastic tablecloth, in a matter of minutes. "There's a lot to be said for going modern," she murmured and stored the trash bag outside the back door. She returned to the dining room, smoothed a lace tablecloth back into place and set the pair of antique Hull candlesticks in the center.

She paused to run her fingertips along the stem of one of the candlesticks, the first of the thirty-four pieces John had given her over the years for their wedding anniversaries. She kept them all displayed behind beveled glass in an old oak cabinet she had helped her father refinish, first stripping away layers and layers of white paint and cleaning tiny specks of paint in each groove in the heavily carved wood with toothbrushes and toothpicks.

Glancing at the cabinet, she smiled. So many memories, outside and inside. Memories of her father, teaching her patience and sharing with her his love for antiques as they worked. Memories of her married life captured with each piece of Hull resting on glass shelves. The small Hull lamp she had gotten their first anniversary for "lighting up his life with joy." The vases she had used to hold the flowers John had given to her for different anniversaries and later, when Rick and Steve had been born.

"Steve."

She choked out his name. Reminded once again of her loss and the breaking news from the police, she fought the swell of grief ever ready to crash over her heart and inflame still-healing wounds. She turned away from the table. Toward the sound of little frogs who had apparently invaded her living room. Toward laughter. Toward the future instead of the past. Toward life filled with more joys than sorrows.

John came back into the dining room and stood beside her. "Russell and Madge are ready to take the children to the puppet show now. It's only a few blocks to the park, so they're going to walk. They'd need two cars, anyway, just to accommodate the four car seats. It's probably best if they leave by the back door."

Barbara nodded and studied the man she had loved all her life. His golden-brown eyes no longer sparkled with the joy of life and his ash-brown hair was flecked with more gray highlights now than blond. She had not seen the laugh lines at the corners of his eyes for months now, and his shoulders drooped beneath the weight of the cross he was carrying, too.

She moistened her lips, searching in vain for the words to have him turn to her instead of his work for comfort. "Will you stay here with me? What if the reporters come?" she asked. Even though the telephones were still disconnected, she was surprised their pizza party had not been interrupted by knocks at the door, and she did not relish being home alone if and when the media barrage began.

"Carl Landon has taken care of the reporters. As soon as I hung up from you, I called him. He scheduled a press conference at his office for five o'clock which should have kept them satisfied. Besides, if any of the reporters decide to come to the door, I don't think they'll get past Rob and Stuart."

She managed half a smile. Carl was a good friend as well as their lawyer, and he had taken on the role of being their spokesperson within hours of John's call after Steve's murder. Their neighbors, Rob and Stuart, bless their hearts, had proven to be as tough and protective as Secret Service agents guarding the president. When they were called to duty, no one got past them to get to the front door.

He kissed her cheek. "Keep the telephones unplugged and use your cell phone if you need to call me. I'll be at the office. I had two appointments for tonight that I couldn't cancel. I'll leave through the back door, too. The walk will do me good."

"Do you have to leave? Tonight?"

"Judy said she was going to do your hair for you, so you won't be alone. It'll do you good to have some time for lady talk. I won't be late. I should be home by nine-thirty," he promised before leaving her.

Nine-thirty. After the girls had been tucked into bed.

She tried, but found it hard to swallow the lump in her throat. Bedtime rituals, from reading stories, saying nighttime prayers and getting that last drink of water, had always been John's alone time with their boys when they were little. He had resumed the ritual with Jessie and Melanie when Steve used to bring them for an overnight visit, whether it was the night before opening remarks or closing arguments in a big case or an occasional weekend when he had to go out of town.

John had avoided the ritual ever since Steve's death when the girls had come to live with them. Instead, he had wrapped himself deep inside his grief, protected by evening business appointments at his office in Whitman Commons—evening appointments he had abandoned years ago. She did not know how long he would continue to grieve alone and avoid bedtime with the twins, and she yearned to see him kneeling at the side of the bed with the girls once again.

She toyed with the edge of the lace tablecloth and watched him lead the parade of guests past the door and through the kitchen to the back door. When the door finally closed, filling the house with suffocating silence, she flinched and dropped her gaze, feeling so very, very alone.

"I've got everything with me. Are you in the mood to be pampered a little?"

Startled, she looked up and saw Judy standing in the doorway holding a large, canvas bag.

Judy smiled and held up her bag. "Tools of the trade. Everything I need to cut and color your hair. I brought them with me when I left the Towers. Madge had called there and left a message with Penny so I'd know to come here instead of Mario's. I stopped at the salon and got the hair dye. I looked up your color. Just in case," she added. "Madge thought it was a good idea."

Barbara ran her fingers through her hair and cringed. "I must look a sight to have everyone so concerned about my appearance. To be honest, I meant to call for an appointment. I just haven't had the time or the . . . interest. I hate to be such a bother," she insisted, although she would have liked nothing better than to have her hair done. "You've already had a long day."

"It seems like every day is a long day." Judy sighed. "I'm also getting used to sitting down to watch a little television at night and falling asleep before the second commercial. I can't remember the last time I saw a show from beginning to end or had enough energy to stay awake long enough to dry the clothes I'd tossed into the washer." She laughed and shook her head. "I'd forgotten how many clothes a young child can go through in a few days. Look, I completely understand. If you're too tired right now, or you'd rather have Ann do your hair, just say so, and I'll pack up."

"No. Not at all. I just don't want to impose. You've been on your feet all day."

"And I'd better stay on my feet if I want to stay awake until Brian gets back from the puppet show," Judy teased. "Shall I set up in the kitchen? I'd rather not risk it here."

Barbara laughed. "I could tell you stories about the havoc two little six-year-olds have managed to unleash in the past two months, but you probably have a good idea now that Brian is with you. You couldn't possibly do any worse damage, but the kitchen would be better, I suppose."

Barbara led Judy into the kitchen and pointed to the granite countertop where Judy set her canvas bag. She laid out a piece of heavy plastic and lined up several pairs of scissors next to familiar bottles of hair dye and conditioner. "We'll color first and cut second, if that's all right?"

"Sure." Barbara pulled a low-backed chair away from the seventeenth-century farmer's table she had found in an antique barn in Connecticut several years back and sat down.

Judy motioned her back up, laid another piece of plastic the size of a shower curtain on the tiled floor, carried the chair to the middle, and smiled. "That's better. Now if any dye drops on the floor, it won't matter. As you can see, I've been known to drop a little dye in the past."

Barbara looked at the splotches that covered the drop cloth, cringed and sat down. While Judy fit a plastic cape around her shoulders, Barbara folded her hands on her lap and toyed with her wedding ring. "You seem to have this down to a real science."

Judy laughed. "I'd better. I've been making house calls for twenty years or more. Most of the time they're at the Towers. Ann and I both still have a few customers who live at home, but don't go out much so we go to them. As a matter of fact, Ann was just at Alice Conner's home."

"How is Ann doing? The last time I was in the shop in the spring, she was just back from being home sick for a few weeks. Gout, wasn't it?"

Judy nodded. "She's been having a rough time of it for the last year or so."

"I don't think I've ever known a woman, other than Ann, who had gout. I thought that was something men got."

"I think it is, but to hear Ann tell it, gout is just another surprise reserved for some very special post-menopausal women." Judy chuckled. "And Ann is definitely a special woman, even though she isn't very faithful about following the diet the doctor ordered or taking her medication. Once she feels better, she's right back to her old habits, I'm afraid," she admitted, and ran her fingers through Barbara's shoulder-length hair.

Barbara closed her eyes and took gentle breaths so she could concentrate on the soothing sensations Judy created with her fingertips.

"Your cut has really grown out, and there's a bit of

a problem with split ends. Nothing I can't fix. I assume you want the same cut?"

Barbara shrugged. "I've worn my hair the same way for so long, I wouldn't know how to manage anything beyond having a center part and just turning the ends under."

Judy played with her hair again for a while before she stopped and walked around her full circle. "You might want to try something new. Sometimes change is good for your hair and it can lift your spirits, too."

Barbara opened her eyes and met Judy's gaze. "Change can be hard, too."

Judy's gaze softened and she nodded. "I guess we both know some changes are harder than others, don't we?"

Barbara swallowed hard and accepted the invitation of friendship and understanding in Judy's eyes. "Losing Steve was the worst nightmare in my life. Everything has changed. Nothing, absolutely nothing is the same as it used to be."

"I know. Or I think I know," Judy admitted. She clenched and unclenched her fists, and her gaze grew distant. "Sometimes, when I wake up in the middle of the night, I wonder where Candy is or if I'll ever see her again." She paused. "I'm so sorry. About Steve. I—"

"In my heart, I know Steve is safe now and happy. He's Home," Barbara whispered. "I can't imagine how difficult it must be for you. Madge told me Candy is in a hospital somewhere in California, but her husband couldn't tell you where or how soon she'll be released."

Judy took a deep breath. "She's in rehab. She's been in and out of rehab for years. I couldn't tell you how many times. I'd lost count long before Frank died and she showed up for his viewing stoned and out of control. She left in the middle of the night and didn't even bother showing up for the funeral. I haven't heard a word from her since. She's somewhere in California. I don't know where. Her husband couldn't or wouldn't tell me. That's my nightmare . . . not knowing . . . being half afraid I'll never see her again and being half afraid she'll show up on my doorstep, stoned or high, demanding to take Brian back into that life again. That's another nightmare."

She sighed. "It's hard being a mother again, but I won't ever let him go back with her unless I'm absolutely certain he'll be safe."

"I'm sorry. Truly sorry," Barbara whispered. "Have you given any thought to hiring a detective to find her, just to make sure she's all right?"

Judy picked up the bottle of hair dye and turned it round and round in her hand. "Detectives cost money—money better spent, if I had it, for Brian. As it is, putting him into day care for most of the summer used up whatever I had saved. It's better now that school has started. I had to hire a sitter for Saturdays, even though it's usually pretty slow and I lose money because the Saturday crowd has switched to the new salon that does both hair and nails. The after-school program is less expensive, but it's still a strain on my budget. I'm not complaining, though. Brian is all I've got left of Candy. He's my flesh and blood, and I'll care for him and protect him any way I have to."

Barbara clenched her own hands. "Sometimes my imagination runs wild, and I have these dreams about Steve's ex-wife suddenly appearing and taking the children away, even though she hasn't tried to contact them since she walked out on them three years ago. They're all I have left of Steve. I don't want to lose them, too."

She swallowed hard, all too aware of the similar challenges she and Judy seemed to be facing. Barbara's loss, with Steve's death, might be very public, splashed in the newspapers for all to read about, while Judy's was more private and perhaps more painful to bear because she was all alone in her grief and struggles. But they both shared the common bond of dealing with the loss of a child, one to death, the other to drugs; their fears about losing their grandchildren; and the ongoing problems of keeping them and adjusting to being mothers again instead of grandmothers. Alone, they struggled in their new roles. Perhaps together, as friends, they might share the struggle and find the path of rediscovered motherhood easier to travel.

Judy held up the bottle of hair dye and read the label. "Summer Sunrise. That's your color, right?" she asked, changing the subject back to the task at hand.

Barbara nodded.

"Just checking. I'd rather find out now instead of later."

"Good idea. Maybe while you're coloring my hair, you could give me some idea of a new style that would be easier to manage?"

When Judy cocked a brow, Barbara smiled. "A little change might be good," she murmured. "Maybe it's time for some good change. For both of us."

Judy cocked the other brow. "For both of us?"

Barbara smiled, but only time would tell if her hopes for a stronger friendship between them would be fulfilled.

Chapter Six

A week after her near-disastrous visit to Grandmother's Kitchen, Judy was on her way to the Towers, and her life was back on schedule. Again. The trouble was that her schedule today seemed to get a little more unsettled and much more complicated with each passing hour.

First, she had overslept this morning, always a bad start to the day. Brian had been late to school by a whopping fifteen minutes, which meant he had to enter the first grade classroom with all of the children already working at their desks.

In between a rush of unscheduled appointments, she had left another message for Mrs. Worth, the school principal, the third in as many days, but the woman did not seem in any hurry to call her back. Judy had met with the school guidance counselor last week and had the first appointment for Brian with a private counselor set for five o'clock this afternoon. Apparently Judy's efforts to report all she was doing to arrange for counseling for Brian ranked low on the principal's list of priorities.

She arrived at the Towers just before one o'clock, right on time, and got buzzed into the office. She took one step inside, looked around at the lavish display of Mickey Mouse decorations that adorned the office: A clock, computer screensaver, coffee mug and even planters holding foliage worthy of blue ribbons at the annual Philadelphia Flower Show. Mickey was on everything!

She grinned. A touch of Disney was just what she needed today. "What a happy place! I always love coming here, Penny, especially after a rough day."

The office manager for the past fourteen years, Penny looked up from her seat behind the shoulder-high counter and laughed. "It's only one o'clock in the afternoon. The day is still young," she cautioned. She got up, retrieved Judy's canvas bag with the tools of her trade she kept stored in the office, and lifted the bag to the counter. She looked at Judy and frowned. "What? No baked goods from McAllister's today? Or are you bringing them later?"

Judy rolled her eyes. "No. Unfortunately, that's only one small part of my day so far. I had a rough morning. Mrs. Sweeney came in for her weekly touch-up, with three elderly cousins visiting from Florida.

Then they all wanted a cut, wash and dry. They even brought their husbands along. Ann's been sidelined with gout again for the past two days, so I had to handle Mrs. Sweeney and company, who proceeded to eat their way through almost the entire box of baked goods."

"Ann's laid up with gout? Again?"

"Again."

"Poor Ann. I'll try to give her a call later."

Judy let out a deep breath. "I was afraid I'd be forced to cancel some of my appointments here today, but somehow I managed to finish Mrs. Sweeney and her cousins all up, scoot them all on their way and still get here on time. I shoved the last two doughnuts down for my lunch."

"The residents on the second floor who were scheduled for the treats today will be disappointed, but they'll survive," Penny quipped. "I'll put a note out in the Gossip Garden for you, but I won't mention why they have to wait for another time. It's safer that way."

Judy chuckled. "Is there ever a topic safe from residents' gossip in the social room?"

"Not really, but they're pretty preoccupied, now that plans are in full swing for next month's Book Fair. Closing down the avenue to promote reading is as worthy a venture as you can get. Authors appear with their books, crafters sell book-related specialties, schoolchildren perform in little plays and food vendors sell everything that tastes good. It's a win-win for everyone, but you'd think the Commissioners had

approved the entire event again this year just to incon-
venience the seniors."

"I suppose a lot of them aren't able to read much
anymore."

Penny pointed to the small stack of newspapers at
the far end of the counter. "There are fifty-seven apart-
ments here. Every day we get fifty-seven newspapers
delivered, courtesy of the Commissioners. See? There
are only half a dozen left, which is about par. I won't
even venture a guess at how many dozens and dozens
of tabloids and magazines come into the building
every week. What does that tell you?"

Judy shrugged. "I guess they're still reading."

"They can't all be lining birdcages or litter boxes,"
Penny teased. "I think many of them are reading, if
only to get a good discussion going in the Gossip
Garden. To be honest, I think there are a lot of seniors
who like the Book Fair, but they get nervous around
crowds. We're not an assisted living facility, but many
of our residents use canes or walkers. The Book Fair
drew what? Four thousand people last year? Even
with the avenue closed to traffic and opened up for
pedestrians, between all the booths and the stage set
up for the children, it's still a bit of a mob scene.
That's why some of the residents just stay put for the
day."

When Penny smiled again, her eyes twinkled. "A lot
of the residents are excited about the Book Fair, and
they've volunteered to help, but the event gives the
grumblers the perfect excuse to sit around and com-

plain. So I got the building manager to agree to add a new element to the day. I'm hoping they'll all be so busy, they'll forget to grumble and my daughter's Girl Scout troop will get credit for a community service project at the same time."

Judy checked her watch. Penny loved to talk and normally, Judy loved to listen, but not today. Still, she would rather be a little late, than rude. "What do you have in mind for them?"

"Adopt-a-Grandparent Day. Each of the girls will come and spend the day with one of the residents who doesn't volunteer or who doesn't plan to attend the Book Fair."

Judy drew her brows together. "You'd know who they were?"

Penny turned, punched a few keys on her computer and pointed to the monitor. "This is a list of volunteers so far. Joan Smith is on the Book Fair committee, and she e-mails updates to me once a week or so. As for the folks just planning to attend, that's even easier for me to find out." She pointed to the pink plastic clipboard halfway down the counter. "Sign-up sheet," she explained.

"They actually sign up, just to attend?"

Penny laughed. "For ten dollars? You bet they do. Actually, we just issue Book Fair Dollars. I make them up on my computer, and we redeem them with some grant money after the fact. Otherwise, someone might take the ten dollars and keep it."

When the telephone rang, she held up one finger to

keep Judy from leaving and answered the call. "Yes, Mrs. Edwards. No, she didn't forget. She's just on her way up now. No problem." She hung up and grinned sheepishly. "Sorry. Guess I held you up."

Judy hoisted her bag from the counter and realized she had forgotten to bring more free samples of hair care products to replace the ones she had given away. Just another part of a bad day. She handed Penny a list of her three appointments today, a minor accommodation she had in her workday after Brian had come to live with her. "Just in case someone's looking for me. I've been playing telephone tag with Mrs. Worth, the principal at Park Elementary. If she calls, tell her I'll call her back and then let me know."

Penny nodded and pinned the list to a bulletin board on her side of the counter and answered another telephone call while Judy left by the side door that allowed residents and workers to enter the office without using the foyer and waiting to be buzzed inside.

She passed the sixty-gallon, freshwater aquarium, a new addition to the inner foyer and whispered a quick prayer for Dan O'Leary whose family had donated the aquarium in his name. Ninety-seven when he died last year, he had been the last of the original residents who had moved into Welles Towers when it had opened years ago. The aquarium seemed a fitting memorial to the avid fisherman and quickly became a favorite with the residents.

She nodded to several women sitting together nearby waiting for the county bus to take them to the grocery store and took a quick glance inside the aquarium while she waited for the elevator. Dozens of fish were swimming in and out of the plants and ceramic decorations. Either the residents had finally stopped raiding the fish food, overfeeding and killing the fish, or Penny had solved the problem after losing a second tank of fish by moving the fish food into her office.

When the elevator arrived, she rode to the third floor where she found Mrs. Edwards sitting in the alcove by the window. Scarcely five feet tall and thin to the point of emaciation, she was a powerhouse of energy. Her mind was still sharp, and she was one of the nicest seniors in the Towers, if not the most talkative. "I saw you walk in a bit ago. Penny bending your ear again?"

Judy laughed and followed her down the hallway. "Just a little. I'm sorry I'm late. She was telling me about the Book Fair."

The elderly woman stopped in front of her apartment door and used the key hanging from a lanyard around her neck to unlock the door. "Handy little thing," she commented as she let the key drop and tugged on the lanyard. "Somebody donated a whole case of them to the residents so we wouldn't lose our keys. I checked it good, though, and made sure it had that safety clip so if I fall when the key is in the door, the strap will snap apart and I won't hang myself like that poor soul out West. Hung there for days before anyone found him. Imagine living eighty-some years, fighting in the war and dying like that. Not an ounce of dignity."

She shook her head. "Awful tabloids. Had a picture of him, too. Looked like they tried to block out his face, but they did a terrible job. Not that it would have mattered much. The poor man's body was all twisted up, plain as day."

Judy shivered. She had gone from a touch of magic to a dose of gruesome reality within minutes, but that was par for the course here at the Towers. She followed her customer into the kitchen and set everything up. She had the woman seated, with a plastic cape around her shoulders within minutes. "When you called, you said you wanted a trim, right?"

"Just an inch or so. Keeps the hair healthy to have it trimmed regularly."

Judy undid the braid of gray-and-white hair wrapped into a crown and slid her fingers through the thinning hair to work out any snags or tangles before brushing the hair that fell just below her customer's shoulder blades. "Your hair feels beautiful, like silk. You must be using that conditioner I gave you."

"It's almost gone. Do you have any more in that bag of yours?"

Judy shook her head. "No, but I'll be back tomorrow afternoon. I'll drop off a few samples for you."

"That would be sweet of you."

Judy misted Mrs. Edwards's hair, separated it into sections, and began to cut while she got filled in on the latest tabloid headlines and Mrs. Edwards's plans to volunteer at the Book Fair.

"I learned my lesson and made sure I signed up early. Last year I waited until the last minute and wound up at a booth selling cotton candy. What a mess! I came home, looked in the mirror and cried until you got here, remember?"

Judy held back a giggle. "I remember. Before I washed your hair, I thought the pink-and-blue cotton candy added a bit of whimsy to your braid."

"And my eyebrows and my ears? Oh, I was one sticky mess. I was so worried you'd laugh at me, like certain other unnamed people who live in my building."

"I would never laugh at you," Judy promised.

When the telephone rang, Mrs. Edwards lifted the cape and pointed to the wall phone. "Be a dear and answer for me, would you? Hannah Damm was supposed to call me this morning, but she never did. That woman is getting more forgetful by the day. Tell her I'll call her back."

Scissors in hand, Judy answered the telephone.

"Judy? Penny. Mrs. Worth called from the school, like you thought she would. I told her you'd call her back, but she was a little huffy. She wants you to call her back right away. 'Immediately,' as she put it."

Judy sighed. "Well, isn't that dandy? I call that woman for three days, patiently waiting for her to find the time to call me back, and now that she's ready . . . Mrs. Worth will just have to wait for me for a change.

If she calls back again, tell her I'm booked until five so I'll stop in to see her in the morning when I take Brian to school. I may not be an important lady like she is, but my customers are."

"Got it. I'll take care of her for you."

"Thanks." Judy hung up and returned to her customer.

"Trouble at school?"

Judy shrugged and resumed cutting. "Nothing that can't wait till tomorrow."

"It's hard being a grandmother and raising your grandbaby, isn't it?"

"Not all the time." She snipped at a few pieces she had missed. "I hadn't seen Brian since he was a toddler, so we're really just getting to know one another. Between school and work, we don't have all that much time together. He spends more time with his teacher every day than with me."

"I was a teacher, you know."

"Really?"

"Fourth grade. I only taught for a year or two before I met James. As soon as we got engaged, that was it. I got called down to the principal's office, and he fired me on the spot."

Judy gasped. "Fired you? For getting engaged?"

Mrs. Edwards laughed. "We were getting married right away and back then, teachers weren't allowed to be married. We couldn't do a lot of things teachers do today, but I didn't mind trading a classroom full of students for married life. Not one bit."

Judy checked to see that the ends were even. "That's it for today. Shall I braid your hair again for you? It's still a little damp."

"Don't bother, dear. I'll sit on my couch by the window and let the sun dry my hair first. Since you're going to Hannah's next, tell her to call me when you leave, will you?"

Judy agreed, packed up and cleaned up. "You're good for another five or six weeks," she suggested.

Mrs. Edwards smiled. "You'll do fine with that boy. You might be his grandmother, but you're a good woman. You'll be a grand mother to him, too."

Judy swallowed hard. "Thank you." She left for Hannah Damm's apartment with a five-dollar tip for herself, all in quarters inside a little plastic bag, and a box of animal crackers for Brian. But the notion she was a grand mother as well as a grandmother was a priceless memento she tucked into her heart.

She rang the bell at Miss Damm's door on the fourth floor twice. No response. She tried twice again, but no one answered. It was not like Miss Damm to forget an appointment, but she was hard of hearing and wore two hearing aids. Judy sighed and decided to go back down to the office again and try calling before moving on to the next appointment with Mrs. Thompson. If Miss Damm was not wearing her hearing aids, she would not hear the doorbell, but she might hear the extraloud bell on her telephone.

If Judy had a cell phone, she would have been able to call from where she stood, but a cell phone was out of the question, along with any hopes for a new winter coat this year. Brian needed an entire winter wardrobe. She retraced her steps, with her quarters jingling in her pocket, and walked back to the elevator that arrived before she had a chance to push the call button. Oddly, the elevator was empty, and she rode back down to the first floor hoping and praying Miss Damm was home and would hear her telephone.

Penny tried calling Miss Damm's apartment. No answer. She tried again. "Still no answer. I know she's here. She stopped in this morning for a package the mailman left and said she was going back to her apartment to wait for you. No problem," she said and jangled a set of keys she retrieved from a drawer. "I'll go up and let you in. She probably fell asleep watching television."

"I don't think I heard the television," Judy countered as she followed Penny to the elevator.

Penny pushed the call button. "She keeps the volume turned down. Don't ask me why. I haven't a clue." When they got to the apartment, Penny rang the bell several times before opening the door with her master key.

Looking over Penny's shoulder, Judy could see the television. The screen flickered with life, but there was no sound. Miss Damm was lying in her recliner, apparently sound asleep. Penny had been right, but how she knew all the little idiosyncrasies of the residents still mystified Judy.

"She's asleep. Just like I thought," Penny whispered

97

and approached the brown vinyl recliner with gentle steps. "Miss Damm? It's Penny. Judy's here to do your hair. Miss Damm?"

While Penny tried to wake the elderly woman, Judy held back and stayed just inside the door. When Penny looked up at Judy, the ashen look on her face confirmed an odd premonition that Miss Damm had slept her way from this world to the next.

"Call 911. There's a telephone in the kitchen. Hurry. She's still breathing, but I think she's suffered a stroke."

The next half hour was a blur of sirens, paramedics, police and fire personnel, who routinely responded to all emergency calls, and hosts of residents who filled the corridor and filed down to the Gossip Garden to share whatever they had been able to see or hear. After Miss Damm had been placed into an ambulance and peace had been restored to the Towers, Judy was not surprised when Mrs. Thompson canceled her appointment. She was simply too upset about her neighbor and friend to have her hair cut.

A bit shaken, Judy stored her canvas bag back in the office while Penny listened to the telephone messages that had been left in her absence. She called out when Judy started to leave. "There was another call from Mrs. Worth for you. She says it's urgent."

Judy stopped and checked her watch. "It's only two-thirty. I suppose I could call her back now. I don't have to go back to the salon to do more than clean up," she murmured, although she had half a mind to make the woman wait until morning, just on principle, pun intended. "I guess it wouldn't hurt to be the bigger person. Can I use your telephone?"

"Sure. Use the one in Patricia's office. She's not in today."

Judy went into the assistant manager's office, found the telephone and punched in the number for the school. This time, the secretary put her call right through to the principal.

"I'm afraid you need to come to school right away," she urged.

Instead of panicking as she had the last time, Judy forced herself to remain calm. "If it's about the counseling for Brian, that's all been arranged. I've met with your guidance counselor and his first appointment with a private counselor is already scheduled for five o'clock this afternoon. If it's about another picture he's drawn—"

"No. It's not about the counseling or another picture. I wish it were."

Judy's pulse began to race. "Is he sick?"

"No, he's not sick or injured. He's been in a fight. I have one of the other children's parents here with me now, and the other one is on the way. I'm hoping you can join us momentarily. Otherwise, Brian will be suspended from school, and he will not be permitted to return until you can arrange to meet with me."

Judy swallowed hard. "Suspended? He's only in first grade," she grumbled. "Since when does a six-year-old get suspended from school?"

"When that six-year-old gets involved in a fight. We have a zero tolerance policy for bullying behavior."

"I'm on my way," Judy murmured. She hung up the telephone and shook her head. Two weeks of school. Two different problems. Two summonses to the school. Maybe a suspension for fighting or bullying. "I wonder where he learned that," she whispered, seeing Duke's image in her mind's eye, and shoving it away.

At this rate, Brian might break his mother's poor school discipline record before he reached his seventh birthday! "If I survive that long. There's a reason why God made mothers young. Some grand mother I'm turning out to be," she grumbled and headed off to answer her summons to the school.

Again.

Chapter Seven

No panic. No fear. Only a dreadful sense of déjà vu.

Judy climbed the front steps of Park Elementary School with her mind playing flashbacks of raising her daughter. Candy had partied hard, fought hard and rebelled her way through high school and graduated next to last in the Class of 1987, but at the top of the list of students with discipline infractions.

Judy reached the top step and took a deep breath. When it came to her own child's outrageous behavior in high school, she had passed embarrassment and humiliation a long time ago. By learning to distance herself, to separate the child from the behavior and the parent's responsibilities from the child's obligations, she had managed to survive with her own sense of worth only slightly bruised and battered. Would she be able to do the same with Brian?

She had a good idea of what lay waiting for her inside the principal's office. Still, the process was never pleasant. She was also certain she was about to face down a pair of professionals and a pair of parents young enough to be her own children, all of whom were educated far beyond her own high school diploma and license as a hairdresser. She squared her shoulders and reached for the door.

"Judy? Wait!"

She turned and saw Barbara Montgomery rushing up the steps. Sunshine danced in the highlights of her hair, a casual, yet elegant layered cut now, but misery and panic shadowed her face. When she reached the top step, she held on to the railing and stopped to catch her breath. "Sorry. The car . . . is in for repairs. . . . I closed my shop . . . and ran here as fast as I could in heels." She took a deep breath and lowered her voice. "Are you here about the fight, too?"

Judy frowned. "I'm afraid so, but please don't tell me the twins were involved."

Barbara's eyes filled with tears. "Only Jessie, but I think Melanie was there. She's too timid to fight. She wouldn't argue with her own shadow." She groaned. "I've never been called to school before. Not once. The boys were always so good at school, but these girls are going to be a whole different story, I guess. This is terribly embarrassing."

"You didn't get into a fight. Jessie did. Keep that in mind. It'll help. Trust me, I know," Judy assured her.

"I'm sorry Brian was involved, but I'm awfully glad you're here," Barbara said. "Facing the principal will be hard enough, considering she's a paragon that the administration lured away from another district this year. The other parent is bound to be a thirty-something, career-building powerhouse. Or a stay-at-home soccer mom whose husband has a six-figure income, while she's a combination of Mother Earth, sultry siren and last year's finalist for Mother of the Year."

Barbara shook her head. "They're going to take one look at me and assume because I'm a grandmother, I'm too old to be raising two six-year-olds effectively. I might think I'm too old once in a while, but I defy anyone else to think it."

Judy looped her arm with Barbara's. "I'd like to see them try. There's safety in numbers and power, too. We're not just grandmothers. We're grand mothers," she whispered, sharing the gift Mrs. Edwards had given to her. "Let's go inside and prove it."

Barbara sniffed. When she reached into her purse for a tissue, she eased out of Judy's hold. "Grand mothers. I like the sound of that," she said and dabbed at her eyes.

"Me, too."

"Okay, I think I'm ready now. I'm not sure I'm up to doing this. It's been a week since John talked with

Detective Sanger, and there's still no news about whether or not they're going to arrest those two girls and charge them with Steve's death. Maybe if I didn't have that on my mind, I wouldn't be so anxious about being called up to the school. Thanks, Judy. I really needed a friend right now."

"Me, too," Judy repeated and led Barbara into the school. When they arrived at the principal's small office, the secretary ushered them to the door of an adjoining conference room. "Mrs. Worth wanted to meet with the adults involved in here. The children are all with Mrs. Booth, the guidance counselor, in her office. They'll be joining you later, after your meeting," she explained and opened the door.

Judy stepped inside, studied the positions of the two women seated at the long, rectangular table, and assumed the woman seated at the head was Mrs. Worth, the principal. Perfectly coiffed and made up, she wore a navy-blue power suit that had to be tailor-made. Mrs. Worth could not be a day over thirty, yet she looked every inch the capable administrator Barbara had mentioned earlier.

Judy's heart sank to her knees as she eased into a chair. Across the table, the other woman met Judy's gaze and offered a brief, tenuous smile. The fact that the woman sat opposite Barbara and Judy implied that she was the parent of the child who had been bullied, but Judy tried not to leap to conclusions or allow the slightest hope to rise that Brian had been the injured party here. The woman was even vaguely familiar.

Judy could not place her. She assumed she had just seen her about in town. Returning the woman's smile, she looked at her closely. Her heart skipped. Another grandmother? Or was she?

At first glance, the woman appeared to be much younger than either Judy or Barbara. She was small and petite and wore a trendy pink-and-black ruffled blouse. Her straight blond hair was long and loose. The fluorescent light caught the rhinestone chips glued to her bright pink nails, and she wore enough gold jewelry to pay for Brian's winter clothes.

When Judy looked closer, the laugh lines in the corners of the woman's eyes, the creases at each end of her lips, and the wrinkles on her face and neck put her well into middle age. Another grandmother?

Maybe.

Probably.

Feeling more than a little relieved, Judy caught Barbara's gaze and smiled.

Mrs. Worth started the introductions and finished with the other woman. "Mrs. King . . . Ginger . . . is here on behalf of her grandson, Vincent. He's in third grade, and he's also new to the school, like Brian and Jessie and Melanie, although he probably won't be staying here for more than another few weeks."

Another grandmother.

Judy relaxed against the back of her chair.

"But Melanie isn't really involved," Barbara asserted.

"Not directly. No," Mrs. Worth admitted, "but we've

included her because she was caught up in the incident." She cleared her throat. "I'm sorry we all have to meet one another under such difficult circumstances, but I'm certain we can resolve today's problem if we all work together."

Her voice was firm, but gentle and calm, unlike the voice Judy remembered from her telephone conversation.

"I've talked to all of the children myself, individually and collectively, as well as the two lunch aides who were supervising the children. Here's what I've been able to learn. Apparently, all of the children were outside in the playground after lunch. Jessie and Melanie were playing hopscotch with some of the other girls. Vincent had brought out a little sketch pad and pencil. He was sitting nearby, drawing away and minding his own business when Brian came up and demanded to see the sketch pad."

"Brian admitted this?" Judy asked, although she suspected he had.

Mrs. Worth nodded. "He did. To me and to the counselor. When Vincent refused, Brian grabbed the sketch pad and ran off, charging right into Melanie. They both fell to the ground, with Brian on top. Jessie rose to her sister's defense and tried to pull Brian off. Then Vincent jumped into the melee to retrieve his sketch pad. There was a lot of yelling, some kicking and punching and name-calling. Inadvertently or not, I can't be sure, Vincent elbowed Brian in the process, as well."

"Then it's Brian's fault, clear and simple," Judy offered, hoping to take some of the wind out of Mrs. Worth's account by acknowledging Brian's guilt. "That's something I will take care of with him."

"I didn't realize Vincent didn't share well, I'm afraid. That's a concern to me. I'm not sure if I've ever even seen him with a sketch pad, though," Ginger admitted.

Barbara shrugged. "I'm probably not aware of half of what the twins do or don't do, or what they have or they don't have. They rely on one another a great deal. Jessie is the more dominant of the two, and she's very protective, so it doesn't surprise me that she rushed to help her sister. I can't condone kicking and name-calling, though."

"All in all, it sounds like a typical school-yard incident to me," Judy suggested. "None of the children were hurt, right?"

"No," Mrs. Worth admitted. "Just a few scrapes and crushed egos, and a few of the bystanders were frightened. I had the nurse check everyone out, but you're all welcome to have each child seen by his or her pediatrician, if you think it's warranted."

Ginger frowned. "I don't think so, but I'd like to see Vincent first."

Barbara and Judy added their agreement, but Judy was still confused by the tone and content of the telephone call she had received from the principal. Thirty years ago, she would have let it go. Not now. "You mentioned bullying when you called," she prompted.

The principal sat a little more erect and passed a folder to each of the three women. "Bullying behavior can be physical, verbal, emotional, or any combination of the three. That includes intimidation and using force, such as trying to take another child's sketchbook, or name-calling, and kicking, which also happened today. In accordance with district policy guidelines, we have a zero tolerance for bullying of any kind. There is a copy of the guidelines in each of the folders, along with suggestions for activities that you can use at home to help reinforce more positive interactions between your children and the other children at school. It's very important for children to know when their behavior crosses the line and just as important for them to learn how to properly handle an incident with a bully. Hopefully, we can put this event today behind us and prevent another one like it from occurring again."

Judy smoothed her hand across the folder and decided against suggesting the principal had blown the whole incident out of proportion. "What now? Can I see Brian?"

"I'd like to see the girls," Barbara said firmly.

"And Vincent," Ginger added.

Mrs. Worth leaned back, reached for a wall phone and pressed several numbers. "Janet? Alicia Worth. Can you bring the children to the conference room now? Oh, that's great. Thanks." She hung up and turned her attention back to the three women at the table. "If you haven't met Janet Booth, she's our guidance counselor. She's been meeting with the children, and she assures me all is well. The children have each talked with her, and she tells me there are no hard feelings between them."

Mrs. Worth stood up, smoothed a nonexistent wrinkle from her suit jacket, smiled and handed each of them her card. "I'll leave you alone with your children . . . grandchildren now. It's almost dismissal time so you might as well take them home with you. If you have any questions or concerns, please call me. My direct line here at school is on the card, as well as my home number."

"What about Brian? Can he stay for the after-school program today? I really should get back to the salon," Judy explained. There was no way she could open up tomorrow, especially if Ann was still out, unless she took care of the cleanup today.

"That might not be a good idea. Overnight, the other children will probably forget all about what happened, but today . . . Is there any way you could take him with you?"

"Yes, I suppose so."

"Good. Thank you all for coming," she said and disappeared out the door.

"Brian can come home with me," Barbara offered.

"No. Thanks anyway. He can help me to sweep up. It might be a good chance for us to talk about what happened today."

Ginger toyed with one of her gold bracelets for a moment. "You've both been very understanding. If

Vincent had just shown his sketch pad to Brian, none of this would have happened. I haven't had a child in school for more years that I want to count. I wasn't sure what to expect when I was waiting for you, but—"

"But you didn't expect to see people like us?" Judy asked.

Ginger raised a brow.

"Grandmothers," Barbara suggested. "We're both grandmothers raising our grandchildren, just like you."

Ginger's eyes misted. "I thought I was the only one. I just enrolled Vincent a few days ago. He started later than the other children, so I didn't get a chance to meet any of the other . . . mothers. A lot of them are probably younger than my own children."

"Well, you aren't the only one," Judy insisted.

The door opened, and Janet Booth stepped into the room. She closed the door behind her and introduced herself, giving Judy an extrawarm smile. "It's good to see you again, though not under these circumstances," she murmured. "I saw Mrs. Worth on my way here. She agreed with me that it might be better if I took you to the children. Follow me. You must be anxious to see them."

She smiled again. "Please. Relax. And don't worry. The children are fine, and they've already patched up their differences." She hesitated and looked over her shoulder as if to make sure the door was still closed. "Look, we've all lived through raising our own children, and I'm confident you'll all be able to raise your grandchildren, too," she said as she pointed to the folders still lying on the table. "Don't be too disturbed about what you read, but do try some of the activities. I've been an educator long enough to know that there are certain issues, like violence in our society, that are reflected in our schools. Sometimes those issues seem to take on a life of their own. School tragedies and lawsuits have made school districts more than a little nervous these days. Bullying as you and I experienced it with our children years ago isn't quite how it's defined or interpreted these days. That's not to say we shouldn't be aware of or concerned about how our children or grandchildren interact with one another. We should, but in this case, I think we can safely say this whole affair was just an old-fashioned school-yard ruckus. All of the children know what they did wrong, and they're truly sorry."

Like the principal, she handed out her cards. "If you have any concerns, call me," she said and opened the door. "Shall we?"

Judy got up and followed Barbara and Ginger out the door, happy to take along a good dose of common sense from the counselor. When they reached the counselor's office, Brian was lying flat, belly to floor, legs bent and feet kicking in the air while he doodled on one side of a large sheet of paper and an older boy, probably Vincent, was on the other side. Melanie and Jessie were seated together coloring opposite pages of a coloring book.

Brian looked up, saw Judy, scrambled to his feet, and ran over to her. "Grandmom! Vincent's grandmom works in a candy store, and she lets him fill his pockets with candy. He said we could go to the store, and she'd let me fill my pockets, too. Can we go? I got big pockets today," he said, tugging on her slacks with one hand and one of the pockets on his camping shorts with the other. "Can we? Please?"

"That would be an interesting punishment," Judy remarked.

Apparently, Ginger was right behind her and over-heard. "Sounds like all has been forgiven," she teased. "I work part-time at Sweet Stuff now that Vincent's in school."

"I thought I'd seen you in town," Judy admitted. "I don't go to Sweet Stuff very often, though. I try not to keep candy in the house. Not that I'm all hung up on keeping candy from Brian," she whispered, only too aware that, given her daughter's name, there might be double meaning to her words. "Candy and children just go together," she managed. "It's me. I'd eat every piece of candy I could find."

Barbara edged into the room and joined the conver-sation. "Did I hear someone mention candy?"

Brian tugged on Judy's pants leg. "Can we go today and get some candy? Please?"

"Not today, Brian. We have to go to the salon and sweep up, then we have an appointment before dinner. Besides, we have a few things we need to discuss first about what happened in the school yard before we even think about getting some candy."

He dropped hold of her slacks and hung his head. Huge tears trembled, then rolled down his cheeks.

Judy knelt down and tipped up his chin with her fingertip. "I said we were going to talk, Brian. Just talk," she assured him. Visions of how his mother, her own daughter, and his father might have disciplined him made her tremble, too.

He drew in shaky breaths. "You're not gonna tell my Dad, are you?"

She pulled him into her arms and held him close. Despite all the challenges and complications and inconveniences he had brought into her life, Brian was exactly where she wanted him to be—safe and loved and protected within her arms. "No, sweetie. I'm not gonna tell your Dad. Not ever," she whispered, along with a prayer this precious child might one day come to love and trust the most important father of all—the Father who had created him.

Chapter Eight

While Tyler supervised Vincent's shower upstairs and had a talk with him about the incident at school before bedtime prayers, Ginger paced back and forth in her kitchen. She checked the clock. Eight-fifteen. Should she leave another message for Lily? She paced faster, stopped to pick up the telephone and hung up.

She had left five messages for her daughter on her

cell phone, starting as soon as she had gotten home from school with Vincent, practically one an hour. No response. Vincent getting involved in a little fracas at school did not exactly constitute an emergency. But Lily was the boy's mother, not that she had been acting like it. Nevertheless, she still had a right to know.

Ginger kept pacing and toyed with the end of a piece of her hair. Disappointment in her daughter for leaving Vincent behind all summer while she was in Boston settling into her new role as Mrs. Paul Taft fueled a host of deeper, darker emotions. Resentment flared for all the changes she and Tyler had had to make in their lives to accommodate taking responsibility for Vincent when Lily was not even able to find the time to call more than once a week. She had never come to see her son. Anger rose that Lily had not kept her word to Vincent or to her parents. Lily and Paul were still living with Paul's parents, who still did not know about Vincent, and consequently the poor little boy had not been able to rejoin his mother to start school on time in Boston.

When pressed on how soon Lily and her new husband would bring Vincent into their lives, Lily had been evasive and distant. Embarrassed by her daughter's behavior and ashamed of all the lies Ginger had told to protect Vincent, as well as herself, and all the lies Lily had been telling her in-laws, Ginger stopped dead. "Not anymore. Tyler is right. It's time you started acting more like a mother, and we got back to being just grandparents," she murmured and headed straight to the desk built into a corner of the kitchen, rifled through the top drawer and pulled out her personal telephone book. She flipped to the *T* section, found the number for the Taft home, and placed the call Tyler had been urging her to make for weeks.

"Good evening. Taft residence."

"Hello. This is Ginger King, Lily's mother. May I speak with her please?"

"I'm sorry. Mrs. Taft is not able to take your call."

"It's important. I need to speak with her right away. Please call her to the telephone."

"I'm afraid that won't be possible."

Ginger clenched her teeth. "It's an emergency. I need to speak with my daughter. Now."

"But she's not at home, Mrs. King. The entire family is spending the week at the family home in St. Thomas."

"Then I'll need the number there," she insisted. "Please." She tried to keep her words polite and her voice calm, but her heart was thumping in her chest.

"One moment, please."

Ginger waited for almost five minutes before another voice came on the line, and she finally stopped twisting the cord between her fingers. "Mrs. King? This is Mr. Harrell. If you'll hang up, I'll call you back and give you the number to call. One can't be too careful today. The media, you know."

She rolled her eyes. She would probably have had

an easier time getting hold of her daughter if she had been a member of the media, especially one of the tabloids. Then again, neither the national press nor the tabloids showed much interest in the Taft family these days. Too staid. Too boring. Too much old money to protect them? "Fine. My number is—"

"I have your number. I'll call you right back."

Ginger heard the click on the other end of the line and hung up. The phone rang less than a minute later. She identified herself again and jotted down the number. She did not have a chance to say thank-you or goodbye. The caller had already hung up. She tapped out the number with the tip of a bright pink fingernail. When someone answered, Ginger went through another hassle, but after fifteen minutes, Lily finally came on the line.

"Mom? Is it Vincent? Is Dad okay?"

"We're all fine. I just—"

"But they said it was an emergency call!"

"It is. Vincent got involved in a little fracas at school today. It really wasn't his fault," she explained and quickly detailed the incident.

Lily gasped. "A school-yard fight? You're calling me to tell me about a little disagreement on the play-ground? Here? Mom, really!" She lowered her voice, obviously trying to keep their conversation from being overheard. "I told you only to call me on my cell phone. I can't talk to you right now. We're on vacation and there's a dinner party tonight with dozens of guests. Important guests."

Ginger's temper got the best of her. "Guests? You're worried about guests? I'm talking about your son. I had to meet with the principal and the other parents today at school, which I did willingly for Vincent's sake, but frankly, that was your job, Lily. You're his mother. Daddy and I love him dearly, but he should be with you. He wants to be with you, and he needs to be with you, and this constant pattern of one delay after another, one excuse after another—"

"I can't talk about this now, Mom. I'll call you when I get back to Boston on Saturday morning."

Ginger's hold on the receiver tightened. "You'll call Saturday? Not good enough. Either you drive down here Saturday night to take your son home with you where he belongs, or Daddy and I will drive him up there ourselves."

"No. Don't. Please don't do that. You have no idea what I've been through this summer. I'll—I'll fly down on the first flight Monday morning. Can you meet me at the airport? I'll call and let you know what time as soon as I book a flight. Please, please give me until Monday."

Ginger hesitated. She had given Lily so many chances to do the right thing all summer long, to no avail, and she had no reason to believe this time was any different. The strain in Lily's voice, however, tugged at her mother's heart. "Monday morning. That gives you until the end of the weekend to make things right with your in-laws. But no excuses this time. I mean it, Lily."

"Thanks, Mom. You're the best mom in the whole world!" Lily whispered and hung up.

Ginger stared at the receiver, hung it back up and let out a sigh. "No, I'm not the best mom in the whole world," she whispered. "If I were, I would have taught you how to be a better mom."

"A better mom? Better than you? She doesn't exist."

When Ginger turned toward the sound of her husband's voice, strong arms embraced her. "Don't worry about Vincent. He's fine. He stood up for himself and got a little more of a reaction than he probably liked, but he's all right now and waiting for a good-night kiss from his Grams. First things first, though."

She snuggled deeper for a moment and looked up at him. He was gray at the temples now, and his hairline had receded a bit, but the look of love in his eyes was as strong as it had been the night he had proposed. " 'First things first'?"

He kissed her. Hard. "There. I had a rough day today, too, but I feel better already. How about you?"

She shrugged her shoulders and giggled. "I'm not sure."

He squeezed her closer and gave her another kiss. "Better yet?"

"Almost," she managed and kissed him back. "Okay, I'm feeling better now," she teased and leaned back against his arms to lock her gaze with his. "While you were upstairs, I talked with Lily."

He smiled. "Wonder of wonders, she finally called back."

117

"No. I called her. In St. Thomas." She gave him a full account of their conversation.

He nodded and pressed his chin to her forehead. "I'll do what I have to do to rearrange my schedule for Monday so I can go with you to meet her at the airport. That way, we can spend the day with her and talk things through before Vincent comes home from school."

She swallowed the lump in her throat. Her shoulders slumped, and she voiced the concerns their other children, Mark and Denise, had expressed the moment each of them had learned that Lily had left Vincent with his grandparents all summer—concerns that had been plaguing her heart all these many weeks. "What if she never takes Vincent home with her? What if she doesn't want him back?"

He kissed the tip of her nose and released her. "She's been his mother for eight years. A new husband, even a rich, society husband, can't compete with that, regardless of what Mark or Denise seem to think. Once the dazzle and the glamour wears off, and once we stop making it so easy for her, Lily will want him back," he assured her.

"But what if she doesn't?"

"Then we'll do the right thing for Vincent. We'll punt, draw up some new plays and draft him so he can stay with us permanently."

She gave him a mock punch to his shoulder. "Wow, it must be football season," she teased.

"First home game is Saturday. I got another ticket

last week so Vincent could go with us. Maybe if he attends a game, he'll develop an interest, but I was thinking maybe it would help more if he took a friend along. I'm going to check around at work or go online and see if I can't swap the three tickets I have for four tickets on an upper level for one of the games later this season. He seemed to like the idea when I mentioned it after he said his prayers."

"Really? Which friend did he have in mind? He hasn't made very many this summer."

"Brian. The boy from the school yard today."

Her eyes widened. "Brian? He's only in first grade."

"Vincent seems to like the boy."

She shrugged. "I guess it would be all right. See if you can get the tickets first, though, before I mention anything to Brian's grandmother. What about the sketch pad? Did you ask Vincent about it?"

"I thought I'd leave that to you." He grinned and looked up at the clock. "It's eight-thirty. The football game starts at nine. I'll get the snacks ready while you go up and kiss Vincent good-night and maybe talk about that sketch pad. I'll meet you in the family room."

When she started up the stairs for Vincent's bedroom, she shook her head. For two sports fanatics like herself and Tyler, trying to entertain an eight-year-old boy with no interest in group activities or sports, as a participant or as a spectator, had been a true challenge. Try as they might, however, Vincent was happiest when left to entertain himself alone. He loved to read, hardly a pursuit she could discourage, although she had made sure the books they had checked out of the library were suitable. The Internet was off-limits, but he loved computer games, again all monitored, and they had gotten accustomed to walking around the roads and bridges he built from one room to the other for his minicars.

She reached the top landing and turned down the hall. After passing Lily's old bedroom, she stopped in the open doorway to Vincent's room and found him in bed, sketching in the light cast by the wall lamp above the headboard.

Caught off guard, Vincent quickly shoved the sketch pad under his pillow and scooted down so his head was on the pillow.

"Ready for a good-night kiss?"

He nodded. "Gramps already talked to me about school today," he offered, as if making sure she knew so she would not bring it up again.

She sat down on his bed. "He did, did he?"

"I'm gonna leave my sketch pad home so nobody tries to take it again."

"That sounds like a good idea," she responded and suspected that idea had been Tyler's.

"Gramps has lots of 'em," he said as he fidgeted about. He pulled his pencil out from beneath his back and stuck it under his pillow.

"What kind of ideas?"

"Maybe taking Brian to the football game with us?"

"Would you like that?"

"He's a good drawer, like me."

She smiled. "Until today, I didn't know you liked to draw. What kinds of things do you like to draw the most?"

He blushed. "Stuff."

"Stuff?"

"You know. Stuff. Like . . . people. I guess I like to draw people the best."

She ran her fingers through his still-damp hair. Maybe he had been drawing one of the children at school and that's why he had been reluctant to let Brain see his sketch pad. "Did you draw any of the girls or boys at school?"

"Nah."

"What about Grams or Gramps?"

He shook his head.

"Your teacher, Mr. Norcross?"

He shook his head again.

Time for more open-ended questions. "Who have you drawn?"

No verbal response. No gesture—until he dropped his gaze.

"It's all right. You're tired. Maybe we can talk about your drawings another time. Good night, darlin'. Grams loves you this much," she said. She opened her arms wide, then enclosed him in a tight hug and kissed his forehead. After turning on the night-light, she switched off the lamp above the headboard and walked toward the door.

"Grams?"

She turned around, but his little face was in the shadows.

"I drawed my mom," he whispered.

Her heart trembled.

Chapter Nine

Another school week. Another difficult Monday morning.

Vincent had no idea how important today was going to be for him, but Ginger was not about to spoil the surprise, even though she was sorely tempted. He sat at the kitchen table with his head bowed and his thin shoulders drooped. The plate of silver dollar hotcakes and glass of orange juice in front of him remained untouched, as if the very thought of going to school today had zapped his spirit as well as his appetite.

Instead of hugging her grandson and reassuring him that his mother was coming for him today, she put a plate of hotcakes on the table in front of Tyler. She met his gaze, gave him a smile pleading for him to intervene and tapped the face of her wristwatch to remind him they had little time to spare.

"Try a bite, champ," Tyler suggested. He poured a little maple syrup on his hotcakes and Vincent's, too. "Sure is nice to be home late enough to have breakfast with you for a change."

No response, other than a shrug.

Tyler started in on his own breakfast and Ginger sat down to join them. She took a sip of orange juice and added more milk to her coffee, but made no comment when Vincent started to push a piece of hotcake onto his fork.

"I can't go to school today," Vincent murmured.

"Why is that?" Tyler asked.

The boy chewed on his pancake and tried to talk at the same time. "You're . . . gonna get . . . mad," he managed.

Tyler frowned. "Chew first, swallow, then talk."

Vincent chewed on that little hunk of hotcake like a cow chewing its cud.

Tyler set down his fork, watching and waiting without saying another word.

Ginger followed suit.

Finally, Vincent took one big swallow and drank half his orange juice in a single gulp. "I—I lost my backpack."

She opened her mouth to ask him how he had managed to lose a second backpack in the space of three weeks when Tyler nudged her knee under the table. She locked her lips together.

"Check with your teacher, Mr. Norcross, today. Maybe you left it at school on Friday," Tyler prompted.

Vincent shook his head. "I brought it home, remember?"

"I remember. We did some math problems together on Saturday morning after we got home from the farmers' market," Ginger offered. "When we finished, you put your math homework into your backpack."

"Then you must have put it in your room," Tyler suggested.

Vincent took another bite of hotcakes and shrugged while he chewed.

"Not there, I guess?" Tyler asked, his voice calm and steady.

Vincent shook his head.

"Finish your breakfast, you two. I'll double-check," Ginger offered and got up from the table. On her way upstairs, she checked the hall closet, did a walk-through of the living room and dining room. No sign of the backpack. Upstairs, she checked Vincent's room thoroughly, looking under his desk and his bed, on the shelf and floor of the closet. No backpack.

She stopped in the hallway and checked her watch. Five minutes left before Vincent had to leave for school. "Two backpacks can't just disappear into thin air," she grumbled and passed the door to Lily's old room on her way back down to the kitchen. She got to the top of the staircase, stopped dead and turned back. The door to Lily's old room was ajar.

She peeked inside. Early-morning sunlight filtered into the room through sheer curtains, but nothing seemed amiss. The quilt on the four-poster bed was drawn tight. The closet door was closed. All the bureau drawers were also closed.

Driven by instinct, she slipped into the room. Surrounded by memories of Lily, she caught her breath. What had happened to the sweet, loving child who had knelt by this very bed to say her prayers every night? Or the teenager who had organized a series of fund-raisers for the church Youth Group to make sure no family went hungry on Thanksgiving?

Tears welled, and Ginger blinked away the echo of Lily's words announcing her pregnancy, just weeks before graduation from college and her refusal to identify the father or consider adoption as a difficult, but selfless alternative to raising her child as a single parent in Chicago, no less. What happened to that determination to be both mother and father to Ginger's first and only grandchild? How long had Lily been putting Vincent second in her life and why hadn't Ginger and Tyler noticed this before now?

Her backbone stiffened. She knew what had happened. The world happened. Without the anchor of faith Lily had embraced as a child to hold her steadfast, she had been swept into a sea of materialism and selfishness while Vincent had been cast adrift.

Ginger crossed the room and opened the closet door. The shelf was empty now, except for a few old sweaters. Most of the hangers were bare. Lily's favorite scent, however, still clung to the old chenille bathrobe she had worn on her last visit. Ginger saw the robe on the floor in the back corner of the closet and got down on her knees to reach it and put it back onto a hanger. When she lifted the robe and saw the two missing backpacks hidden underneath, she gently tucked the edges of the bathrobe back around them.

Tears fell, and her heart ached for her grandson. With her chin to her chest, she closed her eyes and folded her hands in prayer. "Father, help us. Guide Tyler and me today and give us the words to help our daughter. Touch Lily's heart so she will once again embrace You as the source of all love so she may be a good and loving mother." She paused. Her throat tightened with longing. "Please comfort Vincent. Ease the hurt he's endured and bring him joy today as he is reunited with his mother. Amen."

She held very still, loving Him and trusting Him to make this a day of fulfillment, a day when promises would be kept and faith would be renewed and a little boy's broken heart would begin to heal.

Monday was getting worse by the hour. Vincent was late for school. Repair work on the bridge crossing the Delaware River limited westbound traffic to a single lane instead of three which cost more precious time. A tractor-trailer had jackknifed on I-95, the access road to Philadelphia International Airport, creating a snarl of bumper-to-bumper traffic that had Ginger checking her watch every few minutes.

Tyler finally pulled up to Lily's airline terminal and stopped at the curb. "If you hop out here, you can still meet Lily when she gets beyond the security check-point. I'll park the car and meet you where we waited for her last time. That way you both won't have to waste time trying to find me or the car."

Ginger kissed his cheek and hurried from the car into the terminal. Fortunately, she and Tyler had met each of their three children at the airport so often, she knew her way around pretty well. She avoided the escalator. Too many people. Taking the stairs like a marathon runner, she made it halfway up the flight before she stopped. With her heart pumping furiously and her leg muscles screaming, she bent at the waist and gasped for air. She deliberately avoided looking at the people passing her on the escalator.

"Slow down. You're going to kill yourself," she muttered to herself. When her heart no longer felt as if it was going to rip through her chest and spin into orbit, she made her way, slowly, to the top of the stairs. While most of the crowd headed right to join others already in line to go through security, she veered left to the area where she would wait with others for arriving passengers.

She was almost there when she saw her daughter arrive and stop to scan the area looking for her parents. "Lily! I'm here. Over here!"

Lily turned to face her mother, but instead of rushing forward, she stood in place and waited for Ginger to come to her. As she closed the distance between them, Ginger saw that her daughter had changed a great deal since her marriage. The transplanted, Midwestern, all-American girl had been transformed into a Northeastern blueblood.

Instead of wearing her naturally curly hair long and loose, she had had her hair straightened and added fashionable henna highlights. She wore a Capri pantsuit in pale lemon that fit her as though it had been tailor-made to cling to every curve, and the gold choker necklace lying against her throat was a simple, but elegant and very expensive touch.

When Ginger got close enough for a hug, she noted the makeup that concealed Lily's freckles was understated, yet almost professionally applied. She held her daughter close and inhaled a new, more sophisticated scent. "Sorry we're late, sweetie. Traffic was outrageous. Daddy's still parking the car." She stepped back and looked at her daughter. "You're looking very Boston," she teased. "What? No tan? I thought you said you'd been in St. Thomas for a week."

Lily laughed. "No more tanning for me. The sun causes skin cancer, Mom, not to mention wrinkles."

Ginger shrugged. "Seems like everything we used to do causes all sorts of problems we didn't anticipate. I told Daddy we'd wait for him in Granny Alley."

Lily furrowed her brow. "Where?"

Ginger led her away from the crowd to a long corridor that connected the terminal with one of the parking garages. Rows of rocking chairs, separated at intervals by large potted trees and plants, lined either side of the corridor. The secluded area was ideal for travelers who had a lot of time between connecting flights, needed a quiet place to soothe an overtired child or a place to wait for arriving passengers. "Daddy and I call this Granny Alley. I guess it's the rocking chairs. We've spent a lot of hours here," she explained. "Looks like we almost have the place to ourselves today," she noted. Other than an elderly gentleman they passed who had fallen asleep in his rocker, the rest of the rocking chairs were empty.

Ginger pointed to two rockers at the end closest to the crossroads where this corridor and others met just before the security area. "If we sit here, Daddy won't be able to get by us."

Lily sat down, checked her watch and laid her clutch bag on her lap.

"Did you check any luggage?" Ginger asked as she sat down, too.

"No."

Lily's tone of voice suggested she thought the idea was ludicrous, and Ginger stopped rocking for a moment, then resumed. "We weren't sure if you were going to stay the night and go back with Vincent tomorrow or . . . We were hoping you might stay longer. . . ."

With her feet planted flat on the ground and her back rigid, Lily held very still. The rocker never moved an inch. "Mom, I don't have much time here."

Relief that Lily was anxious to take Vincent back to Boston helped to ease Ginger's disappointment. She stopped rocking and put her hand on Lily's shoulder. "I know, sweetie. It's all right. We can all get together later, after Vincent's all settled in with you and Paul. I've been so worried about you since we talked, wondering how Paul's parents reacted when you told them about Vincent and how supportive Paul would be—"

"Mother and Father Taft are wonderful to me," Lily murmured. She toyed with her wedding ring set and smiled. "Paul is the kind of man I've always dreamed about. He's loving and supportive. . . ." She trembled and drew in a long breath. "This hasn't been an easy time for me."

"No, I suppose not," Ginger said gently. The anguish in her daughter's voice replenished the hope that the caring daughter she had raised had not totally disappeared and that Lily and Paul would provide a loving home for Vincent, who would also gain another set of doting grandparents. "It hasn't been easy for Vincent, either," she offered and bit back the urge to tell her daughter about the sacrifices she and Tyler had had to make over the summer. "He's missed you."

Lily closed her eyes for a moment. "I miss him, too. I—I love him so much. That's why this is so hard. I loved him enough to keep him as a baby, and now I . . . I have to love him enough to let him go."

Ginger bolted forward in her seat. " 'Let him go'? Did you say 'let him go'?"

Lily's dark eyes flashed. "Yes, Mom. I did."

Ginger's heart pounded in her ears, and she gripped the arms of the rocker with both hands. "Just exactly what do you mean? Go where?" she demanded. As her mind struggled against all the possibilities, she gave them voice when Lily did not answer. "Vincent is only eight years old. He can't go anywhere by himself. Is he going to some sort of boarding school? Is that what you mean? Or are you going to let him go to live with his father, not that any of us, including Vincent, know who his father is?"

Breathing hard, she stared at her daughter, but Lily

met Ginger's gaze and held her ground. "I don't expect you to understand—"

"Understand what?"

"I didn't tell Paul's parents about Vincent because as wonderful as they are, they would never accept him . . . or me. Vincent is illegitimate. I was an unwed mother. That's not . . . acceptable. Not in their world."

Ginger snorted. "And this is the world you're choosing for yourself as Paul's wife? A world where there is no forgiveness or understanding? A world where a mother would deny her own flesh and blood? Her own son? For what? Tell me, Lily. Is it the status? The money? Or both?"

Lily's gaze narrowed. "Frankly, Mom, it's both. There. Satisfied now? I am. I'm not denying my son. I'm protecting him and his future. Paul and I intend to support him, of course. When he's older, Vincent will be able to attend the best of colleges, with no loans to repay or without trying to hold down a couple of part-time jobs just to have enough to get by until he can graduate. He'll have opportunities and choices I never had until I met Paul," she snapped, venting such bitterness Ginger could scarcely believe this was her own daughter.

Lily paused to take a deep breath. "I want Vincent to go with you and Dad. Will you let him live with you? Permanently? Or will I have to make . . . other arrangements for him?"

Ginger had protective instincts of her own, and they rose full force to stiffen her backbone and every muscle in her body. "Don't bother making other arrangements. Of course I want him to stay with us. He's our grandson, and I don't even want to think about where else you might send him. But you have to talk to Daddy, too. This is not a decision I can make without him."

Lily searched the crowd, checked her watch again and stood up. "Daddy's nowhere in sight. I wish I could stay longer to wait for him, but I have to leave now or I'll miss my flight."

Ginger bolted to her feet so fast she set the rocker in motion behind her. "You have another flight to catch? Now?"

She stiffened when Lily embraced her. "Please try to understand. This is really best for all of us."

Ginger pulled away. "This is best? No. I can't believe that. I don't believe that. If Paul won't stand up against his parents for you, then he's not my idea of a good husband. And he shouldn't be yours, either," she pleaded. "Forget the flight. Wait for Daddy and come home with us. We can talk this through. Maybe . . . maybe Vincent should just stay with us a while longer to give you a little more time—"

Lily shook her head and placed one of her hands over her stomach. "Vincent's not the only child I'm protecting, Mom. I've tried to raise one child on my own. I can't do it again, and I won't risk this baby's future any more than I'd risk Vincent's. Please don't hate me," she whispered, turned and walked away.

Ginger froze in place and watched her daughter

leave. Flabbergasted from the top of her head to the tips of her toes, she felt as if she was outside of her own body watching a nightmare that had exploded into reality. She could not cry. She could not move a muscle. Until she saw her daughter slide her purse onto the conveyor belt at the security checkpoint.

"Lily!" Her cry erupted like a whisper, and she charged forward, only to be stopped hard by a pair of security officers.

"Ma'am, you can't go through here. Not without a boarding pass or ticket."

Frantic, she struggled against strong arms and watched Lily fade into the crowd. "Lily! That's my daughter! I need to see my daughter," she cried.

"Ma'am, if you don't settle down—"

"Ginger? What's wrong? Where's Lily?"

She turned and burrowed into Tyler's embrace. Weeping uncontrollably, she clung to his shirt with her fists. "Lily's gone. Lily's gone," she cried.

Her heart was broken by her daughter's decision, and each sad beat of her heart hungered for reconciliation and understanding.

Her spirit was crushed beneath the weight of so many unanswered prayers, and she struggled with the vision of her own broken dreams for her own future with Tyler as they headed into retirement.

And her soul shook at the thought of telling Vincent that his mother had no room in her new life for him.

Chapter Ten

Ten days had passed since Julia and Augusta Radcliffe had emerged as the primary suspects responsible for Steve's death. Barbara sat with John in an office with Detective Sanger in Philadelphia at ten o'clock in the morning feeling as if she had been yanked into the worst of all possible reality television shows. Both girls were juveniles, but their names had leaked to a media ravenous for details and prepared for breaking news in the case.

Whether the camp of vans and cameras and audio equipment set up by the local, national network, and cable television and radio media in Center City was bigger than the compounds created by the reporters in the print media was hard to tell, but the chaos reminded her that one of the greatest blessings in her life was living in a small town like Welleswood.

Like the legendary circle of wagons that protected migrating families moving West, lifelong friends and neighbors linked together to create a loyal chain around Barbara and John and the twins to protect their privacy. Local police, including a host of auxiliary officers normally called upon as reinforcements for special events, used a variety of methods to keep reporters on the periphery of the town limits. Barbara refrained from having any interest in how far the boundary between legal and illegal methods had been stretched. Instead, she needed all of her resources this morning to focus on Lydia Sanger.

Dwarfed by a mound of folders and stacks of papers on her desk, the petite, African-American detective described the impressive work she had done on the case so far. "I know you're anxious for us to make an arrest, and I wanted to see you today to reassure you both that we're working very hard to make sure our case is rock-solid before we do. We're not going to let the media direct our investigation or force our hand." Her voice was deep, especially for a woman who barely topped five feet. "But I'll be honest with you. This is not going to be an easy case to resolve, which is another reason I wanted to meet with you."

John took hold of Barbara's hand; she held on tight. "The media?" he asked.

"That's only one component," Lydia Sanger admitted. "I don't expect the media circus to abate any time soon, but the last thing we need right now is to have a trial by media, especially now that the family has hired Spencer Crawford to represent the girls."

Barbara looked at her husband. From the quizzical look on his face, he was as unfamiliar with the name as she was, and Barbara offered her own blank look to the detective.

"You two obviously don't watch much television, especially the legal coverage of trials."

John shook his head. "We haven't in the past and to be frank, we've been afraid to turn on the television, let alone the radio, since Steve's death. Between the bottom screen news banners the stations use now, regardless of the program in progress, and the 'breaking news' reports, we don't need to see or hear anything that would make losing Steve any more difficult than it already is, for us and for the twins. Our lawyer has handled the reporters' inquiries for us, and we have no desire to be somebody's idea of entertainment."

The detective's soft gaze met Barbara's. "I understand. Completely. For the time being I think it's wise to keep out of the media glare, although there may be a point where I might suggest we need to have you conduct a news conference or two. It would be controlled and well-orchestrated, of course, and—"

"I don't think I can answer any questions or make any statements, especially to reporters," Barbara insisted.

"And I hope you won't have to, but we may have no other choice. Crawford is an excellent defense attorney with a well-earned reputation for using and manipulating the media, and you need to be prepared for that."

John sat up a little straighter. "We'll do whatever needs to be done."

Barbara swallowed hard and nodded her agreement.

"And so will I," the detective promised. She set aside several folders and crossed her hands atop her desk. "This case is about your son, Steve. He's the victim here. One of my most important jobs during the course of the investigation will be to keep the focus on Steve and make sure we arrest the right person or persons who are responsible for his death. Crawford, on the other hand, will try to deflect the media attention away from his clients and raise questions about the investigation or the criminal justice system in general, or Steve himself."

The knot in Barbara's stomach hurt so badly she could scarcely breathe. "Steve didn't do anything wrong, and it's not fair to make it seem like he did," she argued.

"A good defense attorney like Crawford will do what he has to do to protect his clients. Now let me tell you what we know so far. The girls have denied that there was any personal connection between Steve, the girls, or their parents, but we need to be sure."

Barbara stiffened. She braced herself to hear the woeful tale of the two miserable urban lives that had tragically intersected with Steve's, convinced there was no connection at all.

The detective read from notes she had prepared. "Mom is a pharmacist. Dad is a retired Coast Guard officer and commandant of one of the yacht clubs at the shore. These days, he does private consulting work. No record of any connection between him and Steve's firm. The two girls are their only children. Apparently, all four of them are active in their church. The eldest sister, Augusta, is seventeen. She's a senior at Hale Regional High School, which is in Ocean County, just north of Cape May. She's vice president of her class, secretary of the National Honor Society, and a Merit Scholarship winner who applied very early for admission to the Coast Guard Academy and was accepted. Julia is fifteen, a sophomore at the same school and ranks first in her class. She's all-South Jersey in two sports, soccer and softball, and she—"

"Enough!" John spat out the words. "I've heard enough."

Barbara eased her hand free, even as her mind struggled to absorb the information she had been given—information which exploded every profile she had created in her mind for the people responsible for taking Steve's life. "I've never heard of these people," she managed.

"Me, either," John snapped. "If what you're telling us about them is true, then why in the world were these . . . What would these girls be doing in Philadelphia? With a gun?" he demanded. "It's almost so unbelievable to think that these girls were involved that I wonder if you have even gotten the people truly responsible for Steve's death."

"Oh, we think they're responsible," the detective argued. "The ballistics test has provided a number of leads which I can't discuss at this time, but it confirms the gun that the girls turned in is the gun that fired the bullet that killed your son."

"But why? Why did they shoot the gun? Did they target Steve? Why? Why Steve? Why our son?" Anger and outrage fueled Barbara's questions and her heart pounded against her chest. Tears of frustration welled, and she blinked them back. "Tell me why."

"We're still investigating the motive, but according

to the girls' statements, the shooting was accidental."

John snorted again. "Accidental? Hogwash. They didn't accidentally drive to Philadelphia. They didn't accidentally have a gun which was accidentally loaded, did they?" He held up his hand to keep the floor to himself. "They killed our son. They left our two granddaughters orphans. That's no accident. That's a cold, hard, bitter fact of life we'll have to live with and so will they. I don't care who these girls are. They're murderers, and they should be held accountable," he demanded. With his chest heaving, he glared at the detective who waited until he had regained his composure before answering him.

"If they're responsible for Steve's death, they will be held accountable," she murmured, "but right now, you need to give us time to finish our investigation. We still have a lot of questions that need answers."

Barbara shook her head. "But I thought you said the girls already gave a statement of some kind. If they admitted which one shot the gun that killed Steve, isn't that enough?"

"According to the District Attorney's office, their statement, such as it is, will probably be ruled inadmissible, since they did not have their parents or an attorney present when they turned themselves in to the local police. If we can confirm their statements, then we can charge the girls accordingly. Unfortunately, there's a gaping hole in the investigation that needs to be filled in before we can proceed."

John glowered. "What hole? You have two girls who

turned themselves in with the gun that killed our son and who admit they're responsible."

"True, but we have to corroborate their account of that day, and frankly, we need to find out where that gun has been since July when Steve was shot. Just because the girls had the gun now doesn't mean they had it in July. Maybe they did, but maybe they didn't. And if they didn't, who did? Did they accidentally shoot Steve and now, months later, were so overwrought with guilt they turned themselves in without even consulting with their parents? Or are they covering for someone else. If so, who? And why?"

Detective Sanger straightened in her seat. "Those are the questions that need answers before we arrest anyone. I want to know everything about these girls and every move they've made since July and well before that before I give credence to a single word they've said. If they're responsible, they'll be arrested. If not—"

"The justice system," John argued, "is supposed to be a code of law, not one 'if' after another."

"The justice system is based on law, but the system, unfortunately, does not move as quickly or as surely as the families of victims might like," the detective countered gently. "I know you want answers. You want justice, and you want closure. Please be patient. Be strong. I've got the numbers here for several victims' organizations you can go to for support. In the meantime, give us all time to unravel the truth of what happened that day. That's what you want most of all, isn't it? To know what really happened to your boy and why?" she asked softly.

Barbara lost the battle to keep her tears at bay and let them trickle silently down her cheeks. She took John's hand again. "We do," she whispered. "We'll try to be patient, won't we?"

John turned and met her gaze, and she wiped the single tear from her husband's cheek.

Silence fell between Barbara and John on the ride back to Welleswood. He dropped her off at home and headed straight to the office, once again retreating with his grief and his anger into his work. Instead of going inside her empty house to get her keys and driving to the avenue to open her shop, she went to her room and changed into jeans and a sweater. Seeking comfort, she wrapped herself in the shawl that had been made for her by women who participated in the Shawl Ministry at church and headed for the river that created a natural boundary between Welleswood and neighboring communities to the north.

At nearly noon on a weekday, the children were all in school. Parents were either at work or inside their homes, and she walked the several blocks filled with stately Victorian homes to the river without seeing anyone at all. The air was cool and the breeze was crisp, but her steps were slow and deliberate. She crossed the last street, paused to acknowledge the police officer on bike patrol as he rode by, and crossed over the paved walking path that encircled the river.

She cut through the grassy park and went straight to the giant oak tree at the water's edge. Now mid-September, autumn had yet to paint vibrant colors on the trees that hugged the park or to deaden summer reeds at the river's edge. Waves gently lapped at the gnarled, exposed roots of the oak tree. She pulled the shawl tighter around her shoulders, sat down and leaned back against the trunk to gaze out over the river.

Memories quickly surfaced. Watching Steve learn to sail here on the little twelve-foot, fiberglass sailboat John and the boys had made from a kit. Helping Steve release the frog he had watched develop from a tad-pole for a science project. With her mind's eye, she saw him again, eight years old, soaked to the skin and mud up to his knees after falling into the river while trying to keep the frog in view as it hopped away.

She choked down a half chuckle, half sob, recalling how hard he had tried to train for cross-country by running around and around this river his freshman year in high school, only to suffer an injury in the first event that sidelined him for the rest of the season.

"Steve." She whispered his name, and her heart ached for the sight and the sound of him, just once more. She closed her eyes and felt the gentle stir of the breeze on her face, but despite the shawl she wore, peace and comfort did not caress the anguish in her heart. "I miss him. John misses him. Steve's girls miss him. He didn't deserve to die. Please. Help me to understand," she prayed.

As her mind replayed the morning's conversation in

the detective's office, she bowed her head. She struggled to juxtapose the idea that Steve's death might have been nothing more than a tragic accident with the notion he had been murdered in cold blood. Had those two girls wielded the gun, or had it been someone else, someone who was still unknown? "Help John. Help the girls. Just . . . help us. We can't do this alone. I can't do this . . . it's too hard," she whispered, but her heart was confused.

Was there a difference between seeking justice and wanting vengeance? If so, which did she truly want? Steve was dead, a cold, hard fact, just as John had said. Did it really matter if Steve's death had been an accident or a deliberate act?

With one beat of her heart, it mattered a great deal to her. With the next beat, she did not care at all. Steve had died. That she knew for sure. "I've lost my son," she cried and placed her broken heart in the hands of the One who understood the utter devastation that burdened her heart.

Chapter Eleven

Some days, Judy was tempted to get back into bed, pull up the covers and spend the entire day hiding from the world. Unfortunately, this was one of those days. . . .

Her day started with a call from the plumber telling her that the problem with the toilet was now fixed, to the tune of ninety dollars. His news made the toothbrush Brian had accidentally flushed down the toilet one very expensive toothbrush. She had been interrupted in the middle of giving Mrs. Rosen a permanent by a call from the refrigerator repairman with even better news. Her eighteen-year-old refrigerator was not worth fixing. Unless she wanted to live with several coolers permanently lined up on her countertop to keep her food cold, she needed to buy a new refrigerator.

Torn between relief that the toilet was working again, her annoyance with Brian and anxiety about financing the refrigerator she could ill afford, she needed another call from the school like she needed to have yet another appliance break down.

With Mrs. Rosen now under the dryer, she gripped the telephone receiver hard. "Yes, I'm Brian's grandmother," she replied and braced herself to hear more bad news.

"This is Pam Smith. I'm President of the PTA at Park Elementary this year. Since you haven't volunteered for one of our school activities this year, I thought I'd call and see if we could set something up for you."

Judy sighed with relief that Brian had not gotten into trouble again. "I wish I could help, but I work full-time."

"A lot of our mothers are working. Fortunately, we managed to get all our Room Mothers and library aides this year already. I was thinking that perhaps you could help with the Book Fair. It's the third Saturday in October. Each school sponsors a table offering used books for sale, with proceeds directly benefiting that school. Gail Maguire was going to organize the book donations we've been getting at the school since last year's fair, but she's laid up with a bad back and won't be able to do it for us."

Judy hesitated. "I'd like to help, but I don't know all that much about books, and I work on Saturdays. Perhaps there's something else—"

"It's really very easy, assuming you can tell the difference between a cookbook or a novel or an accounting book," she added with a chuckle. "We'd need you to weed out any book that would be inappropriate, of course. The books are all at the school. All you'd really have to do is organize them by category, affix stickers with the prices, and be able to set them out on the tables early the day of the Book Fair, say seven o'clock? We have all the volunteers we need to sell the books once the fair opens at ten."

Judy heard the door to the salon open, nodded to Mrs. Hart when she entered, and held up a finger to let her know she would be right with her. "I'm sure I could organize them, but I still can't get to the school during the day. I work—"

"No problem. Mr. Fletcher, the janitor, is on duty weekdays from three until nine every night. He can let you in, and you could bring Brian along. You could even get a friend or two to help so it wouldn't take much time at all. We really do need to get started. . . ."

As Pam Smith droned on, Judy waited for the

woman to draw a breath so she could politely decline, but the dour look on Mrs. Hart's face told Judy she needed to end the conversation now or risk alienating a client. "Fine. I'll do it. Let me call you later—"

"Wonderful! There's no need to call me back. I'll tell Mr. Fletcher to expect you and several friends, perhaps. Thank you so much!" She hung up, leaving Judy no choice. She either had to find the time to organize the books or the courage to call back and tell Pam she had changed her mind.

Judy gave Mrs. Hart a smile. "I'm sorry to keep you waiting. The PTA at Brian's school needed someone to organize the book donations for the Book Fair in October."

Mrs. Hart cocked a brow. "And you agreed?"

Judy shrugged, still not convinced she would be able to find the time. "I guess I did."

"Good. I've got boxes of books in my basement and no way to get them to one of the schools. Since you're in charge, I'm sure you'll be able to do that for me." She looked around the salon. "Ann's not here? I have an appointment with her."

"No, I thought she called you. She's—"

"Not that gout again, I hope."

Judy shivered. "No, she's beat that for the time being. She's at the dentist this morning. She broke a tooth. She said she was going to call you at home to reschedule."

"I've been away for a few days. Will you have time? I just wanted a wash and set."

"No problem," Judy assured her and set aside her concerns about volunteering time she did not have to concentrate on using the time she did have today to keep Mrs. Hart satisfied as a client.

By one o'clock, the last client had left the salon, and Judy had two hours to herself before she had to be at the Towers. She ate the brown-bag lunch she had packed for herself, chased the peanut butter and banana sandwich down with freshly brewed iced tea, and packed up the rest of the baked goods from McAllister's without taking a pastry for herself. She left the box behind the reception desk to pick up later, ready to head out to the appliance store, when Ann hobbled into the shop.

"I thought you were going straight home after the dentist."

Ann's novocaine grin was lopsided as she leaned on the cane she had been using while recovering from her most recent encounter with gout. "I thought I'd stop in on my way home. Did Mrs. Hart come in for her appointment? I couldn't reach her to reschedule."

"She just left. She said to give you her best."

"Thanks. Are you ready to hear my good news?" she asked sarcastically.

Judy grimaced. "Don't tell me you had to have the tooth capped."

"Even better. I'm getting a triple crown bridge." She shrugged. "I think that's what Dr. Randall called it. Lucky me. Seems the tooth next to the one I broke is cracked, and the tooth on the other side . . . Well, to make a long, sad story a bit shorter and sweeter, I've got a full-morning appointment scheduled for the end of next week. He just patched me up until then." She shook her head. "Dr. Randall said I just might get the Most Chair Time Award this month. That's one award I'd like to let someone else get!"

"I'm so sorry," Judy murmured.

"Me, too. I'm falling apart, from one end to the other, aren't I?" She chuckled and looked around the shop. "Maybe Jamie is right. Even with a fresh coat of paint, the shop's still just an old gal, like me. I'm not sure how much longer either one of us will hold up before we both just disintegrate. Maybe it's time to really think about what that means and retire both of us."

Alarmed, Judy walked from behind the reception desk and put her arm around Ann's shoulders. "You and the shop are both going to hold up just fine for a long time," she insisted, although the idea that Ann would one day retire suddenly loomed as more than a distant possibility. "You're just feeling a little down. First the gout. Then your tooth. This time next week, when you can put that cane away for a while and you have your new crowns, you'll be feeling a whole lot better."

"I'm not so sure about that." Ann paused and fiddled with the handle on her cane. "Jamie wants me to retire and move down to North Carolina to be near her. She's got plenty of room. I could live with her until I find a place of my own. I told her I'd think about it."

Judy swallowed hard. Ann's daughter had moved south years ago, but she and her mother had remained close—a stark contrast to the estrangement between Judy and her own daughter. Setting aside a tinge of jealousy, she gave Ann a hug and smiled. Maybe getting Ann to help with organizing the books for the Book Fair might take her mind off her health problems long enough to set aside any real thoughts of retirement and moving away. "You're way too young to retire, and I think I know just what you need to make you feel better."

"A new set of teeth and a new set of toes?"

Judy chuckled. "Sorry. I wish I could, but—"

"A big hunk of chocolate?"

"No. Don't even think about it, or you'll be flat on your back again."

Ann shrugged. "So what do you think will make me feel good enough to forget about retirement?"

"I don't know. Maybe having something important to do. Something . . . something that would take your mind off your troubles. Maybe some volunteer work for the school?"

Ann stared hard at Judy. "You're going to try to talk me into doing something you already volunteered to do, aren't you?"

"Well, it's not that I don't want to do it, but I sure could use some help. The president of the PTA called this morning, and I promised I would help organize the books donated to Brian's school for the Book Fair.

You wouldn't have to actually help me to organize them. I could get some of the other mothers to do that. Maybe you could just help by making up the stickers with the prices. That would be a great help. If you feel up to it, that is," she added with a grin.

"If I'm up to it?" Ann straightened her shoulders. "Of course I'm up to it. I can stop and buy the stickers on the way home. You're going to the Towers, right?"

"Not until three, but I was just getting ready to leave. I have a few errands to run," she admitted, although she was reluctant to complain about buying a new refrigerator when Ann was dealing with the much more important issue of her health.

"You go ahead. I'll just rest up here a few minutes before I head off."

"If you're not feeling well, I can stay with you—"

When Ann gave her a no-nonsense glance, Judy held up both hands. "All right. All right. I'm going."

Judy picked out a basic refrigerator, arranged for a late delivery the next afternoon and put the purchase on the emergency credit card she kept just for occasions like this. With careful spending, she might even be able to pay off the cost of the refrigerator in less than a year and keep the finance charges to a minimum.

She left the store, checked her watch, and frowned. She had spent over five hundred dollars in less than fifteen minutes! Feeling guilty after she compared this expense with what Ann was facing, she turned her thoughts to the problem of her new volunteer job.

Ann's help notwithstanding, Judy still needed to recruit some volunteers to help her do the physical job of actually organizing the books. The few friends she had had before Brian came to live with her all had grown children. They had paid their dues to the school years ago, just as Judy had done with Candy. Although supportive of her new situation as both mother and grandmother to Brian, they had far less in common now than they had had a few short months ago.

Madge Stevens came to mind first, but Judy suspected that Madge was already involved with the Book Fair through Sarah's school. She glanced down the avenue, saw the sign for Sweet Stuff and thought of Ginger King, who worked there part-time. Although Ginger had said her grandson was not staying with her much longer that day at the school when they had met, that had been several weeks ago. Judy had seen her from a distance just this morning getting into her car when dropping Brian off at school. Maybe Ginger would like to help organize the books.

Judy could ask Barbara Montgomery, too, although she was not sure if now was a good time. The announcement that the police were investigating two suspects in Steve's death had been in the headlines for over a week now, and Judy was reluctant to intrude on Barbara's privacy, despite their common interests in raising their grandchildren and their budding friendship. If neither Ginger nor Barbara volunteered to help, however, Judy would seriously have to face doing the job all by herself.

After crossing the street, she passed The Diner and waved to Madge who was sitting in a corner booth with her sisters, Andrea and Jenny. Two blocks later, she entered Sweet Stuff, paused just inside the door and let her senses absorb the absolute wonder of stepping into every chocoholic's dream. The air was heavy with the scent of chocolate, and chocolate confections of every shape and size and flavor filled the glass-fronted candy cases on the wall opposite the door. Delicate pink lace curtains on the storefront window matched the painted walls and the carpet beneath her feet.

Directly ahead to her right, an old hutch displayed vintage favorites: Teaberry Gum, Mary Jane sweets, candy cigarettes—though she thought that odd—Turkish Taffy and Necco Wafers still packaged in familiar waxed paper wrappers. Small tables held party favors for every occasion. Shelves on either side of the hutch held gift baskets ready to be sent or delivered to local recipients.

Judy looked toward the back of the candy store, beyond the candy cases and the cash register, to the door that led to the kitchen. When no one came out, she walked deeper into the store, a veritable womb of chocolate that made her want to curl up and consume chocolates until she passed from this world into the next. She was halfway back when Ginger came out of the kitchen wearing a smile and an apron speckled with chocolate.

"I'm sorry. I was busy making some chocolate lollipops for the Book Fair. Oh, it's Judy, right? We met that day at school."

Judy rolled her eyes. "We did, indeed."

"Can I get something for you?"

"No, I—I really came by to talk to you and ask a favor."

Ginger grinned. "In that case, grab a piece of one of your favorites and come on back to the kitchen."

When Judy hesitated, Ginger put one hand on her hip. "Tell me you don't like chocolate."

"I wish I could."

"What's your favorite?"

"Chocolate-covered cherries," she blurted, then blushed. "I really shouldn't—"

"Of course you should," Ginger insisted and headed to the case closest to the kitchen door. "Charlene is pretty strict about making sure I follow company policy."

Judy followed her and watched Ginger put on a pair of disposable plastic gloves and place three large chocolate-covered cherries into a small pink bag. "Company policy?"

"When Charlene hired me to work here part-time, she told me that when she opened Sweet Stuff a few years ago, she had two goals. First, she wanted to make sure there was one place on the avenue where people could go if they were feeling lonely or sad. She wanted to make them feel a little less lonely or a little less sad, so it's company policy. Anyone who comes into the store has to eat some chocolate—on the house. Enjoy!" She handed the pink bag of chocolates to Judy, removed the plastic gloves and tossed them into the trash.

Judy held the bag tight. Despite her best efforts to resist, her mouth began to water. "Her second goal can't be to make much of a profit. Not if she gives away chocolate to anyone who stops in the store."

"It isn't, though you'd be surprised at how well she's doing now that she's added a whole line of gift baskets. Her second goal is really pretty amazing, although if you know Charlene well, it all makes perfect sense."

Judy cocked a brow. "She doesn't live in Welleswood, so I'm afraid I don't know her very well at all. I couldn't even venture a guess," she admitted and followed Ginger into the kitchen.

The room was much smaller than Judy expected. Shelves with ribbons and boxes and wrapping paper lined a small alcove that had a battered white worktable in the center. To her right, a narrow galley kitchen held a sink, a small countertop, a refrigerator with a top freezer compartment and a chocolate machine that reminded Judy of an antique wringer washing machine.

Ginger put on another pair of gloves, opened the freezer, removed a clear plastic candy mold and popped out six chocolate lollipops she placed on the counter atop waxed paper. She smiled as she worked. "I got them out just in time," she noted, filled another plastic mold with sticks and poured melted white chocolate in the mold end. She held up the mold for Judy to see they were lollipops that looked like books before she put the mold into the freezer. "Cute, aren't they? She's donating dozens and dozens to the Book Fair, assuming I can get them all done in time, which explains her second goal."

Judy opened her bag, took out a chocolate-covered cherry and took a bite. The dark chocolate was almost decadent, the cherry inside was crisp and sweet, and the gooey liquid that filled the space between the cherry and the chocolate shell . . . "Oh, no!" she exclaimed as the liquid began to drip. Instinctively, she popped the rest of the candy into her mouth and licked her fingers. Eyes wide, she chewed and swallowed the candy and ended up giggling—an odd experience since her day had been so difficult. "Oh, that was a little messy, but oh so good!"

Ginger's eyes twinkled. "And now you know Charlene's second goal. Everyone who comes in can't leave without forgetting their troubles for at least as long as it takes to eat a piece of chocolate. I take it you're feeling better?"

Judy nodded. "It was a rough morning, but I was hoping it didn't show. Maybe it isn't so rough now," she admitted as she reached into the bag for a second piece of candy. She gave one to Ginger and took the last one for herself. "I saw you at school this morning. I stopped in to see you today to see if you'd be interested in helping me to organize some books donated to the school to sell at the Book Fair, assuming Vincent is going to be at the school for a while longer."

Ginger studied the candy in her hand, took a small bite and turned the chocolate shell sideways to keep the liquid from dripping out. "Actually, he'll probably be here a good while longer," she murmured. She sighed and met Judy's gaze. "Vincent isn't going to be joining his mother and her new husband. He's—he's going to live with us permanently, unless . . . unless Lily changes her mind . . . someday."

The heartache in the woman's gaze met the kindred suffering in Judy's heart, creating an instant bond between them. "I understand," Judy whispered and briefly explained her situation with Candy as well as Brian. "I wish I knew how long Brian would be staying with me or if I'd ever see Candy again, but I don't," she admitted. She polished off her last bite of candy.

Ginger did the same and smiled. "I'll have to do some volunteer work at the school, anyway, and I'd really like to help you with the books."

"I'm glad." Judy glanced at her watch. She still had an hour left. "You met Barbara Montgomery at the school that day with me. I was thinking of asking her to help, too, but under the circumstances, I'm not sure if that's the right thing to do."

"I've been reading about the case in the newspaper. It must be a terrible time for her."

"What do you think? Should I ask her to help us?"

Ginger nodded thoughtfully. "I think if I were in Barbara's position, I might welcome a little diversion." She took the mold out of the freezer, popped out the chocolate lollipops and removed her apron. "Wait for me. I'll go with you," she suggested.

"What about the store? Can you just leave?"

"Company policy," she announced and led Judy out of the kitchen and back into the store.

Judy watched Ginger fill another small pink bag with an assortment of chocolates. After disposing of her gloves, she turned out the lights, fixed the sign in the storefront window to read Will Return at 2:15 and opened the door.

Judy shook her head in disbelief and followed Ginger out the door. "What company policy lets you close the shop in the middle of the day?"

Ginger held up the bag of chocolates. "Any real chocolate emergency. Right now, I think Barbara might need a little chocolate more than anyone else I know. That's good enough reason for me and it would be good enough for Charlene, too."

Judy laughed. "I really think I need to get to know this lady."

Ginger laughed with her, and they walked down the avenue to handle the "chocolate emergency" together.

Chapter Twelve

If it was true that lightning never struck the same place twice, Judy hoped that was true for near disasters, too. There were no customers in Grandmother's Kitchen, but the memory of Judy's last visit here was only too real as she entered the shop. With her arms crossed at her waist, she kept her purse tight against her body and quickly glanced down to make sure she was not wearing the slacks that still needed to be hemmed.

The decor inside the shop had shifted with the season, and instead of the scent of summer roses coming from the candles, she inhaled the mix of cinnamon and apples that hinted at fall. The antique glass display cases were all there, but she still took deliberate care to avoid them.

Ginger stopped just ahead of her, turned about in a full circle, and gaped at the antique canister sets that filled the shop. "I've never seen anything like this," she murmured. She stopped, walked over to one of the display cases, peered inside and gasped. "Did you see the prices? I can't imagine paying hundreds of dollars for canister sets that are so old you probably can't even use them," she whispered.

"I love antiques like these, but I don't know enough about antiques of any kind, except that I can't afford them," Judy admitted.

"Well, I might be able to afford them, but they don't hold any appeal for me." She took a closer look at a garish, two-tone canister set of chartreuse and purple and wrinkled her nose. "These absolutely do not tempt me."

"Some of them are really lovely, though," Judy countered while looking back toward the workroom for Barbara. "I wonder where she is." When the door opened behind them, Judy turned and found herself face-to-face with Barbara, who had a foam cup of coffee in her hand.

Her features were drawn, and her eyes were shadowed with sadness. "Judy! Ginger! This is a surprise."

"Trust me. I'm not going near anything today," Judy promised and briefly described her first visit to the shop to Ginger.

Barbara held up her cup of coffee. "I'm sorry I wasn't here when you arrived. It's midday, and I'm really sagging, in more ways than one, so I went out for some coffee since the cupboard in the back is bare as bones. I don't have any coffee to offer to you, but I have some bottled water in the refrigerator."

"I've got the perfect pick-you-up right here," Ginger announced and handed the small pink bag to her.

Barbara's eyes sparked to life. "Not chocolates from Sweet Stuff!"

Ginger grinned. "Absolutely."

Barbara moistened her lips. "What's the occasion?"

"No occasion. The chocolates are a bribe," Judy offered.

"No they're not," Ginger argued. "They're emergency rations, guaranteed to make you forget your troubles for a little while and maybe even make you giggle."

Judy nodded. "Okay, we'll compromise. They're an emergency bribe," Judy said before asking Barbara to help them organize the books for the Book Fair.

Barbara fingered the top of the bag, set her cup of

coffee down on top of one of the display cases and peeked into the bag. Her eyes widened. "There are at least a dozen pieces of candy in here!"

Ginger nodded. "Twelve different kinds of chocolate candy. I wasn't sure which one was your favorite."

"And all I have to do is agree to help you both organize some books?"

Ginger laughed. "Not really. The chocolates are yours . . . just because . . ."

"Because we really want you to say yes," Judy offered.

"Then, yes. I'll help you, but only on one condition. You both have to help me eat these chocolates. Right now."

Judy sucked in her breath. She could finish the entire bag of chocolates all by herself, even after she had already eaten two chocolate-covered cherries, though she hated to admit it. "Now? I don't think I should. We just had some chocolates at the candy store."

Ginger laughed again. "Oh, please. They were just a small appetizer. I'm always hungry for chocolate."

Barbara looked at Judy and cocked a brow.

Judy held on to her purse with one hand and held up the other in mock surrender while her mouth began to water. "Okay, okay! I'll eat more chocolate. All in the name of celebrating the formation of the volunteer committee in charge of organizing the books."

"And in the name of friendship," Ginger added.

Within moments, Barbara had them all in the back workroom seated on folding chairs in a semicircle at the work counter where she put the chocolates out on a paper plate. She handed each of them a napkin. "If we eat all this chocolate, you know we're going to spoil our dinners, right?"

Judy took a deep breath and inhaled the sweet scent of temptation. "Before Brian came to live with me, this would have been my dinner. Well, not quite," she corrected herself. "I wouldn't have splurged on the more expensive candy like this. But some nights I'd drag myself home from a long day on my feet and be too tired to cook dinner. Instead, I'd lie down on the couch and polish off a big old bag of M&M's or candy kisses or a bag of those mini-chocolate bars while watching television." She sighed. "I can't do that now. I have to cook a good meal to set a good example for Brian."

Ginger stared at the plate of chocolates with a whole lot more interest than she had shown when she had been looking at the antique canister sets. "I always kept a pint of Double Death by Chocolate ice cream in the freezer. Every once in a while Tyler worked late and grabbed something for dinner at work, so I didn't bother cooking for myself." She grinned. "I'd eat that whole pint of ice cream for dinner. But you're right. These days, I'm trying to keep healthier habits for Vincent's sake."

"We all need to indulge once in a while," Barbara argued. "I don't think that's a bad lesson to teach the children, although I haven't really thought about doing that with Jessie and Melanie." Her gaze grew wistful. "When the boys were growing up, we'd let them pick one night in the summertime to indulge ourselves and off we'd go to Scoops. Back then, Scoops didn't sell just ice cream. You could get burgers and fries, too."

"I remember that," Judy said as she tried to decide which piece of chocolate to take for herself.

"So there we'd be, all four of us, sharing an extralarge order of French fries with extra salt for an entrée, followed by ice-cream sundaes for dessert. Rick invariably chose the caramel crater, a gooey concoction as you can imagine, and Steve . . . He always ordered a banana split. . . ." Her voice trailed off, as if she had been caught up in memories of the son she had lost.

"You go first," Ginger prompted and held the plate of chocolates out to Barbara, who took forever to decide which one she wanted.

When she picked up the chocolate-covered cherry, Judy waited to see if Barbara would react the same way as she had. She did not have to wait long. Barbara had scarcely taken a bite before she had to pop the rest into her mouth and when she finished chewing, her giggles filled the room.

With a satisfied smile, Ginger selected a chocolate-covered caramel, took a bite and chewed slowly. "Having Vincent with us for the summer didn't require nearly the adjustment we're making now that it appears he'll be staying indefinitely," she murmured and repeated the tale to Barbara she had told Judy earlier. "I think the hardest part for Vincent and me right now is that I can't answer his questions about his mother. Not in ways that make sense to him or to me, so I just keep reminding him how much his mother loves him and how much we love having him with us. Sometimes I wonder if he shouldn't miss her more, but he doesn't say much. He's almost too content to be here."

"Brian's counseling has helped some," Judy offered. "The counselor seemed to think Brian was handling the situation well enough not to want to see him again, unless there's a crisis. Brian still doesn't talk much about his father, but he's beginning to open up more about his mother. We can talk about Candy and he'll seem fine, but then some nights he still cries himself to sleep, wanting to be with her."

Barbara sighed. "Jessie and Melanie don't seem to remember their mother. They don't mention her to me, but Steve was . . . They really miss him. They don't say too much to me about him, but I hear them when they're playing together. Poor babies. They keep thinking he's coming back for them," she whispered. "It's very hard, isn't it?"

"It is hard," Ginger murmured, "but it can be good, too. I want Vincent to be with us, and to be honest, I like having a child in the house again. I feel like I've gotten a second chance to do things better than I did when I was raising my own children. I love his innocence and his sense of wonder at things I take for granted, like watching a line of ants crossing the driveway."

Judy nibbled on a chocolate-covered nut cluster. "I agree. For all the challenges and inconveniences he's brought into the last part of my life, Brian reminds me every day that life is precious. That as hard as a day can be, there's one moment that's so special you want to stop and hold time still to enjoy it over and over. Like when he says his prayers at night and asks God to bless his grandmother because she makes the best hot dogs in the whole world."

"Or when you're doing some dreary, mundane task, like changing the bed linens. The twins will start a pillow fight, and I join in . . . I'd forgotten so much of what it was like to have a moment that made all the work and the emotional commitment it takes to raise children a little less taxing," Barbara offered.

"Or overwhelming," Ginger added.

Judy finished the other half of her nut cluster and checked her watch. "Or time-consuming," she noted, "which brings us back to one of the reasons I came today. I have about forty-five minutes before I have to be at the Towers. Before I forget, because I'm too busy devouring these chocolates, we need to set a time convenient for all of us to meet at the school to start organizing the books. We don't have to worry about making the price stickers, though. Ann's going to do that for us."

Ginger shook her head. "If it's during school

hours, we wouldn't have to worry about getting sitters, but we all work so that's probably not going to happen."

"We can get into the school between three and nine at night, according to Pam. She was going to alert the janitor, Mr. Fletcher, so he'll let us in," Judy informed them.

"John's had a lot of night appointments lately."

"But Tyler doesn't. I could ask him to watch the children."

Judy cringed. "All four of them?"

"I can ask him," Ginger offered with a shrug.

"Pam said we could take the children to the school with us," Judy noted. "They're certainly old enough to help stack books into piles for us while we sort through them. Later, when we get down to putting the stickers on the books, we could leave the children with a sitter. I mean, really. How long would it take to go through a few books?"

Barbara nodded. "I like the idea of getting the children involved. It's never too early to let them learn the value of helping others."

Judy grinned. "I wonder if having the children work together fits into one of those activities the principal recommended." While Ginger and Barbara each took another piece of candy and rehashed the day they had all been summoned to the school, Judy sat back and thought about the odd trio of women gathered around a simple plate of chocolates.

Although they were all fifty-something baby

boomers, they could not be more different in back-ground or lifestyle. The sense of sisterhood growing between them, however, came from a common bond of circumstances far beyond their control. Their companionship was an unexpected gift. Their friendship was a joy she tucked deep inside to ease the heartache and the loneliness that threatened to consume her and test the very essence of her faith. She would need them to help her handle the uncertainty of what the future might hold for herself, for Brian, and for her daughter, wherever she might be.

One day at a time.

One prayer at a time.

One piece of chocolate at a time.

Chapter Thirteen

A knock at the back door outside of the workroom in Grandmother's Kitchen startled Judy, interrupting their chocolate party, and from the way Ginger and Barbara also flinched, they had been startled, too.

Barbara looked at the half-eaten plate of chocolates and smiled. "It's probably the Good Grandparent Police who have come to arrest us for being bad role models for our grandchildren," she teased. "More likely, it's just an ordinary delivery. This won't take long."

Judy watched Barbara leave and open the rear door to the shop. When she saw Fred Langley, the police chief, standing outside, her heart sank and she exchanged a worried glance with Ginger. "Should we leave?"

"No. It's probably more news about the investigation. I can't believe it's dragged on this long without the police making an arrest. Barbara might need us to stay, unless Fred comes inside. Then we'll leave."

Judy checked her watch again. She had less than half an hour before she had to be at the Towers. "Okay. Let's see what he does."

Barbara sagged against the door frame for a moment, then straightened, stepped back, and let Fred inside.

Taking this as their cue, Judy and Ginger stood up simultaneously.

After Fred followed Barbara into the workroom, Judy took the lead. "Hi, Fred. Ginger and I were just leaving. Call me later, Barbara, and let me know what day is good for you."

Before she took a step to leave, Fred cleared his throat. "I'm afraid I need you to stay, Judy," he murmured. "I've been trying to find you. Fortunately, I ran into Doris Blake. She said she saw you headed into the store here. I would have come in through the front, but with what Barbara's had to go through lately, I thought it might be better to use the back door rather than spark more gossip. I'm glad you're here. I got a call about an hour ago from California. I have some news for you about your daughter."

When Judy's knees buckled, she plopped back down into her chair. Her heart raced straight to triple beats as she braced herself to hear the news he had brought—news that would probably break her heart, one way or another.

Drug rehab. Halfway house. Overdose. Hospitalization.

All these were familiar terms Judy had heard before, and she prayed she would not hear the one word that had fueled her deepest fears the moment she saw the chief of police: fatal. As hard as it was to live with her daughter's battle with drugs, she lived with the hope that her prayers would one day be answered and Candy would be able to beat her addiction. If not, if the drugs won the final battle, all hope would be lost.

When Barbara and Ginger offered to leave, Judy insisted they stay. "Bad news won't seem quite so bad if you're here," she whispered. After they sat down with her, she took a deep breath and nodded to the police chief who had been on the force as a patrolman when Candy had been in high school. She had no secrets to hide from him, then or now. "Tell me what happened to Candy. Is she . . . is she still alive?"

He pulled over the chair from Barbara's desk and sat down with them in front of Judy. His expression was somber, and his gaze was caring. "As far as anyone knows, yes, she's alive. The call I got came from a halfway house outside of San Diego. It seems Candy had been there for about three weeks when she just up and took off. That was last week. She didn't have any next of kin listed, so when she didn't come back, they just packed up her stuff. She didn't have much, but they found a picture of a little boy. On the back, there was an address. No name. Just an address. They tried checking information under her last name and when they came up empty, they contacted us. We checked the address, so here I am. I know it isn't much, but at least you know where she was up to a week ago. Where she is now is anybody's guess."

Washed with relief, Judy blinked back tears. "San Diego. Did . . . did they say if she was . . . how she was doing before she ran off?"

He shook his head. "They wouldn't tell me, but my guess would be that she was keeping herself clean. If she was using drugs again, they would have made her leave."

"Only if they knew she was back on drugs. She's really good at deceiving people," she whispered. She closed her eyes for a moment and shut out painful memories of the past filled with one recovery attempt after another, all of which failed to make Candy stronger than the addiction that ruled her life. When she opened her eyes, she met his gaze and saw her own fears reflected in his eyes. "The reality is that she's probably using drugs again. That's why she left the halfway house. She's done it before. She'll probably do it again, and she'll keep doing it until one day the drugs will take what's left of her life."

He dropped his gaze. "I'm sorry. I wish I'd had better news." He stood up, pushed his chair back to the desk and faced her again. "Is there any chance she's headed home to Welleswood?"

Her eyes widened. "Here? I—I don't know. She wouldn't come to see me, but she might come to see Brian." Her hands balled into fists, and her protective instincts stiffened her backbone. "If she's using drugs, I can't let her anywhere near him."

He nodded. "We'll keep a lookout for her. Just to be safe, though, you might want to contact the school. Let them know you're the only one who can take him out of school."

"I think I did that when I registered him for school."

"Double-check. If she does show up here and starts trouble, call us," he said before he let himself out the back door.

Ginger leaned toward Judy. "What about the locks on your house? Does your daughter have a key?"

"I—I don't know. Probably."

"I can call the locksmith for you," Barbara suggested.

Judy shuddered. "This is all so . . . bizarre. Keeping Brian from his own mother. Notifying the school. Changing the locks. It's like I'm caught up in the middle of a made-for-television movie. I get to live on pins and needles worrying about keeping him safe while Candy is probably in some faraway place, too high to remember she even has a son."

"You don't know that for sure. Maybe she's clean now," Ginger argued.

Judy clenched and unclenched her jaw. "Clean? For how long? Long enough to come to take Brian away again? Then what?" She remembered the picture

Brian had drawn at school and shook her head. "I can't let her take him. I won't let her take him. Not until I'm sure she'll stay off drugs for good and he'll be safe."

"You might not have a choice," Ginger murmured. "She's his mother. If she can convince a judge she's off drugs, I don't think there'd be much chance you could keep custody of him."

"Candy could convince a judge, then she'd take Brian out of the area again so the court, or me, for that matter, wouldn't know if she got back onto drugs."

"You need a lawyer," Barbara announced. "I'll call mine and see if he can—"

"Lawyers and locksmiths cost money," Judy argued. The anger and bitterness she had kept buried the past few months reached deep into her heart and rekindled the old hurt and anger from all the years she had struggled, watching her daughter's addiction and self-destruction. The harsh reality that Frank was no longer here to help her, either emotionally or financially, was almost too much to bear. "The lawyer and locksmith would have to stand in line behind the plumber who just fixed the toilet Brian clogged with his toothbrush and the credit card company that I owe for the new refrigerator I had to buy this morning. Brian will need winter clothes soon, and I already worry all night about how I'll pay for them. I've had it up to here," she snapped and hit the edge of her chin with the back of her hand.

"It isn't fair. Not to me and not to Brian. It's just one

constant struggle for us, and in the meantime, his father is living a carefree biker's life in Florida and his mother is wasting her life away. I'm the one who has to pick up the responsibilities that belong to them and put my own life on hold, again and again."

She narrowed her gaze. "It isn't fair, and I'm tired of pretending any more than I'm perfectly content to raise my grandson. I'm so angry at Candy, I could . . . spit."

When the echo of her angry words faded, Barbara took one of Judy's hands. "No, it isn't fair to you or to Brian, but just imagine where he'd be without you," she murmured as she stroked the back of Judy's hand.

Barbara's words touched Judy's heart and her anger abated. Tears of shame filled her eyes. "I'm sorry. I— I didn't mean to shout or to let my frustrations or my anger get the best of me."

Ginger took her other hand. "You have every right to be frustrated and angry and afraid. I feel that way, too, probably more often than I've been willing to admit, even to myself. It's hard pretending and putting a smile on my face, when inside I'm angry with the way my life and my future has changed. I'm even angrier with my daughter. Lily isn't addicted to heroin or cocaine, but she's hooked on money and status. They're her drugs of choice, and I'm deeply ashamed of her for abandoning her son, too."

Judy blinked back her tears and squeezed Ginger's hand. She was grateful to know she was not the only one who struggled with anger at her situation. When she looked at Barbara, however, she felt nothing but shame. "I'm sorry. We must seem very petty to you, getting angry with our children when you're mourning the loss of your son. He was a good father. He didn't abandon his children like our daughters did."

Barbara let out a sigh. The two women on either side were connected to her, hand to hand and heart to heart, creating a circle of strength she needed desperately. She covered Judy's hand with her own. "No, he didn't, but that doesn't mean I haven't been angry with him, because I have been. Sometimes I still am, for completely ridiculous reasons. Why was he so dependent on using ATM machines? He didn't get cash out once a week. No. He'd stop every day or every other day to get a few dollars."

She shook her head. "Maybe it's a generational thing. People his age don't seem to plan ahead like we do, but maybe if he had taken out more money the day before, he wouldn't have been there when that gun was fired and he'd still be alive. Or maybe he should have listened when we talked to him about marrying Angie. But, no. He insisted she was the one he wanted to have as his wife, and she wanted to live in the city where life was more exciting. If he'd bought a house here in Welleswood . . ."

She smiled. "I told you it was irrational for me to get angry. And it's foolish for all of us to let thoughts of what could have been threaten what we have now."

"Or to think we can do this without God's help," Judy added.

"Amen," Ginger murmured. "I know He's watching over all of us, but it's our grandchildren who really need an extra dose of His love and protection right now."

"Amen," Barbara responded as their conversation turned into an impromptu prayer. "We need help to let go of our anger and disappointments . . . and forgiveness for the times when we can't."

"Amen," Judy replied. "Our daughters need Your strength to turn away from the world and choose a life of faith as His children."

"Keep my son close to You in Paradise. Amen," Barbara whispered.

"Amen."

"Amen."

They all let go of one another, but Barbara urged them to join hands again. "Oh, and if You can, we need a locksmith and a lawyer for Judy," she added, lightening the mood before they let go of one another again.

"You forgot to say a cheap locksmith and a cheap lawyer," Judy teased.

"How about free?" Ginger asked with a twinkle in her eyes.

Judy laughed. "Free is even better, but not very likely."

"No, but you could barter for their services," Barbara suggested. "I saw some ads in the town paper just the other week. There's actually a separate column in the classified section where people can barter their services."

Ginger nodded enthusiastically. "That's right! Like, you could offer to cut or style hair in exchange for new locks for your house."

Judy cringed. "It's a nice idea, but I wouldn't feel comfortable placing an ad like that in the paper."

"Then go in person," Ginger urged. "Tyler is a security consultant. He works with Al Smith a lot, and we socialize as couples. We go to a lot of baseball games together. Al's a good locksmith, and he's a member of our congregation. I think he'd do it."

"I don't know."

"No, you don't. Not unless you ask him," Ginger argued.

The thought of going to the locksmith to barter for services instead of paying for them was about as appealing to Judy as eating a raw egg. "I'll think about it."

Barbara smiled. "I'm sure I'll be talking to our lawyer within the next few days. I'll mention the idea in general. If he's receptive, I'll let you know."

Ginger reached out and took another piece of chocolate. "Time will tell. Who knows? This time next week, you might have new locks and legal advice, all without spending a dime."

"Time?" Judy checked her watch and groaned. "Oh, no. It's two forty-five. I'm going to be late," she cried and got to her feet. "The last thing I can afford to do right now is to miss an appointment with a client. I'll have to go back to the salon later to get the baked goods. I'm sorry, ladies. I really have to run."

After giving Barbara and Ginger a quick hug, she snatched one last piece of chocolate to eat on the way and hurried out the back door. Twenty minutes later, she arrived at the Towers where she found Mrs. Reisch, her first appointment, in the office at the counter getting a receipt for her rent.

The elderly woman apologized profusely. "I'm so sorry. I hope you haven't been waiting upstairs for me all this time." She rolled her eyes. "It's rent day and Patricia isn't here to help."

Judy met the harried office manager's gaze and smiled at her client. "No, I just got here. I'm just running behind today."

"You're not the only one. Let's go upstairs. I'll make us a nice cup of tea and then we'll see about getting this mop of mine back under control."

When Penny, the office manager, handed Judy her canvas bag from behind the counter, Judy told her she would be back later with the baked goods. Then she followed Mrs. Reisch upstairs to her apartment.

"Poor Miss Damm. She passed, you know," Mrs. Reisch murmured as she unlocked the door to her apartment and stepped inside. "She lived next door to me for seven years, not that I'll miss her much. She kept pretty much to herself."

Judy entered the apartment. "I heard she'd been in the hospital," she offered, unable to forget the day she and Penny had found the woman in her apartment and called for an ambulance.

"She lingered awhile, poor soul. The funeral was

lovely, though. Her daughter was such a dear. She had a catered luncheon for all the residents right here in the social room. I think you have a daughter, too, don't you?"

Judy tightened her hold on her bag. She did not know Mrs. Reisch all that well, and she was reluctant to discuss Candy. "Yes, but she lives in California," she offered and followed her client into the kitchen.

Mrs. Reisch turned on the burner under the teakettle. "Pity that. California is no place for decent folks. Not with that movie crowd out there. I read all about them in the tabloids. Makes me want to cry sometimes. Welleswood is a good town and a godly town. If she's as smart as you are, that daughter of yours will move back home."

"Maybe she will," Judy whispered, half-afraid Candy would show up at home, sooner rather than later.

Chapter Fourteen

The following week, Judy left the Towers for the second time on Thursday with a bent and battered gift certificate her last client, Mrs. Fowler, had given to her instead of coins she had saved up since Judy's last visit. The gift certificate, accepted by any of the merchants on the avenue, was for twenty dollars, a tip that normally would be considered very extravagant. There was only one hitch: the certificate expired today.

Exhausted after the fitful night before and a frenzied day at work, she hurried down the avenue toward the school to pick up Brian from the after-school program. Her day, unfortunately, was far from over. After dinner and homework, she and Brian were meeting back at the school with her friends and their grandchildren to organize the books for the Book Fair.

She held tight to her purse as she crossed a side street and continued down the avenue. Still reluctant to barter for the new locks on her doors that she needed, she thought about the gift certificate in her purse. The twenty dollars might have gone a little way or a long way toward getting those new locks, but she had no idea what they might actually cost yet. The expiration date, however, made the possibility of using the money toward new locks almost nil. If she had had the certificate sooner, she could have applied it toward her new refrigerator. Since she hadn't, she could use the money to get something for Brian, but the shops on the avenue were fairly expensive. She would get much more for her money at one of the nearby discount stores, but the certificate was of no value outside of town.

With the way her day had gone so far, however, getting stuck with the certificate seemed about right.

When she arrived at the school, she waved to Mrs. Hemmy, the after-school teacher, as Brian came racing toward her with a paper of some kind in his hand. "Look! I got the Best Student Award today. See?"

He was so excited he almost knocked her over, and she steadied both of them while trying to read the hand-printed award. "I'm so proud of you!"

"I'm gonna get more, too. Miss Addison said so 'cause I'm doin' better. Lots better."

Judy held him against her. "Yes you are! We should celebrate," she announced and had a flash of inspiration of exactly how she might use that gift certificate. She walked him outside and turned back toward the center of town. "Hungry?"

His head bobbed up and down. "Can you make hot dogs tonight?"

She laughed. "I could, but I was thinking maybe we should go out for dinner to celebrate your award. What if we went to Scoops and had ice cream?" she asked, but felt guilty for never taking Candy for an ice-cream dinner when she had been little.

He tugged on her hand and shook his head. "Grandmom, we can't have ice cream for dinner."

"Who said?"

"You did. That time I said I wanted ice cream for dinner, you said no. You said I had to eat my regular dinner first."

"That was different," she insisted. "You didn't win an award that day, did you?"

"Nope. I never got one before today."

"Well, then, that settles it. We're going to Scoops and having ice cream for dinner. Then we'll go home, get homework done, change and go back to school to sort through the books for the Book Fair."

He skipped and hopped his way to the ice-cream store, polished off a sundae with cookie crumbles and gummi bears on top and walked all the way home with her without once complaining about being tired. She had her keys in hand when she got to the bottom of the steps on her front porch, but climbed the porch steps slowly. For a brief moment, she longed for the days not so very long ago when her life had been more settled. If today's hectic schedule was any indication, however, things were not likely to settle down again for her for a good long time.

When she got to the top step, she paused and stiffened her back. Yes, her life was unsettled. It was also unpredictable and a little chaotic at times with Brian here, but her life now was also filled with the love of that little boy and friends like Barbara and Ginger were becoming. She thought about Candy and the danger she could represent, but now firmly rejected the notion of changing her locks and contacting a lawyer, especially if she had to barter for what she needed.

She opened the door and followed Brian into the house. When she closed the front door, she threw the inside bolt. If Candy was on still on drugs and wanted to come here to get her son back, different locks on the doors or a judge's order on a piece of paper would not stop her. That much Judy knew from experience.

But the school personnel could keep Candy from Brian.

And Judy would stop her. She was Brian's grandmother and grand mother now. With friends by her side and faith as her shield, she would protect him better than anyone or anything else.

With a single glance around the basement storage room at Park Elementary School, Judy stood inside the door with her two friends and sighed. Any idea that they could organize the books in a single night quickly withered. What wishful thinking!

"There are hundreds and hundreds of books!" Ginger exclaimed as the four children darted around the room peeking into one box after another.

Barbara pushed up the sleeves on her sweatshirt. "It's a good thing we didn't wait until the last minute. We're going to need more than tonight to get this job done."

Eyes wide, Judy looked from one friend to the other. "I'm really sorry. I had no idea there would be . . . I don't have a clue about how to tackle this many books. Or how to tell Ann that we'll need hundreds more price stickers!" She paused, then turned quickly toward the children when she spied Brian out of the corner of her eye. "No, Brian. Please don't climb into any of the boxes." When he climbed out with no argument, she smiled, took another look at her friends, shook her head and chuckled. "If nothing else, this should be an interesting venture I've pulled you both into. Hundreds of books. Four children with energy to spare. And three tired grandmothers!"

"Maybe all we need is a little adventure to perk us

up and slow them down," Ginger prompted as the children quickly organized a game of tag that had them squealing and racing around the room. She clapped her hands. "Okay, you guys. Hold it and listen up. We've got lots of work to do and we need your help."

"You've got a plan?" Judy asked as the children raced toward them.

Ginger giggled. "No, but I think Barbara probably does." She nudged Barbara with her shoulder. ".You've had to organize boxes of shipments for your shop, right? This shouldn't be much different."

"I guess not," Barbara conceded. She narrowed her gaze for a moment and smiled. "Apparently, we all agree we'll have to do this in stages. Why don't we call it a good night if we can separate the books into fiction and nonfiction piles tonight?"

"Sounds good to me," Judy replied.

Ginger nodded.

With one of the twins on either side of her now, and both Judy and Ginger holding on to their respective grandsons, Barbara glanced around the room. "I think it's probably safe to assume that most of the books will be fiction so we'll need more room for those. Let's see if we can make some kind of divider with the boxes so the fiction will be here, closer to the door," she suggested.

Working hand in hand with Brian, while Ginger and Barbara did the same with their grandchildren, Judy tugged boxes into a row that separated the room, leaving a walkway in two sections to make it easier to move around.

Brian beamed as he helped Judy shove a box into place. "This is fun, Grandmom!"

"I'll try to remember that tomorrow when my back is aching," she teased as she stood up and eased the kink out of the small of her back.

"Can I help Vincent?" he asked as Ginger's grandson struggled on one side of a very wide and obviously heavy box.

"Sure. Go ahead. I'll help Melanie and Jessie," she suggested. While he raced away, she slid in between Barbara's two granddaughters and helped them tug another box into line.

"Will you ask us to help again, Mrs. Roberts?" Jessie grinned. "This is lots more fun than helping do dishes."

Barbara chuckled. "I can't believe you think loading dishes into the dishwasher is work. Back when I was your age, we filled the sink with soapy water and washed dishes by hand, one dish at a time. And then we had to rinse them and dry them with a towel before we put them away," she added. "That was work."

"Cool!" Melanie gushed. "You gave the dishes a bath?"

Judy nodded and suppressed a grin. "We still give dishes a bath at my house. I don't have a dishwasher, so Brian helps me do the dishes every night after dinner."

"That doesn't sound so cool," Jessie admonished before charging off to choose another box to move.

"Yes it does." Melanie grinned. "Can I come to your house some night for dinner and give the dishes a bath?"

Barbara gave the box one final push. "Melanie! It isn't polite to ask to be invited for dinner."

Chuckling, Judy straightened the box into line. "It's always polite to volunteer to do the dishes, though. We'll have dinner at my house soon, okay?"

"Okay!" Melanie replied before following after her sister.

Barbara laughed and shook her head. "I can't remember the last time I thought that doing dishes might be fun."

"Or that washing dishes was the equivalent of giving the dishes a bath."

"Speaking of baths, I know four children who will definitely need a good bath tonight," Ginger noted as she joined them. "Not to mention their grandmothers," she teased as she wiped a smudge from Barbara's cheek. "Now that we've got the books lined up, what's next?" she asked Barbara.

Barbara let out a deep breath and surveyed the room. "I don't know about you two, but I'm beat already. The children, on the other hand—"

"They each have more energy than we have. Combined," Judy noted as Vincent and Brian each started chasing one of the girls.

"Which means we are very smart grandmothers if

we can harness all that energy," Barbara noted and quickly organized them all into specific tasks.

Within minutes, Judy, Ginger and Barbara were stationed in three separate places within the room and the children eagerly assumed their roles as runners. Judy and Ginger inspected boxes, lifted out books and handed one to each of the children, who would run the book to Barbara, who would then direct the child to take the book either to the fiction or nonfiction section of the room. If Barbara deemed the book as inappropriate for any reason, however, she kept the book and stored it in a box marked Discards.

By eight o'clock, the boxes were all empty and the books were in stacks that were separated into fiction and nonfiction. With their faces smudged and their clothes dusty, the children had collapsed against the wall. Subdued, they still had enough energy left to whisper and giggle together.

Side by side on the opposite side of the room, all three grandmothers were smiling.

"A task well done," Judy remarked.

Ginger chuckled. "In more ways than one. I don't think any of us will have an argument about bedtime tonight. Poor dears. They ran themselves straight into exhaustion."

"And their clothes straight to the washing machine," Barbara remarked with a chuckle.

"What? You're not going to give the clothes a bath in the sink?" Judy teased as she brushed the dirt from her own jeans.

When Ginger raised a brow, Barbara quickly explained how Melanie had compared doing dishes to giving the dishes a bath. When she finished, she toyed with the cross at the end of the chain she wore, her thoughts obviously drifting to the son she had lost so suddenly.

"Maybe we should do this more often," Judy suggested.

"I don't think we have much of a choice. We still have to organize the books by topic and put the price stickers on that Ann promised to make," Ginger prompted.

"No. That's not what I meant," Judy countered. "I mean, look at the three of us. With all the problems we have between us, we could be feeling overwhelmed or sad or depressed or angry about how much we've had to give up to raise our grandchildren. Or how much we miss our own children or worry about them. Instead, we're here with our grandchildren, having fun with them and letting them prove to us that being a grand mother doesn't mean we can't just be grandmothers sometimes, too. I'm worried silly about Candy, but tonight, being with Brian and having fun with him was all I could think about."

"You're right," Ginger whispered. "I haven't had a single sad or angry thought about Lily all night."

"For the first time in months, I actually just enjoyed the girls without letting my grief at losing Steven come between us," Barbara whispered.

"That means we definitely have to do this again. And again," Ginger suggested.

"Like next Thursday? We still need to categorize the books," Judy prompted. "I know we didn't plan on including the children, but I think we should."

Barbara nodded. "Agreed."

"Agreed," Judy murmured. "And when we finish organizing all the books, we'll just have to promise to think of something else to do together."

Ginger groaned, even as she smiled. "What? Another volunteering job?"

"Maybe," Barbara replied. "It doesn't really matter, does it? As long as it's something that lets us just be grandmothers. Even if it's only for a little while."

Chapter Fifteen

At the end of October, Judy reviewed the events for that month on the school calendar and smiled. The Book Fair had been a huge success. She, Barbara and Ginger, along with their grandchildren, had worked together for several nights organizing the used books, cementing their friendships with lots of laughter and more than a few tears as each of them enjoyed time being just grandmothers, even as new crises being grand mothers evolved.

Ginger seemed to be faring the best now, although adjusting her carefree, sports-centered lifestyle and trying to find a common interest to share with Vincent was putting a strain on her marriage. Judy counted herself blessed. Candy had not reappeared to threaten or disrupt Brian's new life, and Judy had lived so many years with the uncertainty of not knowing her daughter's condition or whereabouts, she was almost used to it. Almost. With no arrests yet, however, Barbara needed the support the three women offered one another most of all.

With Brian tucked into bed for the night, Judy had nothing more exciting to do on a Saturday night than plan her budget for the next few months. She sat at her kitchen table with a scratch pad and pencil, a pocket calculator, the school calendar and a large wooden box where she kept her tips, otherwise known as her survival funds.

She looked ahead at November and December, months filled with holiday memories that stretched all the way back to her childhood. Rather than dwell on the past, she concentrated on surviving this holiday season, financially rather than emotionally. These two months were also months filled with national and religious holidays, and days for teacher in-service. Brian would almost be out of school more than he would be in!

Jotting down the dates leading up to Christmas break, she noted that the calendar listed the school vacation at Christmas as a "Winter Break" and frowned. So much had changed since Candy had been in school. Judy had known better than to expect there would be any prayer in school these days, but she had not realized they had taken God out of Christmas vacation, too. At least Thanksgiving was still a national holiday and listed as Thanksgiving, but she could not help wondering to whom everyone was supposed to be giving thanks, if not God?

"Just another modern mystery," she mumbled. When she studied the list of days she would need a sitter for Brian, since the after-school program did not operate when the school was closed, her frown deepened and she rubbed her forehead to ease away the beginnings of a headache. Ginger and Barbara could cover a few days for her, and Judy could reciprocate on two Mondays when the salon was closed. Two four-day weekends in November when the school would be closed Thursday through Sunday presented major problems for her budget, especially with Christmas break following so closely behind, and demanded even more money to be set aside for day care.

She lifted the lid on the box holding her survival funds and scanned the coins and bills inside. Even though coin-sorting machines made coin wrappers almost obsolete, wrapping her coins made it easier for her to tell at a glance how much money she had available. Also, she found it much more convenient to use the wrappers so she did not have to make special trips to the bank or the grocery store to exchange her coins for bills.

Two sandwich-size plastic bags from seniors at the Towers held coins to be wrapped. She smiled and wrapped the pennies in the first bag Mrs. Derrick had given to her yesterday, using eight wrappers and leaving the six remaining pennies in the bag. The other bag from Miss Paxton held fewer coins, but they were all silver. She counted the coins, worth $2.10, and added them to rolls not yet filled.

A rubber band held the stack of paper money together, stored in ascending value, and the dollar bills far outnumbered the larger denominations, making it appear as if she had much more cash than she really did. "Business is good, and my clients are generous. Thank you, God," she whispered, although she still needed something akin to the miracle of the loaves and fishes if she was going to make it financially to the first of the year, even with a moderate forecast for holiday tips.

She tapped numbers into the calculator for her usual expenses, like utilities and taxes, a number she hoped would be enough for Brian's winter clothes and food. She shook her head. For a small child, he sure had a healthy appetite!

When she saw the total, compared it to the number she had written down for the salary she would earn, her survival funds, and a projection of future tips, she groaned. She was still short. A lot short. And she had not set aside any funds for Christmas.

When the front doorbell rang, she welcomed the diversion. She was halfway to the door when the possibility that Candy might be standing on the other side occurred to her. Cautiously, she left the inside bolt in place, along with the new chain-guard she had managed to install herself and pulled back the curtain on the living room window a little and peeked outside.

She grinned, dropped the curtain back into place and opened the door to greet her boss, Ann Porter. "This is a surprise! Come in!"

Leaning on her cane, Ann hesitated. "I saw your lights on. I hope it isn't too late to drop in unexpectedly."

"Don't be silly. It's only nine o'clock, and besides, I haven't seen you for a few days. Come in," she urged, stepping aside to let Ann in. "Do you have time for a cup of hot cider?"

"Only if you'll join me."

"Absolutely! I just have to clear off the kitchen table." She carefully locked and bolted the door again before resetting the chain. She followed Ann back through the narrow foyer and the dining room into the kitchen. It was slow going, and Judy could not help but notice how much Ann had aged over the course of the past few months. Worried about why Ann had come to see her, Judy stepped into the kitchen and around Ann to pull out a padded chair at the red Formica table she and Frank had bought as newlyweds. "Here. Have a seat and relax."

Ann plopped into the seat, heaved a sigh and hung her cane on the back of the nearest chair. "Don't get old, Judy."

"Sorry. It's too late," she argued while she filled a saucepan with cider and set it onto the stove to heat.

Ann sighed again. "It's not true, you know."

"What? That I'm not old yet? Ha!"

"No. That 'Life begins at fifty,'" she said, mimicking the slogan most baby boomers had latched on to as they neared retirement age. "In truth, life does begin at fifty. To deteriorate, that is. At sixty, it's even worse. And these are the 'Golden Years'? Forget it. It's all propaganda. I wonder if I can sue somebody for breach of promise."

"Not a chance. Besides, you're just feeling cranky because your foot is still sore. If you'd follow the doctor's orders and eat right and take your medicine, maybe you'd feel better a lot sooner," she teased, grateful that Ann had not lost her sense of humor.

"That's what I mean," Ann countered. "Before I turned fifty, I had no idea what gout was. And I used to eat anything and everything in double portions. Never got sick and never gained an ounce, and I spent twelve hours a day working. I still work hard, but look at me."

Judy cleared the table and set her box of survival funds and other stuff on the countertop before she put a pair of mugs and spoons on the table. "You look fine."

"I'm heavier than I've ever been. Tell the truth. Can you eat like you used to, or do you have to watch what you eat?"

Judy cringed. "Actually, I pretty much eat what I want."

"Okay. Forget about gaining weight. What about

shopping? When's the last time you spent the morning or an afternoon shopping without having to look for a ladies' room? And I don't mean for Brian."

"I'll give you that one," Judy offered as she poured the cider into the mugs and set them on the table. She peeked into the cabinet, found the jar of cinnamon sticks and carried it to the table where she put one of the sticks into each of the mugs.

"What about your legs?" Ann asked with a know-it-all look.

"What about them?"

"No varicose veins or spider veins?"

Judy shrugged. "Maybe a few."

"Hah! You didn't have those at thirty. And take a look in the mirror. Crow's feet. Sagging chin. Turkey neck. It's all there!"

Judy leaned back against the counter and burst out laughing. "Thanks! You make it sound so awful."

"Isn't it?"

"It's just part of aging. It's perfectly normal. It's part of life."

Ann finally laughed with her. "I guess so, but that doesn't mean I have to like it or that I have to buy into the idea that these are the best years of my life. They're not."

Judy took a deep breath. "Maybe not, but they're all we have, and I'm not going to dwell on the past or how it used to be or how it could be better if I were younger. I am what I am, and I'm just thankful for every day I get to be here," she murmured as thoughts of Brian wrapped around her heart and she sat down across from Ann.

As Ann stirred her cider, her mood turned more serious. "Enough about me for now. What about you? Are you really doing okay?"

"I really am," Judy insisted. "Some days are better than others, of course, but overall, life is good. Brian is a handful, but he's a charmer."

Ann's gaze softened. "What about Candy? Have you had any word?"

Judy took a sip of cider. "Nothing new. I'm just taking it one day at a time. Having Ginger and Barbara as friends helps a lot. You, too," she added. "I'm really glad we're friends."

Ann wrapped her hands around her mug. "Me, too," she whispered and dropped her gaze. "This is harder than I thought it would be." When she looked up at Judy, her gaze was deeply troubled.

Judy's spine tingled, and she braced herself to hear the news that Ann had brought. "What's wrong?"

"I'm tired, Judy. Just plain dog tired. I'm tired of fighting gout, not to mention frigid winters that make my bones ache. I'm tired of pushing myself out of bed every morning to get to work." She sighed. "We've worked together now for over thirty years, but it's time for me to face the fact I don't have more years left than I've already spent. I had a long talk with Jamie this morning. I miss her, Judy. She's all the family I have left in the world, and I'd like to spend whatever time I do have left living close to her so . . .

I think it's time to retire, Judy, and put Pretty Ladies up for sale. I—I met with Andrea Sanderson today, but I told her I wasn't going to sign a contract until I spoke with you first."

Judy clutched the edge of the table and struggled for breath. "You're really going to retire and move to North Carolina? And sell the salon?"

"Assuming I can find a buyer, I'd like to retire by summer. The building itself will attract plenty of interest, but the business . . . I worry about that. Even if a buyer decided to keep the salon running, I doubt it would be the same. If the other salons in town are any indication, the new owner would probably add a nail salon, raise the prices and try to attract younger, more affluent clients."

She sniffled and wiped at her tears. "I don't think the new owner will worry about the seniors at the Towers, which truly bothers me a lot, but it's you I'm worried about most of all. There's no guarantee a new owner would keep you on, and I—I'm not sure what to do about that unless . . . unless maybe you . . . you could buy the salon?"

Judy blinked back tears of her own. Through blurred vision, she saw the anguish on Ann's face and got a glimpse of the box with her survival funds on the countertop. All of her worries about having enough money to survive the next two months were washed away by a tidal wave of terrifying questions that swamped her mind.

How could she possibly survive and meet her

responsibilities to Brian if she lost her job? She had not looked for a job for more than thirty years! She had no car and relying on public transportation would be as costly as it would be time-consuming. Her welfare, however, was not Ann's concern. She drew in a long breath. "Don't worry about me. I'll figure out something," she murmured.

"I—I was hoping maybe you'd want to buy the salon yourself," Ann prompted. "I'd feel a whole lot better about retiring if you did."

Judy gasped. "Me? Buy the salon? With what? My good looks? Now that's an idea! If only I'd thought about it twenty years ago when I had any looks at all." She shook her head. "Life doesn't begin at fifty. You said so yourself, and I'm a good seven years past that magic number now. There's no way I could start my own business now."

"But you wouldn't be starting anything," Ann countered and quickly outlined an idea that had Judy's head spinning and her heart pounding with just the possibility Ann was right.

True, Judy had no money of her own, to speak of.

But she did have her own strong will to survive. She had a solid work ethic and a strong commitment to her clients and the seniors. She had friends who would help her, but most of all, she had faith that somehow, someway, God just might lead her past the door that had just closed and open a new one for her, just as He had always done in the past.

Chapter Sixteen

Barbara and Ginger offered much more than friendship when Judy told them about possibly losing her job and her dream of buying Pretty Ladies once Ann retired.

They sat with Judy around her kitchen table in mid-November on a Thursday night. Her two friends did not wear long, black robes like justices in a courtroom or blank, impartial expressions like members of a jury. Judy knew, however, that she could count on both of them to listen objectively, offer critical scrutiny and tell her honestly if her plan of action to buy the salon was more likely to succeed than to fail.

From her seat at the head of the table, Judy spread a number of papers out in front of her, handed a folder marked with her friends' names to each of them, and hit the table with the side of her fist. "The meeting is now officially called to order."

Ginger giggled, tried to put a serious expression on her face and giggled again. "Sorry. You just seem so . . . formal and so in . . . control."

"I'm glad you think so. My legs are so weak I couldn't stand up if I tried, and there are so many butterflies in my stomach I'm nauseous," Judy admitted. "A couple of weeks ago, if you had told me I'd be sitting here with both of you to go over a plan to buy Pretty Ladies, I would have told you that you were out of your minds. I'm not sure I believe it now, even after we've all spent every spare moment gathering all this information."

Barbara peeked into her folder. "I can't wait to see how all the pieces fit together. Let's get started, shall we?"

"Sure, but before we look at all the figures, I want to give you a brief outline of what I could do, maybe, to buy Pretty Ladies and operate the salon on my own. There's no real need to panic, though. Ann's not planning to retire until June. Maybe a little later, if I need the time to work things out."

"You have our full attention," Ginger promised.

Judy took a deep breath, but her excitement kept her heart racing. "Okay, here we go. First, I have at least twenty-five years of experience more than I need to get an operator's license. I got all the information from the state, along with the application. The fee is nominal and the process shouldn't take more than a few weeks."

"So far so good," Barbara noted.

"Actually, Ann helped me a lot. Now second. Doris Blake came out like you asked, Ginger, and looked at my house. I haven't liked all the changes in Welleswood in the past few years, but I certainly can't argue with the amazing rise in property values. Added to the fact that I own the house free and clear, I have enough equity to be able to make a substantial down payment for the building and the business. Ann has agreed to carry the rest as a ten-year mortgage I would pay directly to her."

Barbara's eyes widened. "Are you willing to do that? Put your house at risk for the sake of owning Pretty Ladies?"

"I'm not sure, but I think so. That's why I wanted both of you here—to help me decide if my plan would work and if I should take the risk. But before you do, I just need to tell you the rest. Then after you look at the facts and figures in the folders, we'll talk."

With Ginger's and Barbara's approval, Judy continued. "Now, if I did go ahead with the loans, assuming the bank agrees to a home equity loan, I'd need to update the record-keeping and get a computer. Thanks for calling the women at the county offices and getting all the booklets for me, Barbara. It looks like I'm eligible for free computer training, which starts in January. I might even qualify for a government loan, but I'd rather not get any deeper in debt than I have to. Tell John I really appreciate all the work he did reviewing Ann's books and making sure I wasn't buying into a business that wouldn't return a good value for my investment."

Barbara chuckled. "No problem. He'll be glad to hear you're planning to go modern and use a computer. He said going through Ann's account books was like traveling back to the dinosaur age."

"To be honest, I'm not entirely convinced I can do this." Judy shuddered. "Technology is scary. Buying the business is even scarier, but looking for another job right now and competing with all those younger women to build up a new client base in a new shop where I'd get the worst hours, including Sunday and most nights until eight or nine o'clock, is terrifying."

"Let's look at what's in the folders," Ginger suggested.

Judy knew every item and every figure and every paper in the folders by heart. As she watched Barbara and Ginger read through the material in their folders, she felt the same way she had when she had been in school and watched the teacher grade her test paper in front of her. Her stomach rolled over and over. Her mouth went dry. Her palms began to sweat.

Barbara finished first, gave Judy a wink and waited for Ginger to close her folder, too.

"I'm probably the last person you should depend on to look over financial papers," Ginger admitted, "but the numbers seem reasonable and the business plan looks okay. I didn't see anything that set off alarm bells, did you, Barbara?"

"Not really. I think John may have underestimated the income projections, based on what the salon's done in the past, but that's probably wise. He's the CPA, not me."

"I'd rather be surprised by earning more than I plan for, although it's still going to be tight for a few years," Judy suggested.

"Which brings us back to the reason we're both here," Ginger noted. She folded her hands on top of her folder and toyed with several of the bangle bracelets with her thumb. "In the short term, there's no guarantee that you'll make enough money to support yourself and Brian, although it's likely. It's the long term that bothers me. Tyler and I have only been living here for five years. We've only seen Welleswood as it is now, a thriving community. But you've both lived here all your lives. You remember what it was like not that many years ago."

Barbara met Judy's gaze and nodded. "That's a good point, but like Judy, I've lived here long enough to have seen the businesses on the avenue in Welleswood peak, die and peak again. I would imagine that's a cycle bound to be repeated over and over."

Judy's balloon of hope shriveled a bit. "From what I've seen over the years, I'd have to agree with Barbara, with one exception. Some of the businesses on the avenue did go under. Others moved to other locations in other communities to stay in business, but Pretty Ladies never did. Neither did the real estate office or the bank or the hardware store, for that matter."

"Why is that?" Ginger asked. "Why did some businesses like Pretty Ladies last through the lean years when so many others didn't?"

Barbara shook her head. "We know they stayed open, but we don't know how well they did or how many of them had enough capital to sustain losses until business picked up."

"I can't answer for the other businesses, but I think I know why Pretty Ladies not only stayed open, but remained profitable, even through the lean years."

Ginger and Barbara both leaned forward.

"It's hard to explain to anyone outside of the hair business," Judy offered, "but . . . I've never considered being a hairdresser just an ordinary occupation. Neither has Ann, which is the main reason, other than our friendship, that I suspect she's been so good about agreeing to hold part of the mortgage herself. And I think it's true for other hairdressers, too, at least the old-timers like Ann and me."

She paused to moisten her lips. Since she had prayed with Barbara and knew they shared a common faith in God, she risked sharing her philosophy with them. "I hope I don't sound egotistical or pretentious, but to me, hairdressing is a calling. It's almost like a ministry. When people come to a salon like Pretty Ladies, they want more than a haircut or a permanent or a coloring. They want someone to listen, someone to care."

After clearing her throat, she continued. "My clients aren't shy about revealing their most intimate thoughts or troubles because they trust me not to judge them or to spread gossip. When they leave, they take a peek in the mirror and feel good about how they look on the outside, but it's how good they feel on the inside that really makes them smile."

Ginger dropped her gaze.

Barbara's eyes misted with tears. "That's why you're willing to take the risk and buy the salon?"

"Yes, I—I think I should. Most of the clients who come to the salon can't afford to go to the other new salon. The seniors at the Towers either need me or like me to come to them, and they're even less able to pay any more than they do now. If Pretty Ladies closes for good or a new owner comes in and transforms the shop to compete with the other two, then an awful lot of women will be left without anywhere else to go. I can't let that happen, and with God's help and friends like you to stick by me, it won't happen."

Ginger raised her gaze and shook her head. "When I first met Charlene at Sweet Stuff, I thought she had the most fascinating business philosophy I'd ever heard. Now that I've heard your reasons for wanting to own and operate Pretty Ladies, I'm not sure that yours isn't even more amazing. I do know I feel humbled, and I'm so proud to be able to call you my friend. Buy the salon. Take the risk."

Barbara sniffled and reached into her purse for a tissue. "I wish I had half your faith in God and in people. I think you should buy the salon. I really do. Maybe if I had a different business, I could have . . . Well, it doesn't matter. Now is as good a time as any to tell you both, I guess. I've decided to close Grandmother's Kitchen at the end of the year."

Judy sat back in her chair and lifted both brows. "You're closing your shop?"

"But why?" Ginger asked.

"Lots of reasons. Foot traffic has never been better, but nobody's buying. I get the feeling a lot of the people who stop in are more curious about meeting a murder victim's mother than they are about antique canister sets. Last week, I even had to leave by the back door to avoid a reporter posing as a customer."

She paused and crumpled the tissue in her hands. "I need all my energy to last through this never-ending investigation, let alone if an arrest is ever made, but I doubt anyone in town will be disappointed when my business closes."

"Can't you hire someone to run the shop for a while?" Judy asked.

"Not really. I'm only one of three or four dealers on the East Coast who deals strictly with the canister sets. Trying to train someone or find someone knowledgeable in the field just wouldn't be productive."

"What about selling the shop?" Ginger suggested.

"I don't own the building, and my lease is up in February. Selling the stock would take a while, and I'm not sure I want to sell it. I'd like to think I could reopen someday, but the twins need a great deal of my time right now. John's looking into renting space in one of those new storage facilities that have been popping up everywhere. That way I won't have to make a final decision until much later, assuming I manage to get through the holidays."

She sniffled again and got another tissue from her purse. "I'm sorry. I—I try not to get weepy, but sometimes it just sweeps over me and I feel like there's a concrete block of sadness crushing down on my chest. With the holidays coming and waiting every day to hear of an arrest, I seem to get weepy more and more often. It's getting harder and harder for me to go to the shop every day and hope I won't break down in front of a customer. And to be honest, it's a little hard for me to get excited about china canister sets that are over a hundred years old when my son didn't live to see his thirty-second birthday."

Ginger reached across the table and patted Barbara's hand. "You won't always feel this way. At least that's what I keep telling myself when I feel like I'm neck-deep in quicksand."

"You always seem so cheery and positive, Ginger," Judy countered.

"And you're always smiling or . . . giggling, like tonight," Barbara added.

Ginger shrugged with both shoulders. "That's right now. You should have seen me yesterday afternoon. Charlene had an errand at the bank so I told her I'd make up the last gift basket. It was for Nicole Blinstrom. She just had a baby girl."

"So I heard," Barbara noted.

"After three boys, she must be thrilled," Judy whispered and forced back her own memories of having Candy.

Ginger nodded. "New babies are a blessing, so I thought making this gift basket would be fun. I started filling the basket with frilly pink filler and wrapped up tiny boxes of chocolate and tied them with pink ribbons and *bam!*" She smacked the table with the palm of her hand. "I started crying like a baby myself. I tried, I really tried to stop, but I couldn't. I kept remembering when Lily was born and how excited we were to have our little girl and all the hopes and dreams we had for her . . . and how she grew up to be a woman so coldhearted and so callous, she's turned her back on her own child."

When tears started trickling down her cheeks, Ginger motioned to Barbara, who took a tissue from her purse and handed it across the table. Wiping the tears from her eyes, she attempted to smile and made a sound, much like a giggle caught up by a groan. "I couldn't even finish that gift basket, and poor Charlene! When she got back from the bank and found me sobbing in the back of the store, she almost called 911. She settled for making me a plate of chocolates that I had to eat before she finished making the basket."

Judy listened and empathized with both Ginger and Barbara, but held silent. When the two women looked at her and waited for her to make a similar confession, she shook her head. "I cried all the tears I had for Candy a long time ago. I don't cry for her anymore. I worry about her, and I think about her. I even pray for her, but I don't cry for her. Not anymore. I used to get angry at her, a lot more often than I do these days, but mostly now, I just feel empty and numb when I think of her and wonder where she might be."

She bowed her head. "Sometimes I think I'm possibly the worst mother in the world. Then I tell myself there are a whole lot of mothers in line ahead of me, including my own daughter."

"And Lily," Ginger murmured.

"And Steve's ex-wife, wherever she is," Barbara added.

"But we'd be among the first in the line for good grandmothers," Ginger offered.

Barbara smiled. "I'd like to think so."

Judy got to her feet. "Me, too, which is cause for celebrating, which means it's time for the refreshments that I saved for after our meeting tonight." She took a plate from the refrigerator and set it on the table. While her friends studied the plate filled with slices of tart green apples and several varieties of sweeter red apples with the skin still attached, she tapped the start button on the microwave, set out napkins and a small bowl of crushed nuts.

After she retrieved a bowl of fresh whipped cream from the refrigerator and put that on the table, she only had to wait half a minute before the microwave buzzed. She used a pair of pot holders to carry the bowl of bubbling caramel sauce to the table and grinned. "Help yourselves, ladies. There are a few rules, though. No plates. No bowls. No utensils. We dip, we eat and hopefully we'll all have a good giggle or two before you have to leave."

True to tradition, the women were quickly gabbing and eating and dripping caramel sauce and whipped cream on the table as well as themselves. To a casual observer, the three of them were acting like school-girls, complete with silly comments and more than a few giggles apiece. Judy knew, however, as she glanced around the table, that the silliness and the giggles would not last. They were mature women who were all struggling with crushing new responsibilities, frightening mood swings, or personal tragedies as best they could.

Unfortunately, Judy also suspected that the days and weeks ahead would bring new challenges to each of them. She had no idea what the challenges would be or for whom or that one would arrive so soon.

Chapter Seventeen

The elementary schools in Welleswood had many traditions for marking Thanksgiving as a national holiday. The annual "First Thanksgiving" feast prepared by PTA volunteers for the children to share the day before the holiday was much more of a favorite than the history lessons filled with Pilgrims and Native American Indians. In addition, the school had half days that shortened week so teachers could hold individual parent conferences and distribute reports cards for the first time that year.

Ginger left her appointment with Vincent's teacher, Mr. Norcross, just before four o'clock with a bounce to her step and a smile on her face that deepened the moment she stepped outside and spied Barbara and Judy chatting together on the sidewalk in front of the school. "Are you two coming or going?" she asked as she approached them.

"I'm leaving. Barbara just got here. I guess I don't have to ask how Vincent's doing. You're beaming," Judy noted with a bit of envy in her voice.

"He's doing great. He got an *S* for *satisfactory* in all areas, except one. Art."

"Art?" came the chorus of disbelief.

Ginger shrugged. "I don't understand it, either. He loves to draw and he's about ready for a new sketch pad, although he hasn't been ready to share his drawings with us yet." She wrinkled her nose. "Apparently, he doesn't like drawing whatever Mr. Norcross tells the class to draw. But if that's Vincent's only way of rebelling, I'm not going to complain. How's Brian doing?"

Judy let out a sigh. "Okay, I guess. I feel like I've stepped back in time. Honestly, I'm convinced at this point that there must be a gene for spelling. Candy couldn't spell for beans and neither can Brian, apparently. We're going to try making flash cards. For math, too. But his behavior is great, so I'm going to take that as a positive sign."

Barbara checked her watch. "Oops! I'm late, and I've got a double appointment for the twins. I'll catch up with you two another time," she promised and hurried into the school.

Ginger nodded toward the avenue. "Tyler came home early to watch Vincent. It's such a beautiful Indian summer day, I walked up to the school. Have you got time for a cup of coffee at The Diner?"

"I wish I did. I have to get to the bank to talk to one of the loan officers, George Winston, about getting that home equity loan, but I'll walk with you."

They fell in step and started toward the avenue,

passing younger mothers on their way to Park Elementary. In the distance, the elevated train that bisected the community carried passengers back and forth from deep in South Jersey to Philadelphia. "Everything seems to be coming together for you," Ginger said. "How soon will it be before you know if you can actually buy Pretty Ladies?"

"Unfortunately, I've still got a long way to go. Some days I'm so excited I can't stand still. The prospect of owning my own business is such an unbelievable dream, I'm afraid I'm going to wake up and find out that's all it is—a dream." She shivered. "Today, I'm just really, really nervous. Putting my house on the line and risking the only thing of value I own . . . Whoa! That's got me petrified. I just hope I can keep my head and answer all Mr. Winston's questions today so the bank will agree to give me the home equity loan."

Ginger nudged her friend's arm. "You did your homework, so don't worry. This is the right thing to do. I'm sure you'll do fine and the bank will approve the loan."

"Two hours ago, I would have agreed with you," Judy countered. She stopped talking when they reached the curb, checked for traffic and crossed the side street. "Right now, I'm not so sure." She pointed to a little girl swinging on a playground set in one of the yards they were passing. "That's how it's been for me ever since we all met at my house. One minute, I'm up, close to feeling totally positive this is the right thing to do. The next minute, I'm back to thinking I'm making one of the biggest mistakes of my life." She checked her watch. "In fourteen minutes, I have my meeting with George Winston, so I don't have much time left to make up my mind, do I?"

"Not much," Ginger conceded. "What does your gut tell you?"

Judy laughed. "My gut? Other than the fact that it's telling me to eat a lot less chocolate and caramel apples, it's saying to take a leap of faith and buy the salon."

Ginger put her arm out to stop Judy, stepped in front of her and faced her eye to eye. "Then do it. Jump off the swing, land, plant your feet on the ground and don't look back. Look ahead. You've had to do that to survive after Frank died, after Brian came to live with you, and ever since you found out Candy had run away from that halfway house in San Diego, haven't you?"

"True."

"Then why is this time any different?"

Judy's gaze darkened. "Because I'm not alone any more. I have Brian to consider now."

Ginger tilted up her chin. "Exactly. And all the more reason to recognize what an incredibly strong woman you are." When Judy opened her mouth to argue, Ginger silenced her by holding up her hand. "You are strong. You have drive. You have talent. And you have clients who are depending on you. So jump, will you? Barbara and I will be there if you don't land exactly right."

Judy squared her shoulders and smiled. "You're right. Thanks. For all the nice things you said, too."

Ginger looped an arm with one of Judy's and started them toward the avenue. "You're welcome. Just do me one favor."

"Which is?"

"Promise you'll be in my corner when I think I'm ready to give up the fight."

On her way home, Ginger stopped at the stationery store to buy a new sketch pad for Vincent. On impulse, she also bought a card for Tyler, one of the "I still love you because" cards she used to give him a lot more often. She hesitated for only a moment, then selected a card for Mark and Denise to reassure them that they were not forgotten, even though most of their parents' energies had been focused on their baby sister lately. When she passed the Butcher Bloc, she turned around and went back inside to pick out three steaks to grill for dinner. McAllister's Bakery was too far away in the opposite direction from home to get something special for dessert, so she scooted into The Diner and bought one of their cherry cheesecakes, Vincent's favorite.

Ginger was troubled as she walked home, but hopeful that tonight's surprise celebration would help to ease Vincent's disappointment that Lily had not called him for weeks now. Ginger had only spoken to her daughter once since their meeting at the airport, but Lily had cut their conversation short, as usual.

Although Tyler had spoken to both Mark and Denise, who had each called to say they would not be home for Thanksgiving, he had not spoken to Lily at all. He refused to discuss her, other than to say Vincent was better off without her, a sentiment Mark and Denise both shared.

Apparently, Lily had not made any plans to come home for Thanksgiving. Otherwise, she would have returned the message Ginger had left on her cell phone, with Tyler's reluctant blessing, suggesting Lily and Paul might want to slip out of Boston and spend the holiday here with Lily's family. Since they had already spent so much time with Paul's family, Ginger felt her request was fair, and could be an opportunity for all of the adults to sit down and see if Lily would reconsider her decision not to make Vincent a part of her new life.

Loaded down with packages meant to recognize Vincent's good report card, she managed to get home and inside her back door without dropping anything or running into Tyler or Vincent. She put the steaks and the cheesecake into the refrigerator, wrapped Vincent's new sketch pad, wrote a personal note inside Tyler's card and hid them inside one of the cabinets. Next, she wrote a note inside each of the cards for Mark and Denise asking them to be patient with Lily and reassuring them of their parents' love, as well as sharing the good news about Vincent's report card. When she heard heavy footsteps coming up the basement stairs, she set Mark's and Denise's cards aside, unfolded Vincent's report card and held it out to Tyler when he joined her in the kitchen.

He wiped his hands on his work jeans and met her questioning gaze with a frown. "Good thing I was here. The hot water heater decided today would be a good day to die. I just finished cleaning up the mess. I called Joe. He can't come to put in a new one until tomorrow, so it's cold showers tonight. I sure hope this report card has good news for me."

She kissed his cheek, and she was extra glad she had thought to buy a card for him. "It sure does. Take a look."

He studied the report card and laughed. "He got an N, needs improvement, in art?"

She giggled. "I had the same reaction. Maybe you could have a talk with Vincent about following directions and drawing whatever the teacher wants him to draw?"

Tyler nodded. "Playing sports would be so good for him. He'd learn to follow the rules, follow directions, get a little more self-confidence—"

"He doesn't like sports," she reminded him. "Maybe he would do better in school with art if he took art lessons. If he had some sort of assignment to do for his art teacher, he might be more inclined to do it, which might carry over into school."

"And maybe he'd show his sketch pad to his teacher. I'm still not convinced it's been such a good idea to let him keep it to himself or not to mention we know he didn't lose those two backpacks, that he hid them in Lily's closet."

"We've talked about this before. He'll tell us about the backpacks when he's ready, and the sketch pad is all he has that's completely his own. It's like his diary. He'll show us his drawings when he's ready. It's not like he's been asking us to buy him another backpack or acting out in a way that would make us concerned about his drawings."

Tyler let out a sigh. "Art lessons. I guess it wouldn't hurt."

She kissed him again. "You're a dear sweet man. Do you want to ask him about taking art lessons or should I?"

He glanced down at his dirty jeans. "Why don't you go upstairs and show him his report card while I get changed? We can ask him together. I won't be long."

"Good idea. Oh, I wrote a quick note to Mark and Denise, too. I left the cards out on the counter in case you wanted to add something. And I picked up some steaks for dinner," she told him as they went up the stairs together. "Do you feel like firing up the grill or should I—"

"I'll grill the steaks after I jot something on the cards for the kids."

When they got to the top of the stairs, she kissed him again.

He grinned. "Maybe Vincent should get a report card more often."

"And maybe you should come home early from

work more often," she teased. After he turned to go into the master bedroom, she hummed softly as she made her way down the hall. She passed Lily's old bedroom and knocked at Vincent's door.

No answer.

She knocked again. When he didn't respond, she inched the door open and expected to find him either completely engrossed in his drawing or asleep on his bed.

He was neither.

He was not sitting at his desk. He was not in his bed.

The room was empty. Neat as a pin, but empty.

More confused than alarmed, she walked back to Lily's room and peeked inside. That room was empty, too. Maybe he was in the bathroom. She went to the end of the hall to the bathroom. Empty.

"Vincent? It's Grams!" she cried.

No answer, but her cry brought Tyler out of their bedroom. Ginger hurried to him. "I can't find Vincent. He's not here."

Tyler frowned. "What do you mean, he isn't here? I came upstairs with him only an hour ago and told him to stay in his room until I had the basement cleaned up."

Her heart started to race. "Well, he's not here."

Tyler strode past her and checked all of the upstairs rooms for himself. "He doesn't seem to be any good at following my directions, either," he grumbled as he came back to her. "He wanted to play with Jeremy down the street, but I said no. Vincent must have waited until I went down to the basement before he slipped out. Wait here. I'll go get him."

"No. I'll call. It's faster," she urged. "You check the rest of the house."

"There's no need to panic. He's probably at Jeremy's house playing those video games he's not supposed to play."

"I hope you're right, but it's not like Vincent to deliberately disobey you, or me, for that matter. I'll meet you in the kitchen." She hurried into her bedroom to the telephone while her husband went downstairs.

Her fingers shook as she tapped in her neighbor's telephone number. When the answering machine picked up, she did not bother to leave a message. She hung up the telephone and practically raced back down the stairs. "No one's home to answer the telephone," she gushed when she met Tyler in the kitchen. "He's not with Jeremy."

Tyler's gaze grew troubled. "He's not in the house. I checked the garage and the yard, too. He's not here. Think, Ginger. Where would he go without telling me?"

His words sparked an answer that hit her square in the chest and took her breath away. She rejected the idea at once as being absolutely beyond possible, and too crazy . . . "I have an idea. Wait here," she mumbled and ran back upstairs. She tore into Lily's old bedroom and headed straight for the closet. When she checked inside, both of Vincent's "missing" backpacks were gone. She raced to his room next. The sketch pad he kept under his bed was gone, too.

Terror filled her heart and chilled her soul. She ran back downstairs and met Tyler at the bottom of the staircase. "I think . . . it's time . . . to panic," she managed as she struggled to catch her breath. "His backpacks are gone, and so is his sketch pad. I think Vincent's run away, and I—I think he's going to try to find Lily."

Chapter Eighteen

Almost nauseous with fear, Ginger struggled to keep calm, but she could feel herself sliding close to the edge and falling into pure panic. "We have to call the police. And Lily. We have to tell her he's run away. It'll be dark soon. We need to find him before . . ." She squeezed her eyes shut in a futile attempt to block out images of what could happen to an eight-year-old boy wandering along major highways at dusk during rush hour.

When Tyler wrapped her in his arms, she clutched at his shirt and sobbed. "We'll find him," he whispered. "He can't have gotten very far. Besides, he has no idea where Boston is, let alone how to get there. He's probably wandering around, going in circles, so lost he can't find his way back here."

"B-but we have to find him and we need help," she cried. "Please, God, help us find him. Please."

He hugged her hard until her tears were spent. "It'll

really get chilly after dark. Go on upstairs. Get a sweater for all of us, and I'll call the police. They'll put out an Amber Alert. The more people we have looking for him, the better, but I don't think we should call Lily. Not yet."

Feeling calmer, at least for the moment, Ginger climbed back up the stairs. When she came back down with the sweaters, Tyler was still on the telephone in the kitchen. She stood beside him and watched his expressions, listening to his words, to gauge the other side of the conversation.

Tyler nodded and put his hand over the voice end of the receiver. "They've got all the information now, but I just got transferred to a Sergeant Floyd. I'm not sure—"

He turned his attention back to the telephone. "Yes, Sergeant. That's right. Vincent King." Tyler's body stiffened. "Yes, he was wearing blue jeans and a long-sleeved school shirt. Yes, Park Elementary." When Tyler's eyes flashed with annoyance, Ginger took a step back. "Just stop and listen to me," he argued. "I gave all this information to the first officer. We're wasting time. We need your help right now. What do I have to do to get it?" he snapped.

Apparently, Sergeant Floyd's answer was satisfying enough to keep her husband silent and listening for what seemed an interminable length of time. When his shoulders sagged, however, her heart began to race.

"Yes, I understand . . . No . . . Of course . . . When? Yes, I do . . . Tell me where to meet . . . Yes, thank you.

No, we can be there in five or ten minutes. Thank you," he murmured.

When he hung up the telephone, he bowed his head and kept his hand on the receiver for a few seconds. When he looked up at her, his eyes glistened with tears, and he pulled her to him. "He's fine. They already found Vincent. He's fine."

"Praise God! When you were talking to a second officer, I thought something awful—"

"While I was giving the first officer Vincent's description, another officer called in. Officer Joe, that young cop they hired to work in the school and ride bike patrol. He was riding around the river, saw Vincent and decided to investigate." He sniffled and hugged her harder. "He told Sergeant Floyd that seeing a young boy sitting on one of the benches at the river with two backpacks and a suitcase set off alarm bells."

"Oh, thank you, Father, for a smart, young policeman," she whispered, along with a litany of prayers of thanksgiving that Vincent was safe and well. Weak with relief, she held on to Tyler for support, crushing the sweaters between them. "Where is Vincent now? Can we see him? Are they bringing him to the police station or is he already there?"

Tyler took a deep breath. "Actually, Vincent and Officer Joe are still at the river, at the end of Mulberry Street. Officer Joe thought it might be a good idea for all of us, especially Vincent, if we picked him up there."

After stepping back, she handed Tyler his sweater and put on her own. She folded Vincent's sweater over her arm as the rush of panic receded and the reality of Vincent's disobedience hit hard. "I don't know what I want to do first. Hug him until my arms ache or tell him he's grounded, probably for the rest of his life. Or at least a month," she added, rather than sound too dramatic.

Tyler took her hand. "We'll probably do both, but we shouldn't lose focus on what he did right."

She snorted. "Disobedience and running away are both mistakes. Big mistakes."

"But he didn't get far. When he realized he was lost, he had the good sense to plop himself down on a bench by the river, and he didn't lie to Officer Joe, either. He told him up front exactly what he'd done."

"So we just let it go? Forgive and forget? What kind of lesson will that teach him?"

He cocked his head. "Of course not. Think, Ginger. What did we do when Mark ran away?"

"He never . . . Oh-h-h," she murmured when her mind cleared away today's frightening event and let older memories surface about their son. "I'd forgotten about that," she whispered. "He was just a little older than Vincent is now when he decided to run away to find parents who would let him use his savings to buy a bus ticket to Nashville." If she remembered correctly, big hugs came first when they found him. Punishment, by way of confiscating his guitar for a month, came second. When she thought about Mark now, living in Nashville and still trying to make a name for himself in country music, she smiled. "I never thought that buying that old guitar I found at a yard sale would cause so much trouble."

Tyler smiled before his expression turned serious. "I—I'm not sure what I would have done or how I would have been able to forgive myself if anything had happened to him then or to Vincent today, but I do know this. We know what worked before when we were raising our children and what didn't work. We made plenty of mistakes along the way, but now we have a chance to do it better. No, *I* have a chance to do it better. I'm sorry I haven't been as good as I should have been about having Vincent here. I never even followed through on getting those tickets for one of the football games so we could let him take a friend along. I've just been so angry with Lily that I didn't give Vincent the attention he deserved. I—I never really faced that until tonight," he murmured, "but that changes now. Right here and right now."

Ginger's heart trembled. "You're being too hard on yourself. We've both made mistakes, but we're pros at being parents, right? We can do this."

He chuckled. "Old pros at that, but we still have a lot to learn."

"Old?" She nudged him playfully in the ribs. "Speak for yourself."

He chuckled again and put his arm around her shoulders. "Come on, Grams, let's go get our boy."

Hand in hand, Ginger and Tyler stood on the walking path around the river and waited while Officer Joseph Karpinksi, better known as Officer Joe to the town's children, walked his bike to meet them. Behind him, in the distance, Vincent sat on a bench facing the river. His backpacks were alongside him on the bench. The suitcase usually stored under Lily's old bed was on the ground at his feet.

Before now, Ginger had not really paid much attention to the joint initiative between the school district and the police department to encourage a more positive relationship between young people and the police. They had hired and trained a young police officer who had grown up in Welleswood to conduct special programs in the schools and to ride bike patrol to be more accessible to the children outside of school.

Officer Joe approached them. He was tall and brawny. When he smiled, he was all teeth, but it was the nonjudgmental look in his eyes and his calm demeanor that earned her gratitude and her trust.

"Folks? Joe Karpinski," he said and shook hands with each of them while holding on to his bike.

"Thank you so much," she said sincerely. "That sounds so . . . so little to say when we are so very, very grateful that you found Vincent for us so quickly."

"He's a good boy. He's just a little confused."

She swallowed hard. "Can we take him home with us now?"

"Yes, ma'am. No problem."

"I think I'd like to talk with Vincent here first, alone, just for a few minutes," Tyler suggested. "Is that all right, Ginger?"

She squeezed her husband's hand. "I'll just wait here for a bit."

Her husband smiled, shook hands with the officer again and walked toward the park bench where Vincent was waiting. Since the boy was not facing them, she could not see his face, but from the way his shoulders drooped and his head bowed, she suspected he was not looking forward to facing the consequences of his behavior.

"Ma'am?"

She flinched. "I'm sorry. Did you say something?"

"Only now that you're both here, I was going back on patrol. Unless you need something else?"

"No, not unless . . . You obviously spent some time talking with Vincent. Is there anything you can tell me that might help us to understand what we should do to make sure he doesn't try to run away again?"

He drew in a long breath. "Just love him and let him know it. He's pretty mixed-up right now. Is it true his mother got married, but moved away and left Vincent here with you?"

Shame burned her cheeks. "I'm afraid so."

"Poor little guy. He's hurting pretty bad. I told him how it was for me when my mom and dad got divorced. My mom moved out to Ohio, but I stayed here with my dad. I never saw her much, and I talked to Vincent about that," he murmured.

In his eyes, she saw the pain that still lingered, but she also saw acceptance and empathy for another little boy who was trying to deal with a similar rejection. "I'm glad you were the one to find him."

He nodded.

"What helped you most after your mom left?"

"Having my dad around, mostly."

"Vincent doesn't have his dad."

"But he's got you and his grandfather." He grinned. "And now he's got me. I told him I'd stop by to see him once in a while. I asked him about playing basketball on the team I coach, but he didn't seem to be interested."

"He doesn't like sports. Not even a little."

"What about ice cream?"

She chuckled. "That's different."

"I take a group of kids to Scoops once a month on a Saturday. We eat ice cream, talk about stuff. If it's all right with you, I'll make sure to invite him next time we go."

"I'll check with my husband, but I think that would be wonderful. *You're* wonderful. Thanks again."

He laughed and climbed back onto his bike. "And I'm going to tell my girlfriend your opinion the next time she tries to tell me otherwise," he teased. "I'll be in touch."

As she watched him bike away, she offered a quiet prayer to thank God for sending this young officer to them and turned her attention back to the park bench where Tyler was sitting with their grandson. Above them to the west, the sun was barely hanging on to the edge of the horizon and streaked the sky pink and purple and gold in a glorious display of God's imagination as dusk lengthened, about to drop a veil of darkness to end the day. The river was very calm.

Framed by near-barren trees and a copse of vibrant evergreens, Tyler and Vincent were silhouettes in a picture that she tucked into her heart. Vincent sat cuddled close to his grandfather, who had one arm around the boy while he pointed north. To Boston? Or where the North Star would appear later?

She waited, reluctant to intrude, yet anxious to hold each of them close to her, to whisper words of forgiveness and words of comfort to Vincent and words of love to her husband. Maybe, just maybe, Vincent had been the wisest of them all. By running away, maybe he had forced all of them, however unwittingly, to reevaluate the way they had been living together and the way anger and shame and disappointment had kept them from having what Vincent needed most of all: a family.

A family that loved without conditions.

A family that bonded together by recognizing one another as individuals, each flawed in their own way, yet each with individual talents and needs that should be nourished with love and understanding.

A family she and Tyler could make for Vincent so that one day, when he was a man, he would follow their example and create a loving family of his own.

A family that kept God at the center of their lives.

When Tyler turned and motioned for her to join them, she walked toward them with a renewed sense of commitment and a vow to try to become a grand mother to Vincent, as well as his grandmother. She left behind her, as best she could, all the mistakes she had made so far and all the plans she and Tyler had had for their retirement, but she held on to the dreams they would make together for the years to come.

She would try to be stronger, like her friend Judy.

She would try to be more patient, like her friend Barbara.

And she would try to be more forgiving, like the child of God she was supposed to be, and one day, she would once again be able to love her daughter, in spite of what Lily had done.

When she reached them, she put the backpacks on the ground and sat down next to Vincent. She noticed that Tyler now had the old suitcase on his lap with the lid open. Inside, she saw all sorts of snacks—near-empty bags of potato chips, prctzcls, corn chips and some bars of candy. From the looks of them, Vincent had raided the pantry before he had left home.

Vincent, however, kept his gaze on his grandfather. "What's all this?" she asked.

"Gramps said we needed a *'fess up* party, but we had to wait for you."

She lifted a brow. "Really? What's that?" she asked as she slipped his sweater around his shoulders.

He shrugged. "I never been to one."

"It's simple," Tyler prompted. "Whether you're a

child or a grown-up, you have to take the good with the bad and accept responsibility for whatever you do. At a 'fess up party, you have to confess to something you did wrong, apologize, and then you can take something to eat. That's the good part of a 'fess up party. I'll go first."

She met his gaze, smiled and mouthed, *I love you.*

"Let's see," he began. "I didn't talk to you about your mother very much before tonight, Vincent. I'm sorry." When Vincent did not respond, Tyler nudged him gently. "You get to say it's okay."

"Oh. O-kay."

Tyler grinned and took a pretzel.

"My turn," Ginger announced. "I'm sorry I didn't talk to you about the backpacks you had hidden in your mother's old closet. Maybe if I had talked to you when I found them, you wouldn't have felt so alone."

When her grandson turned and looked at her, she almost melted when she saw the trail of dirt his tears had left on his cheeks. "It's okay, Grams."

She smiled, reached across him and grabbed a handful of corn chips. "Your turn," she said to her grandson.

Vincent started swinging his legs. "I'm sorry."

Tyler nodded, urging the boy to continue.

"I shoulda stayed in my room, like Gramps told me to. I just wanted to see my mom, but I didn't want to make you sad," he whispered.

She ran her fingers through his matted hair. "It's okay now."

"You're forgiven," Tyler whispered.

Vincent sniffled, made half a smile and reached into the suitcase. He took a pretzel with one hand and a handful of corn chips with the other.

The 'fess up party continued until dark. By the time they walked home together, they were well on the way to creating the family Vincent needed and deserved. Ginger had only one new fear—that one day, in the next few weeks or months or years, Lily might realize what she had done and decide to take Vincent away, leaving Ginger and Tyler with a void in their lives that could never be filled again.

Chapter Nineteen

On Sunday night at the end of the extended Thanksgiving weekend, Barbara collapsed on the love seat in the living room and put her feet up on the double-sized ottoman. She was too exhausted after four straight days of child care to get up again to turn on a light, and settled for having dim light filtering into the room from the chandelier in the foyer. Shivering, she pulled the afghan from the top of the love seat onto her lap, eager to see the end of the holiday and resume a normal routine.

The girls would return to school tomorrow. John would go to the office. She would work in Grandmother's Kitchen to start preparations for closing her shop and brace herself for the next holiday she would have to celebrate for the first time without Steve: Christmas.

Before she had a chance to slide down that slippery emotional slope, John joined her in the living room, handed her a mug of warm cider, sat down and put his feet near hers on the ottoman. "Are the girls finally asleep?" he asked.

"Finally. They're so excited about going back to school, they had a hard time settling down."

She took a sip of cider, snuggled closer to him and spread the afghan over his lap, too. She wished she could find a way to close the emotional distance between them, but for now, she settled for having him next to her on the love seat as gift enough for her to enjoy. "I'm glad Rick called on Thanksgiving and had a chance to talk to the girls," she offered, deliberately steering the conversation toward their second son, who was still stationed in Germany with the U.S. Army.

When John let out a sigh, his arm pressed against her. "He doesn't seem to be in any hurry to settle down and have a family of his own, though."

She nudged his shoulder with her own. "I'm his mother. I'm supposed to be the one worried about getting him to marry and have a family. You're his dad. Aren't you supposed to understand how much fun it is to be able to date all sorts of beautiful and fascinating women?" she teased.

He took a long drink of cider. With his expression shadowed, he took her hand. "He might not be able to find a woman as beautiful or as fascinating as his mother, but he's put his career ahead of his personal

230

life for long enough. It's time for him to think about getting married."

His compliment warmed her heart almost as much as the memories of when they had dated themselves. She squeezed his hand. "Don't worry about Rick. He's his father's son. When he meets the right woman, he'll move heaven and earth to marry her, just like you did."

He chuckled. "If I remember correctly, there were four truckloads of topsoil, an equal number filled with mulch, a load of sand and hundreds of paving bricks I had to move that summer."

She laughed with him. "I was only twenty-one when you asked my father for permission to marry me. When he said you had to help him to relandscape and hard scape the backyard before he gave you an answer, I thought you would change your mind."

"I got to know your father pretty well that summer. He got to know me, too, and he taught me a lot of lessons before he finally gave me his blessing."

Touched by memories of her late father, she swallowed hard. "Such as?"

"Responsibility. Taking on a task, any task, and doing your best to see that the job gets done, one step at a time. Or in the case of the brick patio we were installing, one brick at a time." He paused. "Rick is a good son, a good man and an outstanding officer. He's learned to be responsible in his military career, but he has personal responsibilities to meet now for himself and for his family."

She struggled to understand exactly what he meant, turned and stared at her husband. "Do you really think he should get married because it's his responsibility? He doesn't owe us—"

"He owes Steve," he insisted. "They were brothers."

She narrowed her gaze, but with the dim light, it was hard to see the look in her husband's eyes. "What on earth are you talking about? Steve isn't here. Rick getting married couldn't change that."

"No, it wouldn't, but Rick should be married with his own family precisely because Steve isn't here. But Jessie and Melanie are."

Her heart started to pound. "You mean you want Rick to get married so he can take the girls to live with him?"

"No." He tightened his hold on her hand. "No. That's not what I'm saying at all."

She pulled her hand away. "Then what are you saying?"

"I'm saying that I love those little girls, and I want to raise them. But we all have to face reality. I'm sixty-one years old, and you're not that far behind me. The twins are only six years old. Look ahead. There are a good fifteen years, at least, before they're adults. By then, I'll be seventy-six years old and you'll be—"

"Never mind. I see where you're headed now," she insisted.

"Neither one of my parents lived to see sixty-five. Your parents each lived just past seventy. Where would the girls go if something happened to us before . . . before they were old enough to be on their own? Don't tell me you haven't thought about it. You must have."

She leaned against the back of the love seat, closed her eyes and balanced the mug of cider on her lap. She was annoyed with him for voicing one of her greatest fears, but she was also relieved he was sharing a similar one of his own and hopeful his willingness to talk about his feelings was a sign the emotional wall between them was crumbling. "I've thought about it," she admitted.

"And?" he prompted.

"And I've pushed it aside. With the investigation stalled and no arrests yet, taking care of the girls and deciding to close the shop, I just don't have enough energy left to worry about that, too. Not right now."

"Well, I have. I think about it every day. When I go to the office at night . . ." He paused and cleared his throat. "I don't have appointments at night. Not business appointments anyway. Some nights I've met with some friends to review the plans I've drawn up to make sure the girls are taken care of financially if anything happens to us, and I've met with Carl Landon to talk about redoing our will."

She reached out and took his hand again. "What about the other nights?" she whispered and held tight as he struggled to find his voice.

"I think about Steve. How we lost him so . . . unexpectedly. I think about the girls and how much they miss him, too, and how they'd be all alone . . . if we weren't here."

She set her mug on the end table on her side of the love seat and wrapped her arms around his chest. She could feel him tighten, not against her embrace, but against the sobs he held back. "I know," she whispered. "I miss our boy, too, but we still have his girls and we have Rick."

He coughed and cleared his throat. "That's why I wish he would get married and start a family. If anything happens to us, I'd want the girls to have a good home where I know they'd be loved."

She pressed her face against the column of his neck. "Rick would take the girls. He doesn't have to be married or have his own family to do that."

"No, but it would be better for the girls if he did. It would look better, like we anticipated the possibility that we might not live long enough to raise the girls, but we had a contingency plan for them, just in case we needed one."

She held on to him and let go of her disappointment that he had been avoiding her and the girls by working at night. "You're a methodical and exacting man, but you also can be very controlling," she murmured. "I suppose those qualities might make you a good CPA, but this isn't a company you're trying to protect. It's our family. But I agree with you on several points. Yes, we should have a good financial plan for the girls. Yes, we probably should have had our will redone before now, but you can't be paranoid. And you can't expect Rick to get married and start a family out of any sense of responsibility to Steve or the girls or to us. We have to have faith and trust God will watch over the girls for us. How it looks to anyone else shouldn't matter. Besides, we're all still hurting so badly, we need time to heal. We have plenty of time to think about what kinds of plans we need to make in case we don't live long enough to raise the girls."

He put his arm around her and rested his chin on top of her head. "You're right. It shouldn't matter how it looks to anyone else, but I'm afraid it might." He drew a deep breath. "Regardless of how much faith we have, we don't have as much time as you think. I—I talked with Carl on Tuesday afternoon. He's set up a meeting for us in his office for tomorrow morning at nine o'clock, and I told him we'd be there. I didn't want to spoil the holiday for you, too."

"A meeting?" She pushed away from him and sat up so she could face him. "You set up a meeting for us with the lawyer for tomorrow and you're just telling me now?"

"I didn't ask for the meeting. He did."

"So now our lawyer is in charge of us as well as the media?"

"No. That's not . . . It's not like that at all." He shook his head, set his own mug aside and took both of her hands. "Do you remember when Steve brought Angie home to meet us and she told us about being orphaned and being transferred from one foster home to another?"

"Of course I remember." Fear scratched at her wounded heart. "Please don't tell me she's come back. Not after all this time. Not when she made no effort at all to contact Steve or her own children. Please don't—"

"No. She hasn't come back, but her . . . her parents . . . They're not dead. Apparently, they're very much alive and they've hired a lawyer. They know about the twins."

She gasped, even as visions of a custody battle for the girls made her stomach roll. "They're alive? That can't be true. Angie said—"

"I know what she told us, but apparently, she was as good at lying as she turned out to be at disappearing. From what their lawyer told Carl, Angie grew up on a dairy farm in upstate New York. At least until she turned fifteen. That's when she ran away."

"So they claim. These people," Barbara argued. "How do we know they aren't lying? How do we know they're Angie's parents at all? They certainly never made any effort to see the girls when Angie was here, or later, when Steve was left trying to be both mother and father to the twins. Why now?"

She waved her hand to dismiss the entire idea. "I can't believe these two people are anything more than sick charlatans who are trying to take advantage of all the publicity surrounding Steve's death, and I can't believe Carl would get us involved."

"He's had their story checked and double-checked. He's looked at all the documents their lawyer produced. Everything. The birth certificate, medical records, dental records, even the reports from the detectives they'd hired over the years when they could scrape up the money. If we believe Angie is Jessie and Melanie's mother, then we'll have to believe these are her parents."

She huffed. "Of course I believe Angie is their mother. I was in the delivery room with her and Steve, remember?"

He nodded and stroked the side of her arm. "Do you also remember when Angie broke the cap on her front tooth?"

She shrugged, too shaken to think beyond the idea the twins might have another set of grandparents to be able to think clearly. "Not really."

"Sure you do. It was only a few days before the wedding. She was so embarrassed by her smile, she told Steve they would have to postpone the wedding unless she had her tooth fixed."

"Oh, that's right. Now I remember. We called Dr. Wilson for her. He was leaving for vacation the next day, but he stayed late to see her."

"Dr. Wilson still has the full set of X-rays he took that day. According to Carl, when Dr. Wilson compared his X-rays to the ones her parents provided through their lawyer, he said there was no doubt in his mind. The X-rays are a match."

Barbara closed her eyes for a moment to refocus her thoughts. When she reopened them, she held tight to her skepticism. "That only proves Angie is the twins' mother. Like I said before, that doesn't mean these people are her parents or the twins' grandparents."

She remained stiff, disappointed John had kept this from her, even when he pulled her back against his chest. "Lady, you would have made a great lawyer."

With thoughts of Steve, her resistance melted and she accepted the support her husband offered. "My son was a great lawyer," she whispered.

"And he'd be as proud of you right now as I am for being so protective of the girls. The Carrs, they're Angie's parents . . . Except her name wasn't Angie. It was Sharon. Anyway, Micah and Ruth have agreed through their lawyer to submit to a DNA test or anything else we'd want in order to prove they're Jessie and Melanie's grandparents."

Soothed by the steady beat of his heart against her cheek, she sighed. "What does Carl think?"

"He thinks they're legitimate. We'll ask for the DNA test, of course, but the results will probably just prove these people right."

She sighed again. "What about Angie or Sharon— whatever her name is—Steve's wife? Steve's ex-wife," she corrected herself. "Do they have any idea where she is?"

"They've only been able to trace her as far as Las Vegas. She was there two years ago. Since then, her trail has gone cold. When the tabloids ran the story about the girls who killed Steve, they recognized Ang—Sharon's picture and hired a lawyer."

She squeezed her eyes shut, but the fear that they

might lose custody of the girls was too real to block out. "What do they want?"

He set her back from him and put one hand on each of her shoulders. "Right now, they claim they only want to meet us and to learn as much as they can about their daughter, her life with Steve and the twins. Ultimately, they want to see the twins, too."

"They can't see the girls. Not yet," she insisted.

"No, they can't. They know they won't be able to see them unless and until the DNA results are conclusive. In the meantime, Carl said we should bring some pictures of the girls tomorrow. Then, we'll see. If—if they're the girls' grandparents, too, then I guess we really can't keep them from getting to know their own grandchildren."

"No," she admitted with a great deal of reluctance. "We can't, but we can try to convince them that it's in the girls' best interests to grow up with us, right? I mean, these folks, the Carrs, they're virtual strangers. The girls have been through enough. They don't need to be shifted from the family they know to one that's completely foreign to them."

"I agree."

"We'll keep the girls with us, no matter what, right?"

"Absolutely."

"Promise?"

"Promise," he whispered, pulled her into his arms, and rocked her before her tears began to fall.

Chapter Twenty

Barbara could not decide if the conference room in Carl Landon's law office was too small or if the rectangular table in the middle of the room was too big. Either way, they were all wedged in with a wall nearly at their backs and the tabletop in front of them, making it difficult to move around much. She fidgeted in her seat and stretched her legs out straight under the table while the two lawyers debated over a legal point she did not quite understand. Nearly an hour and a half into the meeting, however, she did understand that the facts already revealed and affirmed by both lawyers left little room for any hope this meeting would end without one of the two couples, or both, being badly disappointed.

Even if she set first impressions aside, Barbara still found Micah and Ruth Carr to be exactly as they had represented themselves through their lawyer. They appeared to be ordinary people, like Barbara and John, mired in extraordinary, but heartbreaking events. People of good character. Decent people with old-fashioned common sense. People of faith. Exactly the kind of people Jessie and Melanie needed in their lives.

Carl sat at the head of the table near the door. He had been their lawyer and friend since they had first met over thirty years ago, which was probably just about the time Richard Keith, the Carr's attorney who sat at the opposite end of the table closest to the window, had been born. Keith, however, made up for his obvious lack of experience by being genuine, earnest and completely devoted to his clients, as well as the interests of the twins.

John sat to Barbara's left, completely engrossed in the ongoing legal discussion. On the other side of the table, however, both Ruth and Micah seemed, like Barbara, unable to follow the discussion. The two couples were a study in contrasts. Dressed formally, the Carrs were clearly uncomfortable. Micah wore a dark blue suit and kept running his finger along the edge of his shirt collar and he had loosened his tie twice. Ruth's features bore a striking resemblance to Steve's ex-wife, and her paisley polyester dress looked so new Barbara would not have been surprised if the price tags were still attached. Although her expression was stoic, the woman had fiddled with the silk daisy at the base of her throat so often, Barbara expected the flower to disintegrate.

Both Micah and Ruth looked a good five years older than John and Barbara, but it was hard to know for sure since they each bore signs of the hard work it had taken to operate a dairy farm. Years of working outdoors in the sun had leathered and creased their faces. Lifetimes spent doing manual labor on the farm had created callouses and thickened the veins on the backs of their hands.

Feeling self-conscious about her easier lifestyle and her own soft, freshly manicured hands Barbara rested them on her lap, folded together, and dropped her gaze. For all the differences in their lives and in their appearances, however, the two couples had both been clearly desperate when they had arrived at the meeting to know one thing: Were Angie Morgan Montgomery and Sharon Carr indeed one and the same woman?

How that apparent truth would affect each of their lives remained the last issue to be discussed. At this point, Barbara did not need to hear any more legal opinions to support the idea or to wait for the results of any DNA test. She knew, intuitively, that from this day forward, their lives would be forever entwined like the roots nourishing the branches of climbing roses, with Jessie and Melanie the blossoms that would beautify their existences. Denying either couple a place in the twins' lives would be like chopping away at their roots. Ultimately, the girls would lose and wither away, their lives all the sadder because they had not been given the opportunity to receive the love and support each set of grandparents could give them.

"Is that right, Barbara?"

When she heard Carl say her name, she looked up at him and locked her gaze with his. When he cocked his head, as if waiting for an answer, her heart began to pound. "I'm sorry. I missed your question."

"The pictures of the girls. Did you bring them with you? Micah and Ruth would like to see them."

"Yes, I have them," she replied. She reached into an outside pocket on her oversize purse, pulled out a large brown envelope and laid it on the table. As she undid the clasp holding the envelope closed, her fingers shook, but she managed to pull out the five-by-seven photographs she had ordered from the school when the girls had had their pictures taken at the end of September. "Their school pictures are the most recent," she explained when she handed them to Ruth.

Ruth's hands shook, too, as she laid the photographs on the table close to her. Micah leaned forward to get a closer look and laid his hand on top of his wife's. Ruth's eyes filled with tears she wiped away with the back of her hand as she studied the images, for the very first time, of the little girls she believed were her granddaughters. "Oh, Micah. They're such sweet little girls," she murmured. As she caressed the photographs with her fingertips, her husband whispered words to her Barbara could not hear.

Barbara could not stop staring at the two of them, unable to turn away. When John reached out to hold her hand, she held on tight, as unprepared for the look of total amazement and love on Ruth's and Micah's faces as she was for the moment when Ruth took a picture out of the family album she had brought with her.

Micah slid the picture across the table to John. "Sharon's first-grade picture. We walked her down to the bus stop. Bus driver took the picture for us."

Barbara looked at the black-and-white photograph. When she studied the young man and woman standing on either side of the little girl and looked up at the couple sitting across from her for a moment, she had no doubt they were the same. The image of the little girl staring back at her from the photograph was not a duplicate of either Jessie or Melanie. Rather, Barbara saw dark curls like Jessie's, the same slender build, and that achingly familiar stubborn chin. The girl's eyes, however, held the same tenderness she found in Melanie's smile. Like Melanie, the girl also had only one dimple—in her right cheek. "What do you think?" she whispered to John as the other couple talked quietly to one another.

He cleared his throat. "I think we're in trouble. Double trouble."

She squeezed his hand. "Let's not jump to conclusions," she urged. "We don't know what they want yet." Anxious to find out exactly what the Carrs wanted in terms of custody or visitation, assuming the DNA tests confirmed what everyone at the table already believed to be true, Barbara was relieved when Carl addressed the other lawyer.

"At this point, I think it might be best if we each had time to meet privately with our respective clients."

When Keith nodded, Carl rose from his seat and looked at Barbara and John. "We can talk privately in my office."

Barbara and John both attempted to get up, but Micah urged them all back into their seats. "Before you go, Ruth and I want to make something clear."

Carl sat down again. Barbara and John stayed seated and held hands. Barbara caught her breath for a moment and braced herself by pressing both feet against the floor.

"Mr. Carr, I think it might be better if you waited to speak to me before you say anything more," his lawyer suggested.

"I gather you would, son, but me and Ruth have heard enough from both you and Mr. Landon here to suit us, at least for now," he said firmly before looking directly at Barbara and John. "You're good people. Both of you. Ruth and me, well, we'd like to think we're good people, too. At least we try to be."

"Agreed," John murmured.

"You both lost your son. That's a heartache me and Ruth can understand because we lost our daughter a long time ago. Maybe you think it's not the same for us, but we got no place to go to sit and mourn like you do because she isn't dead, leastways not that we know for sure. But we've been grieving for that girl every day since she took off." He turned and looked at his wife.

When she smiled, as if urging him to continue, he drew a deep breath. "Me and Ruth have heard enough and seen enough to know our girl is the same girl your son married. We can't do nothing now to change the hurt she caused your family, but we're right sorry for the way she ran off and left your son and her babies, just like she ran off from us. But these little girls, Jessie and Melanie, they're our granddaughters, too."

When Barbara nodded, her husband smiled. "Agreed."

Barbara saw Ruth's eyes glisten with fresh tears and blinked back her own.

"The girls have been through enough, losing both their mama and their papa," Micah continued. "The last thing they need is to have a couple of folks like us causing more upset, which is what would happen if we turned this situation into a battlefield. The lawyers might be richer for it if we did, but we'd be a whole lot prouder of ourselves if we could work this out between the four of us."

He paused, took one last look at his wife and squared his shoulders. "We'd be obliged if you'd think about letting us see the girls from time to time so we'd get to know them and they'd get to know us. That's pretty much what we want."

John tightened his hold on Barbara's hand. "A little time with them? That's all?"

He nodded.

"We'd keep full custody of the girls," John said firmly, clarifying Micah's request.

"You're the only grandparents the girls have ever known," Ruth murmured. "We don't think it would be fair to them to even consider forcing ourselves into their lives by asking for custody, too, but we would like to spend some time with them. Or with all of you, at first, if you can find it in your hearts to let us into the girls' lives."

Filled with relief, Barbara smiled. How soon they might introduce the girls to their new grandparents or explain why they had not met before or determine how the visits between them would happen were all matters that could be left for later. Right now, all that mattered, beyond being forever grateful for keeping full custody of the girls, was recognizing the need to share the love and laughter Jessie and Melanie had brought into their lives with Ruth and Micah. "I think there's always room for more love in the girls' hearts and in our hearts. Nothing will ever fill the void left by losing Steve or the loss of your daughter, but being able to love Jessie and Melanie and to watch them grow up is a blessing that will help you, too," she murmured.

"After the DNA tests," Carl interjected, obviously anxious to rein in his clients before they let emotions cloud their judgment.

"I would concur," Keith added.

While the two lawyers retook command of the meeting and made arrangements for the DNA tests, which would yield results by mid-December at the earliest, Barbara offered the rest of the pictures she had brought with her to Ruth and Micah to review. She and John, in turn, studied the pictures in the album. They saw the child in the first grade picture grow into an adolescent of fifteen who undeniably looked like the woman Steve had later married. How the woman who had given birth to Jessie and Melanie had abandoned them or why her life had intersected with theirs was a mystery. But there was nothing mysterious about how or why Ruth and Micah had come into their lives. Miraculous, perhaps, but no longer mysterious.

After the lawyers concluded the meeting, John and Barbara stayed in the conference room while Carl escorted the others into the outer office and to the door. To her surprise, Ruth came back and stood just outside the door to the conference room. "I was wondering if . . . if after the tests come back, maybe I could write and you could tell me if you remember anything more about my Sharon while she was living here."

"Yes, of course," Barbara assured her.

"Thank you," she replied, turned and walked away.

With her heart and mind still reeling, Barbara stored the pictures she had brought to the meeting in her purse again while John walked over to the window. "They didn't even press to see the girls today while they were here," he noted.

"They said they needed to get back to the farm," she countered. "Besides, I thought we agreed it was better to wait until the test results were back before we let them see the girls. Didn't we? Didn't Carl argue that point, as well?"

"Yes, but still . . ." He turned away from the window and faced her again. "But if they really are the girls' grandparents, wouldn't they have asked to see them today?"

"Maybe they're just as overwhelmed as we are," she suggested.

"Maybe."

Barbara got up, edged around the table and joined

him at the window. "They seem too good to be true, is that it?"

He shrugged, but turned to gaze out the window. "Maybe they are," he admitted and raked his fingers through his hair. "Maybe I'm not sure what I think at all. It's hard for me to tell the real from the unreal any more."

"What does your heart tell you about Micah and Ruth?"

"That they're real."

"Mine, too," she whispered and slipped her hand into his. "But I'm glad Carl insisted on the DNA tests, and I'm just as glad the Carrs left without seeing the girls. While we're waiting for the test results—"

"We're not going to have any results until they run the tests, which means we need to get the girls' samples taken as soon as possible," he said firmly, as if he was far more comfortable with organizing and scheduling tasks than he was with handling more emotional issues.

"Carl explained that," she reminded him. "I'm just as anxious as you are. I'll take the girls after school today."

"I could go with you."

"And we'd like the company. Promise me something?"

He looked down at her and smiled.

"Promise me you won't ever keep something like this from me again."

His gaze grew troubled. "I was just trying to protect you and the girls."

"I know you were, and I love you for protecting the children, but I'm not a child, John. I'm your wife. If we can't rely on one another and trust one another, then we have a bigger problem on our hands than waiting for the results of the DNA tests."

He kissed her forehead. "I know. I'm sorry."

"Me, too," she whispered. "I should have known you weren't working so many hours at night to avoid us or because you couldn't deal with Steve's death."

His eyes widened. "Is that what you thought?"

She swallowed the lump in her throat. "Yes. I'm sorry."

He put his arm around her shoulders. "You don't need to apologize. I didn't give you much reason to think otherwise." He paused and pointed toward the window. "Look. There they are."

She watched with him as Ruth and Micah crossed the street. Hand in hand, the couple walked down the avenue together, just an ordinary couple who quickly blended into the shoppers milling along the avenue. "I wonder what they're thinking," he murmured.

"Or how they're feeling," she added. "I can't imagine what it would be like to have your only child run away from home and spend years looking for her in vain, only to discover you'd become grandparents without even knowing it."

"I don't think I want to know."

"I'm glad we had more than one child. With Steve

gone now, having Rick is even more of a blessing . . . even if he isn't married," she teased, hoping to lighten the mood.

He chuckled. "I guess I deserved that."

"Yes, you did."

"I guess I was being a little . . . controlling,"

She grinned. "A lot controlling."

"Maybe even a little paranoid."

"That, too."

"You could cut me a little slack here, any time you're ready."

She laughed out loud. "Don't count on it. Not unless you take me to lunch."

"Lunch? That's all it's going to take?"

"A very expensive lunch. That will be a good start," she teased, but her heart told her that they had taken the first steps on the long journey back to the loving relationship they had always shared.

If that had been the only blessing this day, it would have been blessing enough, but she had the distinct impression that the meeting today held the promise of even greater blessings for them all.

Chapter Twenty-One

Two heavy snowfalls in early December blanketed everyone's dreams for ideal conditions for Christmas, at least for this year.

Owners of businesses along the avenue wailed about losing holiday sales. Working parents scrambled for day care when the schools closed down and used up all the snow days budgeted in the calendar before winter had even officially arrived. Other residents sat trapped in their homes, unable to prepare for the holidays. Swamped by heated complaints about inefficient snow removal, town officials offered proof of their efforts: the mountain of collected snow along the river quickly dubbed Mount Miserable by discontents.

Ten days before Christmas, nature relented, at least temporarily. Under sparkling sunshine and clear blue skies, the last of the snow finally melted before a cold snap returned, bringing frigid air back to town, but no forecast of more snow. Shoppers once again hustled along the avenue and children were back in school, while parents tried to get ready for the fast-approaching holiday. Town officials quickly turned the town meeting for that month into an event to honor all the township employees who had worked so hard during the snow emergencies.

But not everyone looked forward to Christmas this year.

Exhausted by the extended hours she had been working at Sweet Stuff, Ginger lay awake at night and worried about how she and Tyler would mark their first Christmas with Vincent. After another troubled, sleepless night, she struggled out of bed that Monday morning, got Tyler off to work and Vincent off to school. She sat at her kitchen table, stirred her coffee and tried to give herself a little mental pep talk, but failed.

True, there were a whole host of reasons why she was feeling so anxious and conflicted. Their daughter, Denise, had recently been reassigned to overseas flights in the Eastern Hemisphere. She would be spending Christmas in Japan. Mark was on tour as the opening, opening, opening act for some aging country music singer who had taken Ginger and Tyler's son under his wing. With his dreams still alive, Mark would celebrate Christmas somewhere in the Bible Belt.

But maybe it was better that neither Denise nor Mark were coming home, or that keeping contact these days meant occasional messages on the answering machine as they played telephone tag. Lily, her wayward, lost child, had done exactly as she had promised and had virtually severed all contact with her son, save for sending a monthly check that Ginger and Tyler deposited in a special account for him. Apparently, the notes Ginger had written to Mark and Denise had not softened their anger and disappointment with their sister, and they would have no doubt spent much of the holiday denouncing Lily, hardly the mood Ginger wanted to pervade her home over the holidays.

That left Ginger, Tyler and Vincent to fend for themselves here in Welleswood for Christmas—hopefully, a peaceful Christmas.

With few physical and emotional resources left, she felt so overwhelmed, she had to grab hold of herself before she slid from worry into depression. She took a good, long sip of coffee, made two telephone calls before work and set up a meeting for seven that night at her house. She called Tyler on his cell phone, and he agreed to take Vincent to his art lessons at six-thirty and out afterward for a treat, so she crossed that obstacle off her mental list.

Feeling rather satisfied with herself, she showered, dressed and headed out the door to get to work by nine o'clock. She did not quite have a bounce to her walk, but her steps were lighter, her heart was hopeful, and she mustered up all the Christmas spirit she could manage to make it through the day.

At two-thirty that afternoon, the amount of Christmas spirit Ginger had left would not have filled half a thimble. She had used up all her good cheer satisfying rude, demanding and snippy customers who either had crawled out from their homes on Mount Miserable or had no inkling of the real meaning of Christmas.

She checked the clock. Two-thirty. Finally, it was almost time to leave and pick up Vincent from school. Kristen Smith, one of the college students Charlene had hired as extra holiday help, was waiting on the last customer who had a long shopping list to fill while Charlene was busy loading up gift baskets for late-afternoon deliveries.

Grateful for the first lull in business that day, Ginger started to untie her soiled apron. When the door opened and she recognized Miss Grumley, one of the seniors from the Towers, she quickly retied her apron.

Not this customer. Not now. Miss Grumley was sweet enough, but she rarely bought anything and usually just stopped in for a little conversation that might last for the better part of an hour, and Ginger reminded herself that Charlene had opened her shop precisely for women like Miss Grumley.

Nearly crippled with arthritis, the elderly woman shuffled slowly toward the display of vintage candy. Ginger got to the display first and studied the octogenarian who was slowly walking toward her. The frail woman wore a long, matted raccoon coat that seemed too heavy for her and a pair of cracked leather slippers, molded to her misshapen feet, from which a big toe poked through. A purple plumed hat that had seen better days was perched on her head.

Quite a fall from glory, as infamous as it must have been, assuming the rumors about Miss Grumley were true. For the past score and a half years, she had lived at the Towers, but local gossip held that she had been known at one time as Bubbles. According to what Ginger had been told shortly after moving to Welleswood, as the woman's stage name implied, she had been a striptease artist at The Palace in Philadelphia, although the term for what she did on stage today might be exotic dancer. No one dared to ask Miss Grumley if the rumors were true, especially since the rumors also claimed she had been saved and born again when a local minister appeared in the audience one night during one of her performances.

No one could identify the minister or explain why

255

he had been at The Palace in the first place, of course. But not a single soul in Welleswood these days doubted Miss Grumley's faith or her dedication to living a faith-filled life every day by visiting the sick and spending long hours at their bedsides when they had no one else to keep them company during their final hours.

"I'm sorry. These old legs don't move so good anymore," she apologized when she finally got to the display. When she caught her breath, she pointed to the carton holding the Mary Jane sweets. "It just wouldn't seem like Christmas morning without finding one of those tucked under my pillow."

Ginger smiled, took a handful of the individually wrapped candies, slipped them into the woman's hand and wrapped her gnarled fingers around them. "We all wish you a blessed Christmas," she whispered.

"Dear, dear. Just one will do. There's only one Christmas morning," she insisted. One by one, she managed to put all of the candy back into the display except for the one she slid into her coat pocket. "There. Now you'll be sure to have enough for everyone else."

Rather than start a discussion about whether or not parents put something under their children's pillows on Christmas Eve, Ginger simply smiled. "Is there anything else I can get for you? A piece of chocolate, perhaps?"

Miss Grumley leaned so close that Ginger could smell the mustiness of her coat. "I'm not too fond of chocolate, but don't tell Charlene. I wouldn't want to hurt her feelings," she whispered.

Ginger motioned across her lips with her index finger, silently zipping her lips closed.

"Good girl. We'll make this our little secret." A twinkle suddenly appeared in pale eyes clouded with age. "On second thought, maybe I'll take a piece of fudge. I'm going to spend some time sitting with Mrs. Thompson later today. She loves fudge."

"The fudge is right over there," Ginger said and pointed to the case in the front of the store. "Why don't you pick out what you want for Mrs. Thompson?"

"You go ahead. I'll meet you there. Just wrap up a piece of vanilla fudge. No nuts. She can't chew so good anymore, but she's too sick to care much about that, I suppose."

Ginger went behind the case and put on a pair of disposable plastic gloves. After cutting a piece of fudge hefty enough for the two women to share, she wrapped it in waxed paper, put it into a tiny pink bag, and handed it to Miss Grumley. "I hope the fudge makes her feel better. Wish her a blessed Christmas, too."

"I will, but if the doctors are right, she'll have the best Christmas of all of us."

Ginger cocked her head. "Really?"

Miss Grumley leaned close again. "She'll be Home by then." Her gaze grew wistful. "Imagine the glory of being Home for Christmas. The angels singing songs of praise. The heavens themselves trembling with the joy of another soul safely returned Home. Oh, to be in the very presence of God and surrounded by nothing but the very essence of His never-ending love . . ."

She sighed and shook her head. "If we try real hard, we can almost have that kind of Christmas, too, but most folks these days get so caught up with buying gifts and going to parties, they forget what Christmas was meant to be. A time for joy. A time for praise. A time for us to be quiet ourselves, so we can feel His love." Smiling, she patted Ginger's hand. "Thank you for your kindness. Make sure you have a quiet Christmas," she whispered before she turned around and shuffled out of the shop, leaving Ginger alone with a message that snuggled deep within her heart.

With little time to ponder the message, Ginger tore off her apron, got rid of her plastic gloves and grabbed two large shopping bags with the supplies she needed to keep her promise to Charlene. "I'll see you Monday, Kristen," she cried and hurried out of the shop to get Vincent from school.

When the doorbell rang just after seven o'clock that night, Ginger answered the door. Both Barbara and Judy were waiting outside together, and she ushered them in from the cold. After hugs, Ginger stored their coats in the closet and led them into the kitchen where she had set out a box and two large bowls in the center of the kitchen table. The box held ten-dozen candy canes. One bowl held precut pieces of silver ribbon;

the other held tiny jingle bells tinted red, blue, green, gold or silver.

They each sat down on different sides of the table and Ginger grinned. "I'm really glad you could come, but I hope you don't mind working, too. I promised Charlene I'd try to get these done by Monday."

"Show us what to do," Judy prompted.

Ginger took a candy cane and held it upside down so it looked like the letter *J*. "It's easy. Watch." She wove a piece of ribbon through the jingle bell, tied it at the top of the candy cane, and held it out for Barbara and Judy to see. "Charlene is donating the supplies to the church for the children at the Christmas pageant on Christmas Eve so they can each jingle a *J* when they sing Happy Birthday to the baby Jesus. Unfortunately, there isn't any group at church with enough time to get them made before the pageant. Everyone's behind schedule, thanks to the early winter storms."

Barbara nodded, but looked skeptical. "How many are we making tonight?"

Ginger giggled. "There are ten dozen in the box. I have two more boxes, but we don't have to finish them all tonight."

"That's 360!"

"But I already made one, so we need 359 more. What we don't finish tonight, I can get Tyler and Vincent to help me do over the weekend."

"That's 358," Judy announced and put her first completed one on the table in front of her.

Barbara laughed and started making one of her own.

"This looks like a good job for the teenagers in the youth group, but I'm not going to complain. At least we're not sitting here gorging ourselves on chocolate or caramel apples. I've eaten my way through too much of December already."

Judy added another one to her finished pile. "I can't believe I'm agreeing with you, Barbara, but between the clients at the salon and the seniors at the Towers, I've already consumed most of next year's allotment for sweets."

Ginger shook the candy cane she had just finished decorating to make sure the bell jingled. "No problem. I'll save what's leftover from the dessert I made for tonight for the weekend. Tyler and Vincent won't have any trouble polishing off your shares."

Barbara's hands stilled. She sniffed the air, laced with cinnamon, and looked around. "That's not the scent of a candle burning? Oh no, is that what I think it is over there on the counter?"

"I took it out of the oven right before you got here," Ginger admitted. "It needs to cool down a bit more."

Judy looked over at the counter and groaned. "I give up. I'll never be able to sit here and watch you pull that cinnamon cake apart and eat it all by yourself."

"Me, either," Barbara admitted. "We really do have to think about getting together more often, but definitely somewhere safer, like the new ladies' gym that just opened on the avenue."

Judy tied another jingle bell into place. "What gym? Not the one that just opened up next to McAllister's

Bakery, I hope. Talk about silly. We'd end up at McAllister's either before or after we got together." She put the candy cane down in her finished pile. "We'd be better off meeting at the library."

Ginger shook another candy cane and made it jingle. "That's a great idea," she teased. "We couldn't eat in the library, but we couldn't talk there, either."

"Which brings us back to why we're getting together tonight," Barbara reminded her. "Didn't you say you needed to talk about something tonight that was troubling you?"

Ginger put both hands on the table and explained how she and Tyler would be alone with Vincent for the upcoming holiday. "When it was just Tyler and me, we'd either host a big open house or spend the afternoon going from one friend's house to the next. With Vincent here this year . . . I'm not sure what we should do, but filling the house with people who are mostly strangers to him or dragging him around with us just doesn't seem right. I guess I needed to know I wasn't the only one anxious about how to celebrate the first Christmas with our grandson."

"You're not alone," Judy insisted and put her unfinished candy cane down on the table. "I'm not sure what Brian and I are going to do, exactly, but I think we're just going to keep it simple." She paused and toyed with a piece of ribbon. "I wish I could say I wasn't worried that Candy might show up on Christmas Eve or Christmas itself and ruin everything, but I am," she murmured.

"Haven't you heard anything at all about where she might be?" Barbara asked.

"No. Not a word."

"Then why are you so worried that she's coming? She hasn't been home for a few years now," Ginger offered.

"But Brian is here now, and Christmas was Candy's favorite holiday," Judy countered. She took a deep breath. "If she's ever going to head home, it will be this time of year. If I had either the time or the money, I'd be tempted to fly us both off somewhere, but since I have neither, I'm staying put. Brian is in the Christmas pageant at church on Christmas Eve, and I was thinking about volunteering to help serve dinner at the Towers on Christmas Day for the seniors who don't have anywhere to go. I think they'd like having a young child like Brian there, too. I just haven't called Penny yet to let her know for sure, but I think I should volunteer. What do you two think?"

Ginger nodded her approval. "I think it's a great idea and that Brian is very lucky to be with you."

Barbara concurred. "If sounds perfect to me. Christmas is going to be difficult for us, too, so we've decided not to stay home this year."

Along with Judy, Ginger listened attentively as Barbara detailed the startling news about the girls' other grandparents, now confirmed beyond all doubt by DNA tests. "They've invited us all up to the farm for a few days over the holiday, and we've accepted. It's a long drive, but it seems like the perfect opportunity to introduce the girls to the Carrs. We think being at the farm where their mother grew up will make it easier for them to understand who the Carrs are and why they're going to be part of their lives as they grow up."

Ginger looked to Judy to comment first, but she seemed just as speechless. "I had no idea you've been dealing with all this," she admitted. "Are you sure they aren't going to fight for custody?"

Barbara smiled. "Absolutely. They've signed a custody agreement limiting their involvement to visitations, and Carl Landon has just filed it with the court. John and I both believe the Carrs can only bring more love into the girls' lives, and we're looking forward to a country Christmas that should be very, very special for all of us."

Ginger was truly happy for both of her friends, but their plans for Christmas only made her more anxious to have her own. "Since you both have such good plans, maybe you can help me with ours, not that we've made a single one. It's just going to be Tyler, Vincent and me," she said, quickly detailing where each of her three children would be. She also described Vincent's attempt to run away and how important it was to make the holiday special for him. "Okay, ladies. Ideas?"

Barbara shook her head. "Wait. Before we can give you any ideas, you have to answer a few questions."

"Right. Like whether or not you want to stay home like I am or go away, like Barbara," Judy suggested.

Guided by the echo of Miss Grumley's suggestion to find the quiet in Christmas, Ginger answered quickly. "Home."

"Good. At this late date, you'd probably have trouble making travel arrangements anyway," Barbara noted. "What are we talking about? Christmas Eve or Christmas Day?"

"Both."

"Isn't Vincent in the Christmas pageant?" Judy asked.

"He was sick and missed the sign-up so it's too late by now. They probably don't have room for him."

"Yes, they would," Barbara argued. "It's a Christmas pageant. There's always room for one more angel."

"Or another shepherd boy," Judy added. "Call Amy Braxton. She's the director this year. I'm sure she'll find a place for him."

"Okay. That takes care of Christmas Eve. What about Christmas Day? After services in the morning, we have the rest of the day to fill. I'd like to keep Vincent busy so he has less time to think about . . . about his mother."

"That's probably wise," Barbara noted, "but he'll be thinking of her anyway."

"You could help us at the Towers. I could mention it to Penny when I call her," Judy offered.

When Ginger did not respond immediately, in part because Tyler was not particularly comfortable surrounded by the elderly and she was not sure if Vincent would be, either, Barbara interjected her thoughts. "You don't have to volunteer on Christmas this year. Why don't you think about what you did when your own children were little?"

Ginger smiled, recalling memories of Christmas past that warmed her heart. "We didn't do much. We always had our big dinner early, right after services. After that, we pretty much stayed home. Tyler always kept the fireplace going all day. We'd make popcorn over the fire, but that was before the microwave made it easier," she added with a giggle. "Maybe we'd play some of the new board games the children got as gifts or we'd go outside. One of the children invariably got a new bicycle or roller skates or a skateboard."

She paused as her heart opened up to share a special memory she had tucked away. "One year we all got ice skates. That winter we were living in Ohio near a small lake that had frozen solid. We spent the afternoon skating and roasted hot dogs over a campfire. I think it was one of the best Christmases we ever had."

"The lake in Welles Park is frozen," Judy noted.

Barbara nodded. "And there are several campfire pits, so that leads me to ask two questions. Do you still have the popcorn maker for the fireplace and do you all have ice skates?"

Ginger looked from Barbara to Judy and back to Barbara again. "They really allow open fires there?"

"Really. Now what about those ice skates?"

"We haven't skated for years. I'm sure we gave them away, and I don't even know if Vincent can skate. It doesn't matter, though. I'd probably land flat on my face the minute I got to the ice."

Judy scoffed. "Not a chance. It's like riding a bike. Once you learn, you never forget. Just don't try a triple axel or anything fancy," she teased.

"I don't even remember what the popcorn thingamabob is called, let alone where it might be. Do they even sell popcorn you don't pop in a microwave?" Ginger asked.

Barbara laughed. "It's right in the supermarket on the shelf next to the microwave popcorn."

"They sell ice skates these days, too. Not at the supermarket, of course, but Marty's Sporting Goods should have them, if they haven't sold out," Judy suggested.

"It would be an old-fashioned Christmas. A little quieter than what you've been used to in the last few years, but maybe that would be a good thing," Barbara murmured.

As Barbara's words faded, Miss Grumley's words echoed in Ginger's mind again. She mulled them over, along with visions of the Christmas they might have. The joy of Christmas morning opening gifts under the tree. More joy and the songs of praise at morning services. Skating together. Roasting hot dogs. Playing games. Popping corn. Time for quiet. Time to surround themselves with love for one another—love that flowed from the Source of all love.

Ginger grinned. "Thank you so much. It sounds so perfect I'm going to talk to Tyler about it tonight."

Barbara looked around the table and frowned. "In the meantime, we didn't get very far with our work, did we?"

Both Judy and Ginger looked at the small piles of decorated candy canes in front of them, looked back up at Barbara, and shrugged at the same time. "I guess we got so busy talking we forgot to keep working," Judy admitted. "If we stop talking and concentrate on what we're doing—"

"Not a chance," Ginger countered and quickly cleared the table. "Vincent and Tyler can help me do these tomorrow. Right now, we have a cinnamon bubble wreath to enjoy, and I doubt we'll forget to do that while we're talking," she teased. She was gratified now she had actually found the time to run home this afternoon to make a bubble wreath for dessert. Whether or not Miss Grumley had ever been known as Bubbles, Ginger would always associate her with the smell of warm cinnamon cake and the very essence of Christmas.

"John and I want to invite you all back to our house for New Year's Eve after service in the park. We could all meet at the gazebo at seven, attend the service together and then come back to our house for some hot chocolate and goodies," Barbara suggested. "We haven't really followed up on the promise we made to spend time just being grandmothers, and I think John and Tyler would enjoy it, too. Please say you'll come. It'll be fun! Besides, I can't think of a better way to end the old year and start a new one than spending time with all of you."

Ginger set the bubble wreath on the table, plucked a gooey bubble of warm dough and held it high. "I'll have to talk to Tyler, of course, but I know he'll want to come so I second Barbara's idea!"

Within a heartbeat, Judy and Barbara each raised a piece of dough in mutual support before turning their attention to a more serious matter—devouring that bubble wreath!

Chapter Twenty-Two

Just before seven o'clock on New Year's Eve, Ginger pulled into the last open space close to the gazebo in Welles Park and turned off her car. A short distance away, dozens of families were gathered along the shores of the lake, huddled in small groups under a clear sky, with countless stars twinkling around the rising full moon.

Returning to the park for tonight's prayer service, which was scheduled for seven-thirty, resurrected precious thoughts of Christmas Day, along with the not-so-great memory of the hours she, Tyler and Vincent had spent that night in the emergency room.

Before she had a chance to ask him, Vincent had shot out of the backseat and had the crutches ready while Tyler eased himself out of the front seat of the car.

"Are you sure you're up to this?" Ginger asked Tyler as she joined him and Vincent and reached up to rearrange the woolen muffler at her husband's neck.

Tyler grunted a bit before he balanced himself on his crutches. "I'm fine. We can't let a little sprained ankle ruin New Year's Eve, can we?" he asked as he leaned on one crutch to rub the top of Vincent's head.

Grinning from ear to ear, Vincent held on to one of the crutches. "Don't worry. I'll help."

"Me, too," Ginger added.

With Vincent on one side of his grandfather, the three of them made their way to the gazebo, slowly but surely, where their friends were waiting. The twins and Brian raced to greet them, obviously eager to hear the tale behind the crutches. By the time they met up with John, Barbara and Judy, who were waiting inside the gazebo, Ginger and Tyler were spared having to do much explaining to the adults. The children handled telling the details of the accident quite well.

Jessie, ever the leader, spilled the news first. "Mr. King fell and hurt his ankle right here on the lake on Christmas Day!"

Melanie shared better news. "But it's okay. He didn't break it. It's just a sprain. He'll be better in just a couple more days."

"Him and Vincent was having a race," Brian added. "A skating race."

"I woulda won, too," Vincent said proudly, "but I stopped to help him when he fell."

With the children surrounding him, Tyler laughed. "I guess I'm not as good on skates as I used to be, but that about tells it all, folks."

"Not quite," Ginger added as she hugged each of her friends. "Before Tyler fell, we had a wonderful time here at the park. It was the trip to the emergency room that ended the day a little bit differently than we planned, but God is good. Tyler wasn't seriously hurt, and he'll be off the crutches in another few days. I hope your Christmases were a little less eventful."

"Absolutely," Judy replied as she reached over to zip up Brian's coat.

Barbara nodded. "I should hope so. I'm glad nothing was broken, Tyler."

"That goes for me, too," John added. "If you're up to it, Tyler, we should probably take the children over to get our candles ready. Then we'll come back for the ladies."

"We're up to it, right, Gramps?" Vincent asked.

"Right, champ. If you lead the way, we'll follow."

With the four children, John and Tyler made their way to get the candles, leaving Ginger, Barbara and Judy in the gazebo. Ginger pulled her coat tighter around her. "It's a good thing it isn't windy. That would make the chill factor drop close to zero!"

"Not to mention the havoc a strong wind would wreak on the service," Judy added. "So tell us. Other than Tyler's accident, what did you do on Christmas Day after services?"

"Just what you suggested. We came home, opened presents and headed to the park for the afternoon. We skated, using our brand-new skates from Santa and roasted hot dogs on the fire when we got hungry . . .

before Tyler decided that having a race with Vincent across the lake was a good way to end the day."

"I'm glad we didn't suggest that part," Barbara teased.

"So how was Christmas on the farm?" Ginger asked.

"Amazing. Simply amazing. Micah and Ruth were more than wonderful. After a delicious country supper on Christmas Eve, they took us out to the barn where Micah had a creche set up in one of the stalls. There were figures of Mary and Joseph and Baby Jesus and Micah had put in some baby animals. A pair of little lambs, some tiny pigs and a few chickens." She chuckled. "I'm not sure if there were any chickens there in Bethlehem for Jesus's birth, but there were in upstate New York this year. The girls loved it! We took pictures, but I haven't had a chance to get them developed."

"I'd love to see them," Ginger said eagerly. "What about you, Judy? Did you volunteer at the Towers like you'd planned?"

Judy shrugged. "Not exactly. Brian got sick a day or two earlier, and he was still running a fever on Christmas Day. Nothing serious, but I was afraid he might be contagious and the last thing the seniors need is to have a volunteer bring in sickness."

"I'm so sorry. What did you do, then?" Barbara asked.

"Nothing much. We just played some of the games he'd gotten from Santa. He was feeling a whole lot better after he beat me three times in a row playing

Candy Land!" She paused. "To be honest, I spent half the day worrying that Candy might show up, and there's part of me that still thinks Brian got sick because he was worried that she wouldn't. We talked about her, of course, and he was sad, but now that Christmas is over, he seems to have bounced back."

"I'm glad that you had Brian with you for Christmas."

"And that he had *you* for Christmas," Ginger added. She pointed toward the lake. "And it looks like our candles are coming."

Within moments, the troop arrived back with the candles, along with small slips of paper, candleholders made from plastic milk containers, tiny golf pencils donated by the sports shop, and a book of matches. They separated into families, each preparing small messages to loved ones that they tucked into the candleholders beneath the votive candles that would soon be part of the service as luminaries that would cover the frozen surface of the lake. When all the candles were lit, everyone, carried their luminaries to the shores of the lake. There, John led the children across the ice, allowing each child to find a special place for his or her luminaries while Tyler remained behind with the three women.

When John and the children returned, Reverend Fisher took his place in the center of the lake, the crowd hushed, and the service began. "Father God, we thank You for the gift of Your son, who remains present with us even now to guide us and teach us the vast wonders of Your love, for He is the Light of the World. Tonight, we gather together to remember all those who have been called Home to be with You and those who live far away and cannot join us. Like the candles on this lake, let the light of Your faithful love fill the darkness within our lives and our hearts."

As the pastor continued to pray, Ginger edged closer to Tyler and held on to Vincent's shoulders as he stood before them. Her gaze focused on the luminary Vincent had lit for his mother, and she prayed that Lily might one day be touched by the gift of grace and return for the son she had abandoned. Before sadness and loss overwhelmed her, she shifted her thoughts to the luminary that Vincent had made for his new family, and she gave thanks for the wonder of having this child as part of her and Tyler's life now.

Beside her on the right, Barbara and John each held on to one of the twins. No doubt, there was a very special luminary flickering on the lake in memory of Steve, but Ginger also knew there was one there for the girls and their grandparents, as well as one for their new grandparents.

To her left, Judy and Brian stood hand in hand, the boy's face mesmerized by the shining lights of the dozens of luminaries that were mirrored on the frozen surface of the lake, and his gaze centered on the candle he surely had lit for his mother.

Reverend Fisher concluded the prayer service. "And finally, Father God, we also ask tonight for Your unending blessings in the New Year on all those who gather here. Share with them the joy that comes from serving You. Guide us. Comfort us. Continue to nurture us, that may we leave tonight kinder and gentler, more loving and more patient, as shining disciples and followers of Your Word. Amen."

Ginger's voice blended with the others in a resounding "Amen!" even as volunteers brought around baskets filled with small candles, one for each of the attendees. When they finished, Reverend Fisher lit his candle, along with several other people at different points along the shores of the lake who each turned, first from one side to the next, to light the candle of the person next to them. Within moments, the lake was surrounded by light—the light of faith, the light of hope and the light of promise.

When he led them in song, Ginger's voice joined the others. "This little light of mine. I'm gonna let it shine," she began, full of hope that the light of faith would be bright enough to sustain them all in the days and weeks ahead and shine down upon them as they spent time together as grandparents, grand parents and grand friends, indeed.

Chapter Twenty-Three

On the second Monday in January, when Pretty Ladies would normally be closed, Ann and Judy hosted the annual Open House at the salon for friends and clients to stop by to celebrate the start of a new year.

For Judy, knowing this would be Ann's last year as the owner of Pretty Ladies, the Open House was bittersweet. Although Ann was still hoping to retire by the start of summer, she had yet to make any formal announcement to their friends and clients, in part because the bank had not approved Judy's request for a loan. The bank had agreed, however, to review Judy's application again after she completed her computer classes and submitted a revised business plan. Fortunately, Ann had agreed to buy the computer for the salon, assuring Judy that the investment would pay off whether Judy purchased the salon or someone else did.

Whether Judy's venture into becoming a business owner would be one grand adventure or a disappointing misadventure remained to be seen, but the new year held great promise for her and she gladly bid the old year goodbye.

If she had looked ahead one year ago and realized within a twelve-month span of time she would be raising her grandson, trying to buy Pretty Ladies and taking computer classes, she might not have made it through the year.

But she had made it, meeting one challenge at a time, but she had not done it alone. Among all her blessings this past year, she counted Ginger and Barbara's friendship as the best, after Brian, of course. And Ann, too, she reminded herself, not to mention the loyal clients and friends who had been stopping in all day to reminisce and to wish them both well in the coming year.

The fact that Candy had not shown up to ruin Christmas was a blessing, too, although Judy wondered if that thought would be enough to qualify her for worst mother of the year. With the Open House finally coming to a close, however, she simply embraced the idea that this had been one perfect day and for that, she was grateful indeed.

At four o'clock, Judy shooed Ann out the door. "No, you will definitely, absolutely, positively not stay to help clean up! Go home," she urged lovingly and shut the glass door to the salon.

Ann turned, shook her finger at Judy as a mock reprimand, then blew her a kiss before heading home and into a new year that, Judy prayed, would be blessed with better health. After pulling down the shade on the door, Judy turned around to face the remnants of the day's celebration and groaned. Cleaning up would take every minute of the two hours she had left before picking up Brian at the after-school program. She hauled out two large garbage cans and lined them with plastic bags. Before she had a chance to start filling them, a knock at the front door interrupted her.

"The party's over." She hummed a tune on her way to the door, hoping to douse her annoyance before facing whoever had decided to arrive so late. When she opened the door, found Barbara and Ginger standing there, each armed with plastic bags and a broom, surprise and delight instantly changed her mood. "What are you two doing back here again?" she asked, sounding dumb even to herself.

Ginger giggled and waved her broom like a magic wand. "Well, we're not the prize squad or whatever it's called. What do you think, silly? We're here to help you clean up!"

"But don't be too quick to thank us. We have an ulterior motive," Barbara cautioned. "Did you want us to sweep the sidewalk or can we come in?"

Judy stumbled back a few steps to let them in and closed the door again. "You two are amazing. Actually, I'd really appreciate your help. The salon is a mess."

"We're very experienced at cleaning up, too," Ginger remarked as she began clearing off one of the two long tables littered with used paper plates, plastic utensils and trays that had recently overflowed with mini deli sandwiches and baked goods from McAllister's.

Barbara started on the other table, gathering up leftovers she boxed together. "I wouldn't be too grateful. Not until you hear what we want you to do for us."

Judy waved away any objection she might have to returning the favor she owed them. While her two friends attacked the tables, she walked around the salon and picked up paper plates that had been left helter-skelter at different stations and the reception desk or picked up food that had fallen to the floor. "Whatever happened to simply doing good works, without expecting any reward?" she teased.

"That goes both ways, doesn't it?" Ginger asked coyly as she started rolling up the plastic tablecloth.

"We do a good work coming here to help you and you'll do a good work helping us."

This time, Barbara giggled. "I'm not sure how Reverend Fisher would feel if he heard us, but I'm pretty sure we wouldn't be asked to lead a Bible discussion on the topic anytime soon. Not with that logic."

Judy dumped an armful of trash into the can. "I'll help you. There. No more discussion. We're friends. If you say you need help, then I'll help you. I think that falls under the 'Do unto others' umbrella that the reverend always preaches under."

Ginger giggled so hard this time she had to stop working to wipe the tears from her eyes. "The first time I saw Reverend Fisher in the pulpit standing under that bright bright turquoise umbrella, the one with Do Unto Others printed on it, while he preached about how we should treat one another, I knew I was in the right congregation. Ministers don't always have a sense of humor."

Judy groaned as she lugged a large potted plant they had received from a client over to the floor near the window ledge and saw that it had started to rain. She wiped her hands on her already-soiled slacks. "Not everyone thought the umbrella sermon was . . . appropriate."

"Well, I loved it. Maybe we should ask him to help us, too," Barbara suggested before she took the boxes filled with leftovers to the back room.

"Ask him to help clean up this mess? Not a chance," Judy argued.

"No. Ask him to help us with our new assignment for the PTA," Ginger explained. Barbara returned from the back room and helped Ginger with refolding one of the cleared tables before continuing. "I got a call yesterday from Pam, the PTA President. She said since we'd all done such a good job working together for the Book Fair, we might want to work together again," Ginger said before she snapped one of the table legs back into place."

"What did she have in mind for us to do?" Judy asked.

"Apparently, this year it's up to the Park Elementary PTA to host the annual Mother's Day Breakfast for the school district, and she wants us to plan it."

Judy froze in place and clutched the small planter she had been carrying over to the window ledge. She was half-tempted to hurl the planter across town straight at the PTA President to knock some sense into her, but decided not to waste the plant. "You're kidding, right?"

Ginger shook her head. "That was my first reaction, too. I couldn't believe she'd ask any of us to work on something for Mother's Day. It's not like it's a big secret in town that my daughter has abandoned her child, along with us, or that your daughter is still missing . . . and this is the first Mother's Day for Barbara without her son." She paused. "Then . . . then she told me why she asked us."

"As if that could matter," Judy quipped.

Ginger smiled. "She said she admired all three of us

for taking in our grandchildren and raising them. She said . . ." She stopped to clear her throat. "She said we were good role models for the younger mothers and we could help others to see that being a mother means more than giving birth, that any woman who nurtures and loves a child should be included in the breakfast."

Barbara nodded. "And she also said she was absolutely certain we would be able to make this event even more memorable because we planned it."

Judy swallowed hard. The idea that she could be a role model for anyone was so foreign she had a hard time grasping the concept and she felt guilty for thinking the worst of Pam.

"So what else could I do?" Ginger asked. "I told her I had the time, but that I wasn't sure about you or Barbara. Even setting aside the fact that this is a Mother's Day event, which is going to be hard for you to get through, you've got your job and computer classes now and Barbara—"

"I said it would help me to focus on something positive, instead of the investigation," Barbara murmured. "Since no arrests have been made yet and my shop is closed, I really need something to do and good friends to do it with. Planning the event won't be the hard part for me. It's actually attending the event that will be difficult."

Judy's gaze softened. "I'm sorry. I'd hoped they'd be finished with the investigation by now."

Barbara leaned the folded table against the wall. " 'Justice delayed will still be justice.' That's what our lawyer keeps telling us. Even most of the media has moved on to more titillating cases, although that might change when the arrests are finally made." She shook herself as if casting off disturbing thoughts. "Let's talk about the breakfast."

Judy smiled. "Mother's Day isn't going to be an easy day, that's for sure, but if you two can work on the breakfast, then I guess I can, too." She walked to the window and set the planter on the ledge and saw that it was raining harder outside. "I haven't really celebrated Mother's Day for years, except to put flowers on my mother's grave, but this is a new year. Maybe it's time for new beginnings and new traditions. How has the breakfast been done in the past?"

As the women continued to clean up the salon and put the garbage cans outside Ginger explained what she had learned about the Mother's Day Breakfast in previous years. While Judy mopped her way to the back room, Ginger and Barbara waited near the front door, discussing ways to make the event even better. Judy gave the mop one final swish and held it, mop end up, at her side, calling out to the others from just outside the back room. "I think we should each take a week or two to think everything over, come up with ideas on our own, and get together again to compare notes."

She glanced at the brand-new computer sitting on the reception desk and frowned. "I have computer classes on Monday mornings when the salon is closed. Monday afternoons would be good for me, though."

"Now that Grandmother's Kitchen is closed, I'm free any day. Monday afternoons are fine, but I'd have to be able to pick up the girls by three o'clock."

Ginger shook her head. "I work until three."

"Evenings are going to be rough, with running the salon on my own," Judy noted. "Ann's going to limit herself to house calls for the time being so she's not on her feet at the salon all day. And I don't think this is something we can do with the children."

Barbara sighed. "I agree, but weekends are rougher."

"Then I'll just have to talk to Charlene and tell her I'll need to leave early a couple of Mondays," Ginger suggested.

Barbara looked skeptical. "Are you sure she won't mind?"

"I doubt it, especially if we can get together on Mondays this month. There's always a postholiday lull in January. I'll ask her tomorrow and call you if it's a problem. Otherwise, let's say we meet at The Diner next Monday at one. How's that?"

Barbara smiled. "Sounds good to me."

"Me, too." Judy held up her mop. "Why don't you two head home? I just have to rinse out the mop. The floor will be dry in a few minutes, and then I can head home, too."

"What about the leftovers? Didn't you say something about taking them to the Towers?" Barbara asked.

Judy looked at the two boxes stacked behind her,

looked back at the window to see it was still raining outside, and sighed. "I forgot all about them."

"It's raining. Let me drop them off for you on my way home," Barbara offered. "I parked my car about two blocks away. Let me go get it," she said, grabbed her broom and left before Judy could argue with her.

"I'll stay and keep you company," Ginger insisted.

Chuckling to herself, rather than lose another argument, Judy emptied the water into the sink and rinsed out the mop. She was resting the mop upside down in the bucket to dry and propping the handle against the wall when she heard a knock at the door. She sighed and turned her head over her shoulder. "If that's Barbara, tell her I'll be a few more minutes. If not, tell whoever it is that the party is over and I'm not making any appointments until tomorrow," she cried, hoping her voice would be loud enough to be heard at the front of the shop.

She heard the front door open and close quickly and assumed Ginger had heard her. When she heard voices talking again, she thought Barbara had returned. She started putting the boxes into large shopping bags with handles to make it easier for Barbara to carry them when she heard Ginger call out.

"Judy! There's someone here to see you. She says it's important."

"I'm coming," she called back, but she stopped and closed her eyes for a moment. "It's never going to change, is it?" she grumbled under her breath. "Why is it that once a woman decides to get her hair cut or permed or colored, she wants it done yesterday, but waits until today to make the appointment?" She sighed, realized she was beyond tired and tried to put a smile on her face.

She grabbed a shopping bag in each hand, saw the floor was still damp when she came out of the back room. Being very careful not to slip, she kept her gaze focused on the floor and started tiptoeing back toward the front of the salon.

"When you weren't at home, I thought I'd find you here."

Judy froze.

Her hands tightened on the handles of the bags she carried, and her nails bit into the palms of her hands.

Heart pounding, she looked up and stared straight into the face of the only person who could have destroyed her perfect day and made it more perfect, all within a single heartbeat.

With the next beat of her heart, her whole world turned upside down and inside out.

Again.

Chapter Twenty-Four

With her dripping coat clinging to her body and her short, dark hair plastered against her scalp, Candy was a hundred pounds of pure indignation. Her eyes flashed with fury. Her cheeks flushed scarlet, and her lips curled into a snarl. "Don't bother saying hello or introducing me to your friend here. Just tell me this.

Who do you think you are to tell those . . . those idiots running the after-school program that I can't even see my own son?"

Before Judy could answer, the salon door opened again. Barbara was barely inside before Officer Joe Karpinski hurried in behind her and stood off to the side between Judy and the other three women. Drenching wet, as well, he removed his hat, looked at the water he had dripped on the floor and cringed. "Sorry for bringing the rain in with me, Mrs. Roberts. What a downpour! This is definitely not a good day to be on bike patrol. I hope you don't mind, but I needed to see—"

"Cops?" Candy threw her hands up in the air. "Those idiots called the cops? I don't believe it."

The young officer looked directly at Candy. "Ma'am?"

She clapped at her thigh in frustration. "The school. They called you from the school, right? Well, that's just perfect. It's my first day back . . . No, change that. It's my first hour back in Welleswood—"

"Ma'am, please. I'm Joe Karpinksi. The kids call me Officer Joe. I work with them at the school. And you are . . . ?"

Candy flashed her mother a look of pure disgust before letting out a long sigh. "Candy Martin."

"Well, I'm pleased to meet you, Candy."

"It's Mrs. Martin," she snapped.

Still calm and seemingly unflappable, he smiled. "My fault. Mrs. Martin."

Judy kept her gaze locked on her daughter. "Candy is my daughter and Brian's mother," she explained to the officer who was a good fifteen years younger than Candy. It was possible that he did not recognize her or maybe he did not remember her. Or was he responding to the call from the school, fully aware of Candy's identity and relationship with Judy, yet using his training to try to defuse what might be a potentially volatile situation?

In any case, Judy was relieved he was here and very grateful if the school had called him. Behind Candy, Barbara and Ginger stood together, like a pair of tigers ready to pounce if Candy took one step closer to Judy. Barbara held her dripping umbrella in front of her like a sword. From the grim expression on her face, she appeared ready to use it as a weapon, while Ginger held a firm grip on her broom.

Candy's glare remained as bright as a beacon from a lighthouse.

"If you're having some sort of problem with the school, Mrs. Martin, I'd be glad to help, but I only came in here to see Mrs. King. I saw her through the window," he explained, and his statement immediately shifted the tension in the room away from Candy to Ginger.

Shocked, Judy looked away from Candy to the officer and finally to Ginger. Her face was pale and she trembled. Barbara lowered her umbrella and edged closer to their friend.

Ginger's eyes widened with panic. "Me? Why did

you need to see me? Is something wrong? Has something happened to Tyler? Or Vincent?"

The officer blushed and held up his hand. "No. I'm sorry. Please don't be upset. Nothing's happened. I'm sure your husband and your grandson are fine. I just wanted to let you know that I'm taking some of the kids out this Saturday for ice cream. I promised to ask Vincent the next time we got together, but with the snowstorms, I've had to hold off a bit. Do you think he'd like to come?"

Relief washed Ginger's face and restored her color. "Oh! Absolutely. I'm sure he would. I can ask him tonight and talk it over with my husband, just to make sure. Then I'll call you."

He smiled, but shrugged his shoulders. "You don't need to call me. If he can come, just bring him up to the station around two on Saturday. I usually give the kids a little tour of the station house first."

"Two o'clock. We'll be there."

He nodded and looked from Barbara to Candy and finally Judy. "Ladies, I've got room for a few more kids. What about the twins, Mrs. Montgomery?"

Barbara shook her head. "My husband and I are taking the girls to the Adventure Aquarium on Saturday."

"Maybe next time, then. What about Brian?" he asked, looking first at Judy and then Candy.

"I think he'd like that," Judy offered.

"We might have other plans," Candy countered and tilted her chin up as if daring Judy to challenge her authority.

"Good enough. If he can make it, just bring him on up." He put his hat back on and looked out the window. "Rain's stopped. I guess I'd better be going. Let me help you with those shopping bags on my way out," he suggested. When he approached Judy with his back to the others and lifted a brow, silently inviting her to indicate if he should leave or stay, she realized he might indeed have come to follow up a call from the school.

She handed him the shopping bags, which he grabbed and held with one hand. "Actually, I'm not leaving quite yet, but Mrs. Montgomery is going to take these to the Towers for me. Would you mind helping her by taking the bags out to her car?"

"Sure thing." He looked around the floor again and frowned. "I'm really sorry about getting your floor all wet."

"It's not a problem," she assured him. "It's only rainwater. A quick mopping should take care of it."

Reluctantly, Barbara followed the officer out of the salon and Judy urged Ginger to leave, as well. "Thanks again for all your help. I'll see you next Monday, right?"

With her feet planted and her hand still gripping her broom, Ginger stayed put. "I don't mind staying. I could help you mop the floor."

Judy hugged her and opened the door. "If you hurry, you can get to your car before the rain starts again."

"You're sure?"

"Positive."

Ginger slipped out the door, whispered, "Call me," and walked away.

Judy watched and waited until her friend disappeared from view before slowly closing the door. She had no fear of Candy, but she had no great desire to face the ugly confrontation that would inevitably begin once she closed the door and they were alone. In her mind, echoes of angry words from previous arguments collided with heartbreaking memories and the embarrassment of having Candy confront her in front of Barbara and Ginger today.

Trembling, she closed the door and pressed her palms against the shade until determination to protect Brian and maintain her self-control gave her the strength to turn around. As she turned, she caught a reassuring glimpse of Officer Karpinski who was standing next to his bike on the other side of the street, but the sight that waited for her when she looked at her daughter was beyond anything she might have imagined.

She blinked hard several times. "Wh-what are you doing?"

Candy did not look up and continued working. "Isn't it obvious? I'm mopping the floor."

"I—I can see that," Judy sputtered. "I'm just—"

"Surprised?" Candy stopped for a moment and looked up at her mother. Her gaze was hesitant, even wary, but her eyes were clear. Her complexion was also fresh and healthy. She had taken off her coat, and her body had curves again, prompting Judy to assume that Candy had made more than a little progress in battling her addiction. She cocked her head. "It's no big deal. You've been mopping up the mess I've made of my life for a long time. I'm only mopping your floor."

Hopeful, but skeptical by experience, Judy still kept up her guard. Instead of responding, she waited for her daughter to direct the course of the conversation and hoped Candy might offer some explanation about where she had been all these months since leaving the halfway house.

Candy shifted from one foot to the other. "I'm sorry I barged into the salon and yelled at you, especially in front of your friend. I was just so anxious to see Brian that when they wouldn't let me see him at the school, I blamed you and assumed you were deliberately trying to hurt me. I realize now you were protecting him, and I'm sorry."

"You're apologizing?" Judy blurted, as surprised by her daughter's statement as she was at herself for asking the question.

"Just accepting responsibility for my actions." She shrugged, but also managed half a smile. "It's part of my recovery program," she murmured and started mopping the floor again.

"Oh." Judy did not know what else to say. Pointing out that this was at least the third recovery program Candy had experienced would be unkind, at best. At worst, reminding Candy of her past failures might jeopardize the obvious progress she was making now.

The natural bond they shared as mother and daughter remained, but the emotional distance between them was very real. Closing that distance would be difficult. Judy knew she had to tread very carefully, even though she was anxious to know if Brian had been aware of Candy's unexpected arrival at the school and had become upset.

"The halfway house outside of San Diego reported you missing last September. Why did you run away?"

Candy's eyes widened. "You knew?"

"After you left, they found Brian's picture with my address on the back and contacted the Welleswood Police. Yes, I knew, and I've spent every day since then wondering if you were still alive and if you were, when and if you might come for Brian, assuming you remembered you had a son."

"Mom, I'm sorry. I had no idea—"

"No. You never did, did you?" Judy retorted. She kept her voice low and her determination to face the truth was undaunted. "If you're serious about staying off drugs, then I assume being honest is also part of your recovery."

"Sure, but—"

"Then I need to be honest, too. I don't want to hear any excuses or lies, like before. I just want the truth, plain and simple. Why did you run away from the halfway house?"

Candy closed her eyes for a moment. When she looked at Judy again, her gaze was unwavering. "The plain and simple truth is that I didn't run away. I just changed programs."

"So this call to the police was the result of what? A breakdown in communications between one program and another?"

"No. A necessary move because of a difference of opinions. I thought it was time for me to move on. So did my therapist." She let out a sigh. "I've met some incredibly wonderful people who have helped me to get to where I am today, but along the way, I've met a few who . . . Let's just say they aren't working with drug addicts for even one reason that's right or good. Before I found myself trapped by drugs again, I had to leave, even disappear, with the help of a counselor I could trust. If I ever had an inkling that the director at the halfway house would try to find me here and tell the police I was missing, I would have contacted you. If you need to know more than that—"

"No," Judy whispered. The anguish on Candy's face was real, and Judy had heard enough to know she did not need to hear any of the sordid details. Not now. Maybe some day in the future when it would be easier for Candy to explain and for Judy to understand. Instead, she had more immediate concerns. "What about Duke? Did he come with you?"

Candy paused, twisted the handle of the mop for a moment and attacked one last puddle on the floor with a vengeance. "We're divorced. He won't be coming here."

"Oh." Judy kicked herself mentally for repeating

herself, but at least she did not say she was happy to know Duke was now her ex-son-in-law and Brian had no reason to fear being reunited with his father. "I—I mean, I didn't know."

With one final swish, Candy finished mopping the floor and leaned on the handle. "That was part of my recovery program, too."

"Getting divorced?"

"Yes. Staying in an abusive marriage was a mistake. I guess I always knew that, but I never . . . I never had the courage to get a divorce before now. Once I realized he had abandoned Brian, too, I realized I finally had the chance I needed."

As opposed to divorce as she might be in principle and as a matter of faith, Judy had no doubt that Candy's divorce was absolutely necessary to protect her daughter as well as her grandson. Encouraged by the positive choices Candy appeared to be making, Judy focused on her grandson. "What about Brian?"

Candy locked her gaze with Judy's. "He's my baby. He's . . . he's why I'm standing here, completely clean and drug-free now for six months and seventeen days. And he's the reason I intend to stay clean. One day at a time. One week at a time. One month at a time."

Judy looked deep into her daughter's eyes and swallowed hard. She had heard Candy's promises to kick her habit many times, but she had never seen the depth of commitment or strength of will that stared back at her now. Letting go of past disappointments and accepting Candy at her word, however, was more difficult now because of Brian. Judy was not the only one who could be hurt.

Brian's interests were paramount, and if Candy did not understand that, then Judy would have to make sure that she did. Judy bit back the urge to make any demands or to tell Candy what she could or could not do. Instead, she did something she had never done before. She simply asked, "What are your plans?"

Candy's eyes widened, obviously surprised by Judy's new approach. She raked her fingers through her wet hair and brushed it away from her face. "That's hard to say. Not that I don't have any plans. I do. I have short-term plans and long-term plans, but . . . but I guess I need to know . . ."

She paused and straightened her back to stand tall. "In the long term, I plan to be able to raise my son and to be able to support us both."

"And in the short term?"

"In the short term, I know I need to prove myself and get involved in a program here. I need a place to live. I need a job. I—I need to convince Brian that I love him and that I'm really sorry for leaving him and that I won't ever leave him again." With tears welling, she choked and cleared her throat.

Judy battled tears of her own and struggled to get air past the lump in her throat.

"But most of all, I need your help. I know you've tried to help me in the past, and I'm really, really sorry for what I've done to you. I wouldn't blame you if you didn't want to try to help me again, but it's different this time. Will you help me, Mom? Please? Just one more time?"

Judy stood still, her emotions balanced precariously on a thin wire separating belief from disbelief that. Could she give in to the cries of her heart and help her daughter?

Yes, she could help Candy. Judy could give her a place to live. She could even ask Ann to let Candy work in the salon, at least temporarily, until she found a permanent job. Judy could support her, emotionally, as Candy reestablished her bonds with Brian, and Judy could offer encouragement as Candy continued her struggle against her addiction.

Should she help her daughter?

Judy had dozens of memories to convince her otherwise, but as a mother, how could she say no to Candy? Did Judy's responsibilities as Brian's grandmother conflict with her role as Candy's mother, or were they so intertwined she could not be loyal to one without the other? Should she take the risk and offer to help her daughter one more time or should past experience be her guide and remind her there would always be promises that would be broken and pleas for one more chance and then another and another?

Torn between what she could do and what she should do, Judy had to decide here and now exactly what she would be willing to do in answer to her daughter's plea.

Would she be willing to risk failing again as Candy's mother or would she be able to use the mistakes she had made in the past to help her to know how best to help Candy succeed? Would she be able to take one giant leap of faith and trust the Lord to watch over all of them and guide them?

The risks were great.

The chance of failing again was real.

But the opportunity of succeeding was too precious to deny . . . just one more time.

She could, she should, and she would help her daughter by taking one day at a time, one week at a time, one month at a time, and most importantly, with one simple, faith-filled prayer at a time.

"Father, we need You," she whispered.

When her spirit filled with warmth and peace, she took the first step with faith and started walking toward her daughter. "Why don't you put that mop away so we can go pick up Brian together?"

Chapter Twenty-Five

There are deep truths to be found in a child's spontaneous expressions. Within the innocence of childhood, there exists a fountain of purity, unspoiled by guile or selfishness, which flows with unconditional love and forgiveness or joy and wonder.

Wise adults know to look for these truths, to take them to heart and accept them at face value.

Judy did not necessarily believe she was wise, but she was smart enough to know that she needed to see Brian's expression the moment he realized his mother had returned. After clearing their way into the school, Judy spoke directly to the teacher in charge. She stood off to the side, just inside the doorway to the playroom, and watched Brian building blocks all by himself while other children were still doing homework or painting or playing.

The moment Brian saw his mother approaching him, his dark eyes lit with surprise and immediately sparkled with joy. A huge smile almost turned his dimples inside out. He jumped up, knocked over the castle he had been building and whooped and hollered and charged across the carpet. "Mom! Mom! Mom!"

Candy held out her arms and scooped him up. He wrapped his arms around her neck and she hugged him to her, turning round and round in a circle and murmuring words of love Judy could barely hear.

Brian's reaction cemented Judy's decision to give her daughter one more chance, albeit with one major condition Candy had agreed to before coming to the school. Any type of relapse, using any kind of drugs, just once, and Candy would have to leave Judy's house. Without Brian. In the meantime, Judy would retain legal custody. They would work out the other conditions later tonight after dinner and after Brian had gone to bed.

Finally, Brian's feet touched the ground again, but he held on to one of Candy's legs. When she pointed to Judy, he waved, tugged on his mother's hand and dragged her with him as he closed the distance between them and Judy. "Look, Grandmom! Look! It's my mom!"

Judy laughed and ruffled his hair when he almost ran into her. "Yes, I know."

Grinning, he gave her a look of pure delight, as if his mother's reappearance had turned on an inner light in his spirit that their separation had dimmed. "Can we have ice cream for dinner tonight? Can we?"

Candy scowled. "Ice cream? That's a treat, not dinner. Besides, it's pretty cold out to be eating ice cream."

He shook his head. "Me and Grandmom had ice cream for dinner when I got my 'ward, didn't we, Grandmom?"

Candy looked at Judy and raised a brow.

"W-well, Brian got the Best Student Award that day, and we were celebrating," she offered.

"We never had ice cream for dinner when I was growing up," Candy countered.

"No, but . . . maybe we should have." Judy met Candy's gaze and held it for a moment. They were connected, here and now, by the reality of what had been in the past and the hope for what could be in the future. Resolving the past was a great challenge. Judy's ability to balance her role as Candy's mother, Brian's grandmother and his grand mother while they blended into a family again would be an even greater challenge.

Having ice cream for dinner, however, was not an issue Judy wanted to battle over with her daughter.

She looked down at Brian and shivered for effect. "But your mom's right, Brian. It's a little cold outside to be eating ice cream."

"But it's not too cold inside Scoops, if it's even still there," Candy suggested. "Maybe we could even have a hamburger first."

Eyes wide, Brian nodded. "That's where we had our ice cream. Scoops. Right, Grandmom?"

Judy chuckled. "Yes, it was, but they don't have burgers anymore. They only serve ice cream these days."

"Then it's settled. We're going to Scoops to celebrate Mom coming home. Why don't I help you put the blocks away first?" Candy suggested.

"And I'll meet you both in the foyer. I need to stop in the office to talk to Mrs. Moffett," Judy offered and retraced her steps back to the school office.

Once inside, she found Jean Moffett behind the counter at her desk, talking on the telephone. "Yes, that's right. . . . No, the after-school program ends at six. . . . I'll see you from the office and buzz you inside. . . . You're welcome." She hung up the telephone and smiled. "I'm sorry. We still get three or four inquiries a day. I'm glad you stopped back to see me. I didn't want to say anything earlier when you were with your daughter, but I hope you're not angry with me for not letting her take Brian earlier . . . or that I called the police. Candy was very, very upset. I tried to call you at home, but you weren't there. I know the salon is closed on Mondays, but I was so rattled, by the time I remembered you were having the Open House today, it was too late. I knew the police would already be handling the problem."

"On the contrary," Judy insisted. "That's one of the reasons I wanted to see you before we left with Brian. I truly appreciate the fact that you followed the rules and wouldn't let Brian leave with anyone other than me."

"I wouldn't make an exception. Not in today's world. It's not like it was when we were raising our children. But I saw that she was with you when you both got here a few minutes ago and buzzed you both in. I gather everything is settled now?"

"For now," Judy replied. Fortunately, Jean was an old friend, and Judy did not have to explain Candy's erratic behavior in the past or earlier today, for that matter. "That's another reason I wanted to see you. Candy will be living with me again, temporarily, and sometimes she'll be picking up Brian from school or the after-school program. I wonder if we could change the instructions in Brian's records?"

"Yes, indeed." Jean opened a desk drawer, flipped through a number of file folders and pulled one out. After leafing through the papers, she found what she was looking for. She carried it with her to the counter and pointed to a section near the bottom. "Here. Right now it says you're the only one who can take Brian out of school or pick him up from the after-school program. Should I just add Candy's name?"

Judy hesitated, then decided her original idea would

be best, at least for now. "Actually, it's a little more complicated than that."

Jean handed her a pen. "Here. Cross off what's written there now. As you can see, there's plenty of spare space below. Just write down what you want us to do, and we'll follow your instructions."

After drawing several lines through her previous instructions, Judy wrote her new ones and turned the paper around for Jean to read the changes. "How's that?"

Jean read the new instructions to herself and nodded. "Sure thing. If Candy comes to pick up Brian again, either during school or the after-school program, you'll call me first. If I'm not here, whoever is covering for me will call you back either at home or at the salon to make sure you were really the one making the call."

She tucked the paper back into the folder and smiled. "I hope everything works out. For you and Candy and Brian," she murmured. "Candy looks good. Like she's doing good."

"I think she is." When Judy heard Brian's voice, she turned and saw Candy and Brian waiting for her in the foyer. "Thanks for everything. I've got to go. We're heading out for dinner."

"The Diner has the meat loaf special on Mondays. We went there last week. You should try it!"

"Maybe another time. We're going to Scoops." She grinned and slipped out the door, but not before she tucked the surprised look on Jean's face into the memory book in her mind.

Judy was not sure if Brian was unable to go to sleep out of pure excitement at his reunion with his mother, from eating too much ice cream topped with crushed candies, or out of fear that his mother might not be here when he woke up. Maybe it was a combination of all three reasons, but she left Candy in charge of putting Brian to bed for the night and getting him to go to sleep.

Instead, Judy had stayed downstairs to call Ginger to reassure her all was well and to ask her to call Barbara to ease her concerns, too. After making her calls, she went upstairs, dry-mopped the hardwood floors, and dusted the bureau in the spare room where Candy would be sleeping. The master bedroom where Judy had slept every night since moving into the house years ago was at the front end of the narrow upstairs hallway. Brian's room, Candy's bedroom as a child, was sandwiched in between the other two bedrooms, along with a bathroom that separated his room from Candy's.

After she emptied her summer clothes from the bureau and postage-stamp closet, she pulled down the foldaway steps and stored her summer clothes in the attic. By the time she got back to the bedroom to put fresh sheets on the double bed, she needed to stop and gather up enough steam to finish the job.

When Candy entered the room, she sighed. "He's finally asleep. Need some help?"

Judy arched her back and stretched her muscles.

"Only if you insist on having sheets to sleep on tonight. I'm beat."

"Long day?" Candy asked as she started nudging the fitted sheet into place at the bottom corner of the mattress. "I thought the salon was closed on Mondays."

Judy fit the sheet onto the opposite corner. "We had our Open House today. Just between us, Ann Porter is hoping to retire by summer, and I'm trying to buy the salon."

The sheet slipped from Candy's grip. "Really?"

Judy shrugged. "I'll have to take out a home equity loan and some to do it, and I still have to come up with a new business plan that the bank will like. But I think I can do it. I also think Ann might be willing to let you help out at the salon until you find a permanent job, especially since she's going to concentrate on working in clients' homes now."

"Mom, that's so . . . so cool! You might actually get to own Pretty Ladies!"

"Don't get too excited. Lots of things still have to be worked out yet, but yes. I just might get to own the salon." She chuckled. "When I think about how old I'll be when the home equity loan is finally paid off, assuming I get one, I think I'll wind up at settlement laughing. But I guess it doesn't really matter. I'll be long gone before I'm eighty-seven."

"Don't say that," Candy argued. She waited for Judy to fit the sheet on her front corner of the mattress, then struggled to fit the final corner. "Think about what you're doing. You might actually own your own business. That's . . . impressive," she grunted before the sheet snapped into place.

Judy had the folded top sheet in her hands and pressed it against her chest. "I'm pretty excited. And scared. And a little nervous, but thank you." She shook her head. "I can't remember the last time you gave me a compliment."

Candy dropped her gaze for a moment. When she looked up, her eyes were misty. "I can't remember the last time you gave me one, either, but that's not your fault. It's mine. B-but I want that, you know."

Judy swallowed hard. "You want a compliment?"

Taking a deep breath, Candy shook her head. "No. I don't just want a compliment from you. I want you to be proud of me. *I* want to be proud of me. And I want Brian to be proud of me, too. I'm getting there, I think, but I still have a long way to go. I know that, but I've really tried hard to change these past six months and I'm excited . . . and scared . . . and a little nervous, too."

Judy's heart skipped a beat, and she worried the edge of the sheet in her hands. Having an open, honest conversation with her daughter, without anger or disgust, was so rare she barely knew what to do or to think, beyond the desperate need to hold on to this moment. "It sounds like we're both ready for a change, for a new beginning. Maybe . . . maybe it's time we tried working together on the same side as a team instead of being opponents. I—I never wanted it that way," she admitted.

"I never did, either. Not really. I'm sorry, Mom . . . for everything."

When a long silence ensued, each of them apparently unsure of what to say, Judy opened up the flat sheet and started tucking in the bottom on her side of the bed.

Candy followed suit. "I wish . . . I wish it wasn't too late for me to tell Daddy that I was sorry, and that I loved him."

Judy squared the corner of the sheet. She smoothed the top of the bed with the palm of her hand, as if she were caressing the memory of her late husband, even as bitter memories of his viewing tried to surface. "I think he knew, sweetie. He knows now, though."

Candy smoothed her side of the top sheet into place and folded down the top. "I wish I could say something to apologize for making such a scene at the viewing, but between the drugs and Duke and the sight of Daddy lying there so cold . . ." She shivered. "I can't honestly remember what happened or why. It's all a blur. All I can remember is feeling so empty and so dumb, like I'd lost any chance ever to make Daddy love me again or be proud of me."

Judy blinked back tears. "He always loved you. I've always loved you. We didn't always like you or what you were doing or what you'd become. We just felt so helpless watching you destroy yourself with drugs. We made lots of mistakes. All parents do. But we loved you," she insisted and cocked a brow. "We really didn't like you a lot of times, and we sure didn't understand you, but . . . but we always loved you."

Candy swiped at her own tears. "I wish I could believe that."

Judy slipped the case on each of the two pillows and tossed one to her daughter. "Believe it."

Sniffling, Candy tossed the pillow back. "It's not that easy."

"How much do you love Brian?" Judy asked, lobbing the pillow across the bed again. "For all your yesterdays, and today, and all your tomorrows. How much do you love him? Enough to forgive him when he does something wrong?"

Candy threw the pillow sideways at Judy. "He's my son. Of course I do."

Judy tilted up her chin and tossed the pillow back again. "Enough to let him make his own mistakes, even if they're big ones, and watch him suffer through the consequences without saying, 'I told you so,' and praying with all your heart that he can do it, and crying yourself to sleep at night when he fails?"

Candy squared her shoulders. "If I have to." She hugged the pillow to her chest. "Is that what you and Daddy did?"

Judy cringed. "No. You know we didn't. We tried, but in all honesty, I know I wasn't as good a parent as your father. I know I didn't miss an opportunity to say, 'I told you so.' I tried to soften the consequences and make excuses for you when you missed a curfew or said you weren't smoking or . . . or worse. I cried myself to sleep at night, though, and I prayed sometimes. But that wasn't enough, was it? And I'm sorry, Candy. I wish I could do it over again. Maybe things would have been different for you if I'd been a better mother, but at the time, I guess I did the best I could."

Judy's words hung in the air like a curtain separating the past from the present. She waited, patiently, to see whether or not Candy would accept her mother's apology and pull that curtain back to let the light of honesty and forgiveness shine on the present and guide their way through the future.

With a sigh, Candy laid her cheek on top of the pillow she held. "I spent a lot of hours in therapy talking about us, about growing up, and about growing apart. I've spent a lot of hours talking about Brian and the kind of mother I've been to him so far. I wish I could do it all over again, but I guess I just did the best for him that I could, too. But I want to do better. I want to be a better mother, a better person, a better daughter."

Judy tossed a second pillow at her daughter. "Believe it."

Candy was so surprised when the pillow hit her shoulder, she let it fall to the bed. "Are you picking a fight with me?" she asked, holding her own pillow in front of her like a shield.

"Only if you want one. If you don't believe in yourself, if you don't believe God will never let you struggle alone, even if no one else seems to care, then you've given up the fight already."

With a twinkle in her eye, Candy tossed her pillow at Judy with one hand and grabbed the pillow from the bed with the other for protection. "Okay. I believe. Do you?"

"Me?" Judy snatched the pillow, tossed it up in the air and let it land on the floor behind her. "Yes, I believe. I believe in God. I trust Him to help me to believe in myself, and I trust Him to help me believe in you. It's not going to be easy. Not for either one of us," she warned. "This old house is chock-full of memories and not all of them are good. Brian's really happy you're here, but you have a lot of mending to do with your son. And somehow, we've got to work out exactly how we're going to manage living together again for a little while and how soon you might be able to live with Brian on your own."

"I know," Candy murmured and stood up straighter.

"And living in Welleswood again means you're going to need a pretty thick skin, too. This is a small town, but people have big memories and lots of folks, unfortunately, like to gossip."

"Daddy always said I had more guts than brains," she argued.

"Well you'll need both, along with a good dose of faith."

Candy put her pillow at the top of the bed. "That's easy."

"Really?" Judy picked up her pillow from the floor, dusted it off, and put it on the bed.

"Sure, Mom. Any time I run short of guts or brains or

faith, I'll just borrow some. You've got plenty, right?"

Judy smiled. Whether it took guts or brains or faith or just a whole bunch of love, she had plenty of each and no one she would like to share them with more than her daughter. "One day at a time," she cautioned, praying each day would lead to weeks and then months and perhaps years of a drug-free life for her daughter.

"What about tomorrow? Were you really serious about asking Ann to let me help out at the salon?"

Judy laughed. "Sure I was serious. I'll call her tomorrow. You can't do much with the customers, though. Not without a license. Since Ann will be working in clients' homes, you could open up in the morning and get everything ready for me, make appointments and clean up. I could teach you how to order the supplies, too."

"Great."

"No, *great* would be if you were computer savvy and could not only put all of our old records on my very new, very neglected and very confusing computer, but get it up and running to handle the current business."

Candy's grin stretched from ear to ear and back again. "Get ready for great, Mom."

"Y-you know computers?"

"Compliments of the great state of California. Sleep in tomorrow. All I need is the key to the salon. After I get Brian to school, I'll open up the salon and start the computer work before you get there."

"Pinch me. I must be dreaming."

"Only if you'll pinch me back," Candy teased.

Judy picked up a pillow. "Would you settle for a pillow fight?"

Candy's eyes widened. "Mom! Are you serious? First we have ice cream at Scoops for dinner. Now you want a pillow fight?" She shook her head. "You're losing it, Mom."

Judy swung a pillow at her. "And it feels good, too!"

"Mom!"

"Come on, Candy. It's fun! Give it your best!"

"Mom, you're acting crazy. This is silly!"

"Just making up for missed opportunities," she countered and squealed when Candy swung a pillow in her direction. There would be plenty of days ahead when serious issues would arise, when they would lock horns and disagree, especially where Brian was concerned, and it would take a long time before Judy truly trusted her daughter again.

But right now, their tomorrows would have to wait.

Right now, today was all that mattered.

Today, joy and laughter felt just about right.

Chapter Twenty-Six

The following Monday had *detour* written all over it.

Despite all her efforts to carefully plan out her day, Ginger met one roadblock after another, and she had to scramble again and again to reorganize her day. Vincent's three-thirty dentist appointment, a routine six-month checkup, had to be rescheduled for the next day when the dentist had an unexpected emergency. Tyler's business trip was still on, but his flight to Atlanta had been canceled. He had managed to book a later flight, which meant she would be cooking instead of taking Vincent out for a quick supper. When she realized she had left all the notes she had made for the Mother's Day Breakfast at home on the kitchen counter, she left work even earlier to rush home before meeting Barbara and Judy at The Diner.

She slipped in the back door and headed straight for the folder. A steady beeping challenged the silence in the house to announce there were telephone messages and led her from the counter to the telephone. Despite the national Do Not Call list, she and Tyler usually had several solicitations on the answering machine daily. She would barely be on time as it was, and she was half-tempted to erase the messages without bothering to listen to them. The very nature of her day, however, encouraged her to take the time to check the messages, but she did not bother to remove her coat.

About ten seconds into the first message, announcing that Vincent was entitled to a full year's supply of vitamins, she hit the skip button. Ditto for the second message announcing Tyler had won yet another free trip to Florida. She had her hand poised to hit the skip button one last time for the third message—until she heard Lily's voice.

"Mom? It's me. I know you're at work, but I need to talk to you. Please call me back on my cell phone as soon as you get home. It's important, but don't say anything to Vincent. Thanks."

Ginger pressed Save and replayed the message. There was no sense of urgency or sadness in Lily's words, but Ginger did detect a high level of stress. Worried about Lily and the baby she was carrying, yet hopeful Lily had finally realized she had made a mistake by hiding Vincent away, Ginger checked the caller ID for Lily's number and called her immediately.

Lily answered on the first ring. "Mom?"

"Yes. What's wrong? Are you all right? Is the baby—"

"We're fine. Look, now's not a good time for me to talk. I thought you wouldn't be home till after three. Can I call you back in a little bit?"

"No. I have a meeting. I'm already late. Can't you at least tell me—"

"I'll call you back in five minutes. Please wait. It's important," she insisted and hung up.

Ginger stared at the telephone in her hand for a moment, gritted her teeth and prayed for patience as yet another roadblock detoured her plans for the day. "It's important to you," she grumbled. "It's always important to you." Frustrated and close to anger at her daughter for being so selfish and at herself for letting Lily impose her will, Ginger channeled her negative emotions into positive action. After she put her coat on the back of a kitchen chair, she pulled the café curtains open to let in the afternoon sun and started to empty the dishwasher.

Her mind, however, raced through a barrage of thoughts, which she sorted into useless and constructive. As she stacked the dinner plates and put them back into the top cabinet, she tried to filter out useless thoughts such as how selfish Lily had become and how difficult it was to understand Lily's ease at walking away from Vincent or how unfair it was that Ginger would never really know Lily's new child, her own grandchild. Mercy, Ginger did not even know when Lily's baby was due, although she guessed sometime between early to late spring.

She lined up the mugs and glasses in the cabinet, one by one, and shook her head. She used to be an optimist, seeing every glass half-full instead of half-empty. But one abbreviated call from Lily and every glass looked totally empty, just like any hope she'd had that Lily would come to her senses.

She carried the utensil basket to the drawer. While she sorted the flatware into the appropriate sections, she whispered the little prayer she had learned as a child. "All I need is a forkful of faith, and a knife to slice through my fears. With a spoonful of God's precious mercy, I'll be patient and kind all my years." She bowed her head and repeated the prayer silently again, afraid she would need the drawerful of flatware to make it through her conversation with Lily with both patience and kindness.

After ten minutes passed with no call from Lily, Ginger called The Diner and left a message for Barbara and Judy telling them she had a problem at home and would not be able to meet with them today, but she would see them next Monday. When the telephone finally rang a long fifteen minutes later, Ginger saw Lily's cell phone number on the caller ID, picked up the receiver and closed her eyes for a moment to help her concentrate. Patience and kindness. "Yes, Lily."

"I'm sorry, Mom. Things are pretty hectic right now. Paul and I moved into our own home last week, but there are still workmen everywhere."

Ginger did not respond.

"Well, anyway, here's the problem. Mother Taft wants to meet you and Daddy. I've been putting her off for months now, but she's been pressuring me pretty hard lately to have you both up for a weekend. I—I'm running out of excuses, and I was wondering . . ." She paused to take a deep breath. "I was wondering if you and Daddy could come to Boston this weekend to meet the Tafts. It'll only be this once."

Ginger clenched her free hand into a fist and battled tears. "I wasn't aware your Daddy and I were such a problem to you, or that you needed to make excuses for us or that you even cared to see us."

"That's not what I meant." She huffed. "You have no idea how hard it's been for me, and with the baby coming in April—"

"It's been hard on everyone here, too." She paused before she lost her patience. Maybe she had misunderstood what Lily meant. Maybe Lily was really reaching out and trying to bring her son back into her life. "What about Vincent? Are we supposed to bring him with us for this weekend get-together?"

"Mom, you know he can't come. Couldn't you get a sitter for him? It's only for the weekend."

Disappointment filled Ginger's spirit. "No, it's not just the weekend. It's more than that. My problem is that you want us to come up to Boston and lie for you and pretend he doesn't even exist. I won't do that, and I don't need to talk to your father to know that he wouldn't do that, either. Besides, what would we tell Vincent? That we're going to see his mother, but he can't go with us because she doesn't want to see him?"

"Vincent wouldn't have to know you were coming to see me. Mom, please. This means a lot to me."

"And you mean even more to me," Ginger countered, "but I won't lie to the Tafts for you and I won't lie to Vincent, either. I've done quite enough of that already, hoping you'll realize how foolish you've been before I have to tell him he won't ever be able to go home with you. Apparently, you still don't have a clue about what you're doing to your son, do you?"

Lily's voice turned shrill. "I'm doing what's best for everyone. I'm sorry if you don't understand that, but . . . never mind. You've actually made it easy for me. Now I won't have to make up an excuse. I can tell Mother Taft the truth this time. You were invited, but refused to come."

Ginger blinked hard, but tears still blurred her vision and she lost her final grip on patience. "Don't delude yourself. You can't claim to tell the truth unless you tell the whole truth, Lily, and that means telling your in-laws about Vincent. You can't build a life on a foundation of lies. Sooner or later, when you can't tell the truth from the lies, it might be too late and the very things you want will slip out of your grasp," she warned.

Drawing a deep breath she went on. "Daddy and I love you, but we don't understand you anymore. More importantly, Vincent loves you and he needs you. You're his mother, and as much as Daddy and I try, we can't take your place. That's the truth, the only truth you need to think about."

"You're so, so wrong, Mom. The truth is you're— you're jealous," Lily snapped.

"Jealous? Of what?"

Lily snorted. "Don't be absurd."

"No, you're absurd if you think for one moment you can continue to act like a selfish brat and blame anything that happens when you don't get your way on me or your father," she said, losing her struggle to be kind or understanding. "You want the truth? Take a good hard look at yourself in the mirror. I don't think you'll like what you see. I know I sure don't like what I see in you anymore."

"Just . . . just forget I called, Mom, and I'll do my best to forget, too. But don't count on it. In the meantime, I'm going to contact a few of those boarding schools again and see if I can't find a better place for Vincent to live. That way you won't have to worry about ever seeing him again, either, because I'll make sure you won't," she threatened and disconnected.

Trembling, Ginger barely managed to hang up the telephone before she collapsed into a chair at the kitchen table. She was ashamed of herself for losing her temper and she was beyond distraught to think that her last words to her daughter had flowed from a fountain of anger—words she could never take back. She cradled her face in her hands, muffling the sound of her deep, chest-rattling sobs that filled the air. Overwrought, she made no excuses for herself and faced a bitter truth of her own. Because of her anger, she had lost more than her daughter, probably for good. She may have lost her grandson, too.

Gradually, her sobs subsided into quiet weeping.

If only she had been more patient with Lily.

If only she had been kinder to Lily.

If only . . .

Startled by an urgent rap at the kitchen door, she stiffened and sat up straight. She wiped her face with her hands and pressed the palm of her hand hard against her forehead. She couldn't let anyone see her now. She did not have to look in the mirror to know her eyes were red and swollen and her makeup was smeared beyond repair.

"Ginger? We know you're in there. It's Barbara and Judy."

Ginger groaned softly and caught her breath for a moment. Maybe if she held very still, they would think she was upstairs and could not hear them at the door.

Judy, however, made that idea impossible when she suddenly appeared outside the kitchen window, peeked inside and waved.

With no choice left to her, Ginger got up from the table and opened the door. She even managed half a smile. "I'm sorry. Didn't you get my message?"

"They told us at The Diner you had a problem at home so we thought we'd see if we could help," Barbara offered.

"You look like you might need someone to talk to," Judy suggested.

Close to tears again, Ginger swallowed hard. "I'm a mess, inside and out," she murmured. Self-consciously, she wiped at her cheeks again. "I'm not sure talking about it would solve anything."

"It might make you feel better," Barbara countered.

Judy shrugged. "But maybe not. Talking about it might even make you feel worse. Probably will, since neither one of us has a single problem in our lives big enough to make us cry our hearts out in the middle of the day," she warned sarcastically. "Come on. Grab your coat. The sun's warm. Let's just take a long walk together. You won't have to say a word, and the fresh air will do you good."

Barbara smiled. "Just a walk sounds good to me. How about a stroll around the park?"

Outnumbered and anxious to avoid talking about her disastrous conversation with her daughter, Ginger grabbed her coat and a house key. Once she was outside, she locked the door behind her and followed her friends around the side of the house to the front sidewalk.

Judy, however, led them into the street. When Ginger and Barbara hesitated, she laughed. "Come on. We're all big girls. We can walk in the street without getting hit by a car. The sidewalk isn't wide enough for all three of us to walk side by side."

Ginger was too drained to argue. She fell in step with Barbara on one side of her and Judy on the other. As promised, neither of her friends attempted to start a conversation. Within a block or two, Ginger relaxed enough to set aside her troubled thoughts and concentrate on just walking and enjoying the fresh air.

The sun was warm for January. The air was cold, but not biting, and the desolate landscape matched her mood. Barren trees and gardens gave the neighborhood an open feel and provided good views of backyards no longer blocked by lush summer foliage. Overhead, nests abandoned by birds and squirrels lay waiting to be filled again when another cycle of birth began in the spring. Still early afternoon, the day was hushed, except for the sound of their footsteps on the paved streets which were still stained by road salt and littered with sand along the curbs—streets that would again be covered with snow before winter's end.

When they finally reached Welles Park, Ginger slipped her hands into her coat pockets and followed Judy's lead across the crisp, short grass to the lake at the center of the park. The gazebo at the opposite end of the lake offered seating, but also shadowed the sun. Ginger was glad they continued to walk instead. The lake was no longer frozen, and a flock of Canada geese pecked along the shoreline just beyond the reach of the cold gray water.

The fountain in the middle of the lake had been turned off for winter, and in her mind's eye, Ginger saw the lake as it had been on New Year's Eve for the prayer service. The memory of all those luminaries on the lake, however, did not lift the darkness from her spirit.

Ginger paused for a moment, spied the log near the shore of the lake where she and Tyler and Vincent had perched to put on their skates on Christmas Day and ambled toward it. When she sat down, her friends joined her, one on either side of her like bookends. "We made a lot of memories here," she whispered. She glanced at the lake, numb to all thoughts now save for her conversation with Lily and the possibility that Vincent would be taken away from her and Tyler.

Although Ginger knew she could tell Barbara and Judy almost anything, she did not want to rehash her conversation with Lily. Not right now. Her despair at this moment ran too deep. Her thoughts wandered back to the early years of her marriage when her three children had been babies—years when she and Tyler and the children had been so happy together. She sighed. "When you first became a mother, did either of you think there would ever be anything that would come between you and your baby? That there would come a time when you would be estranged?"

"Never," Judy whispered.

"Not once," Barbara murmured. "Any more than I ever thought I'd outlive one of my sons."

"Why is that?" Ginger asked. "I mean, if the bonds were so strong between us, what went wrong? What could I have possibly done to deserve this kind of pain? That's what I don't understand. I'm not an evil person. I try to keep my faith strong, but I don't understand why this is happening to me any more than I could try to explain what's happened to each of you. I know lots of women, and they don't have these problems with their children. Why me? Why both of you?"

Barbara let out a long sigh. "First of all, you don't know what problems other women might or might not have with their children. Still, I wish I knew the answers to your questions, but I'm afraid I don't."

"Neither do I," Judy agreed. "But at this point, I'm not sure I worry so much about why it's happening to me or whether or not I deserve it. I'm having enough trouble living day to day with the reality that it has happened." She shook her head. "With Candy home now, it's no different today than it was the last time she tried to stop using drugs. I still love my daughter. I just can't trust her. Not completely. Maybe I never will, but I still have to think twice about leaving my purse lying around for fear she'll take money again for drugs. I'm not totally comfortable leaving her alone with Brian, not for very long. When I go to bed at night, I'm half-afraid that I'll wake up in the morning and she'll be gone . . . and so will he."

She picked up a pebble and tossed it into the lake, sending ripples across the still water. "Candy is helping out at the salon now and getting the records onto the computer. She really seems to know what she's doing. I started computer classes this morning anyway. Not because she can't teach me herself, or even because the bank insists that I finish computer classes in an accredited program before reviewing my application for a loan again. It's because I don't trust her to show me everything, so I would know if she was cheating us or not. How sad is that?"

"It's very sad, but it's also very smart," Barbara suggested. "Once trust has been betrayed, it's very hard to get it back, especially when it involves one of our children. Remember, you'll be taking a very big risk buying Pretty Ladies. Protecting that risk for your sake as well as Brian's will be important."

"True," Ginger noted and fidgeted on the log to find a more comfortable spot. "But that's exactly my point. Judy's worked hard all her life. She's a good person. She doesn't deserve to have this kind of heartache and stress, especially at this stage of her life."

"But maybe that's not the point," Barbara argued. "Maybe it's not about whether or not anyone deserves to have heartache or disappointment. Maybe it's more about having faith that you can endure it," she said softly. "I think that's where I'm stuck, at least today. I worry about my faith. I worry that I won't be able to endure the heartache that lies just below the surface on some days and on others . . . I feel like I have no faith at all and I'm being strangled with grief for the son I've lost. I just want my faith to be strong enough to stop that."

Ginger snorted. "What good is faith if it doesn't stop the heartache or the grief or the stress?"

"Faith is just faith," Barbara argued. "I guess it's pretty easy to have faith when everything is good in your life."

"It's not so easy when everything falls apart, though," Ginger observed.

"But it's only difficult if you expect faith to erase all the heartache. Maybe we shouldn't expect faith to do that," Judy insisted. "I'm not sure if it will help, but here's how I'm trying to see it. Life is one bumpy road, full of potholes and sharp curves and more than a few dead ends. Having faith doesn't mean the road miraculously changes into a smooth one. And faith isn't like some road crew that comes along and fills in all the potholes or eases the curves or puts up barricades to keep you out of the dead ends. Faith just means you bump along, get stuck in a pothole once in a while, take a curve too fast, or find yourself backing up after reaching a dead end. With faith, you just know, deep in your heart and soul, that faith will get you to the end of the bumpy road and lead you safely back Home."

Ginger bowed her head and closed her eyes. She thought about what Judy had said and embraced her wisdom. She looked up and smiled, first at Barbara and then Judy. "And if you're truly blessed, faith might even give you a friend or two to travel with you," she added, along with a silent prayer that each of them might hold on to their faith, as well as their friendship, in the weeks and months ahead.

For now, however, she needed to hold tight to her faith, if only to help her face the possibility that Vincent would no longer be part of their lives and be forced to grow up away from the grandparents who loved him.

Chapter Twenty-Seven

After cooking dinner, supervising Vincent's homework and tucking him into bed, Ginger got one last hug from Tyler before he left for Atlanta. "Call me when you get to your hotel," she told him.

He pressed a kiss to her forehead. "At two o'clock in the morning? Not a chance. I'll call you around eight while you and Vincent are having breakfast."

She held on tight, reluctant to be alone tonight. "I wish you didn't have to go."

"I'll be back Wednesday. Now listen. I don't want you to keep beating yourself up for what happened today with Lily. Maybe it was time for somebody to tell Lily the truth. I just wish I'd had the courage," he murmured.

"It wasn't courage," she argued. "I told you earlier. I just lost my temper. What if she never calls again?

What if she decides to take Vincent away from us and put him into a boarding school?"

"Stop." He set her back and locked his gaze with hers. "Lily is making her own choices, as bad as we think they are. Whether or not you got angry with her and said things you might regret now won't make her choices any better or any worse."

"No, but I shouldn't have pushed her so hard. I only wanted to make her understand—"

"You can't make Lily understand anything because you can't change her heart. Only Lily can do that. We've tried being patient with her, but maybe we've been too patient. Maybe we've made it too easy for her to put Vincent out of her life."

Ginger stiffened. "How? By keeping him with us instead of letting her ship him off to some academy where he'd grow up alone?"

"No. Well, maybe." He raked his fingers through his hair. "At this point, I honestly don't know."

When she glared at him, he smiled sheepishly. "Now don't go losing your temper with me. I love Vincent as much as you do. I'm not saying I don't want him here with us, but maybe we gave in to Lily too easily when she threatened to send him away the first time. Maybe we should have called her bluff."

"She knew us well enough to realize we'd never let her send Vincent away to live with strangers," she argued.

He raised a brow and silently challenged her to listen to her own words and take them to heart. When she did, she realized Lily's threat today had probably been an empty one. Her eyes widened. "Do you think she didn't mean it today?"

"I think that's a very strong possibility. Think about it. You got angry and refused to do what she wanted, so she got angry in return. She wanted to hurt you back. What's the one way she's got left to hurt you, other than continuing to exile herself and our next grandchild?"

"Taking Vincent," she murmured.

He raised a brow again.

She sighed and leaned against him. "You're a very wise man."

"Married to a very wise woman."

She looked up at him and furrowed her brow.

He chuckled. "You married me, didn't you?"

She nudged him away from her. "Go to Atlanta. I've got things to do."

He grabbed his suitcase and gave her a kiss. "I've got my cell phone with me so call me if there's a problem. Why don't you take a hot bath and go to bed early tonight? You'll feel better in the morning."

"I feel better already, but I'll feel much, much better after you call us in the morning," she reminded him. She watched him leave and stayed at the window until his car disappeared from view. Although it was only eight o'clock, she followed his advice. After a long, hot bath, she got into an old flannel nightgown. When she went down the hall to check on Vincent, she saw the light under his door go out and smiled. By the time she got to his room and peeked inside, he was perfectly poised in bed, feigning sleep.

Tears welled. She swallowed a lump in her throat. As hard as it would be to send him back to live with his mother, if and when Lily came to her senses, Ginger knew it would be the right thing to do. She could not stand by and let Lily pack him off to some year-round academy because it would break her heart, if not her spirit. They could fight Lily legally to keep custody of Vincent, if she tried to send him away.

She would have to fight Lily another way, but Tyler had been right. She could not change Lily's heart. But God could. Faith and prayer were Ginger's only weapons and she carried both with her back to her room. She climbed into bed and spent the next half hour in the dark, curled under the covers, deep in prayer that helped to lift the veil of sadness she had worn since earlier that afternoon.

As she was drifting off to sleep, she heard little footsteps out in the hallway. Vincent, however, was not heading toward the bathroom at the other end of the hall. He was coming toward her room. Concerned, she reached up and turned on the light. She had just slipped into her robe when he knocked at her door.

"Grams?"

"Come on in, sweetie."

He opened the door and poked his head inside.

"Having trouble sleeping tonight?"

He shook his head and came into her room carrying

his old sketch pad. She sat down on her bed and patted the quilt. "Sit down here with me."

He put the sketch pad on the bed, climbed up next to her, and sat cross-legged. When he looked up at her, his gaze was troubled. "Are you still sad?"

She tussled his hair. "What makes you think I'm sad?" she asked, all too aware of how badly she had failed to mask her emotions in front of him.

"I get sad sometimes, too," he murmured.

She sighed. "Yes, I guess you do. I think everybody gets sad once in a while, and today was my day," she admitted. "Do you want to talk about what makes you sad?"

He stared at his lap. "No. Not tonight. Do you?"

"No. Not tonight," she whispered, taking her cue from him. "But I think I won't be sad tomorrow. That's what happens, you know. One day you can get real sad, but the next day is usually better."

"But I gotta go to the dentist tomorrow."

She chuckled. "You don't like going to the dentist?"

"Nope."

"Me, either, but we have to take good care of our teeth, don't we?"

"I guess."

"There must be something about tomorrow that will make you not feel sad," she insisted. "Don't you have a spelling test tomorrow?"

He grinned. "I'm a good speller."

"See? Getting a chance to prove you're a good speller will make you happy, won't it?"

He nodded. "What about you? What are you gonna do tomorrow that won't make you sad anymore?"

"Hmm. Let's see. I have to work tomorrow while you're in school. Maybe I'll eat a piece of chocolate. That usually makes me happy."

"Don't you have any chocolate you can eat tonight?"

She frowned, even though she seriously considered going downstairs and raiding the cupboard to find the bag of chocolate kisses she hid for emergencies. "Even if I did, it's too late to eat chocolate. Besides, I already brushed my teeth."

"When I'm sad, I look at my pictures." He reached over and pulled the sketch pad onto his lap. "Maybe you could look at them so you won't be so sad tonight."

Moved to tears, she had to blink them away. Once he had started art lessons, Vincent had shared his new drawings, but he had never shared the pictures in his old sketch pad with them before. She was incredibly touched by his concern for her and just as curious to see what he had kept private for so long. "Are you sure you want to share them with me?"

Instead of responding, he opened his sketch pad and started at the back with the last page. "This is Gramps, but I'm not done yet. I still gotta finish it."

Speechless, Ginger stared at the pencil portrait of her husband and tried to reconcile the childish sketch she had expected to see with the startling image Vincent had drawn. Though the portrait was not as good as a professional one, Vincent's talent was nothing short of amazing—if indeed he had drawn this picture by himself. "Y-you drew this? Mr. Andrews didn't help you?" she asked, suspecting his art teacher might have helped him more than a little.

"Mr. Andrews makes me draw pears and apples sitting in a bowl, but I like to draw people better," he explained and quickly turned the page, working toward the front of the sketch pad. "See? That's you, Grams."

Sure enough, her own image stared back at her. He had even drawn her favorite pair of dangle earrings. "Yes, it is. You're a wonderful artist, Vincent."

"Wanna see more?"

She smiled. "Who's next?"

He hesitated, then turned back a page. "Do you think this looks like my mom?"

She caught her breath for a moment and traced the features he had drawn with the tip of her finger. How could he have captured that look in Lily's eyes so well? "I think it looks just like your mom," she managed after she swallowed the lump in her throat. "You miss her a lot, don't you?"

He rubbed the tip of his nose. "She's pretty busy right now, but I think she misses me a whole lot. Do you think she gets sad sometimes, too?"

"Yes, I'm sure she does," Ginger murmured, unable and unwilling to crush his hopes and tell him his mother was not coming for him any time soon. Not now. Not tonight. "Who else have you drawn?"

"Lots of people, but you don't know them. They live in Chicago."

"I'd still like to see their pictures," she suggested, curious about the people who had been important in his life before he had come to live with his grandparents.

He continued working forward in the sketch pad. "This is Mrs. Washington. She had five cats." He shivered. "They were mean old cats, too. See?" He held out his hand and pointed to a very thin white scar on the tip of his baby finger. "I got bit once right there."

She grimaced. "I guess that hurt!"

"My mom got mad and said I didn't have to get babysitted by Mrs. Washington any more, but we were moving soon anyway so she let me live at Mrs. Washington's house for a little bit more."

"You lived there at Mrs. Washington's house?" she asked, certain she had misunderstood him.

He nodded. "My mom was always real busy, but she came to see me sometimes. Once we went to the aquarium. We liked the turtles best."

Stunned to learn her daughter had left Vincent to live with a sitter, Ginger embraced Lily's threat to enroll him in a boarding school as very, very real.

"I liked Nancy better," he offered and turned back another page, revealing the image of a teenage girl with short spiked hair and a nose ring. "She had seven holes in one of her ears. See?" He pointed to one of her ears and counted each of the holes. "She said it didn't hurt when she got them holes, but I think it did."

"Smart boy! Did you live with Nancy, too?"

"No. She babysitted me when Mrs. Washington had to go out."

He introduced six more babysitters, one picture at a time. First, Mrs. C. Her last name was too hard to pronounce. According to Vincent, she had a lot of children to watch every day, and he had made lots of friends at her house, naming Hannah, Dillon, Kaylee, Colin and Mikey as the friends he missed most now. "Me and Mikey had bunk beds at Mrs. C.'s house," he announced. "I wanted to sleep up top, but Mrs. C. said I was too little." He lowered his voice as if Mrs. C. might overhear him. "One time, after Mikey fell asleep, I tried to climb up the ladder, but I got scared. I'm bigger now. I don't think I'd get scared if I tried to climb the ladder again."

"I don't think you would, either," she assured him. "Would you like to have bunk beds for your room here?"

His eyes twinkled. "Could I sleep in the top bunk?"

"I don't see why not. We'll talk to Gramps when he gets back from Atlanta, how's that? Show me who's next in your sketch pad."

He identified the next woman, who appeared to be in her late fifties as Mrs. Garinetti. He loved her spaghetti. Good thing. She served it every day for dinner, but he had his own room at her house, which he liked a lot. Betty, another adolescent sitter, was one of his favorites because she took him to the mall with her to hang out with her friends.

"Did she babysit you when you lived with Mrs. C.?" Ginger asked, wondering how he had survived layer upon layer of caregivers.

"Betty lived with me and my mom for a little while, but then she had a baby and we didn't have enough room, so I went to live with Mrs. Scott." He went on to describe how the woman, who looked rather grumpy, had a menagerie of reptiles, including snakes and lizards, which she used to threaten to turn loose to keep some of the children she cared for in line. "She made the snake eat a real mouse," he exclaimed and proceeded to demonstrate by lying down and wriggling about on the floor like a snake and using his fist to represent the mouse.

"Why didn't the mouse run away?" Barbara asked, trying not to laugh.

Flushed and breathless, he stood up. "'Cause she freezed the mouse first."

"Oh! That sounds awful!"

"Nah. It didn't hurt the mouse. She fed the snake goldfish, too, but the lizard ate crickets. Sometimes I helped her catch them in the garden. Crickets like to hide under rocks." He plopped back up on the bed and sat down beside her again. "That's all I drawed 'cause I don't remember my babysitters when I was little."

She shook her head. "No, I suppose you don't," she murmured.

"I like you and Gramps the most," he whispered. "You're the best babysitters I ever had."

She hugged him hard. "We're not babysitters, Vincent. We're your grandparents. Your family." Almost overwhelmed with guilt for not knowing how her own grandson had been raised and not intervening before now, she fought back more tears. Knowing the sheer number of caregivers during the eight years of his life certainly helped to explain how he had adapted so easily to living with his grandparents. His allegiance to his mother, however, remained strong which only served as a reminder of the strength of the bond between mother and child and the need for Vincent to maintain contact with his mother, even if he could not live with her.

Missing from his collection, oddly, was a picture of Lily's husband. "What about your stepfather? Now that you have a new sketch pad, are you going to draw him?"

Vincent closed his sketch pad. "I think I wanna draw Officer Joe. He's cool."

Her eyes widened. Vincent had not said much after coming home from spending time with the young officer last Saturday, and she was pleased Vincent was willing to talk about it with her now. "Cool?"

He grinned. "He's got a real gun and handcuffs. Me and Brian wanted to get cuffed together, but Officer Joe said we had to wait a while."

She laughed. "Wait for what?"

"Till after we had ice cream. Then he let us take

turns sitting on his bike and we forgot to ask him again. Next time I see him, I'm gonna remind him." He tilted up his chin. "I wanna be a policeman when I grow up."

"Like Officer Joe," she added, grateful that the young officer had taken an interest in her grandson.

"He comes to our school sometimes and tells us stories. But when I'm a policeman, I'm gonna arrest all the bad guys and lock 'em up with handcuffs."

"You really did like those handcuffs, didn't you?" she teased.

He grinned. "But I like ice cream better. Do you think Gramps is gonna have ice cream on the plane tonight?"

"I doubt it. They usually don't give the passengers ice cream. Maybe a small bag of pretzels and something to drink."

His eyes lit with mischief. "Like soda?"

"Or coffee or tea or a glass of milk."

"Milk and pretzels? Yuck!" He wrinkled his nose. "Ice cream and pretzels is better. Want me to show you?"

She laughed out loud. "We both brushed our teeth, remember?"

"We could brush them again."

Still laughing, she got up from the bed and held out her hand. "Forget about being a police officer, Vincent. You'd make a fine lawyer."

He scooted off the bed. "Do lawyers get to use handcuffs?"

"No. Now stop. Enough with the handcuffs!"

He giggled. "Wanna know something, Grams?" he asked as she took him downstairs for some ice cream and pretzels.

She held up her hand. "Only if it has absolutely nothing to do with handcuffs."

"Nope."

"Okay, tell me."

"I don't think you're so sad anymore."

"Not anymore." She hugged him to her, closed her eyes, and wondered if Lily would ever understand she was missing out on a very great blessing indeed—a blessing named Vincent.

Once she was certain Vincent was finally asleep, Ginger slipped downstairs at ten o'clock. Tyler's plane was still in the air, so she left a message for him on his cell phone to call her back tonight, making it clear that it was not an emergency.

While she waited for him to call her back, she sat at the kitchen table and leafed through yesterday's Sunday newspaper again. She tore out several ads for furniture stores likely to carry bunk beds. Her thoughts, however, remained troubled as she recalled her conversation with Vincent, along with her conversations with Lily and Tyler. Then an idea came to her—inspired and devious—and she set the paper aside. She rushed upstairs to the attic and rooted through some old papers until she had what she needed.

Prepared, yet uncertain whether or not Tyler would share her enthusiasm for her idea, she went back down to the kitchen. While she continued waiting for his call, she clipped coupons from the newspaper circulars to donate to the coupon box at church where members could help themselves to the coupons they needed.

When the telephone rang just after two o'clock, it startled her awake. She had fallen asleep at the kitchen table with the scissors still in her hand. She tossed the scissors aside and picked up the telephone before it woke up Vincent.

"Tyler?"

"I just got to my room and checked my messages. What's wrong?"

"Lily isn't bluffing." She gave him a synopsis of her talk with Vincent. "That's why we have to take her threat seriously," she said when she finished.

"After what you've told me, I'm afraid I have to agree with you."

"I don't like being threatened, and I don't like Vincent being used like a pawn, either. I've thought about what you said earlier, and I think you were right. Up to now, we've made it too easy for Lily, and I think we've let her manipulate us one time too many."

"So what should we do?"

"We call her bluff and force her to agree to our terms," she replied. "When you finish your meetings in Atlanta on Wednesday, is there anything at the office here that can't wait for a day or two?"

"Probably not. Why?"

She drew in a deep breath. "There's no reason to doubt what Vincent told us, but we need proof. I want you to go to Chicago," she replied and outlined her idea which relied in no small measure on Tyler's contacts in the security business. When he agreed, she gave him Lily's social security number, all the old addresses for Lily she'd been able to find, the names of the babysitters Vincent had drawn, and the name of the school where Lily had said she had worked.

"That's probably all I'll need, but I'll call you tomorrow night," he promised. "I think we both need to think this through very, very carefully. If we make a single mistake, we could lose our grandson for good. Are you willing to take that risk?"

She swallowed hard. "I love him too much not to try."

Chapter Twenty-Eight

Barbara arrived well ahead of time for the meeting for the first Mother's Day Breakfast.

Finding a table or booth at The Diner at one o'clock in the afternoon was a lot like finding an open pew in church five minutes after holiday services had begun. So, Barbara had arrived at noon, before the lunch rush. She spent the hour drinking coffee and reviewing her notes. She was so engrossed in her work, she only realized someone had joined her when she heard the whoosh of the red vinyl seat cushion across from her.

She looked up, expecting to see either Judy or Ginger, but it was an old friend who returned her smile. "Madge! I haven't seen you in ages. How are you?" She laughed. "Forget I asked. You've got a great tan and look totally relaxed which means you must have gone south for the holidays."

"We took Sarah to Aruba. After all the snow we had, I told Russell if I didn't get these old bones good and warm at Christmas, I'd never make it until spring." Her gaze softened. "How are you doing?"

Barbara drew a deep breath. "This is a good day. Actually, most days are pretty good. I'm waiting for Judy and Ginger." She pointed to the papers she had spread out in front of her. "We're getting together to plan the Mother's Day Breakfast for the PTA. I'm sure you know the drill. Do one good job for the PTA and you're always asked to do another. Would you like to join us for lunch?"

"No, thanks. I can't stay. I was just passing by on my way to the store when I saw you sitting here. I popped in to see how you were doing." She glanced at the papers. "Are you sure the breakfast is something you want to work on? It's awfully soon . . ."

With a sigh, Barbara leaned against the back wall of the booth. "When Pam called Ginger to ask the three of us, she had the same concern."

Madge frowned. "Pam's doing a great job as PTA president, but she shouldn't have asked any of you to work on the breakfast. Sometimes I think my Sarah, who is only five, has more common sense than that woman."

"I have to admit I was a little taken aback, at first, but now I think it might be a good thing for all of us. It's not going to be easy, but I realized that one way I could honor Steve and his memory was to make this Mother's Day very special instead of trying to ignore it. Working with Judy and Ginger helps me a lot because I know I'm not the only one who's going to find the day . . . difficult."

Before Madge could respond, the waitress arrived. "Sorry. It's been busy. Can I get you something, Madge?"

"No thanks, Caroline. I'm not staying."

"More coffee, Barbara?"

Barbara put her hand over her cup. "I'm good for now."

"Give a wave if you change your mind," she said and left to clear another table.

Before Madge left, she took Barbara's hand. "Call me if you need anything. Help planning the breakfast. A sitter. Or just someone to listen. Promise?"

Smiling, Barbara nodded.

Madge's seat was still warm when Ginger and Judy arrived together. They hung up their coats and slid across from Barbara. "Looks like you got started without us," Judy noted.

Ginger giggled. "Good. I'm sure Barbara's ideas are going to be a whole lot better than mine," she teased and laid her folder on the table next to Judy's, leaving little room for anything else.

Laughing, Barbara scooped up her papers. "I think we might need a bigger table."

"We need lunch," Judy countered. "I'm starving."

Caroline immediately appeared with pen and pad in hand. "Do you want to know the specials?"

Barbara looked around the table. Judy and Ginger shook their heads. "Not today."

They placed their orders and chatted throughout their lunch. By the time Caroline returned to clear away the dishes, the crowd of diners had thinned. "I guess I'll go first," Barbara suggested. "After I looked over the programs from the past few years, along with the notes made by the women who have organized the breakfast before us, I thought we might follow the same basic format, but with a few changes. Instead of Reverend Fisher starting with an invocation and a speech, I thought it would be nice if he did the invocation, but we asked his wife, Eleanor, to say a few words."

Judy nodded enthusiastically. "She's a mother and a grandmother and a very funny lady. She could keep the event from being too serious or too formal."

"Do you think she'd be willing to do it?" Ginger asked.

"I think she will, but I'll ask her," Barbara offered and jotted down a note to call Eleanor Fisher. "The organizers, that would be the three of us this year, usually sit at the head table with Reverend Fisher, the PTA President, the school board president and the mayor, with all of their spouses, of course. I'd rather sit at a regular table with my family, especially with the twins being here now. How about you? Head table or family table?"

"Family," they replied in unison.

Barbara wrote that down, too. "That means we'll need a smaller head table."

Ginger opened her folder. "Speaking of tables, we need a color scheme and flowers. The ladies who will be coming to the breakfast usually get corsages at church from the youth group, so I checked to make sure that's still planned for this year and it is, so we don't need to worry about it. We could save money and use the rolls of white paper tablecloths and add a little sparkle and color with fresh flower arrangements," she began.

One by one, they discussed and settled almost every detail of the event, from tickets to the meal to organizing the cleanup until they had only two items left. They would not be able to set the final price of the tickets until they had each followed through on their assigned tasks. Expanding the event to include any woman who had nurtured a child in the past or was nurturing a child now was perhaps their biggest challenge, which was why they had left it for last.

Judy was the first to offer an idea. "I talked with Penny at the Towers."

"You already said her daughter's Girl Scout troop volunteered to be servers," Barbara reminded her.

"Right, but I also asked her about the seniors, who are mostly women, by the way. Including them would be one way to expand the number of women who attend. Some of the seniors have children living in the area, but many of them don't. A few have either outlived their own children or never had any. Penny thinks there might be thirty or forty seniors, at most, who might want to attend. She also said there's money in the budget and she thinks the Commissioners might approve buying tickets for the seniors so they could all attend, if they wanted to, providing we could offer some sort of discount."

"I don't think offering a discount has ever been done before. At least I didn't read anything like that in the notes," Barbara responded.

"Me, either," Ginger added. "But I don't think that's a problem. We'll make up the money we lose in the discount by having more women attend."

"Absolutely. I think you have a great idea, Judy." Barbara cocked her head. "I've read a number of articles about programs in which seniors volunteer as tutors in the schools, giving them something meaningful to do and providing extra help to the children who need it. Involving the seniors at the Towers in the breakfast is a great way to introduce the idea that Welleswood's seniors might be an overlooked asset to the schools."

Ginger smiled. "Pam is going to love the idea."

"She'll probably take credit for it, too, but that's fine by me," Judy quipped. "At least we've got one good idea about how to make more women feel welcome at the breakfast." She checked her watch. "It's almost two-thirty. I really have to go. Candy's been working on the computer at the salon all day, and I promised her I'd stop by after our meeting so she could show me what she's done." She rolled her eyes. "Like I really want to spend one more minute staring at a computer after arguing with one in class all morning."

"You'll get the hang of it soon," Ginger reassured her.

"That's what I'm hoping. Anyway, if you have a minute, Barbara, maybe you could come with me. I told Candy that you'd closed Grandmother's Kitchen and stored your stock away. She said she had an idea that you might like."

Barbara held up her hand. "I'm not sure I can handle anything more complicated than using the computer for e-mail or surfing the Internet or typing a letter."

"That puts you way ahead of me," Judy countered.

Ginger giggled. "I'm not even in the game. I don't even know how to turn one on."

"Candy gets so frustrated when I act like she's speaking a foreign language. Maybe you can help translate a little?"

Barbara shrugged. "I could try, but I have to be at the school at three to pick up the twins."

Judy turned her attention back to Ginger. "You're welcome to come along."

"No, you two go ahead," Ginger replied. "The less I know about computers, the happier I am. It's my turn to pay so I'll wait for the check and take care of it. Are we still planning to meet again next Monday? That might be too soon."

Judy slid out of the booth and put on her coat. "How about two weeks from today?"

Barbara picked up her folder and grabbed her coat. "Same time, same place?"

Ginger nodded. "Done. Go on, you two. And have fun with the computer!" she teased as they hurried out of The Diner.

Walking the few blocks between The Diner and Pretty Ladies took less than five minutes. When they reached the salon, it took just about as long for the awkwardness between Barbara and Candy, who had not met again since the day Candy barged into the salon, to turn into enthusiasm.

With the three of them gathered around the computer behind the reception desk, Candy pointed to the computer screen. "This is the site I wanted to show you."

On the screen, delicate gold letters set against a lavender background announced the name of an online store, Mandy's Heirlooms, and a brief paragraph describing the store as the best place on the Internet to purchase antique ladies' jewelry. Candy scrolled down the page to a list of offerings: rings, bracelets, watches, necklaces and earrings. "Pick one," she urged.

Barbara shrugged. "Rings."

With a click, another page opened with a list of available antique rings. Without asking, Candy clicked on the first one and yet another page opened, revealing the picture of a delicate pinkie ring, a description and the price.

"I've done a little shopping on the Internet, although

mainly for books, so I'm familiar with how it works," Barbara explained, hoping she would not hurt Candy's feelings.

"Most people have, except for my mother, of course," Candy replied.

"And I've survived quite well. Imagine that," Judy teased.

Candy shook her head, but kept her attention on Barbara. "Mom told me you had to close Grand-mother's Kitchen since you can't spend regular hours at the store anymore. I thought this might be an option for you."

Barbara furrowed her brows. "What? A Web page?"

"An online store, like this one. They're easy enough to set up. I e-mailed a couple of the stores I found, just for fun. You'd be surprised how willing some people are to share their experiences. Some of these business owners use the Internet to supplement their actual stores, but several of them have had so much success online with the worldwide market that they've closed their regular stores."

"I—I wouldn't know the first thing about how to set up an online store," Barbara countered.

"You've got a computer, right?"

"One at home, which my husband mainly uses, and one in storage."

"What about a digital camera?"

Barbara shook her head.

"Never mind. They're cheap enough to buy. If you're interested, I could help you set up your online store and you'd be back in business again, except you could run the business right from your home." Candy paused, grabbed a paper from on top of the appointment book and handed it to Barbara. "You might want to visit these sites to get a better idea of how to operate a business online. I checked them out. They're pretty helpful."

"Thank you. I suppose it's worth a look," Barbara said, her instincts telling her to seriously consider Candy's idea. "I'd want to talk it over with my husband before I go ahead with anything, though."

Candy clicked off the Internet and returned to the desktop. "No problem. Mom, do you want me to leave the computer on so you can practice what you learned in class today or turn it off?"

"I thought you were going to show me how to keep track of the supplies on the computer."

"I got an e-mail from the human resources department at a company in Center City. Someone saw the résumé I posted online, and he wants to see me at four o'clock. I need to go home to change and still get to the train by three-thirty at the latest."

Judy's eyes widened. "An interview? That's terrific! Go ahead. Turn that thing off. Maybe I'll just take the rest of the afternoon off and pick up Brian early from the after-school program."

Candy shut down the computer. "Thanks, Mom. I'll probably be home by six or so for dinner. Bye, Mrs. Montgomery. Call me if you have any questions," she offered and rushed out of the salon.

"I guess we should leave and get to the school," Barbara suggested.

After Judy locked up the salon, they headed down the avenue.

"That was really nice of Candy to spend all that time researching on the Internet on my behalf," Barbara said. "John mentioned something a while back about trying to sell some of the canister sets online, but I never seriously considered it. I like what Candy showed me so much I think I should make Grandmother's Kitchen into an online store."

When Judy stopped dead, Barbara turned to face her. "What's wrong?"

"Nothing . . . Everything . . ." She twisted her hands together. "Look. I think it was great that Candy offered to help you, but I—I'm not sure it's such a good idea. It's one thing for me to take a risk and let her organize the salon's business on the computer. She's my daughter, and I'll repay Ann if anything goes wrong. But . . . but if anything happened to you or your business . . . if Candy relapsed and abused the trust you put in her, I'd feel absolutely awful."

"Somebody needs to give her another chance," Barbara argued. "She certainly seems to know what she's doing. She's enthusiastic, motivated and—"

"And a recovering drug addict," Judy argued. "Right now, she's doing very well, and I'm proud of her. But everything could change and she could go back to using drugs in less time than it takes to change a lightbulb. If she's using drugs again, she'll lie, cheat and steal to get the money she needs for the drugs. She's stolen from me in the past, and she'd steal from you. I don't want anything to interfere with our friendship."

"Me, either, so let's get that out of the way. Ann is obviously comfortable taking the risk, isn't she?"

"Yes, but—"

"Look, if I do decide to go ahead and work with Candy, I'd have John check and double-check everything Candy sets up, and he'll audit the business for me, of course. If that makes you uncomfortable or if you'll worry about it every day, then I won't even consider working with Candy. I'll just hire someone else."

Judy sighed. "I'd hate to have Candy miss out on an opportunity because I'm so paranoid, but—"

"Then she won't, assuming I actually decide to take the plunge into the cyberworld. Maybe you should think about getting a Web page for the salon once you own it. I'm sure Candy would help you, too," she suggested.

"Me? You want me to get a Web page? I can barely handle the computer as it is. I'd be better off looking for a pearl in a clam shell," Judy retorted, "and since I don't like to eat clams any more than I like computers, I think I'll pass and concentrate on praying for something a little more likely to happen and a whole lot more important."

"Which would be . . ."

Judy smiled. "Having Candy come home tonight and telling me she got the job."

• • •

When John came home for dinner that night, he told Barbara that the call they had been anxious to get for the past six months had come late that afternoon, and immediately unplugged the telephones in the house.

With the twins at home, Barbara had no opportunity to discuss the call from Detective Sanger that John had gotten just before leaving work in any detail. The minutes dragged as they followed their usual school-night routine, although this night would be far from ordinary. Tonight, Barbara hoped to learn exactly who had been arrested for killing their son.

She managed to get through dinner, although the little bit she had eaten seemed to be lodged painfully behind her breastbone, making it difficult to breathe. While she cleared the leftovers from the table, John helped the twins load the dishwasher. He settled the little girls around the dining room table to start their homework while Barbara packed lunches for school and finished cleaning up the kitchen.

As she wiped down the countertop, she heard the twins chatting in the next room. Both Jessie and Melanie loved to recount their daily classroom experiences, and their animated voices helped to assuage Barbara's anxiety about facing whatever news John would share with her after the girls had gone to bed.

Hearing their voices as they were gathered around the dining room table, however, reminded her that it had only been a short while ago when she and John had been at that table, exploring opportunities for sailing their way through retirement. The maps and brochures had been put away along with their dreams, but so much more had changed in their lives over the past six months.

Steve was Home, sharing in the glory of eternal life, but his passing had left a wound in her heart that would not be fully healed until the day she and her son were reunited in heaven. Jessie and Melanie were the center of Barbara's and John's lives now. Loving them, caring for them and watching them grow up was a blessing that Barbara was willing to share now with the girls' other grandparents, people whose lives were forever linked with their family.

She wiped the kitchen table and put on a fresh table-cloth while she thought about Grandmother's Kitchen, the shop she had enjoyed so much that was now nothing but a memory. She intended to follow up on the idea of creating an online store, but any plans she might make hinged on the news from Detective Sanger. Had the police made an arrest? If so, who would be charged? Would Barbara and John finally know the circumstances that had led to Steve's death? Would justice be done or would the system be manipulated to favor the defendants instead of the victim and his family?

Before she got twisted up in a whirlwind of questions that could not be answered, she smoothed the wrinkles from the tablecloth and decided to help with the homework. When she got to the dining room, the girls had already packed up. "Finished already?"

"I helped Mel with her math," Jessie announced proudly.

Melanie pouted. "I don't like math."

"Neither did I," Barbara confessed. "Let's go, ladies. Bath time."

Without further prompting, the girls raced for the stairs, and John laughed out loud. "For the life of me, I can't ever remember the boys being so willing to take a bath."

"You're right. It must be a girl thing," Barbara conceded. "Shall I have the girls come back down for a good-night kiss?" she asked, hoping he might offer to handle the bedtime routine as he used to do with the boys.

"Sure. I'll check my messages and sort through today's mail while the girls take their baths."

Disappointed, she helped the girls through bath time and had them ready for bed, as usual, by eight o'clock. "Go on. Run downstairs to kiss Pappy good-night, then we'll—"

John poked his head into the bedroom. "Who's ready for prayers and a good-night kiss?"

"Me!"

"Me!"

Barbara caught his gaze and held it as he entered the girls' bedroom, and her heart swelled with joy.

"I was thinking I should say prayers with you and Grammy before you go to bed at night," he said. When he knelt down at the side of Melanie's bed, the girls knelt down beside him, one on each side.

Barbara knelt down on the opposite side of the bed to keep all three of them in view.

John led their granddaughters in prayer. "Heavenly Father, we thank You for all the blessings we have received today, and we pray You will forgive us all if we have not followed Your Word the way we should have. Help us to be kind and loving, and help us to be patient."

"Amen," the girls whispered in unison with their grandparents and finished the first round of prayers before adding individual prayer requests.

"God bless Jessie and Melanie," he whispered.

"God bless Grammy and Pappy," Jessie added before she craned her neck and motioned for Melanie to take her turn.

"God bless Grandmom and Grandpop Carr and the baby pigs at the farm," Melanie offered with a shy smile.

Barbara suppressed a grin. "God bless us all."

"God bless Miss Addison," Jessie said with a smile of her own.

Not to be outdone, Melanie offered another request of her own. "God bless our Daddy and tell him I miss him."

"Tell him I miss him, too," Jessie said quickly before scrambling across Melanie's bed into her own.

Moved almost to tears, Barbara tucked Jessie into bed while John did the same for Melanie. After a round of good-night kisses, she went downstairs with John, and she was still glowing from the experience they had just shared together for the first time since Steve's death. She followed her husband into the family room, less anxious than she had been earlier, but still curious to hear what news Detective Sanger had given John earlier.

John stood in front of the fireplace and faced her as she stood behind a wing chair and held on to the back for support. "Detective Sanger called to tell me they made an arrest late this afternoon," he murmured. "She wouldn't tell me much over the telephone, but she said that the media would probably run with the story tonight on the evening news."

Her spine tingled. "I'm sure they did," she quipped, uncertain if she was any more prepared for the media frenzy that had already been unleashed than she was for the emotional roller coaster she was about to ride. "Did she say who had been arrested? Or when we could expect the trial to begin?"

"No, she was pretty busy. She asked if she could talk to us first thing tomorrow morning."

Barbara sighed and prayed for patience. "When and where?"

"She said she could meet us at my office since the media is less likely to look for us there. Unless you'd rather go back to Philadelphia and meet at police headquarters."

"No. Your office is fine. She didn't tell you anything else?"

He shook his head. "With all the commotion in the background, I could barely hear her as it was. I figured if we waited this long, one more night wouldn't matter much." When she sighed again, he nodded toward the television set. "We could watch the news."

She closed her eyes for a moment. "No. I think I'd rather wait to hear what the detective has to say."

"Me, too. Scared?"

"A little."

He opened his arms, offering comfort. "Me, too," he whispered.

When she stepped around the chair and moved into his embrace, he held her close.

Chapter Twenty-Nine

Some things never change. Candy was late. Not even a telephone call to explain why she was delayed or when she would be home.

For Judy, watching the hands on the kitchen clock was nothing new. Becoming more and more disappointed, instead of angrier with each passing hour, was very new—but experience, like age, it seemed, had its advantages.

At six-thirty, she and Brian ate dinner. Judy washed the dishes. He dried them. She put them away.

By seven-thirty, he had finished his homework and taken a bath.

At eight o'clock, after he said his prayers, she tucked him into bed.

His head had no sooner hit the pillow, when he sat right back up again. "I forgot something!" he exclaimed and scrambled out of bed. He sorted through the clothes in the hamper next to his closet door, found the blue jeans he had worn to school that day and rifled through the pockets. He smiled when he found what he had been looking for. He handed her a paper that had been folded and crumpled into a thick wad. "Miss Addison said I hadda have this back tomorrow."

She carefully unfolded the paper. "Why didn't you have this in your backpack?"

He shrugged. "Can you sign it for me, Grandmom? If I have it back tomorrow, I get a sticker."

She nodded as she scanned the wrinkled message, a list of directives concerning the Valentine's Day celebration in school, along with a roster of the names of everyone in the first grade class, which ensured that no child would be slighted. Judy's signature on the bottom would mean she had read and understood the guidelines. She took a pencil out of Brian's backpack, signed the lower portion, tore it off and stored both the pencil and the signed paper in the outside pouch of his backpack before she put the top section into her own pocket.

"All set. I guess this means we have to make some Valentines soon. But not tonight," she said and pointed to his bed.

He leaped back into bed, crawled under the covers and drew them up to his chin. "My mom helped me make Valentines once. Is she coming home soon?"

Judy smiled in spite of her disappointment. "She had

a very important interview for a job today. Maybe it just took longer than she thought it would, but you need to get to sleep now because you have to get up early for school tomorrow."

He snuggled against his pillow. "Tell my mom about the Valentines, okay?"

She kissed his forehead. "You can tell her at breakfast. Sleep tight."

She left his door open in case he called out while she was downstairs and slowly descended the steps. Why Candy had not been home at six as she had promised and why she had not called was almost irrelevant now, compared to knowing where she was and when or even if she might be coming home. Candy had only been home for a week—long enough to inspire hope, but briefly enough to suggest her recent effort to maintain her recovery would fare no better than her previous attempts.

The heavy weight of déjà vu threatened to push Judy back into the past, full of old fears, disappointments and anger that could all be so easily reawakened by present circumstances. When she got to the bottom of the steps, she crossed the living room and went out to the front porch without bothering to put on a coat. She stood at the front railing and drew in a huge gulp of frigid air that chilled the burning desire to scream in frustration.

One week. Is that all it had taken for the bubble to burst and for Candy to have relapsed? What a cruel possibility. Judy lifted her face to the dark sky. Clouds

hid the stars and kept a pale sliver of moon from pro-
viding more than a blush of light as she whispered a
pleading prayer that He would keep her daughter safe
tonight.

Shivering, she went back into the house. When she
closed the door behind her, she automatically threw
the bolt and latched the security chain. She was
tempted to leave them in place, to force Candy to
knock when she wanted to come into the house;
instead, she undid the bolt and chain and went to the
kitchen to pack Brian's lunch for school tomorrow.

When Judy went to bed at eleven, she would set the
bolt and chain back into place. If Candy was home by
then, fine. If not, then Candy would get a very strong
message when she tried to let herself in with her key.
If Candy had not come home by morning . . .

She pushed that thought away because, frankly,
she did not know what she would do or how she
would explain Candy's absence to Brian and concentrated on making Brian's lunch. She lined three
small plastic sandwich bags on the counter. After
smearing chunky peanut butter and grape jelly on
bread, she cut the sandwich into quarters and stored
them inside the first bag. She peeled an orange, separated the sections and slipped them into the second
bag before she emptied some yogurt-covered raisins
into the last one then she put all three bags into the
refrigerator.

After wiping down the counter, she took out the
trash, remembered it was trash night and dragged the

metal can to the curb behind the garage rather than trying to lug it all the way out front. By the time she got back to the kitchen door, her teeth were chattering and she was stiff with cold. She hurried inside, only to find her daughter standing at the sink filling the teakettle. She was still wearing the winter coat she had borrowed from Judy that morning.

Candy looked up and frowned. "It's cold out there. You should be wearing a coat. Where were you?"

Judy's temper was temporarily frozen, along with her hands. "Taking out the trash. Funny. I was just about to ask you the same thing. You told me you'd be home at six," she snapped and glanced at the clock while she rubbed her hands together to warm them. "It's quarter to nine."

"Is Brian asleep?"

Judy frowned. "His bedtime is eight. Of course, he's asleep," she managed.

"I'm sorry, Mom. I would have called—"

"You should have called. Period."

Without answering, Candy turned, set the teakettle on the stove and adjusted the flame on the burner. When she turned back, Judy saw that her daughter's cheeks were chafed and her nose was almost scarlet, as if she had been out in the elements for way too long. "Look, Mom. I don't want to fight. Can we please sit down and talk this out? Calmly?"

Feeling inappropriately chastised, Judy held her temper, which had thawed sufficiently, and her tongue, resisting reminding Candy who was at fault here. "Calmly?" she repeated. "Sure. But no lies. The truth is all I want to hear."

Without removing her coat, Candy sat down first and shoved her hands into the coat pockets.

Judy took a seat across from her. "Go ahead. I'm listening."

"It's not my fault that I'm late," Candy began.

The weight of déjà vu got a little heavier, but Judy kept her shoulders back and tried to keep an open mind.

"I got out of the interview and back to the train station by five-thirty. I got through the turnstiles, but I couldn't get near the loading platform. There were police and paramedics everywhere. Apparently someone had fallen off the platform onto the tracks. At least, that's what I heard. So I figured I'd go back up to the street and walk to the next stop, but the stupid machine took my ticket, and I didn't have enough money left to buy another one."

Candy's tale sounded plausible enough, if indeed someone had fallen off the platform, but Candy always had such a flair for concocting dramatic excuses that Judy was not sure if her tale was true or not. She held silent and nodded for Candy to continue. When she did not, Judy finally asked, "Why didn't you call me?"

Candy rolled her eyes. "Have you tried to find a pay phone lately? Half of them are disconnected and the other half are vandalized. At least, the few I found had been destroyed. The first thing I'm going to buy with my first paycheck is cell phones for both of us."

"If you didn't have enough money for another ticket and you couldn't find a pay phone to call me or anyone else, how did you get home?"

"I had just enough to take a bus across the river. Then I walked."

Judy gasped. "It's not even twenty degrees outside. You walked? At this hour? It isn't safe."

"Next time I'll take a cab and ask the driver to wait while I run inside to get money from you to pay for the ride. You've got an extra twenty or thirty dollars lying around, right?"

Judy was shaken by the idea her daughter had traipsed home in the dark through rough neighborhoods along dangerous highways and all the while, she'd been picturing Candy taking up her drug habit again. "Don't be flip. I'd rather pay for a cab than a funeral," Judy snapped.

Candy flinched, then studied her mother closely. "You . . . you thought I was out doing drugs again, didn't you? Is that why you look so terrified and so guilty, all at the same time?"

Judy's cheeks flamed. "I wish I could say the idea hadn't occurred to me, but yes. I was worried you somehow had been disappointed by the interview—"

"And decided to feel better by getting high?"

Judy nodded, remembering her vow to be honest, whatever the cost.

With a sigh, Candy sat back in her chair. "I guess I can't blame you for that. If our situations were reversed, I'd probably have thought the same thing. It's not like it hasn't happened before, right?"

"This isn't going to be easy, is it?" Judy asked.

"What? Living together?"

"Yes, living together. Learning to trust you. Helping you, but not . . . enabling you," she said, recalling the phrase she had learned previously, dealing with Candy's addiction.

"You're helping me a lot, Mom. I know that, but we can't worry about every little thing we say or do. We just have to be honest with each other and take one day at a time. If something I do bothers you, you have to tell me so we can talk about it, and I'll do the same."

"I didn't want to think the worst tonight, but I did," Judy admitted. "I was scared, and when you told me you'd walked all the way home, I didn't know what scared me more. Losing you to drugs again or losing you forever to some mugger or to a freak accident because your wallet was almost empty."

Candy patted Judy's hand. "You're not going to lose me because *I'm* not going to lose me, all right? And if I feel like I'm starting to slide, I'll tell you and I'll do something about it."

The teakettle whistled, and Candy got up from the table. Without asking, she poured boiling water into two mugs, added tea bags and put the mugs on the table. Judy watched as Candy set out the milk and sugar before she sat down again. "Aren't you going to take off your coat?"

Candy wrapped her hands around her steaming mug. "Not until I drink this. I think my bones are frozen."

"You're lucky if your toes aren't frostbitten."

Candy chuckled and wrinkled her nose. "I could probably manage without a toe or two, but I think I'd look pretty funny without my nose. I kept switching hands, trying to keep my nose from freezing and falling off my face."

"Very funny," Judy murmured. "I'm not sure how we'll swing it, but tomorrow I want you to look into getting some cell phones for us. As long as there's no deposit—"

"I told you, Mom. I'm getting the cell phones for us with my first paycheck."

"Right. Except your first paycheck, which Ann will be giving you Friday, won't be enough. Besides, you need to start getting some warmer clothes, remember? Welleswood isn't San Diego."

Candy shivered and took a sip of tea. "You don't have to remind me, but I wasn't talking about my paycheck from the salon. I meant the paycheck I'll be getting two weeks from Friday for my new job, assuming you can do without me at the salon."

"Do without you? Why . . . ?"

"I had an interview today, Mom. Remember?"

"Y-you got the job?"

"I got the job!" Grinning, she tapped her own shoulder. "You are now looking at the newly employed Candy Martin, who will be reporting to work next Monday as the assistant to the assistant producer for the soon-to-be launched cable news show, *All Around Town.*"

Chapter Thirty

Early Tuesday morning, Barbara and John arrived at Whitman Commons, where John kept his office. Located within easy walking distance from the elevated train, the former school building had been renovated and turned into an office building a few years back. The sound of the trains rumbling by every seven or eight minutes during rush hour added a sense of urgency to a day already filled with anxiety.

They entered the building through the rear door and used a back staircase to avoid running into other people who were arriving for work in the other offices. When they reached the third floor, she followed him to his office. He had called his secretary last night and asked her to come in an hour later than usual so his office was dark and quiet when they arrived just before nine o'clock.

While he turned on the lights and the office equipment, Barbara hung their coats on a hall tree just inside the door. She paused, held on to the sleeve of her coat and closed her eyes. She had been waiting for months to hear what the police had determined to be the true circumstances of the day Steve had been killed and to learn who was responsible for his death. Now that the moment was nearly at hand, she was tempted to bolt. Run away. Disappear. Do something, anything that would make the dread pooling in the pit of her stomach and the awful visions her imagination had created go away.

She opened her eyes and let go of her coat sleeve. If she ran away now, the wrenching pain in her heart would never be eased and her desperate need to see justice done for Steve and the daughters he had left behind would never be satisfied. She had no choice. She had to stay and bear the pain today's meeting would bring and pray that God's love and mercy would sustain her now and in the challenging days ahead.

"We can wait in my office."

She turned toward the sound of her husband's voice. He was standing in the open doorway that connected his office with the waiting room where his secretary worked and greeted clients.

Detective Sanger entered the office before Barbara had a chance to join her husband. "I'm a little early. I'm glad you're both here." She slipped out of her ankle-length, quilted coat, stuffed her gloves into the pockets and hung it on the coat tree next to Barbara's. In a dark pantsuit, she moved with an ease and confidence that Barbara envied in this moment, as knots were tightening in her stomach.

After they all stepped into John's office, the petite detective closed the door and took control of the meeting. She signaled John and Barbara to sit in the club chairs that faced his desk. For herself, she pulled the executive chair out from behind John's desk and joined them.

"We really appreciate your coming here," John offered.

"It's the worst part of my job and the best part," she replied. "It's been a long and tedious investigation, and I know it's been hard for you to wait, but I'm hoping our meeting today will finally give you some peace of mind. You may not find it easy to hear the details we've learned about your son's death, but I have to caution you that the process is far from over."

Barbara reached over and took her husband's hand. "We know."

The detective continued. "The district attorney's office may or may not be in touch with you later, but for now, let me assure you both that we wouldn't have made the arrests yesterday unless we were absolutely certain and the district attorney's office was satisfied that we had sufficient evidence to proceed."

John squeezed Barbara's hand. "We understand."

Sitting upright, the detective watched both of them closely. "Despite anything you might read in the newspapers or see on the news, here's what we believe happened. You've lived in South Jersey most of your lives, if not all, so I'm assuming you're familiar with Senior Week at the shore?"

"That's when the kids who are graduating from high school more or less invade the resort communities and generally run wild. We have some friends who have summer homes at the shore. We've heard the horror stories," John replied.

The detective nodded. "It's a rite of passage, of sorts, I suppose. There are hundreds of kids there from high schools in South Jersey as well as Philadelphia and beyond. It's usually pretty harmless. Loud music. Big parties. Some underage drinking. The local police have clamped down in recent years, so it's not as bad as it used to be."

"I guess that depends on whether or not you happen to be on vacation that week or have a year-round home there and have to deal with all those kids," John countered. "What does Senior Week at the shore have to do with Steve's death? He was killed in Philadelphia."

"As a result of our investigation, we know that one of those kids at the shore was Jason Whittle. He hadn't actually graduated. He'd dropped out of school in Philadelphia the previous February when he turned eighteen, but he decided to crash the scene and join up with some of his old friends who had graduated. That's where he met Julia Radcliffe, the younger of the two sisters. I believe she was fifteen at the time."

"Jason Whittle?" John repeated the boy's name out loud. "Is he the one who killed Steve?"

"No, but it was his gun," the detective replied.

"But he didn't kill Steve. You're sure?"

She nodded. "He has a rock-solid alibi. He was at work when Steve was killed. But he's involved," she added. "From everything we were able to learn, Julia and Jason met at a party and had a fling that didn't end when Senior Week did. In fact, we can prove that Whittle spent the weekend before Steve's death with Julia at the Radcliffe home outside of Cape May while her parents and sister were away."

Barbara gasped. "They left a fifteen-year-old girl at home alone?"

"She was supposed to be staying with a girlfriend and her family."

"So she lied to her parents," Barbara charged.

"Yes. We believe she did. In fact, neither her parents nor her sister had any idea Julia had been sneaking off to any of the Senior Week parties or that she had met Jason, either."

"Then she's an accomplished liar," John snapped.

The detective cocked her head and waited a moment before she continued. By then, John's breathing was no longer rushed and his cheeks were not quite so flushed. "After Jason left that Sunday afternoon, Julia cleaned up the house to make sure there was no sign they'd been there all weekend. That's when she found the gun."

"Jason's gun?" John asked.

"Yes. The girl's only fifteen. She panicked. Apparently, she was too upset to go to school the next day. That night, she broke down and confessed what she'd done to her sister, Augusta, and showed her the gun."

Barbara closed her eyes for a moment and tried to keep her mind from racing ahead toward the possibility that Steve's death might have indeed been an accident. When she opened her eyes, the detective met her gaze and held it for a few moments.

"Augusta was seventeen. She was older, and she should have known better. That's not to excuse Julia. Either one of the girls could have prevented the tragedy that ended with the death of your son if they had gone to their parents, right then and there. Or they could have disposed of the gun. Or they could have gone to the police right away instead of waiting until later."

She paused and shook her head. "These are kids from a good neighborhood, with good parents, good upbringings and good future prospects. But they're still just kids. Like Julia, Augusta panicked. The next day, that would have been Tuesday, both girls played sick and stayed home from school. After their parents left for work, the sisters drove to Philadelphia to return the gun to Jason. They'd only been to the city once or twice before with their parents so neither one of them had any idea how to find Jason's address. To make matters worse, the air-conditioning in the car was broken so they had all the windows down as they drove around and they got turned around in some really rough neighborhoods. They were hot. They were scared. And they were totally lost. Julia was so frightened she took out the gun and held it on her lap for protection, despite Augusta's protests."

The detective paused. Her expression softened, and she lowered her voice. "At three-thirty, the girls found their way back to Center City where Steve was at the

ATM. When they stopped at a red light, Augusta and Julia's argument exploded. When Augusta tried to grab the gun and take it away from her sister, it discharged. The bullet passed through the open window and struck your son."

Barbara struggled to breathe, but suddenly, it seemed as if all the air had been sucked out of the room. She looked at her husband. He was so pale she wondered if he were breathing at all.

He let go of her hand and waved away the detective's account. "Are you serious? The chance that the bullet hit my son and didn't strike either one of the girls or something inside the car or—or a building or a passerby is almost beyond comprehension. What are the odds? One in a million? A billion? A trillion? Are you sitting there and telling us that after months and months of investigation that's what happened? You expect us to believe it?" He snorted and glanced up at the ceiling, refusing to look at either the detective or his wife.

Barbara realized at once that she had mistaken his expression. He had not paled from shock. He was angry, furiously angry, as he voiced her own disbelief. But beneath his outrage and disbelief, she knew, he was also as distraught as she to learn that Steve had lost his life in an idiotic, completely preventable accident.

Despite John's bitter fury, the detective never flinched. When she spoke again, her voice remained low. "I wouldn't be sitting here if we didn't believe this is what happened. We've uncovered absolutely nothing to indicate otherwise, and with their lawyer's permission, the girls have been very cooperative helping us reconstruct every circumstance of Steve's death. The girls did not drive to Philadelphia with the intent to kill anyone. They were only trying to return the gun to Whittle."

"But the girls have been arrested, haven't they?" Barbara asked. "They'll be held accountable? Someone needs to be held accountable. Even if the gun was accidentally fired—"

"Yes, they've been arrested, but it's up to the district attorney's office to decide on the specific charges they'll face. Remember, both of the girls are under eighteen and fall under the jurisdiction of Family Court."

"Unless the district attorney's office petitions the court to see that the girls are tried as adults," John argued.

"True, but that's something you'd have to discuss with the district attorney's office."

"What about Whittle?" he asked. "It was his gun. If he hadn't left the gun behind, none of this would have happened."

"Whittle is a whole different story. Legally, he's an adult. The ballistics test confirms the gun that killed your son is also the gun that was used in a robbery in North Philadelphia in which a storeowner was shot and badly wounded." She smiled for the first time since she had arrived. "If it's any consolation to you, the investigation into your son's death led directly to Whittle's arrest yesterday for robbery and attempted murder. In addition, he'll face charges for the statutory rape of Julia Radcliffe and any other charges the district attorney's office can justify related to your son's death. I don't think Whittle will be on the streets to hurt anyone else for a very long time."

John stared down at the floor and shook his head.

Her emotions in turmoil, Barbara folded her hands together to keep them from trembling. "Wh-what do we do now?"

"Go home. Grieve for your son. Let the justice system do what it's supposed to do—find justice. How involved you become as the process unfolds is entirely up to you. I've seen some families of victims stay very involved, others don't. Do whatever feels right for you and for Steve's daughters. Don't let anyone pressure you into anything. In the end, no matter how this case is ultimately charged or the punishment is decided, the most important thing for you to remember is to celebrate Steve's life, not his death."

She stood up and pressed a card into Barbara's hand. "I put my cell phone number on the back. If you have any questions or you just need to talk, call me. Whenever," she whispered and quietly left the office.

John suddenly got up and followed the detective into the waiting room, leaving Barbara alone with her thoughts. She had never really given much credence to the girls' early claims that the shooting had been accidental, but she could not afford to waste any of her limited emotional energy on finding fault with the results of the police investigation. If the police and the district attorney's office were satisfied that they had uncovered the truth, then Barbara would simply have to accept that.

The truth, however, did not bring the peace of mind she had hoped.

The truth only opened up a whole host of disturbing thoughts that led Barbara down a path littered with questions that all began with one word: why. Why had Julia lied and sneaked out of her parents' home to go to the parties at Senior Week? Why, out of all the young men she might have met, had she met Jason Whittle? Why had she lied again and disobeyed her parents again and had Jason spend the weekend at her home? Why hadn't she or her sister immediately turned the gun she found over to her parents or the police? Why had they gone to Philadelphia on that specific day and driven down that specific street at that specific time when Steve would be at the ATM? Why had the bullet chosen one path in a million or more that had led straight to her son? Why? Why? Why?

If she knew the answer to just one question, she might begin to understand the answer to the greatest question of all: why had Steve been taken away from them at all?

Was it mere coincidence that the lives of these girls and Jason Whittle and Steve had intersected in such a tragic way? Was it something that happened to remind everyone that evil existed in this world, an evil that claimed the good and the innocent, to test their faith? If so, was it necessary for Steve to be part of this? Or had the pastor been right when he had told her that there were no accidents or coincidences that were not part of God's plan for the greater good?

Deeply troubled, she cradled her face in her hands, unable to pray, unable to think beyond the pounding of her heart and the throbbing in her head. She did not know why, but her spirit no longer cried out for vengeance, rather it sought understanding and acceptance, even forgiveness for the ones who had caused her and her family such grief.

She only knew her heart hurt.

When she heard a sound in the outer room, she got up and went to investigate.

John was standing at the window in the waiting room with his back to her. His shoulders shook with sobs that he was trying to muffle. She went to him, laid her face against his back, wrapped her arms around his waist and held him tight as he wept.

Somehow, through faith, they would find their way to understanding.

Some way, through faith, they would find their way to acceptance.

And some day, through faith, they would be able to forgive Julia and Augusta and Jason for the roles they had played in Steve's death.

But for now, Barbara and John needed to let go and grieve, to accept all they had learned today.

Together.

Chapter Thirty-One

Near the end of their session, Ginger had one last question for Ed Raymond, the counselor Judy had recommended. "In case Lily does not want to take Vincent home with her, I just want to be sure that anything we do or say will make it easier for Vincent to understand he'll be staying with us, more or less permanently. We want to help him to accept the idea that he can't be with his mother right now, but we don't want him to give up hope because maybe Lily will change her mind someday."

The counselor set aside his clipboard. "Vincent is only eight years old, but from everything you've told me about his relationship with his mother so far, he seems to have adjusted quite well to living with you and your husband. Making that arrangement more secure and reinforcing his relationship with the two of you is not only important, it's imperative. I'd also like to see Vincent. Just for one or two sessions, so if there's a dramatic change in circumstances, I'll be better prepared to help."

"Yes, I think that's a good idea."

"In the meantime, keep in mind what we talked about. When you're answering Vincent's questions about his mother, remember to ROAR, but gently," he teased, reminding her what each letter stood for by holding up one finger at a time. "*R*eassure him of his mother's love. *O*nly answer the specific question he's asked. *A*nswer his questions honestly, but consider his age and his cognitive and emotional development. *R*espond to his feelings with empathy and compassion."

She held up the notes she had taken. "I've got it. ROAR," she murmured. The acronym inspired a mental image of herself as a lioness protecting her cub against predators, with Tyler standing guard, ever faithful and vigilant. That picture, beside the image of the carefree lifestyle they had enjoyed up to six months ago, was startlingly different, but a call to duty she and Tyler had embraced with renewed enthusiasm since he had returned from Chicago on Sunday night.

More strongly committed than ever to issuing an ultimatum to Lily that would affect all of their futures, Ginger left the counselor's office. She sat in her car in the municipal parking lot and called Tyler at work on her cell phone to give him a rundown of her session with the counselor. She got his voice mail and left him a message to call her back. Eager to carry out the plan she and Tyler had formulated, and which the counselor had supported, she made one more call to the furniture store, then left her car and headed to the avenue.

Her first stop was Sweet Stuff, to thank Charlene again for the afternoon off and to purchase a pound of chocolate-covered pretzels and a small gift card. While Ginger wrote out the card, Charlene boxed the pretzels and wrapped the gift in bright pink paper.

Next, Ginger shopped at the stationery store, where

she picked up a supply of note cards. Then she tried several gift shops before she found the turtle night-light she had seen a few weeks ago and had the clerk wrap it up in colorful paper with a huge blue bow. Loaded down with packages now, she passed Pretty Ladies and looked in the window. When Judy waved back from behind the reception desk, Ginger hurried inside. "I thought you'd be gone by now."

Judy's smile was forced, and she glared at the computer screen. "So did I. Unfortunately, I'm smack in the middle of an argument." After she punched several keys with the tip of her index finger, the computer shut down and the screen went dark. "There. Take a time-out, George."

Ginger giggled. "George? You named your computer?"

"I most certainly did. I may not be the smartest woman on earth when it comes to computers, but now it's personal. With Candy working at another job now, it's just me against George, and I'm not going to let him get the best of me. I will get him to do what I want when I want and how I want or he's history, and I'm going back to using my cute little recipe box and index cards, whether the bank likes it or not."

"I guess that means everything is still at a stand-still?"

Judy let out a deep breath and shook her head. "At least until I finish my computer classes."

Ginger laid the gift from Sweet Stuff next to the keyboard. "Here. When you try working with George again, I think you definitely need reinforcements."

Judy grinned and tucked the box between her hands. "Bless you!"

"You're welcome."

"Wait. Don't tell me you brought this because you heard me yelling at George all the way down the avenue at Sweet Stuff!"

"No, silly. I just wanted to thank you for referring me to Ed Raymond. I met with him this afternoon, and he was very helpful."

"I'm glad, but you didn't have to bring me anything. Not that you can take this back," she teased and put the box on the other side of the keyboard. "I'm not finished with George yet, and I have a feeling I'll need this."

"Maybe you should try being a little sweeter to George."

Judy sighed. "Maybe I should pay better attention in computer class, but it's slow going. Candy offered to come to the salon with me a night or two, but I hate to bother her. She's putting in long enough hours at her new job."

"And you're not?"

"Well—"

"Let her help you. After all you've done and continue to do for her, the least she can do is to help you with the computer. Give her the chance to repay you."

Judy rolled her eyes. "You're right. I just don't want to put too much on her plate right now. She's doing so well."

"So you'll suffer alone, with too much on your plate, so Candy doesn't have to?" Ginger cocked her head. "What kind of message does that send to your daughter?"

Judy hesitated for a moment, furrowed her brow as if she was thinking over Ginger's question and eventually let out a sigh. "The wrong message. You're right again. Thanks. I'll talk to Candy tonight about helping me with George. I guess we could bring Brian with us. He could do his homework while we work at the computer."

"Good idea. I haven't heard from Barbara again. Have you?"

Judy shook her head, but looked long and hard at Ginger. "You seem different today. More confident. More assertive. More in control. Maybe I should go back to Ed Raymond for a session or two."

"He helped, but . . . Tyler and I have had to make some decisions about Vincent and Lily. We probably should have done something about this whole situation before now. . . ." She squared her shoulders. "The point is, we're ready now. I'm ready now. I've never been a strong or determined woman. Not like you are. But I've never had to be. Not until recently. Getting to know you and seeing how strong you are and how you've struggled to build a life for yourself and meet every challenge along the way really helps me to believe I can do almost anything."

Judy blushed. "I treasure your friendship, too," she murmured. "Did you say 'anything'?" she added with a sudden twinkle in her eyes and a nod toward her computer.

Ginger backed away from the reception desk and held up her hand. "Don't push it. George is a problem you'll have to handle without me. I have to leave to get Vincent at school," she teased and hurried out the door.

That night, while Tyler tucked Vincent into bed, Ginger set the kitchen table again. Instead of plates and utensils, she lined up all the paperwork she needed at her fingertips to implement the plan that would force Lily to make a decision. Lily would have to take Vincent fully into her new life, or he would continue to live with Ginger and Tyler—on their terms, not hers.

Either way, Vincent would have the most to gain. The first option, which would reunite him with his mother, was the ideal. Lily had yet to demonstrate, unfortunately, that she wanted him in her life. Thanks to Tyler's fact-finding mission in Chicago, he and Ginger had enough sad documentation now to corroborate much of what Vincent had reported about living primarily outside of his mother's home for the first eight years of his life.

Still, Lily was Vincent's mother. If she was prepared to start over and to make a real home for her son, as she was apparently ready to do for the child she was carrying, Ginger and Tyler were prepared to let Vincent go.

If Lily refused, then Ginger and Tyler were equally prepared for the second option and to dictate the terms under which Vincent would remain in their custody.

In her mother's heart, however, Ginger knew which option Lily would choose.

She surveyed the paperwork, arranged in chronological order, to make sure nothing was missing and sighed. What sad testimony to the life Lily had lived in Chicago. Her ability to deceive her parents about how she was living and raising Vincent in the past explained how readily she could deceive her in-laws now. Ginger had a copy of Vincent's birth certificate, in addition to a statement from three of Vincent's caregivers whom Tyler had been able to locate. A list of jobs Lily had held after leaving the teaching job the second year she was in Chicago included full-time positions in sales and waitressing and part-time jobs, the most lowly of which had been bartending. Another paper listed five addresses where Lily had lived. The last document was the custody agreement Lily had sent them months ago, giving Ginger and Tyler the legal right to raise Vincent, to enroll him in school, and to secure medical treatment for him, if necessary.

Once Ginger was satisfied nothing was missing, she used a fresh notepad to list the points she needed to cover with Lily, then put that document at the head of the table. On impulse, she filled a glass half-full of water, and put it in the center of the table, just as Tyler walked into the kitchen.

"Is he asleep?" she asked.

"I'll go back up and check again in ten minutes to make sure, but I think he is. What's with the water?"

She smiled. "Just a visual image I wanted to keep in mind."

"As in the glass is half-full?"

"Exactly. The glass is half-full because I know that with God's help tonight, we're going to do what's best for our grandson."

"We said we'd call Lily tonight, but there's no guarantee she'll take our call. She might not even be home," he cautioned.

"It's her cell phone. She'll have it with her wherever she is," Ginger countered. "If she doesn't take our first call, we'll leave a message and then another and another until she realizes she either has to call us back or wait and answer the phone when we call again. I've done this before, when Vincent had that trouble at school, remember?"

He glanced at the paperwork on the table. "You were a lot less sure of yourself then."

"Weren't you?"

"I guess I was." He shook his head. "My grandmother used to tell me that people were 'too soon old and too late smart.' I hope we're not too late . . . for Vincent's sake," he murmured, still clearly troubled by what they had learned about Vincent's life in Chicago.

She crossed the room and gave him a hug. "My grandmother used to tell me something, too." She leaned back and looked into his eyes. "She said never to be afraid to make a mistake. Just don't make the same mistake twice. We made lots of mistakes raising Lily. Both of us. We can either wallow in self-pity and guilt or we can try to fix those mistakes by making her accountable for her life and holding her to it. And if Vincent is going to stay with us, then we have a second chance to make sure we don't make the same mistakes with him. This time we'll do it better and we'll do it together."

He took a lock of her hair and brushed it back over her shoulder. "I think my grandmother was right," he whispered.

She bristled and tried to pull away, but he tugged her into his embrace. "Don't get all bristly. Hold still. I'm trying to give you a compliment."

With her eyes wide, she looked up at him. "By telling me we're old and stupid?"

He laughed. "No. By telling you something else my grandmother said." He cleared his throat. "She said, 'Tyler, that girl's got a good heart and a good soul. You better marry her, because if you don't, you'll be making the worst mistake of your life.' So I did. Bless her heart, she sure knew what she was talking about. I'm not sure what I ever did to deserve you, but I'm very sure I wouldn't want to find out what my life would have been like without you."

Battling tears, she pressed her cheek against his heart. "I love you."

He gave her a squeeze. "I love you, too. Now let's

call our daughter. Do you want to do the honors or should I?"

She sighed. "It'll probably take hours until we reach her. Let's alternate and take turns. Maybe if she gets a few messages from each of us, she'll be more likely to call us back tonight."

"Go ahead," he urged. "You can make the first call while I go upstairs and check on Vincent. You're the one who usually calls her anyway."

She glanced back over her shoulder at the table. "Where's the cordless telephone from the bedroom? I thought you were going to bring it down with you so we could both be part of the conversation."

"Sorry. I forgot. I'll bring it down with me," he suggested and started for the stairs.

"I'll wait for you to get back before I call."

He waved behind him. "Don't bother. Make the call, leave a message and heat up some cider for us. I'll be right back."

She shrugged, tapped out Lily's number on the kitchen telephone and carried it with her to the refrigerator to get out the cider. By the fourth ring, she had the cider on the counter and started to fill two mugs. By the seventh ring, she had the mugs in the microwave, anxious for Lily's voice mail to kick in.

"Mom?"

Ginger flinched and frantically looked at the doorway, but Tyler was gone.

"Mom?"

"Sorry. Yes, it's me," she murmured, just as Tyler picked up the telephone upstairs. "Your father and I wanted—"

"If you've called to apologize for not coming for the weekend, don't bother. I've already started making plans to enroll Vincent in a boarding school, so you won't be taking care of him anymore."

"Actually, Lily, your mother and I have a lot to say to you, and I suggest you listen very, very carefully," Tyler cautioned from the extension upstairs. "And don't hang up. If you do, your mother and I will drive through the night to be in Boston in the morning with Vincent, and we'll be going directly to see your in-laws."

Lily hissed. "You wouldn't dare!"

"Yes, we would," Ginger insisted, if only to present a united front.

"Th-that's blackmail!"

"No," Tyler said firmly. "It's an ultimatum. Look. All you need to do right now is to listen to your mother. I'm on the cordless phone upstairs. While I check on Vincent to make sure he's asleep, I can't say anything, but I'll be listening. Once I get back down-stairs with your mother, I'll be able to answer any of your questions. Agreed?"

"I don't seem to have much choice about anything at the moment, do I?"

"Yes, you do," Ginger countered. "As a matter of fact, your father and I have decided there are several choices you can make and we want to discuss them with you. What you choose will be entirely up to you, but you will make a choice. Tonight."

Chapter Thirty-Two

Lily's response to her parents' demands was as loud as it was shrill. "Are you both out of your minds? I'm thirty-one years old. I'm not a child. You can't treat me like one and issue ultimatums or threaten me to make me do anything I don't want to do."

"There's no need to yell. You're absolutely right," Ginger murmured. "You're an adult. You're a married woman and you're about to be a mother again very soon. We want you to be happy in your new life, but you can't continue to turn your back on Vincent and pretend he doesn't exist. He's not a pet you've out-grown or a friend you can cast aside. He's your son, your own flesh and blood."

"When I met you at the airport, I thought I explained what I was doing. I'm protecting Vincent and pro-viding for him in a way I'd never be able to do on my own."

"That's an excuse, not an explanation. There is no excuse for abandoning Vincent," Ginger argued.

"I didn't abandon him, Mom. He's with you and Daddy. You're his grandparents. He's your flesh and blood, too."

"Yes, he is, which is why your father and I cannot and will not allow you to send him away to some year-round boarding school where he'll grow up alone without you and without us. It's not an option. Period," she added for emphasis. She kept her gaze locked on the doorway and prayed Tyler would be here with her soon.

Lily let out a long sigh. "So that's what all the fuss is about. Why didn't you just say so instead of acting like a pair of drill sergeants?"

The relief in her voice had softened her tone, much to Ginger's own relief. Putting Lily on the defensive at the start of their conversation was not how she or Tyler had hoped to begin, but there was no undoing that now.

"I'm sorry I got mad at you for not coming up to visit for the weekend. I shouldn't have threatened to send Vincent away from you, all right? I'm sorry. I didn't realize how much you and Daddy wanted to keep Vincent with you. I'll drop the whole idea of boarding school. Look. I can't really talk right now. Tell Daddy I'll call you back in a day or two."

"No," Tyler said on the cordless phone as he entered the kitchen. "Your mother told you that you have some choices to make tonight, and you will," he insisted as he walked over to Ginger and took her hand.

"Weren't you listening? I've made my choice. Vincent can stay with you."

"I heard every word," he said and nodded to Ginger to pick up the conversation.

"We love Vincent, sweetie," Ginger began. "We love having him in our lives, but our first choice has always been for you to keep Vincent with you. You're his mother. He needs you. He should be able to grow up with you and with his new baby brother or sister and with Paul. Now that you're married, Paul should accept his responsibilities as Vincent's stepfather."

"Your first choice? I thought we were talking about me. About my choices," Lily charged. Her voice tightened. "This isn't about me at all, is it? This is about you and Daddy. It's probably about Mark and Denise, too. Some things just won't ever change, will they? I have my own life to live. You and Daddy can't keep trying to get into my business, and Mark and Denise need to realize I'm not the baby they can boss around anymore. None of you ever understood that before, so why am I surprised you all don't understand it now?"

"Don't try dragging Mark and Denise into this conversation. Right now, the focus is on you and Vincent and your mother and me," Tyler warned. "What business are you talking about? Understand what?" he demanded and held up his hand so Ginger would let him continue. "Do you mean what you did after you left teaching your second year in Chicago? Or did you mean we couldn't possibly understand why you sent Vincent to live with one caregiver after another instead of keeping him with you? I've been to Chicago, Lily. I've talked with Mrs. Washington and Mrs. Carpatto, just to name two. You've never made a home for Vincent before, but that doesn't mean you can't do it now. You should do it now."

"We'll help you every way we can," Ginger offered.

Alarmed that Lily had not exploded the moment Tyler mentioned Chicago and his investigation, Ginger tried to fill the silence coming from the other end of the line. "Let us help you, Lily. Please. For Vincent's sake," she pleaded.

When Lily finally answered, her voice was frigid. "Help me?" She snorted. "You spied on me. You invaded my privacy. You investigated my life in Chicago like I was a criminal. How could you? How dare you lecture me on being a good parent?"

"You didn't give us much choice," Tyler replied, "but you do have choices you can make tonight."

"Don't use the word 'choice,' Daddy, and don't lie. I don't have any choices to make because you and Mom have already made them for me, haven't you? I wouldn't be surprised if you told Mark and Denise what you were going to do, just as you always discussed me with them when I did something wrong when I was little. Why can't all of you—"

"That's not true," Ginger protested, ignoring Lily's attempt to change the focus of the conversation again. "We want you to choose to take Vincent to live with you."

"Forget it. My answer is the same as it was six months ago. No."

"Then Vincent will stay with us. Indefinitely," Tyler said, clarifying their grandson's status for all three of them.

Lily sighed. "Unfortunately, yes. Vincent can stay with you. But again, with your threat to bring him to

Boston still standing, that's your choice, not mine, isn't it?"

Rather than provoke an argument that would only deter them from the greater purpose of their conversation, Ginger ignored Lily's question. "Your father and I have certain conditions under which Vincent will continue to live with us."

"Conditions?" Lily cackled. "Now you have conditions?"

Tyler held on to Ginger's hand. "You haven't contacted Vincent for months. You haven't called or written or acknowledged his existence in any way. That has to change. Once a month, we expect you to write to him or call him. Which will it be?" he asked.

"I can't promise to call him," she protested.

"Fine. Then you'll write him a short note. Keep it simple, but be honest. Just tell him you love him and miss him. Don't make any promises you can't keep," Ginger said firmly, keeping her session with the counselor in mind.

"Send it along with your check each month," Tyler suggested.

"Oh yes, the check. I assume you have another choice for me to make about the amount of the check? No. Don't tell me. Let me guess. You want me to send more so you won't have to use any of your own money—"

"Nonsense," Tyler snapped and let go of Ginger's hand to wave his in the air. "We don't touch that money. We deposit that check directly into an account we've set up for Vincent."

Ginger put her hand on Tyler's arm to calm him. "I've bought some note cards for Vincent to use to write to you. I'm not sure how often he'll want to write, but—"

"Don't mail them to me. I don't want him to have my address. If he wants to write, keep his note cards there. I can't afford to have anything like that here. At least you can promise to do that for me."

"We don't even have your new address," Tyler countered.

"You're such a good detective, I'm sure that won't be a problem. Is there anything else or can I go now?"

Ginger was so rattled by their conversation, she walked over to the table and glanced at the list she had made. "There's one more thing."

"Surprise. Surprise."

"Watch your tone. Don't be disrespectful to your mother," Tyler warned.

When Lily did not respond, Ginger continued. "I want you to send me something of yours that I can give to Vincent. Something small enough for him to hold. If he can't be with you and he can't talk with you, he needs something tangible, something concrete to reassure him that you're real and your love for him is real. It doesn't have to be anything expensive. Just a trinket will do, but it has to be something he'd recognize as yours."

"Where did you get that idea, Mom? Visit a shrink?"

Ginger held on to Tyler's arm, this time to keep herself calm. "As a matter of fact, I did meet with a counselor. I wanted to make sure my instincts were leading me in the right direction, but the idea that Vincent might need something of yours to hold wasn't mine. It was Vincent's."

Lily groaned. "His idea? You talked to him about this? He's only eight. What could he possibly know about—"

"I didn't have to talk to him," Ginger interrupted. "I just watched him. After school started, he told us he had lost his backpack. When he lost a second one, I found both of the backpacks in the closet in your old bedroom. He'd wrapped them in your old yellow robe. The one you left behind. To be honest, I didn't think any more about that, even when he tried to run away to find you right before Thanksgiving."

"He ran away? Why didn't you call me and tell me?"

"Because we found him almost right away," Tyler replied. "We would have told you when you called again. But you didn't. Not for Thanksgiving. Not even for Christmas. You didn't call again until you needed us to come to Boston for the weekend. Without Vincent."

No response. Only silence again.

"When you first told us you didn't want Vincent to be part of your new life, we thought you would change your mind. We were afraid to do anything to upset you, even when you didn't call over the holidays.

When you did call and told us you were going to send Vincent away to a boarding school because we wouldn't come to Boston, we were still afraid to do much of anything," Ginger explained.

She drew in a long breath. "We're not afraid anymore. Vincent deserves more from you than what he has now, and we're both prepared to see that he gets it. Your father and I both pray every night that you'll realize you want Vincent to be with you one day soon. When you do, we want to do everything we can to make sure that he wants to be part of your life, too. I'm not sure what he'll need when he's older, but right now, while he's still living with us, I just know he needs something from you to hold on to."

No response again. Only silence.

When Ginger looked at Tyler and motioned for him to say something, he shook his head. After several long heartbeats, Lily finally replied. "I've packed away most of the stuff I brought with me from Chicago, but I have a few things I kept out. One Christmas, Vincent gave me a pin he'd gotten at school where they had a Secret Santa Shop. I can send you that."

Ginger swallowed hard. For all her bluff and bluster, Lily was not quite as hard-hearted as she appeared to be, even to herself. "No. Send him something else. Don't send him the pin, but you should mention you have it in your note and that the pin is special to you. He probably needs to know you have something he gave you to hold on to, too. What about a bracelet you wore?"

"I'm not the bracelet queen, Mom. You are."

"But you like to wear a lot of rings. Or you used to," Ginger suggested.

"I think I have some of those old rings packed away. Wait. There was one he liked a lot. I used to let him play with it."

"Send that one," Ginger urged.

"I'll need a little time to sort through the boxes."

"Make the time tomorrow and send the ring, along with your note. Make sure you send it to be delivered overnight," Tyler prompted. "We're painting Vincent's room this week and having bunk beds delivered Saturday afternoon. We'd like to give him your note and the ring then, too."

"Any other orders?" Lily snapped, her patience now apparently stretched thin again.

Ginger frowned. "We're not the enemy, Lily. We're only trying to do what's best for your son. It's not too late to change your mind. Just say the word and we'll bring him to you."

"I know you don't believe me when I tell you that I'm doing what's best for him, either one of you, but I am. You don't have to like it. Just accept it, like I do," Lily suggested.

"We don't like it. But that doesn't mean we don't love you. We just don't like what you're doing. There's a difference," Tyler murmured gently. "Please make sure we have your note and the ring by Friday."

"Or else you'll carry out your threat and bring Vincent to my in-laws. Don't bother to repeat the details.

I got your message loud and clear," she replied and disconnected.

Trembling, Ginger hung up the telephone. After Tyler disconnected the cordless phone, Ginger welcomed the support of his arms around her shoulders. "I thought for sure Lily would put up more of an argument," he murmured and glanced at the paperwork spread out on the kitchen table. "I really think she has no idea what she's doing by putting Vincent out of her life." He shook his head. "I'm not even sure she loves him. How can that be?"

"She loves him," Ginger argued. "She might have packed him off to us and boxed up most of the remnants of her life in Chicago, but remember what she said she didn't pack away?"

He shrugged. "Not really. I was trying too hard not to yell at her for being so selfish."

Ginger looked up at him. "The pin. She kept the pin he had given her for Christmas. If she didn't love him, if she really didn't care about him, she would have packed up anything and everything that would remind her of him. That tells me Vincent isn't the only one struggling right now. We just have to have faith and continue to pray for her. It might not be soon, but I have to believe that someday she'll want Vincent back in her life. When she does, there won't be enough money in this world to stop her."

He cocked his head. "And if she doesn't?"

"Then you and I will be here for him," she whispered.

"A few years from now, he's not going to be satisfied with an occasional note that says she loves him and misses him or a little token from her. He'll want to know more. What are we going to tell him then?"

She turned, put her arms around his waist and held him tight. "Let's not worry about that right now. Let's use the time we have with Vincent to show him how much we love him."

He chuckled. "I can't believe we're both looking forward to taking the next two days off to paint his room. This time last year we were getting ready to fly to the play-offs, remember?"

She laughed with him. "Sure I do. I hate to burst your bubble, Gramps, but Vincent did not let you talk him into painting his room green and white because he's become a die-hard Eagles fan."

He pulled his head back to look her in the eye. "I know he doesn't like football, but he said he liked the team colors."

"Sea turtles are green, too," she teased. "Remember? He told us how much he enjoyed going to the aquarium in Chicago. He likes all kinds of water animals—turtles, fish, dolphins, whales. . . ."

Tyler sighed. "I think I see some weekend trips coming up. There's a great aquarium in Baltimore Harbor. I think they run whale-watching cruises out of Cape May, but we'd probably be better off going to Florida to see the manatees. He'd love them."

She giggled. "Wait. Wait. Wait! Maybe we should start a little closer to home. The Adventure Aquarium is fifteen minutes away from us. Barbara and John took the twins there recently."

He grinned. "And the aquarium is almost walking distance from Campbell's Field, the minor league baseball stadium. What's a little visit to the aquarium without a little baseball, too?" he teased. "If we go in the spring, we could ask Vincent to bring his sketch pad along. He could sketch at the aquarium first and then at the baseball stadium later. He might not be crazy about watching the game, but he won't be able to resist the mascot—it's a shark! Just you wait. Sooner or later, I'll change that boy's mind about sports."

"Let's get the room painted, the bunk beds in place, and see if Lily follows through with her first note to him before we get too optimistic and start planning trips," she warned, but it was hard not to get excited. For the first time in months, the future held great promise for all of them. Even for Lily.

Chapter Thirty-Three

Curiosity. Fear. Dread. And relief.

For Barbara, these emotions rose and swelled in succession from one heartbeat to the next, robbed her of sleep and drove her from her bed in the early hours before dawn on Sunday morning. She slipped into her robe and tiptoed out of her bedroom so she would not wake up her husband. After she stepped into the hallway, she leaned back against the door frame.

Her emotions changed so quickly and erratically, she did not know whether she should take something to ease her wicked tension headache, her acidic stomach, or both. Unfortunately, there was nothing she could take to mend her broken heart. The passage of time would help her to escape the darkness cast by despair and doubt, but only if she allowed the light of faith to shine upon the path she should follow and guide her steps along the way.

She slid her hand into the pocket of her robe and wrapped her fingers around the source of her emotional and spiritual turmoil. Considering its importance, the folded envelope was not very thick. She was curious about the messages contained within the two letters inside the envelope, but she dreaded the prospect of reading them. She was afraid to read them. She had been afraid to read them from the moment John had brought them home with him on Friday night and handed them to her. She had steadfastly refused to read them with John that night. Or all day Saturday. Or Saturday night.

Tightening the belt on her robe, she glanced down the dimly lit hallway toward the bedroom where Jessie and Melanie were sleeping. In a few hours, the whole family would get up, have breakfast together and dress for Sunday services. Barbara trembled and bowed her head. How could she enter the Lord's house and worship today when she did not have enough faith to trust He would give her the courage and the strength to open those letters and read them?

What kind of hypocrite had she become, claiming to be a woman of faith, yet failing to act like one? What kind of role model would she be for the twins if she turned out to be nothing more than a Sunday Christian?

She pressed the palm of her hand against her forehead to ease the pain tightening like a band of metal around her head and drew in a deep breath. Whether by impulse or inspiration, she tiptoed back into her bedroom and went directly to the closet. She pulled down the shawl she had stored away months ago and carried it with her downstairs to the living room. After turning on a light, she curled up on the sofa and tucked her legs beneath her before she tugged the shawl around her shoulders.

She toyed with the fringe of the shawl, letting the soft strands slip between her fingers. Each stitch had been knitted by her sisters-in-faith, with love, and the shawl itself offered comfort for Barbara's spirit that went far deeper than the warmth of the wool. Wrapped in both faith and love, she took the envelope out of the pocket of her robe, removed the two letters and laid them on her lap. She placed the palm of each hand on top of a letter, closed her eyes and let her mind sort through the surprising events of the past week.

With a plea agreement now, there would be no trial. Her relief was real, and she was incredibly grateful for being spared the ordeal of spending days or weeks in court. She still did not know whether or not she agreed with the judge who had ordered both girls to remain within the jurisdiction of Family Court. She did agree that sealing all the proceedings related to the case, including the final sentences, was very wise.

She smiled. At first, confounded by the judge's ruling, the media had collectively sulked for a few days, but was quickly galvanized by an even more tragic case. Two teenage girls had been charged with murdering their grandparents—a case that had already been ruled beyond the jurisdiction of Family Court and into proceedings that would be televised.

She glanced down at her lap and stared at the letters beneath her hands. If she did not read the letters, she herself would be trapped forever by the past where she would languish in grief. She would be unable to free herself to share in the promise of the future that beckoned in the beautiful, smiling faces of her granddaughters. Or the silent pleas in her husband's loving gaze that begged her to help him quench their thirst for vengeance and justice, once and for all, with the life-giving waters of acceptance and forgiveness.

Snuggling deeper within the folds of the shawl, she shivered. For months now, she had struggled with the idea that she would be able to make the journey toward acceptance and forgiveness at all. Now, however, she knew she must begin that journey by reading the letters from Julia and Augusta Radcliffe, the two girls who had accepted their responsibility for Steve's death. Her faith alone must give her the courage to take the first step, and she bowed her head for a moment before holding the first letter to the light. She glanced immediately to the bottom of the single-page letter, saw Julia's signature and realized the letter was from the younger sister whose actions had led her older sister down the same path to tragedy. Tears welled as she read the brief, but poignant message:

Dear Mr. And Mrs. Montgomery:

I'm not sure if you will read this letter soon, but I pray every day that you will read it someday. To say that I'm sorry for everything I did will not change the fact that because of me, your son, Steve, lost his life and his two little girls lost their daddy. I am truly, truly sorry. I know I have horribly disappointed my parents and my sister, as well as myself, and I know God must be very, very angry with me.

My pastor keeps telling me there is no sin too big to be forgiven and that God's mercy and forgiveness is freely given to all who repent. I hope he's right. I also hope that one day you will be able to forgive me for the pain and heartache I have brought into your lives. I will understand if you can't, because I'm not sure I will ever be able to forgive myself. I will pray for you every day. If you can, I hope you can pray for me, too.

Weeping silent tears, Barbara pressed the letter to her heart. It would have been easy to dismiss the young girl's letter as nothing more than a message designed to ease her own conscience or to meet one of the terms of her plea agreement. But there was something about the letter that tugged at the cords of Barbara's heart and drowned out the echoes of doubt and suspicion. Perhaps it was the girl's reluctance to believe she could be forgiven, not by Barbara or John or even the twins, that rang true. Or was it her reliance on hope and her plea for prayer?

Barbara wiped away her tears with each of her shoulders. She kept Julia's letter pressed to her heart and moved Augusta's letter into the light. The salutation was the same. The signature was just as clear, but the tone of her message, if not the message itself, gave Barbara a glimpse into the distinct differences between the two sisters:

If I ever doubted that one day could make a difference, I know better now. In one day, within the space of one short moment, my world and your world collided and changed forever. If I ever doubted the existence of sin, I know better now. Because of my sins, you have lost your son forever and his daughters will grow up without him. If I ever doubted that life would be unfair, I know better now. It is not fair that so many people are suffering because of what I did that day in Philadelphia, but they are.

The burden of my guilt is a cross I will carry for the rest of my life and carry to my grave. I do not dare ask you or God for forgiveness. Killing your son, even accidentally, is unforgivable. I won't ask you to accept my deepest and most sincere apologies, because words alone cannot ease your pain. I can't promise that I will pray for you because I don't know how to pray. Not anymore. But I will never forget the wrong that I have done or the lessons I have learned, and I accept my punishment as just and deserved.

More tears. They flowed silently again down Barbara's cheeks, but they were tears she shed for Augusta, too. Where Julia had found hope and the promise of redemption in her faith, Augusta had found only despair and rejection, reflecting the dual struggle of faith Barbara had experienced all these long months. For the first time since Steve's death, she finally realized that finding and practicing true faith was a process. Faith was not an instant cure for despair or a guarantee of hope, but the essence of faith nevertheless held the promise of redemption and eternal life, even for the sinners who had committed the most grievous offenses against the laws of man and the Word of God.

If ever Barbara had known that before, she embraced the very nature of faith she had rediscovered now in the letters she had just read. Instead of turmoil, she found peace. Instead of despair, she found hope. Instead of fear, she found courage.

Her headache was gone.

Her stomach had settled.

And the ache in her heart had eased.

She smoothed each letter before carefully refolding it and sliding it back into the envelope and placing it in her pocket again. After she turned out the light, she tightened the shawl around her shoulders, steepled her hands within the folds of the shawl and closed her eyes. She had been wordless before God for months now, unable to recall the simplest of prayers, but the greatest of all prayers came easily to her now. Slowly, she recited the prayer God Himself had given to all of His followers and paused from time to time to silently add prayers of her own.

" 'Our Father, who art in heaven, hallowed be Thy name. . . .' " *You alone are the light of the world. Guide us all with the light of Your love.*

" 'Thy kingdom come. Thy will be done. On earth as it is in heaven. . . .' " *I trust Your wisdom and Your will above mine, Father. Help me and my family. Help Julia and Augusta and their family to submit to Your will freely, with joy, as we rebuild our lives with faith in You.*

" 'Give us this day our daily bread, and forgive us our debts as we forgive our debtors. . . .' " *We cannot come to You with our hearts tainted with ill will toward others. Forgive me for doubting You and questioning You. Forgive me for not being able to forgive Julia and Augusta until . . . until now, and lead them back to You, the source of all forgiveness and love.*

" 'And lead us not into temptation, but deliver us from evil. . . .' " *I know we will face many trials in the days ahead, but I know You will be with us. When we are weak, be our strength. When we are sorrowful, be our joy. When we are filled with doubt and fear, fill us with the sureness of Your love and the promise of life everlasting.*

"'For Thine is the kingdom and the power and the glory forever. Amen,'" she whispered and lost herself in thoughts not of herself or her loved ones, but of the two girls who had written the letters and the parents who had lost not one child, but two.

Barbara had breakfast on the table when John and the twins came downstairs at seven-thirty. "You're all up early," she teased.

"We smelled breakfast, didn't we, girls?"

Jessie was the first to plop into her seat. "I love bacon!"

Melanie sat down next to her sister, but her gaze was locked on the stack of waffles Barbara had put on the table. "Are they your waffles, Grammy?"

"Yes, they are. I made them from scratch because I know how much you both like them," she replied and filled each of their glasses with orange juice.

John pulled out his chair at the head of the table. "This is a feast. What's the occasion?"

"It's Sunday. We're going to Sunday School today, right, Pappy?" Jessie asked.

Barbara sat down across from the girls. "That's right. We're all going to church." After John led them in prayer, she fixed the girls' plates and passed one to each of them. "I thought maybe we could do something special together this afternoon. How about it, Pappy?"

"The movies! Let's go to the movies!" Jessie cried before he could answer.

Melanie wrinkled her nose. "I don't want to go to the movies. I want to go ice-skating."

Barbara laughed. "It's cold outside, but the lake in the park isn't frozen solid enough for skating, and going to the movies won't work, either, because there isn't anything playing that I want you to see. Besides, Pappy and I have to talk it over first, remember?"

"That's right," he added and looked at her askance. "Are you sure you're up to going out today?"

She fixed a waffle with butter and syrup for herself and smiled. "Absolutely. I even have a few ideas. We'll talk about them after breakfast."

As soon as the girls finished and were excused from the table, they raced upstairs to brush their teeth and pick out dresses to wear to Sunday school.

Now that she and John were alone, he spoke openly. "I guess you still haven't read the letters."

"I read them a few hours ago," she contradicted. "I probably should have read them when you did, but I— I just wasn't ready."

He patted her hand. "Did they really make a difference?" he asked.

When she looked at him oddly, he smiled. "The letters. Did reading the letters really make a difference?"

"They did. After I read them, I couldn't stop thinking about those two girls and their parents, and I kept comparing their lives and their futures to ours and to Jessie's and Melanie's. That family has lost so much."

He let out a long sigh, his gaze etched with sorrow that was all too familiar. "I'm going to miss Steve forever, but I can't dwell on why he died or how those girls should be punished. Not anymore."

She turned her hand over and laced her fingers with his. "Me, either."

"Were you—did you want to write back to Julia and Augusta? Carl said he'd get the letters to them through their lawyer."

She shook her head. "I'm not ready to do that quite yet, but maybe in a few months . . ."

He nodded, lifted her hand and pressed a kiss to her fingertips. "Let's talk about this afternoon before the girls tumble back downstairs with ideas of their own."

"Follow me." She tugged on his hand and led him into the dining room where she had spread out all the maps and brochures that had been stored away for so long. "Well? What do you think?" she asked in a voice filled with hope.

"I think retirement is at least twelve or fifteen years away, not two like we'd hoped. By then, these maps and brochures will all be badly outdated."

"What about this summer when the girls are out of school? They'll probably want to spend some time with the Carrs at the farm, but why couldn't we take them on a short trip to see if they like sailing as much as we do? We could take a trip with them every summer. I know it's not exactly what we planned to do originally, but it might be even better. The girls are young enough that we could actually go on that two-year, sail-around-the-world trip we wanted and take them with us. I could homeschool them. Just imagine what it would be like. They'd have the world as their classroom. History would come alive. They'd learn so much more from experience, rather than reading a dull textbook."

Laughing, he pulled her into his arms. "Slow down! You're on fast-forward," he teased. "Let's take it one step at a time. There's a boat show in Philadelphia next weekend. Why don't we take Jessie and Melanie over to look at the sailboats?"

She smiled and patted his back, quite certain that they had both taken the most important step of all—the step toward reclaiming and living the faith that would sustain them for the rest of their days.

Epilogue

By custom, families across the nation celebrate Mother's Day on the second Sunday in May. Also by custom, the Welleswood PTA hosts a Mother's Day Breakfast that day. This year, however, the event that honored the women who loved and nurtured the children in the community went far beyond previous efforts.

Families and friends, neighbors and residents, as well as a choir of schoolchildren, welcomed women of all ages to the cafeteria at the high school for the first time to accommodate the largest number of attendees since the event began more than fifteen years earlier. Some women were mothers of biological or adopted children. Others were foster mothers, grandmothers, aunts, or cousins. Long-term caregivers or occasional babysitters were not overlooked. All but one senior woman from the Towers attended. Since she was in the hospital recuperating from surgery, she received a bouquet of flowers and a gift certificate good for a free breakfast at The Diner whenever she was well enough to return home.

Beneath a rainbow canopy of paper flowers made by all the elementary school children in the district, everyone enjoyed a good meal together after Reverend Fisher said grace, and listened to a wonderfully funny speech given by the pastor's wife, Eleanor. Exhilarated by their success, exhausted by their hours and hours of work, but extremely pleased by the whole affair, Barbara, Judy and Ginger gave a collective groan when the PTA President called them all up to the head table. They lined up together behind Pam and stood shoulder to shoulder. She asked the audience to stand and give the three women a round of applause that, once started, did not seem to have an end.

Ginger giggled and nudged Barbara's shoulder. "You know what this means, don't you?"

"I imagine we get to do this again next year," she replied and leaned toward Judy. "Didn't I warn you about doing a good job? You two better think of something quick, or Pam is going to ask us in front of everyone so we won't turn her down."

Judy craned her neck to get both Barbara and Ginger in her sights. "Don't worry. I already told her we couldn't possibly work on the breakfast next year."

Ginger grinned. "I knew we could count on you. Just exactly what excuse did you use?"

"And when did you tell her?" Barbara added, still skeptical.

Judy laughed. "I told her yesterday. Right after I promised to convince both of you we would help the PTA Executive Board organize some events to raise money to expand the after-school programs in each of the elementary schools."

Barbara gasped. "You didn't! All of the schools?"

Ginger groaned. "What kind of events?"

"As a matter of fact, I did. Yes, all of the schools. As for the events . . ." Judy waved her hand in the air and jingled the keys to Pretty Ladies. "As the proud, heavily-in-debt, new owner of my very own salon, I thought we could start with a special event where the salon would donate all the proceeds on a given event day to the after-school programs. That's just one event I have in mind, though. I'm sure the two of you will be able to come up with others. It'll be a snap."

Ginger's eyes widened. "A snap?"

"A snap? For whom?" Barbara huffed.

"For three grandmothers who can outwork, out-think, and outplan all of the men and most of the women in this room. We're all grand mothers, too. Doesn't that say it all?" Judy teased.

Absolutely.

Afterword

According to the U.S. Census 2000, grandparents who are raising grandchildren under the age of eighteen are a growing phenomenon that is reality for more than two and a quarter million grandparents in the United States. Help for those grandparents is available online at a number of sites. I highly recommend the AARP (American Association of Retired Persons) Webplace, Grandparents Information, which is especially helpful, offering advice on different challenges and links to related Web sites. If you or someone you know is raising his or her grandchild, please visit *www.aarp.org* for further information.

The Shawl Ministry is not fictional. To learn more information about this loving ministry, please visit the official Web site at *www.shawlministry.com.*

For those interested in recipes, below is the recipe for the Cinnamon Bubble Wreath. Recipes for other goodies are posted on my Web page, *www.delia-parr.com.* Enjoy!

Cinnamon Bubble Wreath

Preheat oven: 350°
Ingredients:
$\frac{1}{4}$ cup sugar
$\frac{1}{2}$ tsp. ground cinnamon
1 can (11 ounces) refrigerated French bread dough
$1\frac{1}{2}$ tbs. melted margarine or butter

Grease 9-inch tube pan. Combine sugar and cinnamon in small bowl. Cut dough into 16 slices and roll into balls. Roll balls in sugar-cinnamon mixture and fill tube pan. Bake 20–25 minutes or until golden brown. Note: For an extra treat, top with vanilla ice cream and sprinkle with caramel and crushed pecans.

Center Point Publishing

600 Brooks Road ● PO Box 1
Thorndike ME 04986-0001 USA

(207) 568-3717

US & Canada:
1 800 929-9108
www.centerpointlargeprint.com